The Story Thus Far

When last we encountered the mismatched lot that were to be the saviors of the Carotian Union, they had completed the first leg of their quest. Their ultimate objective? To free a prince from the planet Thalas before that world descends into the civil war that would destroy the entire solar system.

One adventure lies behind them. On Astra, a world shared in an uneasy truce by humans and dragons, the questors discovered an ancient ruin littered with time traps. By reaching into Astra's past, they were able to assemble the elements of a fabulous chalice that could heal virtually any disease known to man or dragon. And the dragons of Astra were dying.

The questors fought mere pirates to win the chalice on Astra, but before they set out, each had a dream of an adventure that lay along the path to freeing the prince. With six adventures to go, pirates may prove to have been the least of their worries.

And thus begins...

Tapestry of Enchantment

Adventurers of the Carotian Union: Book II

Karen Anne Webb

Tapestry of Enchantment

Karen Anne Webb

WWW.DRAGONMOONPRESS.COM

Tapestry of Enchantment

ISBN 13 978-1-897492-08-6

Dragon Moon Press

Printed and bound in the United States
www.dragonmoonpress.com
www.chaliceoflife.com

For my mother, who never quit believing.

SAGE AND CHRONICLER

ERI PUT ASIDE THE huge tome in which her story of the Quest for the Lost Prince of Thalas was taking shape and considered her fingers. *Ten,* she thought. *Eight fingers, two opposable thumbs. It doesn't make sense.*

She held up her left hand and, on the theory that the human harpers she knew only used three fingers and the thumb, caused her pinky to phase out. Giggling outrageously, she compared left and right hand, flipping them palm outward and back several times in rapid succession. "That's better," she finally murmured in satisfaction.

"What's better?" came the voice of the old sage. "What are you doing, young Peri? What are you about?"

She had advanced to flipping her hands back and forth in opposition now: thumbs right, thumbs left, thumbs right, thumbs left... "I'm thinking about the number nine," she said complacently.

"Hmph," said Tuhl, seating himself on the log next to hers and staring at the scene that remained floating in the air above the fire. In that scene, the questors were still milling about the wooded interspace that separated the first leg of their journey from the second: an odd group, to say the least. "Nine?" he prompted after a moment.

"Yes. Do you know my people call it simply 'the Unity'?"

He chuffed a bit. She had learned long ago that sound represented laughter. "Tuhl knows the ninety and nine meanings of every number in creation, and what those numbers are called by every race in this corner of the cosmos."

"Oh, yes, I forgot. You know everything." The remark was neither as awestruck nor as sour as it once might have been.

"And well for you I do, young one." His eyes twinkled. "But why nine? Why now?"

"Well, Torreb remarked early on in the quest he was surprised at the number of questors being seven rather than nine. The human folk of the Union have no special name for the number nine, but he indicated the number held some spiritual significance to their faith, akin to our concept of the Unity."

"That is so. The largest single-digit number has profound significance for many cultures, no matter their system of counting or the base they use. The Unity, the Oneness, the Many-in-One, the One-as-Many: in many symbologies that number means the unity of many and the strength that is found in being unified. What made you think of that?"

"Well, as the questors ended their first adventure, they really found that they *were* nine."

Tuhl's eyes shifted as if he were counting. "Ah, yes. I see." He chuffed a bit more and grinned.

"Seven picked by the Divine directly," Peri enumerated, "one given as a gift by you. And one, well, *acquired* along the way—by accident or Providence or Divine Will, or sheer dumb luck."

Tuhl swirled his staff through the image that hung suspended above the flames; it swirled like bright smoke. The figures lost their discrete edges, and the hues defining them ran together—a watercolor exposed too soon to its final wash. "Acquired," he mused, making the chuffing sound she had come to take for amused laughter. "Yes, you might say they *acquired* Anthraticus." Bright eyes snapped up to impale her. "Have you decided how you planned to describe this acquisition in your Chronicles? As accident or Providence or Divine Will, or sheer dumb luck, or something entirely other?"

"Oh, well, I—" She fumbled a little with the words, tore back through her pages of notes. "I hadn't worked it out yet," she confessed finally. She felt no shame in the admission.

"Ah," he said with a sagacious nod, as if he thought more of her for not trying to jump to a conclusion—one he had demanded she make without analyzing the evidence, at that.

"I mean, there seems to be evidence on both sides. And, well, *my* people believe both fate and free will exist, but the extent to which each influences any individual event is a Mystery."

He nodded again. "The humans would tell you the *Book of Life* and the *Book of Wisdom* say just that—that it is a Mystery not to be deciphered on this side of the grave, even by sentient creatures of great insight. See? You and they are not so very different!"

"No," she agreed with a wistful sigh. "No so very different, not now. As for Anthraticus' appearance being an accident, I truly believe there *are* no accidents. And yet..."

"Speak your thought."

"Well, Mistra released her consort because the High Queen had assured her any not marked with the Stag would surely die if they attempted the Quest of the Lost Prince. Goddess bless! She suffered the Nonacle to shatter the consort bond!"

"'As bad as that was, I wish this were that good,'" he mused, recalling the vision they had just watched in which Mistra compared the loss of one consort to death and another to forcible termination of the bond.

"Yes. Yet Anthraticus passed the second Portal and lived, and I have never seen the mark of the Stag upon him at all, though the others bear the mark as a trophy of honor."

"Mistra," he said after a moment's thought, "has more than once made the observation that the test of the Lesser Worlds is to learn the Will of their Creator and to prosecute it with a high heart, while the test of the Later Worlds is possession of complete knowledge of that same Will." He grinned. "She and Mosaia had many long talks about that one, believe me! He would tell her the men of his world would go to their graves blithely doing the Will of their Lord if they could know it with such clarity as the Pantheon often gives. And she would answer that complete certitude in that sense was not the boon his folk imagined it to be. 'When people claim,' she said to him on a time, 'that they would exert their utmost endeavor if only the Pantheon or the One or whatever they call it would divulge its Will, they envision that Will as being consonant with their own, or at least not contrary to it. The true test of faith for our people lies not in the search for that Will but in its glad prosecution, though the doing of that Will break your own heart.'"

"She does not look very heartbroken these days."

"She persevered in the prosecution of that Will," he said, "though at times she thought her heart lay dead in her breast. And in the prosecution, she came to understand."

"Understand what?"

He raised his staff again and swirled it through the smoke above their small fire. She watched as a shape like a cream-colored trapezoid formed. "Can you tell me what this is?"

She frowned. Obviously, he was leading up to one of his Lessons, which could assume any one of a myriad obscure shapes. She had learned to play along. "Of course not. It could be any one of a dozen things."

"Such as?"

"Oh, by the Lady, Tuhl, I don't know! It could be the side of an eggshell or the petal of a flower or the Royal Thalacian Opera House seen from a great distance above, or just a pretty geometric shape."

He raised his staff again and a second trapezoid, the mirror image of the first, sprang up a small distance away. "And now?"

"A butterfly with a very fat middle," she said drily.

A third gesture, and an entire circle of the shapes appeared; now the ground upon which they sat took on the hue of an emerald sparkling in the sun.

"Ah!" She felt the spark of recognition come. "A snowflower from Dantos

I." She frowned, counted the number of trapezoids in the circle. "No, wait a bit. They have ten petals, not twelve." She cocked her head; he had engaged her interest now, and she was making a serious attempt to find the solution to the puzzle. "Except for the colors, it could be the rosette used by some of the clergy to symbolize the Pantheon."

"As the athletes competing in the Games might say, you are in the ball park." A final gesture and the resolution of the image hovering above them improved. Now the cream of the trapezoids and the green of the ground were broken by discrete, identifiable features: a fountain here, a balcony there.

She burst out laughing. "That's an aerial view of Holy Hill!"

He chuffed. "So irreverent you are."

"Irreverent? I've heard Caros' highest royalty use the phrase. It isn't *my* fault they collected all their holiest temples and crowned the same hill with them. Such excess invites such epithets."

"It will be *Tuhl's* fault if you do not understand the point he is trying to make."

She sobered, pondered. "You're saying doing the Will of the Divine is like this? If we don't understand the reason for what's being asked of us, it's because we see only the first small shape and don't know what to make of it? Or even if all the pieces of the puzzle lie before us, we may still not know what to make of *them*? Is that it?"

He nodded.

"And that maybe—maybe if we *did* see, our hearts would not break at all?"

He nodded again. "What Mistra came to understand was just so, that contingent beings do not always see the end in the beginning, or the whole pattern in the smallest fragment. Contravening the Will of the Pantheon serves no one, and if one contravenes enough in one's life, one will never *see* the pattern, or the reason one sacrifice or another was required in the first place. Yet if one endures with patience, if one is obedient to Their commands even when he looks around and believes himself forsaken by Them—*especially* when he looks around and believes himself forsaken by Them—the most glorious of designs will come to full fruition."

She took a moment to collect herself, found within herself the strength to address the Guardian of the Orb of Caros as if he were an equal, or as if their difference were one of degree rather than station. "I do not like it that good people suffer from doing the right thing." She quirked him a smile. "Is that short-sighted of me?"

He gave her a benevolent smile in return. "It shows you have a kind heart."

She perked up a little at that.

"But, yes, it also shows you are short-sighted—ah, ah, ah!" He held up a hand to forestall her when she would have taken umbrage. "But no more than is reasonable for any of us," he amended, cackling a bit as she struggled not to look like a deflated balloon. "In the case of the truly great ones," he went on in a more philosophical tone, "those tests bring suffering *as* great, for they suffer not only that they might be tested and perfected like the rest of us: they suffer that sentientkind might live. They take on themselves the burdens of a harsh universe that their fellow beings may be set free. They consent even to be shackled that the rest of us might know release from bondage." He rose. "Come. The first Portal took the adventurers to a different world; the second took them to—well, it is a place more easily visualized in the Well of Eliannes."

CHAPTER 1

Where Are We?

*"Those who journey in the garden land of knowledge, because they
see the end in the beginning, see peace in war and friendliness in anger.
Such is the state of the wayfarers in this Valley, but the people of the
Valleys above this see the end and the beginning as one; nay, they
see neither beginning nor end, and witness neither 'first' nor 'last.'"*
—The Book of Life

THE EIGHT QUESTORS FOR the Lost Prince of Thalas stood gaping at the inadvertently-acquired ninth member of their party. Prior to their trip to planet Astra, none of them had ever seen a spragon, a creature like a small coatl with butterfly wings and a telescoping neck. The sight of a spragon drunk, giggling, hiccoughing, and using Deneth's pack as a portable hostel struck most of them so silly that their first response after the initial shock was to burst out laughing.

"How did he get through the Portal unharmed?" asked a befuddled Mistra, who alone refused to find humor in the situation.

"Getting through the Portal" was, in fact, a slight misrepresentation of their circumstances. The questors had learned early on that the path to the Prince's plane of incarceration was littered with Portals which magically gated them through space. When they stepped through the Portal on Astra, they found themselves in a quiet wood that seemed disconnected from any other reality. Within the wood stood a second Portal—the egress from what they had now dubbed "the interspace," and the entry to the next stop on their journey. Even before they crossed the threshold of the Portal leading to that first interspace, Deneth, with his strange bardic magic, had discovered that these tranquil spots were places of refuge and respite, places to mend, places where restoration that had eluded them in the outside world simply happened on its own. Only his discovery had allowed them to save the life of their comrade Alla, who had expended much of her life energy performing a risky ritual at the end of their last adventure. The ritual had accomplished its purpose, allowing them to make a final elixir that would heal Anthraticus' ailing kin, but it had nearly cost the *aranyaka* her life.

Deneth tried, out of respect for Mistra's sobriety, to still his mirth. He failed miserably. "Well, he settled in my pack, and I guess the packs are *sort* of magical. Maybe it protected him."

"And his system is obviously more than adequately cushioned against physical shock," Mosaia, their *de facto* knight-protector, chuckled. He poked Anthraticus in the ribs. The dragon doubled over, giggling more loudly and begging him to stop tickling. "What did you do, Deneth? Force some of the local shrubbery down his throat?"

"No. It was only wine, I swear. Just little bitty thimblefuls." He rummaged in his pack and came up with the thimble Anthraticus been using as a glass and a bottle they had previously dubbed the Bottomless Bottle of Brandy for the spell of plenitude Mistra had placed on it during their last adventure. It now stood nearly empty.

"I didn't mean for the spell to keep replenishing it once we took care of the dragons on Astra," Mistra explained with a chagrined look.

"And a good thing," the bard said dryly. His look of consternation—the spragon must have continued to imbibe while Deneth got swept up in their frenetic efforts to cure Alla—was wasted on the others. No one was frowning accusation; in fact, the discovery triggered a resurgence of good-natured laughter.

"Is it safe to take him through the other half of the Portal?" asked Mistra, still the only one among them who seemed inclined to treat the matter seriously. "I mean, we can't take him the rest of the way if it's going to kill him."

"We can't just leave him here," Habie protested. "Wherever *here* is."

"Yeah," Deneth said sourly. "He'd have no one to play his jokes on. Die of terminal lack of mirth, no doubt."

T'Cru nuzzled the dragon. "What say, cousin? Will you risk another trip in Deneth's pack?"

Anthraticus flashed his toothy grin at the Tigroid and proceeded to pass out.

T'Cru bowed Tigroid-fashion to Alla. "Lady, I would trust your judgment."

Alla, fully recovered from her ordeal, settled herself next to the spragon and stroked his underbelly. "My only fear is the Universe permitted him to pass the Portal and live because it was an honest mistake—the first *half* of the Portal, anyway."

"He was," pontificated Mosaia's sword, which they had grudgingly unsheathed so it could contribute to the discussion, "just curling up in the closest place to hand, to... er, I believe the human term would be 'to sleep it off.'"

"Now that we know he's here, is that knowledge a danger to him?"

"You are seriously asking my advice?"

"Much as I hate to admit it." said Mosaia. "You are, after all, a sentient construct of goodly magic."

The sword could not truly locomote, but something about the aura around it said it was preening. "I was forged at the dawn of time by—"

"Ereb himself," they chorused.

"And Phino," said Deneth, as if he were repeating the most boring of litanies.

"And Strephel," chortled Habie.

"The point is," Mosaia cut in before anyone could launch into the rest of the sword's lineage, "you were forged by members of the Pantheon whose goodly influence now seems to permeate these Portals and interspaces. You may be in the best position to judge of all of us."

The sword considered. "Well, then, I tend to think not, from what I know of Minissa, though she is only cousin to the gods who forged me. Ereb, of course, would hardly consider it just that we abandon him here in this nether world, pleasant though it is to you organics. Whether he can continue on safely after our next adventure I cannot say: we may have to leave him in whatever place we find ourselves next."

"I agree," said Mistra. "I just wish he were coherent enough to decide for himself."

"In the field," said Mosaia, "we wish for many things, but we fight with whatever means we have to hand."

"Maybe a few words from Torreb before we go, then?" Habie suggested. "You know—prayers, or a blessing from Minissa or one of the others, or all of them, or something...?" Her voice trailed off as she took in the amused or astounded looks the request garnered, not for its peculiarity, but for its peculiarity coming from *her*. "Well, it's *their* Portal and *their* quest," the diminutive thief retorted, though no one had maligned the suggestion. "Can't we ask them to be nice to a poor little drunken, well-meaning spritely dragon?"

At that remark, Torreb laughed for no reason but heart's ease. "Habie, you'll be asking to take holy orders before the quest is over."

"Me? Puh-*leez*!"

In the end, the priest incanted a blessing and begged the gods for pity, and they passed the egress Portal. Anthraticus, once again curled up inside Deneth's pack, seemed none the worse for wear when they looked in on him, although he was still sound asleep. They breathed a collective sigh of relief and set about preparing to make the next leg of the journey.

They found themselves in yet another wood, pretty but pathless and featureless. Everyone knew they needed to look to the Portal Stone for direction, but when Deneth first looked up to ask Mistra why she was taking such a long time extracting the locator device from her pack, they discovered she had disappeared.

Relief was, in fact, Mistra's first reaction to the news that Anthraticus had made the passage safely, but fury and grief quickly displaced it. Both smote her in a wave she had not seen coming, a wave of such magnitude she could neither avoid it nor fight her way clear. Its very inexorability left her with few options: she could not quiet the outburst that threatened to burst forth, she could only refuse to burden her friends with its onslaught. She slipped quietly away, plunging into the forest before the worst of the violent sobbing took her, fleeing with the sense she could outdistance the pain if only she could run fast enough.

Images flashed before her eyes. They obscured her vision and dizzied her so her knees buckled before she had gone more than a dozen meters. She stumbled, sank to her knees, and threw her arms across her face to blot out the scene that pushed its way violently to the forefront of waking memory. She did not succeed: when she lowered her arms, she stood no longer in a quiet forest but in a secret chamber in the palace in Caros City, surrounded by a sea of faces in which few were familiar.

"Minissa has elected you to the quest," Ariane intoned in a voice like a death knell.

"Fine," said Mistra. "We'll be off in the morning, then."

"She designated you, Mistra—not your consort."

A beat of silence, then: "What?" None of the small cluster of dignitaries, great folk and high from all over the Carotian Union, moved to contradict the woman who was Mistra's sister—and their own High Queen. Nor did any attempt to answer Mistra's outburst. She waited the space of three heartbeats anyway just to give them the chance: no one was going to like what she had to say next if she did not get a response to that simple query, least of all her. Still, no one spoke. Her next words tore into the silence, daring it to persist. "But if I try to run off alone, he'll follow me!"

"Then he will die." In making this statement, Ariane had not wanted for compassion; she sought only to make absolutely clear Mistra's position—and her consort's.

"He won't believe that. He'll come after me."

"It is a choice he must make, or else you must make the choice for him. Minissa did not visit him with the mark of the Stag. If he follows you, he will die.

Mistra never knew how much time passed before she felt a gentle hand on her shoulder. The secret chamber faded. Through tears that still partially obscured her vision, she saw Mosaia. A question was in his eyes, as were concern and compassion. "Princess?" he asked. "Mistra?"

"They *lied* to me!" she sobbed. Her heart felt ripped in two; her mind could barely compass the enormity of the injustice that had been done her. "Anthraticus passed the first Portal and lived, and no goddess of any race marked him for this quest or any other. They *lied*!"

She caught the nuance as he took her in his arms. He did not understand the exact nature of her problem, nor had he great experience with women, of holding them to express affection or to comfort them when they sorrowed, yet he acted: it was enough that she grieved. She found something inexpressibly sweet about the gesture—it lacked consciousness of self to such an extent that it became a completely selfless act. The knight acting so on her behalf coupled with his strong, reassuring presence dispelled half her heartache on the spot.

"Ah, your consort," he said after taking a moment to piece it together. "I see. You think he might have come after all, if Anthraticus has not come to harm."

She nodded, knowing with her face buried in his broad chest, he could do no more than feel the movement.

"Oh, dear," he said with more consternation than rancor.

She felt him stroke her hair as he rocked her gently, letting the sobs run their course. She felt a second nuance: her tacit acceptance of his comfort was bolstering his confidence. "It was all for nothing," she said once she could speak again. "The fiction of my death, the hours of planning, the creation of the replicant, the severing of the bond by the Nonacle..." *And the ache in my psyche that throbs like an open wound.*

"You don't really think they lied, do you, lady?" He tilted her chin up so her eyes met his, and she offered no resistance. His voice and manner were infinitely gentle. "Your own good gods and priests and loremasters, those whose praises you sing? Anthraticus came with us by accident, and who knows what else we will meet on the road that may kill us all, marked with the Stag or not? Your consort was learned and resourceful by all accounts, but not invulnerable, for all that. I think we must count it a mercy of your gods that Anthraticus took no harm from his passage of the Portal. A deliberate attempt by someone who bore not the mark of the Stag might have resulted in disaster."

Something in his words made sense to her so she nodded, but she could not bring herself to pull away from the sheltering circle of his arms. "I said on the day I accepted my fate I would enter this valley of despair with pain as my steed and denial as my mantle. I think I was just finding my seat and getting my cloak adjusted when we realized Anthraticus had come with us! I think I've already blundered too far into that valley to turn back, yet my steed of pain has suddenly grown so great and wild I think I shall be thrown to the ground and trampled." She flashed him a rueful smile. "The well from which I draw my meager strength seems to have run dry; to whom can I look to replenish it?"

He smiled kindly down at her. "To your own self, which I think is a greater wellspring than you know. And to your loving companions. And to—well, a knight of my persuasion should say to your faith, I suppose. But how can one person exhort another to faith at a time like this? My heart tells me it would sound like nought but empty platitudes. How does one who has never known the pleasure of love counsel one who is grieving its loss? Yet you are courageous and high-hearted, Mistra, or your Minissa would not have elected you to the quest. Can you think that in the moment she elected you, she also decided you had attained perfection and could go to your grave with no further tests of your faith? Yet, can you believe she would test you beyond your capacity to endure? It is to the strong the harshest tests are given, that they may grow ever greater in the sight of God. It is only our own imperfections that make us feel as weak as newborn kittens while the storm buffets us; did we not need the test to grow, we would be as secure in the storm as a globe of imperishable crystal anchored to the bottom of the sea."

She could only stare for a moment: she was used to men of war being prosaic, and he was giving her poetry as beautiful, as deeply moving as any ode written by any master bard who ever set pen to paper. She was also used to men of war having about as much true insight as the glue with which her pointe shoes were stiffened. However Mosaia had learned the letter of his Law, its spirit had gone straight to his heart! She crooked her mouth into what felt like the wriest of smiles. "I would have said this particular test should have held me for at least a few months, but..." She sighed. "You are very wise. I feel like I'm courting disaster, Mosaia—disaster and madness. You may have just thrown me the rope I needed before I went toppling over the edge. It should have been *my* rope, one I spun for myself." Another crooked smile. "Grief seems to have blunted the edge of my rope-making skills. I keep thinking I'm working with the best hemp when what I really have in my hands is something as insubstantial as a butterfly's cocoon. In *your* hands, the rope has substance and weight—and a pleasing form."

"Then please catch it and hold on with all your might," he said, smiling as though he found amusement in the metaphor. "The party cannot bear to be deprived of your company just yet."

She rested her head on his shoulder once more, content in his warmth and solidity, in the sense of his great spirit enfolding hers like a quilt of eiderdown, in their companionable silence. *Perhaps this is the* real *test,* she thought, *that in my hour of trial I learn to find comfort in the words of a stranger, an outworlder who knows nothing of the Greater Mysteries as we understand them in the Union. I am not encumbered by despair and lost love but by pride...*

She could have rested content in his arms for long hours but for the urgent shouts of their companions calling to them to return.

Mistra and Mosaia returned to the spot where the rest of the party had remained assembled. The other six were standing motionless and rapt; it took the returning pair mere seconds to join in the display of mute reverence. Mosaia even partially drew the sword so it could share in the experience. For once, the loquacious blade found nothing to say.

Before them, living and breathing, stood the Stag of Minissa.

He said nothing but regarded each of them in turn with his great, solemn eyes. He made no sign, although he may have been indicating approval for completion of their first task and sizing them up for their readiness to go on to the next. Only when a curious Anthraticus, still recovering from his bout with Deneth's brandy, fluttered shakily from his perch in the trees and landed on the Stag's antlers did the vestige of a grin appear on the great beast's mouth. The little spragon snaked his long neck down so he could look the Stag in the eye, cocking his head one way and the other as if to ask what manner of being the stately creature was. His purchase, however, proved tenuous; the act of tilting his head caused his grip to falter. He did not go crashing to the ground—his claws still clung loosely to the Stag's antler—but instead looped 180° so he came to rest hanging upside down staring the Stag full in the face. He looked appalled for a moment, as it struck him that this was a divine creature whose antler he was using for his gymnastics. He tried to recoup by covering the grimace with his broad, silly grin. The Stag merely flashed a cervine smile of amusement. With a toss of his mighty head, he sent Anthraticus the other 180° around the circle so he landed upright. The spragon now perching on his great rack like a hood ornament, he beckoned to the others to follow.

As the Stag led them along, the forest thinned. Now, rather than picking their way through closely spaced trees and dense underbrush in a line, they could walk several abreast. A respectful, almost reverent hush had fallen over them when the Stag had appeared, and they walked now in silence. Even Mistra's pained resentment abated in the face of the Stag's majestic grace.

As they walked, surrounded by the whisper of the wind in the trees and the chirps and squeaks of woodland creatures who came to pay homage to the Stag, Mistra pulled the Portal Stone from her pack. To her surprise, it lay dormant in her hand. She nudged Mosaia, who frowned thoughtfully.

"Too far?" he whispered.

She gave a thoughtful shrug as if to say his was a reasonable supposition. "A guide?" she asked him quietly with a nod in the Stag's direction.

He, too, shrugged thoughtfully, for exactly the same reason. "The gift of a benevolent God—or Pantheon—to those lost in the wilderness." He may have meant that as remark or question; whichever, a look of understanding passed between them before they moved on.

The sun had just begun to wester when they came to the edge of the trees. Ahead lay a grassy plain broken by a hill so broad they could only guess at its diameter from where they stood. Its slope was gentle, but it reached so high above them the midday sun would soon be hidden from their sight. Deneth gave a low whistle.

"Over it or around it," he mused aloud. "Either way, it looks like a long walk."

They drew to a halt, waiting for the Stag to continue on, but the Stag turned to face them. He fixed his gaze on Deneth. It took a moment for Deneth to register that the Stag was communicating with him. He cocked his head and frowned, as if trying to catch some nuance of sound just on the edge of hearing. The others felt a crackling in the air around them, as though the atmosphere were being charged with electricity. The tension mounted till the sense of anticipation became so strong they felt they must prepare to fight or flee, or else go mad from their inability to defuse the pressure that threatened to overwhelm them.

And then it was gone, like the snapping of an elastic band stretched suddenly beyond its limit. They stood dazzled, as if the sun for a moment shone directly into their eyes. When the world righted itself, they noticed simultaneously that they could breathe again—and that the Stag had vanished. Mistra pulled out the Stone again, hopeful that it would now direct them, but it still lay quiescent. She sighed audibly. "Now what?" she asked. She meant it rhetorically, but, while the others seemed at a loss, Alla noticed the distracted, distant look that Deneth still wore.

"I think," she said to him, "that the Stag has left us in your hands."

Deneth heard Alla speaking to him as if from a great distance. He contemplated the words that seemed to swoop down on him from the very Ether, the tune and lyrics he had seen revealed to him as if through a dense fog. He had never thought of the Ether as a physical place, but the odd sensation came to him that these words, this great music, had been composed on the Day of Creation, then anchored here in this spot to await his arrival, as if, in all the cosmos, his mind alone could perceive them.

As he forced himself back from that place between one reality and the next, he forced his brow to smooth a little; he shifted his focus so his companions would know that wherever he had been, he had returned to them. "I think so, too," he replied. "Phino knows why! I feel as though the Stag gave me a puzzle with all the pieces but with no directions and no clue as to what sort of puzzle it might be."

"Did he *speak* to you?" Habie asked, a rare note of awe in her voice.

"Yes. I suppose he did. Here." He touched his brow absently to indicate a telepathic contact of some sort. "He told me—" He stopped himself, looking from face to face to reassure himself these people would not try to haul him off to the nearest asylum for what he was about to say. Whatever reassurances he needed, he must have found, for he plunged ahead after a moment of intense scrutiny. "He told me to sing the stones asunder, to move rock and grass with but a phrase."

"Our bard waxes poetic," Torreb said with a benign grin.

"Not this time. Those were his exact words. I wonder... The right musical tones *can* produce enough sympathetic vibrations to shatter certain substances, like glass." He regarded the hill, assessing the odds that such a structure would be made of glass and deciding it wasn't the way to bet.

"What kinds of notes would it take to shatter a great big pile of dirt?" asked Habie, her voice skeptical.

"I heard music," he said, running over the melody in his mind but thinking it would take more than his voice to move mountains with it. "When I was..." He waved his hand vaguely to indicate "out there."

"If you heard it—" Mistra waved her hand to indicate the same nebulous place. "—then maybe you must look less to physical science for an answer and more to the magic of your own soul."

A further moment of thought, and he brightened. "Of course!" He unslung his pack and pulled from it the lute that had been Tuhl's gift to him.

"Tuhl said it would give you powers over the elements!" she exclaimed.

He cocked an eyebrow first at her, then at the hill. "Elements?" He inflected it so she could see the picture the word brought to his mind and understand it more to do with spring breezes and dancing brooks than with a hill the size of Thalas City.

Mistra bit her lip and gave him a helpless little shrug, but Habie said, "Hey, why start at the bottom and work your way up when you can start at the very top?"

"Top," he muttered, glaring briefly at her. "Right." He directed his attention to the lute but did not position it. He had played it since Tuhl had presented it to him, but only to entertain: he had not yet taken it up thinking to invoke any of its powers. Having the continuation of the quest depend on his doing so was a little frightening—the lute actually felt different now that he was planning to call on its magic—but it was also a little thrilling!

He touched a tentative finger to the lowest of its 14 courses. Plucking the tandem strings produced a tone of such compelling purity he felt his heart might break from the sheer beauty of it. Looking up, he saw the enraptured expressions on the faces of his friends and knew the spell was drawing them in.

He felt suddenly acutely aware of his own shortcomings; he felt as if he might be defiling something holy with his meager skill and tainted hands. He was tempted to put the instrument away, to *throw* it away, or at least to hand it over to someone like Torreb or Mosaia, men who had long ago dedicated their lives to the Divine. But in the instant before he would have yielded to the impulse to put the lute from him forever, he felt a gentle touch on his arm. He looked up to see Mistra smiling encouragement. He heard echoing through his mind something she had said to him once upon a time: that when she heard his music, she could see into the magnificence of his soul. Worldly she might be, but in some ways, he thought she was even purer in spirit than the two who had taken holy orders: her stalwart belief in him meant more. If she thought that, if Tuhl had entrusted him with the lute's keeping, then perhaps he *did* dare play it. Seen in that light, perhaps he dared not refuse!

He cradled the lute tenderly a moment, then positioned it and proceeded to play. As he sought to reproduce the melody and words he heard in the Ether, it struck him how akin the tune was to one he had learned in the days of his apprenticeship—an old Thalacian work song about the cutting and laying of brick, about the building of a mighty edifice by the humble efforts of many, each doing his own small share.

He framed the piece fully in his own mind, then lifted his voice and began to play in earnest.

As the sight of the Stag had held the little company rapt, now the sound of Deneth's music riveted them. His voice—a sweet, resonant tenor that would have stood on its own merits in the greatest concert halls in the galaxy—blended with the magic of word and melody to make the very dust motes around them vibrate with joy. If his voice seemed loud in his own ears, he knew it also sounded more true than he could ever recall it having sounded in his life. Lute, voice, and song of the very Ether rose to the Home of Homes and rivaled in grandeur the music Phino made for the One on the Day of Creation.

Deneth was just finishing the last phrase, the final strains of the lute feathering off into silence, when the ground quaked. The tremor was so violent none but T'Cru kept his footing. It felt as if the ground might break asunder at any moment and swallow them whole. So they were surprised to see the ground open not at their feet, but in the side of the hill: about halfway to its summit, a horizontal cleft straight enough to have been cut with a laser was forming. From it issued a light bright and rosy: first a seam, then a thread, then a ribbon, till it became a veritable river. Paler than the light of the sun it was, yet it dazzled them more than any sun's rays could have at noon on a bright summer's day.

The air shuddered as though a huge gong had been struck. As the sound faded, the cleft stopped widening. Now they could see that above them lay no mere fissure. The light issued from the heart of the hill itself; its entire crest was lifting into the air! No trick of levitation, this. Rather, the crest of the hill perched on a thick column so it looked like a gigantic bumbershoot, or like a tree being thrust out of the ground by its own tap root.

All of them save Deneth looked on, gaping, but the bard, with the self-assured air of one who had not only *made* this happen but had *intended* it to happen all along, said, "Well, it's a much shorter climb now. Come on." He ignored the several histrionically murderous glares his friends aimed at him and led the way.

They ascended the lower half of the hill to find themselves looking down and across a wide bowl-shaped field. The only object in all that immensity of tall grass was the column that supported the top half of the hill. Whether by design or chance, it did indeed resemble the bole of a huge tree.

"The Hollow Hills," Mosaia mused. It came out in a voice no greater than a whisper, but in that whisper awe resonated. He found Mistra, Alla, and Deneth staring at him, their looks somewhere between amused and accusing. "You've caught me out," he admitted with a grin. "We *do* have legends of Faerie where I come from, and of the Hollow Hills that are said to be the entrances to that world." Although the women accepted the explanation, he stared Deneth down and still got a skeptical "R-I-I-I-ght..." from the bard as he turned away.

They descended and crossed the field till they stood under the column, a trunk-like structure of massive girth. Only once, in the Meadow under which lay the Orb of Caros, had any of them seen a bole of such diameter. Holding hands (and paws and claws) the eight of them could not have encircled it. Not a living creature could be seen either in the "tree" or upon the plain.

They were at a loss over how they should proceed till Habie, on a whim, rubbed her hand against the column. Her original intent had been to see whether it felt like a tree, since it looked like but could not reasonably be one. Her expression changed from one of idle curiosity to interest quickly. "Here, Alla," she said. "Feel this. It's like it's *singing* to me. Someone like you could probably tell its entire family history," she added with a grin.

With an indulgent smile, Alla, too, touched the column and found Habie's assessment to be quite accurate. She nodded to the others, who variously touched and sniffed and listened. Even Mosaia, who thought of himself as the prosaic and citified man of war, was soon exulting in the joy of life and growth the tree—they supposed they must call it that now—emanated.

Their period of respectful silence drew to a halt as another tremor shook the ground. However, just as they were looking at one another as if to say, "Oh, no, not again," and bracing themselves to keep from falling should the tremor escalate, what had seemed the start of a quake became no more than a steady vibration. The rumbling resolved itself into a discrete sound: the pounding of many hooves. They looked all around the field several times before they discovered the source of the disturbance. There, down the side of the bowl opposite the one they had descended, came galloping six of the most splendid horses any of them had ever seen. Their coats glistened with the sheen and hue of precious metals and gemstones. A large stallion colored like ebony shot with gold and silver ran at the head of the line. Behind him galloped two blood mares, one the color of lilacs in spring, one the deep blue of sapphires in starlight; two smaller stallions in shades of topaz and garnet, and one smaller mare (or perhaps a large pony) of translucent aquamarine shot with platinum. Zigzagging toward the adventurers in an unbroken file, the horses thundered down the incline, then made a sharp turn and headed straight for the tree. They veered off just as it seemed they would either collide with the tree head-on or trample the small party. As the questors watched in amazement, the horses circled several times, then came to an abrupt halt almost nose-to-tail. A beat, and they pivoted with military precision to face the questors.

The company considered the horses as they stood in a neat line, stamping occasionally but otherwise standing as if at attention and awaiting orders. "By all that is holy!" gasped Mosaia. "What magnificent creatures! I have never seen their like." He reached out a hand to the ebony stallion. The gesture was tentative, almost shy, so amazed was he, but the stallion trotted forward and nuzzled Mosaia's hand as if the paladin were a long lost friend. Mosaia's touch became more confident, and he made the sort of soft cooing sounds one makes to babies, or to animals whose fear one is trying to ease. Turning back to the others, he said, "Do you suppose they have been, um, sent? Sent to bear us to the Portal?"

Mistra ran a hand along the flank of the sapphire mare, a knowing grin on her face. "Our clerics are served by horses very like these."

"But none so, well, *magnificent*, as Mosaia said," Torreb added. "Their true colors are evident only in starlight, though they are still the finest steeds in the Union, truly beautiful even by day. Perhaps these are more pure-blooded forebears." He frowned. "Forebears," he repeated. "Odd I should say that."

"Why?"

He shrugged. "Well, they *could* as easily be a race co-existing in time with our own, couldn't they?" He sounded only marginally convinced.

Mistra spoke softly to her mare for a moment, communing with her, divining, and, in fact, asking her permission to ride. The mare whinnied and nodded her shapely head, whereupon Mistra sprang lightly onto her back. Mistra had just been getting reacquainted with her own horse, a Tobiano Pinto mare named Windwalker, when destiny and the quest had claimed her. Rather than finding her seat and cantering the mare about the dell, however, she sat with her head bowed in concentration.

"Having a private conversation there, Mistra?" Deneth hazarded after a moment of this.

The sorceress shook her head as if awakening from a trance and gave them all a rueful smile. "I was just trying to find out something about them and their intent. This one is a little mum on the subject of where they came from, but she says she and the others will make it their business to keep their riders seated. So even those of us with little riding experience should be safe riding bareback."

"We don't get saddles if we ask nicely?" Torreb asked with a nervous laugh.

"No." Pointed but not ill-humored.

"You said 'a little mum'?" Deneth prompted.

Mistra looked heavenward as if trying to figure out how best to translate something for which she simply didn't have the vocabulary. "What she communicated—they speak in images, not words—is something like 'We were There, but now we are Here, and we have been commanded to bear you to Another Place before we return There.' 'There' seems to be synonymous with 'Home,' but whether that's someplace in the material world or not, I can't quite pick up. It's very pretty, though—green and peaceful, a bit like what I saw of the Home of Homes on my Dreamquest."

Torreb's eyes lit. "Then perhaps they are like Minissa's Unicorns and live at once with one foot—one *hoof*—in the spirit world and one in the material."

Deneth looked thoughtful. "Well," he said, "it's been a while since I've ridden bareback, but..." He approached the topaz stallion and mounted with an easy grace that belied his words. He and Mistra cantered around the dell for a few minutes while the others chose their animals (or while their animals chose them). Torreb felt at ease with the other stallion, but he and Mosaia had to all but bribe Habie to get her near the smallest mare, and then were obliged to assist her to mount. Habie only became comfortable after the pony itself shut its doe-like eyes and attempted to communicate on its own behalf.

"That's deeply weird," she commented as she relaxed into a reasonable posture for riding.

"What?" asked T'Cru, who was finding comfort himself in the novelty of the horses not shying from him.

"I don't think I've ever felt around in the mind or heart or wherever of an animal. It's almost like she knew I was an empath and was designing images just for me. They were all—y'know, *horsey*, like oats and hot mashes and rolling on springy grass and stuff. But it was like she knew that wouldn't mean much to me, so I *saw* the horsey stuff, but I *felt* more like hot meals and safe harbor for the night and no one trying to beat on me and take advantage." She screwed her small face up in thought. She took some gentle instruction from the others and was soon trotting around the bole of the tree with greater and greater confidence.

At last, all of them were settled except Alla. The lavender mare had indicated Alla should mount, but the shape-changer looked uncomfortable. "I have never liked the idea of one creature using another for transportation," she confessed solemnly. The matter clearly carried great weight to her, to the point of violating principle and ethic.

"Lady Alla," said Mosaia, "I believe these good beasts have been sent to us by some divinity—my God or your Minissa. Surely it would an affront to either not to make use of them."

"Could you shape-shift to your feline form and run alongside us?" Mistra suggested. Although she did not share the *aranyaka*'s concern over this particular use of beasts, as a true daughter of Minissa she understood it on a more fundamental level than the others.

"My dear Princess," said T'Cru, "I think *I* shall have trouble keeping pace with these creatures, and I am in my natural form. What of that, Alla? Does it not require a measure of strength and energy to maintain your alternate shapes?"

"Yes," Alla agreed. "I'm sure I could never keep up." She seemed on the verge of tears.

"Well, who says we have to run all the way?" Habie offered. "We'll go at your pace."

But Alla's attention had been captured, as had the lavender mare's, by some other Presence that had just manifested in the dell. The mare looked from one to the other of the questors, finally settling on Mistra as the one whose ability to commune with this Presence was the most profound. Drawn by the mare's gaze, Mistra nudged her own horse closer and placed a hand on the mare's brow. Again, she bowed her head and concentrated. As she did so, Alla looked up, rapt, as though she were listening to something at once deep and mysterious and heartbreaking in its sheer blinding beauty. Light came to her eyes, and tears. Minutes passed. Finally she nodded as if in assent to some command issued for her ears alone. She bowed, not to the mare but to the other Presence, one the others could sense but not see or hear. Smiling apologetically at the others, she mounted.

"What did you see, Alla?" Deneth asked as they set off. But Alla could only look beatific, and Mistra kept to herself the opinion that Minissa had come among them.

CHAPTER 2

When Are We?

*"One righteous act is endowed with a potency that can so
elevate the dust as to cause it to pass beyond the heaven of
heavens. It can tear every bond asunder, and hath the power
to restore the force that hath spent itself and vanished..."*
—The Book of Life

THE HORSES KNEW THEIR business. Once over the lip of the bowl, they turned southwest across a vast heath. They ran with such great speed that, had the terrain been rockier, sparks might have flown from their hooves. T'Cru had doubted his ability to keep up, but whatever magic propelled the horses swept him up in its tide; he kept abreast of the leader with no more exertion than he would have used had he been chasing butterflies in one of the pleasant meads of Caros.

Presently, a cluster of hills appeared in the distance, a rough circle of them with a taller summit amidmost. They made for this landmark, but Mosaia reined in abruptly when the formation still lay a league or so ahead of them.

"By God and all His angels in Heaven!" Mosaia breathed. "*That* is a familiar place!" For a moment, all he could do was stare.

"What is it, Mosaia?" asked Mistra, drawing up alongside him.

He shook his head, obviously hoping when he focused again, the view would have changed. He even looked back, considering the distance they had covered and the time in which they had covered it: the hollow hill had disappeared completely from view in the first hour of their ride. At their current speed, they would easily reach the circle of hills and the town he knew must lay beneath them by nightfall. "There is a village that nestles within the arms of those hills, I think."

"Do you know it?"

"More to the point," said Deneth, "is there a good inn?"

"Oh, an excellent one," replied Mosaia, his tone dry. "One of the best on Falidia to this day."

"Have we, by any chance," queried Torreb, "stumbled onto your ancestral home?"

Mosaia nodded. "'Twill be difficult to explain another hasty departure to my family and prospective bride." His eyes flickered with amusement. "Or, rather, it would if..." He trailed off, surprised he should make the surmise before these other folk who were so used to the workings of magic.

"So you *do* have a past," Deneth chuckled.

"Not yet, I don't." He seemed to take some pleasure in the discomfiture the remark caused the bard.

Anthraticus at this point fluttered up out of Deneth's hood, where he had been sleeping off his affliction for most of the afternoon, and came to rest on the paladin's head, the easier to address them all. "I believe he means," the spragon offered, "he may have no *present*. You—*we*—must have traveled across time as well as space."

Once they got over the shock of the spragon's lucidity, they found themselves sobered by the thought. They had expected magical interplanetary travel, but the possibility of travel in time had only just occurred to them. From Mistra's visions alone had they received a glimmer that they might journey across eons as well as parsecs. *What next?* They asked as a collective unspoken question. Mistra pulled out the Portal Stone again, sighing in resignation when it lit brightly as she held it facing the ring of hills.

"I have a doomed feeling about this," Deneth muttered as they exchanged uncomfortable glances. "Too bad that thing doesn't have a calendar attached to it."

Anthraticus sprang into the air and came to rest on Deneth's shoulder, exclaiming, "Gadzooks, man! Did you learn nothing of the Stone's lore when you cast the spell I taught you at it?"

"He learned how we might save Alla's life," Torreb said pointedly. "You were indisposed for that part."

"Did I miss something?" asked Deneth. "Like that it functions as a chronometer?"

"Perhaps, perhaps!" the spragon chirped.

He sucked in his cheeks. He had meant the comment to be as rhetorical as it was sarcastic, but he could play along in the face of the little coatl's suggestion. "OK." He held his hand out to Mistra, who surrendered the Stone, then reoriented his horse so he sat facing the cluster of hills. He looked at the Stone a moment as if expecting it to morph into a calendar.

"Try holding it here," Mistra suggested, touching a point between his brows. "It's a contact that facilitates the Sight."

His gave her a look that said *thank you, we do have a counterculture on Thalas that teaches all about things like energy nexi and the Third Eye*. But, to everyone's surprise, he thanked her without cracking wise and did as she suggested. The others waited while he divined what he could. It took a few minutes, during which Anthraticus snaked his head over and pressed his ear to the Stone, as if he might learn something by listening.

"If this fails," Mosaia said quietly, "I may be able to glean a better idea of the time period by seeing the exact state of development of the town. Our lands lie just to the west, and I know something of the history of the area."

But the Stone saved Mosaia the trouble of digging more deeply into his memory. In less than a minute, it began to throb with a faint blue light. Deneth's concentration deepened. A few minutes more and the light dimmed. He lowered the Stone, frowning and shaking his head. "I'm getting something, but it doesn't make sense to me. It confirms that this is Falidia and the town is called Waterford, and the Clear Water lands are off that way somewhere, but the date isn't in Galactic Standard, or in any planetary scale that I know of."

"Perhaps neither exists as yet," Mosaia suggested. "Tell us anyway."

"E.E. 760?"

He arched an eyebrow. "We *are* deep in the past. The date makes sense to me, Deneth, though it is a frame of reference naught but scholars even on Falidia would recognize. The calendar Falidia keeps in our era—the one that corresponds to Galactic Standard—dates from this year. We are come on the threshold of a new era."

"What happened?" asked Alla. "Was there a revolution?"

He looked troubled. "Unfortunately, my knowledge of Falidian history will avail us little more. The events leading to this new epoch are shrouded in mystery." He lowered his voice and looked around, as if the grass itself might be listening. "It is my private opinion, after having studied the matter, that the authorities of the time, secular or religious or both working in concert, obscured the facts purposely. The practice of magic existed on Falidia once—it may have even been commonplace, though I doubt as commonplace or worked with such ease as on Caros and Ereb, but the Falidians of the day saw it as magic nonetheless. The church of the time, such as it was, accepted its use; it may even have been sanctioned, or somehow bound up with the dominant faith, as it is in the Union. But that dominant faith differed widely from ours, for this part of Falidia at least seemed to believe in a multiplicity of gods—only a few, and, like your Pantheon, benevolent. This era that is so shrouded in mystery is what we now call the Dark Time, the Era of the Emari."

"Ah," said Deneth. "E.E."

"Yes. It was a dynasty of sorts, a loose theocracy whose heads were the prophet Emar and His descendants. In 760, a new prophet arose—the One Whose teachings on monotheism and conduct form the foundations of the mainstream religion in my land today—and a new era began. But known only to a few who have sought, I think, is the fact that a ban on all magic use arose from incidents that occurred at that time. One must search the church archives in my time very thoroughly to find even that much. And I came to believe that what arose was not a simple ban but a total disappearance of magic—you might say mana, for like you, my forebears drew their power from the very elements—as if something had stripped the very ability of your Orbs at home to mediate all of your special abilities." He saw Mistra pale at the thought. "Believe me, lady, by the time this happened, what you revere as the Art had degenerated into something utterly malign. We know from open records at the beginning of the period that magic began as it seems to have on Caros and Ereb and that mages saw it as their duty to act for the common weal, actions certainly in consonance with the teachings of the Prophet Emar. But by the end of the age, usurpers had taken over much of the direction of the church in the great centers of thought, wresting the reins of authority from the hands of the Prophet's family itself. Its most powerful practitioners used it for dark and evil designs, often seeking to undermine the Emari themselves, and the Prophet's family had begun to dwindle." He shuddered as if the sun had suddenly gone behind a cloud. "It does no credit to a good man of the church to find such things in his faith's history."

"You smell of shame, if I may be so bold," remarked T'Cru.

Deneth quirked an eyebrow at the paladin. "How would such a thing dishonor you? Ask Mistra here. She's had intrigue in her family in the last quarter century, not millennia go, and she doesn't agonize over it."

Mistra snapped her eyes around toward Deneth, then softened and let the tension drain from her posture. Still, she drew breath raggedly. "The blackest magician Caros ever produced nearly saw my sister assassinated," she explained for the benefit those who did not know the story. "My own cousin aided him. Stripped of their powers by the Nonacle, they found a way to regenerate those powers, a way that would be anathema to the rest of us. My cousin died in battle with my father when he tried to take the throne. The mage came to serve the last Thalacian king, the one who started the war. He almost undid both my sister and the High King, threatening them with torture, with magical compulsions so Thalas could unite the system and two royal bloodlines by force. My sister would have committed ritual suicide before she let that happen, had Avador not gotten them free." She sighed. "The Toths gave him safe harbor, used him, conspired with him—but *we* produced him." She rolled her eyes upward, as if drawing tearful strength from the Ether. "For all Caros is an idealized, peaceful society, we do get—well, *miscreants* from time to time, throwbacks from a more savage time."

Taking in Mistra's sudden show of introspection, Deneth flashed her a rueful grin that widened to include first Mosaia, then the rest of the party.

"Sorry, Mistra, all of you. I was trying to make Mosaia feel less wretched about Falidia's past, not open old wounds between Mistra's folk and mine." He touched Mistra's hand lightly and waited till she gave a small nod of acceptance. Something—his words, the sincerity in his voice—made her smile up at him shyly. Reading what only her eyes said, he found himself brightening at the thought he had destroyed nothing between them with his misdirected ire.

"Go on, Mose," he encouraged once the moment had run its course. "You're doing well for 'knowing little that could help us.'"

"There's not much more to say," Mosaia continued. "The histories indicate some intrigue between a practitioner of the Black Arts and a daughter of one of the noble families. I think he tried to bring her within his sphere of influence but some agency thwarted her somehow. It must have been quite a plot to have provoked the reaction it did."

"Taking the mana from the very land," Torreb mused, knitting his brow.

"According to some very obscure, restricted texts," Mosaia reminded him.

Torreb perked up. "But don't you practice a form of magic in your clerical arts?" he asked. "And haven't we heard you refer to, well, to witches whom you believe traffic with your god of evil?"

"The Fiend is no god as either of us understands the term," he corrected the priest, "but, yes, he is believed to be the source of their power—a mediator, if you will. The powers of our priests and holy knights come directly from the Father in Heaven, without mana, without mediation—at least, in our day."

"If there *were* a source for the magical powers of your ancestors," reasoned Torreb, "that may mean they were what we would call physical magicians: they couldn't just shape the Ether with a thought. They would need objects and incantations." He brightened at the thought of a new area of learning he could explore. "How very interesting! But, er—" He broke off as he saw the indulgent smiles his friends cast him, a sort of collective "There goes Torreb again" look. "That *could* be good strategic information, couldn't it, Mosaia? From a practical point of view, I mean, if this Black Magician—however powerful—still needs the trappings of physical magic to work his spells. And if we are to defeat him."

Alla's eyes twinkled. "Are you suggesting our little band proves the downfall of this dark worker of magic, that Falidian history would be changed but for our intervention? Such hubris!" But she meant it humorously, and the others laughed.

As they approached the town at an easy walk, Mosaia pointed out the features that had tipped him off as to the place's identity: the tall hill upon which the University of Waterford stood in his day, the cramped configuration of what even in his day was extant as "the old city," the curve of the river (and ford) that gave the town its name, the general contour of the rolling hills that lay to the west of the city—hills in which he had grown up. In his time, most of the city extended outward onto the plains and rolling green country that surrounded the current village. The University of Waterford alone had been built on and around the tor that served as the city's geographical (and, later, intellectual) heart, as the tor constituted a discrete part of the landscape where the seat of learning could be kept separate from the hustle and bustle of the town. Later, he told them, an entire sub-section of the city would arise between the University and the old city—a colony unto itself where students and artists, teachers and philosophers might be heard debating the great tides of history at any hour of the day or night.

"That is an area from which the most radical, forward-looking thought reaches out to my poor, benighted land," he told them. "So great a force have the people in that quarter become, though their numbers are not great, that the church dares not move to silence them. If revolution comes to Falidia in my day, it will start not with good barons like my father striving to mete justice, but with students and scholars and scientists who dared to dream and were left to do so in peace." As the words left his mouth, he looked more thoughtful than any of his companions had ever seen him, and they suddenly saw him in a new light. Where most assumed he would be the first to uphold the status quo, they could now see him as a shining beacon poised on the cusp of social change.

When they reached the town of Waterford, they found the inn—the one Mosaia had described for them, the one he counted on being there—had, indeed, already been built. Time, of course, had barely touched it, so it looked far less worn than the soldiers' retreat he remembered from his era, but it lacked for neither atmosphere nor the quality he had promised. Waterford itself turned out to be a cozy little nook nestled at the foot of the hills.

As Tuhl had promised, their packs had been magically re-supplied with contents suitable to their changed surroundings, including, significantly, ample amounts of the local coinage. They found enough in their purses to secure for them pleasant rooms for the night, the use of a private dining room, and an excellent supper. If the weight of those purses also invited the interest of the few unsavory-looking characters who loitered in the dark corners of the tavern, one look at T'Cru's fangs and claws or at the Retributor strapped to Mosaia's back served as all the encouragement they needed to look elsewhere for prey.

A thick curtain separated their private dining room from the common area of the tavern. They did not try to eavesdrop, but they kept catching snatches of conversation through the barrier or whenever one of them went to alert the innkeeper to the need for more food or wine. Little of the local gossip sounded good. Patrons were complaining about the way the number of hedge wizards in the area had dwindled sharply in the last fortnight. From the tone the complaints took and from what little Mosaia had been able to tell them, the companions drew a picture of a society in which these itinerant country magicians and their skills were integral to daily life. They were not only benign practitioners but supremely useful ones: they painted signs, shod horses with shoes that would magically resist wear, took in mending by the basketful, even aided priests in the upkeep of their parishes. Where formerly they had numbered in the hundreds, now they had vanished virtually overnight. Whether their powers had deserted them or they had simply left the area, no one knew. Rumors suggested they had somehow lost the ability to draw their magic from the soil here and so had moved on to find greener, more mana-laden pastures elsewhere. Some few visitors in the common room favored the darker idea that the wizards had been driven out or even killed by someone who wanted to harvest their abilities. The companions, when they questioned visitors to the common room, found all of those ideas to be at best hearsay and at worst idle speculation.

What seemed to be neither rumor nor speculation was that a very small number of mages had suddenly attained tremendous power, and that these few were neither benign nor useful to anyone but themselves. Worse, their leader, Sigurd, once a surreptitious practitioner of the dark arts, now practiced them openly. A long-time resident of the province, he had gone so far as to make demands that the local barons acknowledge his authority and treat him as equal and fellow ruler. If hubris motivated the demand, underpinning that hubris lay remarkable, terrifying power: according to those few mundanes he had allowed to see him work his dark wonders, his powers excelled those of the rest of the remaining mages combined. None sitting in the common room that night voiced the thought that Sigurd would be using any of this tremendous power to advance the common weal. Any who were able, in fact, were making provision to flee; those who had not the means to flee were busy fortifying the defenses of their homes. The few witnesses Sigurd had released had spread the word that the mage was making plans to strike down every other power in the province.

"And I've found another interesting connection for you, Mose," said Deneth as he brought a fresh flask of wine to their table. "Someone called Gwynddolyn seems to have attracted this Sigurd's dark affections." He did his histrionic best with the last two words.

"And my connection to her would be what?" asked the paladin.

"Not much. Only her family name, that's all."

"Gwynddolyn *Clear Water*?"

"Youngest daughter of your ancestral House." The bard made a theatrical bow.

"Then this Sigurd—"

"I reckon we've found both your dark wizard and the member of the noble house he tried to—how did you put it?—bring within his sphere of influence."

"Then if our job here is to save her," reasoned Torreb, "you'll be saving not a stranger but one of your own forebears." He frowned. "So if we don't save her, perhaps you will cease to exist."

"Oh, I don't know," said Deneth. "Maybe we'll just learn that Sigurd is one of Mosaia's forebears, rather than someone noble like him and his dad."

"Deneth, please," Mosaia cautioned, although he looked unsure whether to smile or frown at his friend for voicing the thought.

"I think that unlikely in the extreme," Torreb chuckled as he uncorked an excellent port the innkeeper had unearthed for them. "'Tis said that true love and evil cannot abide in the same heart, so what can this mage really feel for the poor girl? Although perhaps I'm speaking out of turn—I myself am woefully inexperienced in such matters and have at best an academic's grasp of the whole notion of love."

"And Mosaia's less inexperienced than he let on," said Deneth, deliberately staying mute on the point that it required somewhat less than true love to get a relationship consummated. "Come on, Mose, give—what's this about a bride you left at the altar?"

"*Prospective* bride, Deneth," Mosaia replied. It was obviously a matter of some weight that he make that distinction. "She is my fiancee by virtue of an arranged betrothal. It is the custom among the noble families here—at least, it will be. The quest forced me to put off the ceremony."

"The girl from the castle next door?" quipped Mistra.

He laughed in spite of himself at her apt turn of phrase. "Something like that. If we were to climb the tor here, on a clear day we could make out my ancestral home on the one hand and her castle on the other—or, could, if it's been built yet. House Bright Star has a somewhat shorter history in this province than House Clear Water."

"You put off your wedding?" asked Torreb, an unspoken note of tragedy in his voice.

"Yes. We hadn't set an exact date, but everyone expected us to marry well before the next harvest."

"Wouldn't the warm weather normally be a time of battles?" asked Deneth.

He smiled wistfully. "My father reached an accord with the surrounding baronies this year past. Everyone thought a summer wedding would be a nice symbolic gesture to honor the fact that we are at peace."

Torreb ploughed ahead, showing a better grasp of the romantic than a mere academic should have possessed. "Why aren't you pining?" The fact that the marriage was one of convenience rather than a love match seemed not to have sunk in.

He shrugged. "Well, I do not know her well—less well, I would say, than I know Anthraticus here as our most recent addition to the party. Certainly less well than I know the rest of you already, although we did know each other as children."

"I can just see it!" Deneth chuckled. "You used to use your toy sword to rescue her dollies from whatever mortal danger her big brothers put them in. Am I right?" This brought a chorus of laughter.

"Sorry, Mose, but this sounds real dumb," Habie decided. "I mean, suppose she's a complete twit or she's insane or ugly or something?"

"She is none of those things," he returned blandly, although he gave her a small smile for the dose of perspective.

Torreb still seemed to want to hear the match had something beyond convenience to commend it, and said so.

"She has—our parents' wishes." He smiled wanly, as if he knew how lame this might sound to a less provincial group.

"And quite right, too," T'Cru said lazily from his spot on the hearth rug. "Humans and other two-legs have the oddest ideas about romance entering into it."

"Well, you must know *something* about her you can tell us," Deneth pressed. "Come on, give. Is she pretty?"

"Pretty?" Habie chortled, whapping Deneth on the shoulder. "Who cares? Is she *rich*?"

"As a matter of fact, her father, like mine, is a ruling baron," said Mosaia, "so I expect her dowry will be substantial. But she is quite comely, really. Here." He pulled from his pack a holograph, which ran an image of a petite, buxom, blue-eyed blonde plucking several sprays of lilacs and braiding them into her hair, then smiling brightly at the camera. "It doesn't do her justice," he added, though the others "ooh"ed and "aah"ed appreciatively. He regarded the image as if to refresh his memory. When he spoke, fondness colored his voice, but it was more the fondness of a child for a well-loved pet than of a suitor for his betrothed. "Her skin is like new cream, her hair like the wind on waves of amber wheat, her eyes the blue of berries in spring—"

"Sounds fine if you're hungry for lunch," Habie said in a loud aside to Deneth.

"—her figure..." He stopped, abashed, realizing there were women and a priest present.

"Not athletic?" Mistra suggested good-naturedly.

"Curvaceous?" Deneth tried. "Makes you think of melons and pears rather than bananas, to keep with your description of the rest of her?"

Mosaia nodded rather shyly. "The men in my command tell me what a lucky rascal I am. They encourage me to be more—forward? At least, those suggest it who have taken no holy vows as I have," he added hastily. He was aware of several solicitous smiles. He suddenly found his wine glass to be of immense interest.

"We do shelter our women on Falidia," he finally went on, "overly so, I think, sometimes. My Johanna is very unworldly. She would think ill of no one. If she were forced to fight to defend what she held dear, she would have the will, but in terms of practicalities, I think she would be lost, and I sometimes wonder if a thought beyond the keeping of our future home ever enters her sweet mind." He sighed. "She will make me a good Falidian wife, I know. She is skilled in all we deem the feminine arts—use of the needle, the loom, the cookstove. Still, now that I have met the likes of you ladies and the noble and erudite Dr. Roarke, I wonder if I shall ever be content as I once would have been. Truly, this quest is fraught with more perils than the danger to mere life and limb!"

"Ah," said Mistra, resting her head on her stacked fists, "you're treading the most dangerous ground of all, Mosaia. You've begun asking questions that have no black and white answers." Her eyes twinkled.

"Well," Deneth pointed out, "we *all* thought we were on paths other than the one we landed on, Mosaia. You were on your way to an altar of convenience, Mistra was about to marry a man of her own choosing, T'Cru was learning to rule the Tigroids, Habie was merrily stuffing her pockets with other people's belongings, I'm still pretty sure Minissa meant this bloody mark for someone else. Habie's turned honest, Mistra's resigned herself to having love wrenched from her very soul, I still don't think Minissa intended me for this quest, but I've found you clowns fun to hang out and solve problems and split heads with. You, though—maybe you'll come to the end of your road and find Johanna is what you wanted and needed all along."

Habie guffawed. "And if not, you know you're the sort that has women falling all over him. It's not like you'll lack for choice. Hell, I'd fall all over you if I reached higher than the bottom of your sword harness!"

The image of the two of them as a couple lifted the pall of pensiveness that had threatened. Habie's raucous laughter proved infectious; Mosaia refilled his glass, passed the wine around again, and proposed a toast to new friends and inopportunely diverted life paths.

The humans in the party had a difficult time convincing the innkeeper (and the beasts) that the beasts should stay inside the inn for the night. T'Cru wanted to curl up in the stable or prowl the woods that lined the hills, and Anthraticus wanted to roost in the trees, but the humans advised against this on the grounds that they would either frighten the locals or invite capture by some enterprising woodsman. The innkeeper, on the other hand, was appalled at the prospect of having either stay in the inn proper. But T'Cru spoke to him—first civilly, then regally, and, when that didn't work, growled (regally) and allowed the fur on his back to rise the slightest, most tasteful bit. To the Tigroid, choosing to spend the night outside was a much different matter than being forced to stay outside because he had been barred from the inn! It was at that point (and after some gold had surreptitiously changed hands) that the innkeeper saw reason, although he went away muttering something under his breath about "people of the Tribes and their strange ways with animals."

Once they had settled that, the companions ambled into the common room to mingle with the locals and see what further news they could pick up. Deneth fell in with the troupe of musicians seated on the small stage; when he had dropped enough clues about his vocation that they guessed it, they invited him to join them.

"What's your instrument?" asked one.

Habie's ears pricked up at the question: unless she missed her guess, there was money to be made here. "He plays *anything*," she assured them. She kept mum on something she had heard Mistra once claim: that Deneth's compositions were changing the very nature of music on the faces of the Three Worlds. He was *that* good at what he did!

Deneth looked modest but did not deny the claim.

"I'd like to see the color of your money on that one," said a fellow with a lap harp.

Habie pulled out her purse and jingled it in front of his face. "It's the prettiest shade of yellow—all sparkly-like."

"Gold?"

"Gold."

"Anything?"

"Anything."

"A wager?"

"Lots of them, if you're game."

The harper laughed. "You're suggesting he run a gauntlet of our instruments? For money?"

"He would say something stupid like money and art don't compare and shouldn't mix, but—yup."

The harper exchanged glances with his fellow musicians, all of whom either looked thoughtful or nodded with varying degrees of enthusiasm. "All right, then, Missy—"

"Habie. And this is Deneth bent Elias."

"All right, then, Habie and Deneth bent Elias. If you'll put up your pouch of shiny coins, we'll see if he gets so much as a sound out of them all, or makes sweet music, or sends these nice patrons screaming into the night with their fingers in their ears because of his caterwauling."

Habie came back with, "Don't be daft, he'll outplay the lot of you." Surveying the assortment of instruments— everything from the harp and viol to a set of Uileann pipes—she mouthed surreptitiously, "Right, Deneth?" She did not truly doubt, but found herself reassured when he mouthed back "Hey, it's *me*."

Rather than ask for the exact color of *their* money, Habie did a quick assessment of the group. She guessed they held no professional standing but represented that much more congenial entity, a loose confederation of musicians from all walks of life drawn together by their common interest in music. Judging from their garb, some came from wealthy houses and some could have been not much more than street musicians. She suggested a betting structure that would have them start with a small ante that would double each time Deneth successfully played an instrument. If he struck out three times in a row, she would concede their entire purse to be distributed to the group at large: the gold inside would easily cover the all of the bets if he made it through the score or so of instruments arrayed before him. At this show of fair play, the richest members of the group said they would cover all bets should any individuals not be able to meet their obligations.

"To make it fair," she added, "I'll just pick what comes next based on what I think looks like the next hardest thing."

"How's that fair?" asked a woman with a penny whistle.

"I've got no musical training like my friend here. I'll just be guessing." That was what she said. What she planned was to start with the least affluent-looking musician and work her way up to the richest. Fair was fair, after all.

Now Deneth took over, running through the first seven instruments Habie designated in rapid succession. That got him through the less well-off people and well into the middle class, through most of the woodwinds and to the first instrument that used a bow. He faltered a little while he placed his fingers on the bow, made a truly horrendous sound with one pass of the bow across the strings, and stopped.

"You know, a bowed instrument is much harder than a woodwind," he remarked, "even one with a reed or a slide-y bit. What say we make this a little more interesting?"

The gamba player agreed eagerly to advance the wager by two factors, then looked completely crestfallen when Deneth's initial attempt—a sound like cats being scorched alive in boiling oil—resolved into a spritely folk melody played without fault.

The musicians realized at this point they had fallen for the great-granddaddy of all cons. They had him continue to run their gauntlet for the novelty of hearing one man play like a master on such a wide variety of instruments; in the end, they surrendered the money without begrudging him his win. They came out on the right end of the wager in one way—the longer the contest went on, the more interested the patrons became, and the more interested they became, the more drinks and snacks they bought and the more tips ended up in the group's tip jar (which rarely netted more than would buy them beer and pretzels).

The contest over, Deneth pulled out his lute and joined them. Their style of music was close enough to that with which he had grown up that he was soon playing with them as though they had been making music together all their lives. News had spread, and the common room now had people hanging from the rafters.

Her work accomplished and her purse twice as heavy as it had been, Habie moved on to greener pastures: she hustled the others into a game of poker. Her skill soon had the locals interested in cards as well as music, so, as her friends dropped out one by one as their cash reserves ran low, she did not lack for opponents. And no one in the common room left that night with anything near the number of valuables he had come in with, and no one turned in but with a good thought for what a memorable night this evening had become. The innkeeper, while not happy to see his best customers shorn of their money by strangers, brightened considerably when he realized the strangers had provided his regulars with some welcome diversion from the oppressive gloom that had settled on the district.

Only Mistra had become restless early on. She watched the contest with amused interest, listened to the music once Deneth joined the ensemble, and played a few hands of poker (the only ones during which Habie's pile of valuables shrank noticeably), then bade the others good night.

Deneth, who had been performing at the time Mistra called it a night, had noted her departure, wondered at it, but ultimately decided not to interfere. He played out the set, finished off his wine, and sat in on a few hands of Habie's cutthroat poker game. Only then, when he knew she had taken some badly needed time to be alone, did he go upstairs. He was not surprised when he returned to his room to find a note on his door:

Borrowed the lute. Hope you don't mind.

Mistra had signed not with her name or initial but with the Murzik, the formal character that would begin her name had it been written in Old High Thalybdenocian. He decided to interpret the note as an invitation, or at least as permission to approach.

When he came to her door, he found it closed but unlocked. To his surprise, when he stopped to listen, he heard her not strumming diffidently as a beginner might, but plucking out a complex accompaniment to her own voice—a meltingly sweet, light lyric soprano. That a voice so beautiful could be singing so mournful a tune smote his heart. He put his hand to the door, listened, then thought better of making his presence known when he recognized the words as phrases from the epic poem *The Rainbow Warriors*. It was one he had long ago fallen in love with for both the poetry of its composition and its subject matter. The story spoke of conflict, of good opposing ultimate evil, but it was colored with the tenderness of love that dared find expression in a landscape of fear, with courage that defied insurmountable odds, with the mixture of bitter and sweet that motivated the choice of life for a princess' people and lifemate over life and love for herself.

> "Melora poured water from the sacred spring
> Into the basin blessed to receive it
> Passed her hand over it, blew on it
> Gently, till the image of her lover appeared.
> He was in Flight.
> She said,
> 'Seek not to find me again in this life
> Be not grieved that I chose thy life above my
> own.
> My first duty is to my people.
> But I choose for thee to have life
> as well as they.
> Go thou, therefore.
> Remember me not in bitterness, but in love,
> And know that I shall be beside thee always.'"

His heart clenched, and a tear came unbidden to his eye at both the poignancy of the lyrics and the sweetness of the execution. It was his favorite passage; he had tackled the daunting task of memorizing it years ago in bardic college. It had had a strange effect on him. He could not say he had truly chosen to learn it; it had been more like a compulsion had seized him to draw all that startling beauty inside him. He thought of the lay as blue—not "the blues," but blue. He had seen the exact shade in his mind's eye the first time he read it: it was the color of the shadow cast at dawn by a glacier while the aurora borealis danced overhead. That is to say, it was a color that could never have existed in the physical world, but he thought—just maybe—it existed somewhere beyond.

Hearing Mistra sing it had a similar strange effect. Because of its sheer length, very few had tried to learn it by heart, and those who did chanted it. Now he was hearing a complete non-bard *singing* it. He had occasionally speculated, always keeping the thought to himself, that something about Mistra transcended the mortal; now he wondered briefly if he was about to enter the presence not of a human, but of an angel.

He opened the door and slipped inside.

She had extinguished all the lamps, but a fire laid on the hearth cast a warm glow so shades of bright copper seemed to play tag with the shadows. The effect dazzled his eyes and it took him a moment to locate Mistra. When he finally sighted on her, he found her curled up on the window seat, her back propped against the pane of the open window. She might have been unaware of him; even after she strummed the final solemn arpeggios and allowed the strings to resonate away to silence, she continued to stare out the window at the stars.

"Don't you know it's dangerous to touch a bard's instrument without his consent?" he asked quietly after a moment of stillness. He could think of no gentler way to announce his presence. He stuck his hands in his pockets and tried to look nonchalant when she fixed him with a stare whose import he had difficulty interpreting in the dim, lambent light. Between the silence and the stare, he felt she was regarding him as stranger or intruder rather than friend. He gave her an amiable and, he hoped, winning smile. "There might be any manner of booby traps on it that you wouldn't even know how to look for, let alone defuse," he felt compelled to add under the intensity of that gaze. To his relief, her lips parted in a grin, and he knew they were OK again.

"I altered my energy field to resonate with the lute's," she said simply. "It effectively, um, thinks I'm you."

"The more fool it!" He said it with a friendly leer.

"Well—wasn't it trapped?"

"Yes." He shrugged. "It would only have given you a little shock. I would have desensitized it for you if I had known you played *that* well. Of the lot of us, you're the one I'm absolutely sure I could trust with an instrument of that caliber."

"Thanks. I'm sorry I took it without asking your leave. I just—" She shrugged; he suspected she was at a loss to put her feelings into words after having poured them into the music. She proffered the instrument to him as if in apology.

"Hey, you don't need to explain." He took the lute, pushed himself up on the window ledge, and plucked a little. He knew he gave the impression his fingers had some special way of communicating with the strings without the intervention of his conscious mind, and that that alone often dazzled his listeners. Mistra did not seem dazzled, but he knew she was listening intently, appreciating his art in a way few could. She leaned her head against the window casement so she looked at him only obliquely. The light breeze ruffled her hair. He had rarely seen it loose before. It cascaded to her waist, catching the red glow of the firelight so it looked like a river of molten gold. It surprised him that he could take that all in and still go on as he had started, comforting a friend rather than letting desire crest and consume him. "Bards are bards because we *have* to make our music and our rhymes, as if they were bouncing around our hearts clamoring to be given voice. We—*I*—would feel like something inside me had died if I couldn't play my instruments and sing. You don't have to explain to me what it feels like only to *need* to." He regarded her a moment and knew somehow she had absorbed his words and the sentiments behind them and let them go straight to her heart. "Um– I've only heard *The Rainbow Warriors* recited or chanted before, never sung. Where did you come by the music?"

"I wrote it." She waved her hand vaguely, as if indicating another time, another place. "Once upon a time."

He arched both eyebrows, impressed. "You moved me to tears, with—well, with everything. The melody, the chord structure, your voice. You sing like an angel. It's more than a pretty voice. It's haunting, almost, did you know..." He trailed off, realizing he was rambling, set down the lute, and touched her hand. "Mistra, what is it? What's wrong?"

He felt her hand close tightly on his, saw the tears glistening on her cheeks. He knew she was trying to hold them back still, though he didn't fully understand why. Compassion welled in his heart then, and he held his arms out to her. She came as if she had only been waiting for the invitation, finally letting the tears flow once he enfolded her, then sobbing convulsively and clutching at him so he felt he had become her only anchor in a stormy sea. He cradled her head on his shoulder.

He knew less of his people's mysticism than a five-year-old Carotian child, but he supposed good intentions and the sense of connection they had felt since the day they met must count for something. Stroking her loose hair, he reached out in thought and let the Ether guide him till it drew his fingers to the psi points at the base of her skull. With very little encouragement on his part, they opened to let loose a torrent of psychic pain whose magnitude he had barely guessed before this. Waves of anger, of bitter resentment, of sorrow so profound he almost buckled under its weight swept him. For the first time, he could visualize the site the Nonacle had ruptured so she might preserve for her consort the fiction of her death. It looked like an amputated limb whose scab had been ripped off forcibly every time it started to heal. It felt like some sadistic power was lobbing salt at it every few seconds. He heard an involuntary groan, but only in focusing intently did he realize that he, rather than she, was its source.

Mistra felt his hand travel to the psi points at the base of her skull. Despite his imperfect touch, her pain was such that it flowed out readily, as if he sought to puncture with a blunt knife a balloon filled to the breaking point with water. The pain, though a trickle compared to what she had been keeping dammed up, flowed out with such force it wedged the points open, or he was too willing to assume the burden, or—

She gave up trying to mar with intellect what Deneth offered with such greatness of heart. She sobbed a bit more but relaxed very gradually as she felt the pain diminish. There were layers upon layers there from her severed consortium. If her pain were like an onion, she thought giddily, this would be like having him peel away the skin and not much more, but—oh, the blessed relief of having even *that* much of it stripped away!

How can a psychic wound be so raw? His thought echoed in her mind. He seemed to know she heard, for he spoke his next words aloud. "You said before that as bad as losing one consort to an abrupt and fiery death was, you wished this were that good. I think I must have assumed you were exaggerating!"

She shook her head glumly.

"I feel," he said, sounding like he was choosing his words with infinite care, "like the bonding site has never sealed over. You're leaking no vital fluids as you would be if a limb were suddenly amputated, but the wound itself is staying fresh. Is it the *tal-yosha*?"

She laughed wanly, marveling once again at his insight. "There's a reason the phenomenon is called that—'hunger of the soul'— rather than simple hunger of the body, or even hunger of the mind. I told you before, it's not simply a compulsion to unite physically with a man; it's a yearning of everything not of the body to find a life's mate. My mind and body aren't rationally looking for a bond-mate, but the ruptured site where the Nonacle severed the bond won't seal over because my psyche has to stay prepared, just in case Mr. Right comes along." Another laugh that was more of a grunt of self-derision. "And I think that's the grim truth."

He made a few more soothing noises and held her closer. A sense of decision came to his manner, as if he were saying, "I can do better than this." A moment later, he shifted his hand to a contact that would bleed the pain off much more directly. Knowing where he was going, she forgot her own pain long enough to do the moral thing.

"That site," she whispered, catching his hand. "You'll experience it much more directly. You'll be overwhelmed."

"Don't worry about me. I feel the pain as I draw it off, but it dissipates easily. It's not *my* pain, after all."

She met his eyes, endured his mental query, finally relented and let him touch his first two fingers to the contact over her heart. She giggled, only partially in relief at the sudden diminution of the psychic pain: he had noted only with detachment the pleasant contours that lay but a hair's breadth away from his fingertips, then commented silently on the fact that he was only noting and not acting. He seemed to think the reaction showed how thoroughly he had doomed himself!

He continued with the Discipline for a few more minutes. As she felt more confident in both his mastery of the technique and his ability to handle the pain, she gave herself over to his ministrations. She knew she had been resisting, but she did not realize till that instant of utter surrender how much she had been holding back so he would not be crushed under the weight of the psychic agony. The pain flowed freely out of her now, a torrent where it had been a stream. *We'll never make the center of the onion,* she thought with a sense of drowsy euphoria, *but I think he's peeling enough away that I can sauté it up with some mushrooms and have the beginnings of a lovely omelet...*

Abruptly, Deneth became so overwhelmed he was forced to break the contact. It was not a voluntary act; it was more akin to jerking one's fingers away from an open flame they have unconsciously strayed too near. He actually found himself blowing on his fingers a little as if he *had* been burned. He gasped, fearful the reflex would have hurt her, but he looked into her eyes and saw there only peace and understanding. She jerked, too, but settled back immediately. For her, the abrupt breaking of the contact was no worse than being yanked from a state of deep slumber to one of complete awareness, then discovering her surroundings were safe and she had no cause for alarm.

"Sorry," he said, waggling his fingers as if they still stung. "I guess I reached my saturation point without warning."

She stretched in her lithe, feline way. "I can't believe you're apologizing," she chuckled, then grew suddenly diffident. "Of course, if you *do* feel you have something to make up to me, there *is* one other thing you could do."

"Oh?" He arched his eyebrows outrageously several times but refrained from uttering any of the *double entendres* her suggestion brought to mind. Something about the sudden change in her manner cued him that this was not the time to respond in kind, however innocently.

She lowered her voice and pressed a little closer, as if what she was about to say amounted to the disclosure of a shameful secret. "I've been having horrible nightmares since the night I had that first vision of—*him*." She had no need to expound on who "he" was. The mage Syndycyr—a man who, like their Lost Prince, existed outside the flow of normal space-time, who had developed an intense interest in Mistra and in the quest even before they had embarked—had appeared to them as a group the day the last of them had come to Tuhl's wood. Though he had made only one attack many days ago, as they set out, Deneth himself agreed with Mosaia's earlier phrasing, that the mage was somehow dogging their footsteps. The bard shuddered, more on Mistra's behalf than his own. Now he knew why that feeling of vague dread had pursued him.

"And not just nightmares," she went on. "They're almost like full-out psychic attacks. I visualize myself standing on a storm-swept plain fighting off these dark, winged monstrosities, and however many I kill or fend off, more keep coming. I've kept it to myself, but truly I haven't gotten a decent night's sleep since before we left Caros."

His brow lined in concern. "What is it you know I can do for you that you're afraid to ask me for directly?" he asked, brushing a stray hair from her face, an infinitely tender gesture. "A Sleep of Peace?" He said it very solicitously; the mental contact required for the ritual was so intimate he knew this couldn't be an easy request for her to make of anyone, let alone a Thalacian. With the Discipline he had been using, the healer only allowed his subject to cast off negative emotions. With a Sleep of Peace, the healer actually insinuated his consciousness into his subject's.

She dropped her eyes and nodded.

He tilted her chin up so her eyes met his. "Say no more, and look no farther." Smiling fondly, he kissed her on the nose and set her on her feet. "If you've never had a Sleep of Peace sung to you by a ranking bard of the Emerald Brotherhood, you haven't lived—*slept*, I guess I should say. Not to mention that the companionship couldn't be better."

"Ah," she said drily, "once I've had it from a bard, I'll never go back? Is that what you're saying?"

Seeing from the comment that she had gotten past the brief bout of vulnerability, he laughed, making no effort to conceal the earthiness of the sound. "In no uncertain terms. Come along." He took her hand in one of his and grasped the neck of the lute in the other, then led her to the bed. "You sleep in that?" he asked of the short robe she wore. It was more a poet's shirt than a robe, frilly the way nightgowns were, but cut modestly enough to be worn to a garden party.

She flashed him a smile, and this time she made it overtly seductive. "When I sleep in anything."

"Don't feel compelled on my account," he rejoindered, doing his best to keep a straight face. "A Sleep of Peace will work much better if we get you as comfortable as possible before we start." He made a little feint toward the laces at the shirt's neckline.

She swatted him lightly but laughed as she did so.

He raised his hands in a show of jovial concession. Abruptly, though, his manner changed. "Sorry," he said, rubbing his brow in a way that said he was struggling to frame his thoughts. He flashed her a wan smile. "Poetic, tragic beauty isn't something you can expect a bard to resist for too long."

"Maybe my outsides only look so good because you've been prowling around my insides," she said kindly.

"You know I think your outsides always look pretty good, but—yes. I, on the other hand, must look grim indeed by the same token."

She poked him in the ribs, as if to upbraid him for angling so outrageously for a compliment. "I told you before: when I hear your music I see into the greatness of your soul"

"Mistra, I—" he began, then stopped, discomfited by the way she kept taking his glib tongue and tying it in knots.

"Ssh." She put a finger to her lips, but her eyes twinkled. "Sleep of Peace."

She got herself to the bed, but it was Deneth who tucked her in, and with as much tenderness as ever any mother tucked in her newborn babe. She curled up on her left side, whereupon he retuned the lute to the odd open tuning he used for his version of the Sleep of Peace. He had created his own tuning and his own arrangement, one that would allow him to play the accompaniment he used with one hand while contacting the psi points over her temple with the other. Propping himself against the headboard, he began to chant softly as he plucked out the opening arpeggios.

He felt her remaining tension ease almost immediately. As he sang, he wove into the images he was projecting all the things he knew she loved: ballet, unicorns, flowers in spring, the fresh smell of a meadow after a sudden storm, the rampant ki-rin that formed the central image of her personal sigil, the hidden falls with its rainbow that he knew without her having told him formed an integral part of her Dreamquest name. When he felt certain that she not only slept but dreamed peacefully, he removed his hand from her temple. He rose, pulled a chair up to the bed, retuned the lute more conventionally, and dug into his vast repertory of music and rhyme. And there he stayed, playing for Mistra, singing softly, and keeping away the evils of the night.

⚜

The others disturbed Deneth so many times throughout the rest of the evening inquiring after Mistra's well-being that he finally hung out a note. It read:

> *Mistra's OK. I'm spending the night, and I wish it*
> *were what all of you think, but it's not, so get lost.*

However, at about midnight, someone chose to disregard the note and knocked anyway. Deneth's initial inclination was to ignore it, but whoever it was continued to hammer at the door—not heavily, but so insistently Deneth feared the noise would wake Mistra. Furious at the thought that all his hard work might suddenly be rendered useless, Deneth finally rose and stomped to the door, intent on clobbering whoever he found.

"I should have known," he said a bit sourly when the unwelcome guest turned out to be Mosaia. However, he couldn't keep from cracking a smile at the paladin's poorly-concealed attempt to look surreptitiously past him. Deneth stepped back, opening the door enough that Mosaia could peer in and see what he would. The look of relief on Mosaia's face at the sight of the lute (rather than Mistra, he guessed) in Deneth's hands and of Mistra asleep in bed (alone and clothed) amused him more than he supposed was fair.

"She's sleeping," he explained quietly. "She was upset and having trouble settling down. There's a ritual we have at home that can help. It's best performed by a bard, though Torreb might tell you differently."

"Nightmares?" Mosaia asked.

Deneth nodded.

"I thought as much. I've been aware of her groaning in her sleep, being wakeful, ever since we met. I sleep rather lightly when I'm in the field."

"And you never said anything about it? Never asked her? Never offered to help?" He stepped out into the hall, truly irritated with the paladin but afraid their conversation would wake Mistra. "For the love of Thalybdenos, Mosaia, you're the paladin, the one besides Torreb who has the pure motives and the power to heal. What's the matter with you?"

Mosaia seemed at a loss: he was unused to being the recipient of a reprimand!

He shrugged, a gesture of helplessness rather than dismissal. His brow lined with concern. "I wanted to do all of those things; I simply didn't know how. She was functioning, to all appearances; she never asked for my help or Torreb's, not that I know of; and if she has a—well, a special friend in the company, it is you, not I." He frowned. "You mean *you* weren't aware till now?"

Deneth shook his head. "I'm a heavy sleeper. The only thing I tune in to that will wake me is physical danger—to myself. Years of training in the streets of Thalas City will do that to you! Mistra and me—it's not what you think. It's just what you said: she's a very special friend." He grinned. "Not that I don't enjoy giving the impression there's more between us."

"Well, that's, er, understandable."

"It *is*?" He had been expecting the paladin to call it something like "reprehensible" or "childish."

"Well, er, she is most comely."

"Comely. Uh-huh." He folded his arms across his chest and leaned against the wall. "I thought you fellows weren't supposed to notice such things, especially those of you who were engaged." He kept his face neutral, but mirth flickered in his eyes. This paladin-baiting had possibilities!

The hint of a blush came to Mosaia's cheeks. "I'm a man, Deneth, not a saint. I realize my innocence in that area amuses you, but it certainly doesn't exist because I'm immune to temptation. It is a choice."

He considered a witty rejoinder but opted for honesty. "It amuses me less than you think, Mosaia," he said with a kind smile. He cast his eyes heavenward, again searching for the words. "She came up here to be by herself because she's in such profound pain. I helped her with that, a little." He shook his head and summarized for him the story about the consort bond ruptured by the Nonacle and how ragged it left her psyche—how like an open wound, or even akin to a battlefield amputation. "I thought she was being poetic about the extent to which she hurt," he said. "Now I wonder that she could find a way, poetic or not, to describe it at all."

"It may be worse than you think."

"Oh?"

"When she ran off into the wood when we first arrived, she was attempting again to distance herself from us while she grieved. She likes not inflicting her grief on others, I think. When Anthraticus arrived here safe and whole, she suddenly believed everything she had been told about her consort not surviving if he pursued her amounted to a blatant lie. Like you, I did what I could to offer comfort, but then the rest of you called, and the Stag had already appeared, and then there was the hill and the tree and the horses, and the ride, and the shock that this is my own world, my own country. She had no time—"

A sudden muffled groan issuing from Mistra's room cut him off. "Oh, bloody draffing drek!" Deneth swore. "I shouldn't have left her." He pushed open the door and rushed to her bedside, Mosaia on his heels. They saw that, while she still slept, Mistra had begun to thrash and moan.

"What devilry is this?" Mosaia demanded. He took her hand, meaning to wake her, but Deneth restrained him.

"No. Better to help her work it out in the dream, or she'll keep being haunted by whatever is troubling her."

"But how?"

"Watch." He touched a slightly different set of contacts than those he had used to get her to sleep. Mistra settled down almost immediately, but she continued to breathe heavily, and strange words escaped her lips. Deneth concentrated deeply for about a minute, after which he slumped, flashed Mosaia a disgruntled look, and shook his head. "Maybe you're right. This is more than I can help her to set straight by myself."

"What is it? You could see into her very dreams?"

He nodded, and his expression grew grim. "Yes. She's fighting some sort of strange, evil phantoms. She tried to describe them to me earlier. I didn't know then that she meant they truly had substance, but that's exactly what she was trying to tell me. It's not a simple nightmare; it really is a full-out attack. What she's mumbling are fragments of some spells—short, powerful ones like Words of Command—she's using to try to fend the creatures off. A word of advice for you, mate: if you ever hear of a Carotian this powerful using words or signs or knickknacks to work her magic, or doing anything beyond pointing and concentrating, you know she's about to pop several major gaskets."

"What are the creatures? Demons?"

"Yes."

He considered. "Perhaps our nemesis is only restricted physically—it is he who troubles her hours of sleep, is it not?"

"The best I can say is these things bothering her felt the way Syndycyr's castle looked, but, yes—that's the way I'd bet."

"In the Dreaming, the veils between the worlds are thin indeed."

Deneth gave him an odd look. "More stories of Faerie you didn't want to admit to?"

He shook his head. "I had that from a shaman of one of the Tribes I encountered once while on retreat in the wilderness. The Otherworld is a place where you not only encounter your ancestors but a place where your spirit can be set free to wander all the worlds of what your folk call the One."

He didn't quibble over the fact that, while some Thalacians swore by the deities of the Pantheon as a matter of habit, it was really Mistra's and Torreb's folk who owned the concept of a Supreme Being. "But you believe," he ventured.

Mosaia nodded. "I think I do, despite my conventional Falidian upbringing."

"Yeah, well—I'm not sure I don't. Despite my conventional Thalacian upbringing." He grinned, thinking he suddenly wanted very much to buy Mosaia a drink and share the ways in which they were both less cultural stereotypes—*archetypes*—than he had been thinking. For now, though, he frowned, gazing at Mistra with pity (and growing alarm) as her thrashing worsened. He took her hand and kissed it, then gently stroked her brow. "Oh, Mistra," he sighed, his heart aching. He wondered if Torreb knew anything about healing that reached beyond the physical. Even if he did, Deneth thought it likely the priest would rush in and start taking notes rather than being any real help.

Mosaia merely looked thoughtful, as if someone had set him an elegant chess problem that lay just at the limit of his abilities to solve. "These techniques you have for joining minds—could *I* do it?"

"Oh, sure, with a little guidance."

"And these phantasms—truly evil, not just poor dumb creatures doing their master's bidding?"

"I'd say so, but really—what's the difference if the effect is the same?"

"I can banish many powerful evil creatures, where I would have limited effect against those acting with no ill intent. Perhaps between us...?"

Deneth jumped on the idea. "I'd get us into her mindscape and then let you add your skills into the mix?"

"Yes, that was what I was—"

"Mosaia, that's brilliant! We'll make a complete pagan of you yet! Here—interlace your fingers with mine and touch here and here. And don't be too drekked out by anything you see or hear."

Together, they probed again for the contacts.

Mosaia, unused to mentalic contact, wanted to protest he was not easily "drekked out" by unusual experiences, but before he could speak, he felt himself being swept off into the psychic maelstrom. The room swam before his eyes; he retained an awareness of his body, but it seemed to be floating, sitting on the cusp between the edges of this reality and one he had only seen in dreams and moments of fervent prayer. As he attended to his surroundings, he saw the room blur, then darken, then go utterly blank. Slowly, a different scene replaced it.

Before him sat a grassy plane, and above it, a stormy sky. The grass bent before the onslaught of the wind; the air smelled of rain. The plain stood deserted but for a lone figure. *Lone?* he thought. So, but not so, for around his own solid frame swirled demented shapes born of nightmares and the Abyss. Talons they had, and leathery bat's wings and fangs. Their eyes, when he could see them, were colored in lurid shades of green and yellow, shot with veins of blood red. Still, they appeared insubstantial even in this place where substance had limited meaning: they phased in and out of their material forms like ghosts, as if they were donning and discarding clothing, though their menace never abated.

He would have turned away in horror but for the inspiration of the lone figure standing her ground in the face of the attack. A sword gleamed in one hand; from the other leapt a glorious white light. His suspicions about the motives or nature of any of his companions had left him long ago, but he thought if he had still harbored any doubts about Mistra's essential purity of spirit, this one sight would have dispelled them forever: he saw that light as Holiness Incarnate. Still, for all its splendor, it was like a candle guttering in the wind. Even supported by her not inconsiderable skill with the sword, she could muster only enough power to defend, not enough to defeat or even discourage her attackers.

"OK, Mosaia," he heard Deneth's voice, and suddenly the bard stood beside him on the grassy plain. He was having to shout above the rising wind. "You're on."

Mosaia reacted as Deneth flourished the lute and began to play. *He's encouraging me in his own brusque way,* he thought. *He truly believes I can help her!* Deneth's absorption in his music served as further affirmation of his utter conviction that Mosaia could find a way to do what needed to be done. Deneth had put him in charge and was using his own skills only to bolster whatever talents Mosaia chose to employ.

He felt rage build in his heart then. Rather than quelling it, he let it blaze forth—rage at so fierce an attack on so gentle a woman, alone, unaided, in what should have been her few quiet hours of sleep. He prepared to wade in to defend her, looked down to see he was now arrayed in his field armor. It showed no wear but shone brightly; his old sword appeared in his hand, and he saw his warhorse grazing so near at hand a mere whistle would summon him.

But before he went charging to Mistra's rescue, he stopped to consider. It may have been his own thought, or Deneth's, or some synthesis of the two; it may have been his own common sense rebelling. Whichever, he had a sudden clear sense that she must fight this battle herself or risk its recurrence. *I'm here in a support role only,* he thought, and, *How can I best serve her?*

Tentatively, he let his mind reach out to Mistra's. He felt Deneth's mind there beside him, not guiding as a child might assist his blind grandfather but ensuring, like a lantern-bearer, that his steps did not falter. Closer he came, and closer... He felt the connection the way he might hear a key snick in the lock for which it had been made. For a moment, he lost his sense of purpose as his mind wandered helter-skelter through the vast panorama into which he had just stumbled, a panorama in which he would willingly lose himself for long hours. Was that not the light of the Divine he saw hovering in the distance, and was it not brighter and more radiantly lovely than the soul of man had a right to be? God the Father must have accorded her a great portion on the day He sent her soul forth from the Void...

He felt a sudden sharp sense of admonition from the bard that he had just trespassed where it was not meet for an outsider to go without invitation. *Of course*, he thought. *What was I thinking?* Oriented once more, he came to grips with the problem. *I am in her mind already,* he thought. *Is it possible I can arc one of my own banishment spells directly to her mind. Yet she is enchantress, not cleric. Will such spells avail her?* A nudge from Deneth and he recalled that, though she denigrated her own powers, she had been consecrated priestess as an infant. All the children of the royal houses were. It could work.

Taking a deep breath, he began to murmur the words of one of the most powerful banishment spells he had ever had come to him in his hours of prayer.

And he sensed what he could only call bounceback. He could actually sense her mind recognizing it, absorbing it, embracing it. He watched as she shook her head a little in bemusement, moved her eyes as if she were following words on a page and making sure she had them memorized, then turned to him and smiled a smile that spoke volumes.

Mosaia watched, fascinated, as she lowered her sword and chanted the words—haltingly at first, as if she spoke a language for which her vocal apparatus was unsuited, then with greater conviction. She took the symbol of the Tree from her wristband and inscribed the proper figure in the air before her. A living brilliance issued from the symbol. As he continued to watch, that brilliance disappeared, not so much retreating or dissipating but flowing into her upturned palm. Seconds later, her entire body began to glow with the same soft, pure, holy light. It pulsed, throbbed, reached out with arms of effulgent glory to smite her foes from the very sky. One by one they fell, emitting wails—not only of pain, but of the dread of souls being consigned to the Abyss.

The pace accelerated. Now entire waves of the Hell-spawned creatures were dropping from the air around her. For long minutes, they would attack and fall, attack and fall, and always as individuals. It was as if, while mean and single-minded, they were too stupid to realize their ranks were being decimated. He thought vaguely their master must have created them with an inborn sense of their own invulnerability: even if some of their number fell, the horde would go on. What need strategy or adaptability when they could overwhelm with sheer force of numbers? But now, that limitless, ever-replenishing number was declining rapidly. Finally, he noted what must be the dawning realization that their ranks had been severely depleted. They rallied for one last feeble assault. Mosaia thought he saw confusion on their faces, but he also saw grim determination. Where the demons had been attacking piecemeal before, this group dived as one. The leading half met the ever-widening nimbus of light that surrounded Mistra like a halo, made a horrible sound like a thousand mosquitoes being fried, and vanished. Mistra, a look of grim satisfaction on her face, slashed two from the sky with her sword. The rest fled.

Mosaia felt his vision cloud again. The next moment, he found himself back in Mistra's room. Deneth was easing him down onto a chair. He looked up and nodded a weary thanks. He had rarely felt so spent after a day's pitched battle! He looked over at Mistra. She was resting peacefully now, and for that, he felt an immense sense of relief sweep him. Deneth again took up his lute and began singing and playing quietly. Under the spell of such music, Mosaia laid his head back, first shutting his eyes and then simply dropping off where he sat. As he did so, he had the odd sensation that, if he chose, he could still see into not only Mistra's mind but Deneth's.

"Deneth?" Mosaia asked when he roused a short time later.

"Yo."

"Do your folk also have the potential to form these deep spiritual bonds like consortium? And do your women also undergo the *tal-yosha*?"

Deneth thought about that for a moment while he strummed and plucked. "I reckon," he said finally, "Thalacians must have the same capacity to bond— we, the Erebites, and the Carotians were all one people in the beginning, you know. Do we do it? No. Mysticism and magic are so bound up on our worlds that when we began to deny the one as being unbecoming a warrior race, we lost out on the other completely. All the lore about these bonds has been all but lost. Our women miss the *tal-yosha*, and I guess none of them would tell you that was a bad thing! But the union of man and woman has become a thing of the body. That's all most of us are willing to share, anyway. The melding of mind or spirit or heart Mistra would tell you about—or Torreb, going by what he's gleaned from his books!—no, it's not the Thalacian way."

"More of that rejection of things unbecoming a warrior race?"

"Exactly. And yet, since the Carotians and Erebites decided to make nice and not enslave us after we lost the war—since they're bent on seeing us reunited as a people—there are at least a few of us who are starting to reassess."

"You?"

"I'd have said no, till I met up with you lot." He chuckled in mild self-derision.

"But you accept magic—at least bardic magic—when you were raised to abjure it."

"I am what I am, Mose, and magic that requires some physical component—" He lifted the lute slightly, "—seems marginally more acceptable to my countrymen. Or maybe it's that *we*'re acceptable." He grunted. "Let my mates Bradys or Kort tell you sometime about what it takes to make a man acceptable on my world! As to the bonding, I'd have said it was one more of those polite fictions and codifications the Carotians like to embrace as born mystics—you know, a bond for every relationship and a term to sanction every degree of intimacy. I'd like to hate all of you for making it so I can't say that anymore, especially not after poking around in Mistra's mind!" He turned his sight inward for a moment. "But how do you rationalize hate of being shown truth? I've started to think—and on some days since I hooked up with you people, my thinking is changing about every ten seconds—that, on Thalas, we deny ourselves those bonds and all the mysticism that goes with them because they would let Thalacians get *too* close. But now I also think in denying ourselves the bonds that could incur that pain, we have lost much that could be making us a better people and a less barbarous society." And he thought it odd that he could share such intimate feelings with a man he had known less than a month, whose societal norms were so at odds with his own.

Mosaia, for his part, was as surprised to hear such sentiments coming from Deneth's lips as Deneth was. Beneath his veneer of brashness beat a great and poetic heart. *But I should have known that,* he thought, *or how could he make music of such power the very earth obeys him? Surely his own gods have favored him!* "I, too, have reassessed. Consortium does not exist on my world, nor, to my knowledge, does this hungering for a life partner—at least, not as the true physical or psychic need Mistra describes. Chastity is a vow we paladins take very seriously, yet I have long thought physical innocence does not necessarily connote purity of mind or heart, and I think the one without the other is a meaningless exercise. I could also conceive of circumstances where one would be technically no longer innocent and yet still be chaste. You may laugh to hear this from a holy knight who has consented to an arranged marriage with a woman I barely know, whose culture has no analogue for consortium, but I think that to unite physically with a woman and not open oneself up to the greater possibilities of intimacy of the spirit is a kind of perversion in itself, and not what the Almighty intended to come of the act." He grinned diffidently—he had exchanged fewer words on the subject with fellow paladins he had known since childhood. "I guess I have more in common with the Carotians than I expected to, on that point! But I see your point about the pain of letting someone get that close. I think it cannot be an easy thing. Yet I also think the rewards could be very great."

Deneth nodded agreement, and a thoughtful frown came to his face. He found himself looking at Mosaia with new eyes as he suspected the knight was looking at him. "It's always seemed to me that people who choose that path tend to revel in their own morality. It's like they're wearing the psychic equivalent of a banner that says 'Don't tread on me,' or relying on a rote set of laws without ever having given thought to what motivated them in the first place. Don't let this get around, but what you've said... I think you understand without ever having been with a woman more than I've grasped in an adulthood peppered with experience. You've a poetic soul for a fighting man, Mose." Smitten with the sudden realization that he and the paladin could actually become great friends, he grinned. "Here's another tidbit of mysticism for you: not all the bonds people from our stock form are meant to be for the purpose of solidifying the unions of bond*mates*. Some are just meant to seal extremely deep friendships."

"Really?" he asked, interested.

He nodded. "Of course, on Thalas, things are usually a bit more straightforward. You drink and brawl with your mates, you bed your women, and anyone who doesn't stick a knife in your ribs you get to call friend."

"And now?"

He chortled. "I think I've quit believing what once seemed so simple and straightforward. If the Carotians and Erebites go overboard with this stuff, at least they're trying to honor the right things."

"I couldn't agree more." Rallying, he rose to go but was forced to catch himself on the bedpost when he staggered.

Deneth came immediately to his feet to help him. "You need sleep, mate," he chuckled. To his glance at Mistra, Deneth went on, "I'll stay with her. I think I can handle anything else that comes up."

"Call me if you can't."

"I will. Mosaia?" he called as the paladin opened the door.

"Thank you. For helping her."

"Thank *you* for showing me how."

"I was wrong to chew you out."

He grinned. "No, where you were wrong was in threatening to make a pagan of me."

He shrugged innocently. "A man has to have his dreams."

CHAPTER 3

Who Are We?

*"You do not see things the way they are; you see things the way you
are—and what determines that is where you stand on the Wheel."*
—Strephan of Caros

*"What you see depends a lot on where you stand.
I think I'll stand over here near the bar."*
—Deneth bent Elias

ENETH KNEW FROM MISTRA's occasional bouts of restlessness that the
attack during which he and Mosaia intervened was not the last she
endured that night. Yet, to judge from her response, each time she
grew restive, it was for a shorter period of time, and he got the impression she
was rallying faster with each pass—the attacks were dwindling in severity. By
dawn, they had ceased altogether. After a quiescent hour, he took a spare pillow
and blanket and curled up on the floor beside her bed, the lute within reach in
case he had misjudged.

And so Mistra found him when she woke later that morning. She smiled
fondly down at him. He must have stayed there all night to protect her, and she
hadn't really needed protection.

Wait a minute, she thought. And it all came crashing back.

She leaned over the edge of the bed and tickled Deneth's rib cage. It took a
few seconds for him to respond. He tried to pull away, then grabbed drowsily
for her wrists, then yanked with all his strength, which was less than Mosaia's,
but not by much. Mistra came tumbling down atop him, first gasping, then
breaking into a fit of giggles. Presently, she calmed herself and lay pushed up on
her elbows studying him closely. She hesitated just one more second before she
bent down to kiss his brow. "You kept vigil for me all night."

"Oh, yes." His voice and manner were very much the sort lovers use in the
afterglow. "Well, that and more."

She cast her mind back to the strange dreamscape. "You were there with me, weren't you?" She frowned, still trying to piece it together. "And not alone."

"I'd tell you Mosaia helped, but I'd be afraid it would mean you'd give him the same warm reception."

"At least you admit it," she laughed. "Tell me."

He gave her a brief account of the way he and Mosaia had worked together to help her fend off the attacks.

Her brow furrowed a little at his account, and she searched around the corners of her mind a bit. "I remember Mosaia's spell; it must have imprinted somehow. And without it, I don't think I could have fended the creatures off. You haven't been in my mind before, so you wouldn't know, but the creatures had –well– a clarity to them they haven't had before, as if someone nearby were crafting them. Before they've been—nebulous. Still horrifying, but nebulous."

"If Syndycyr is attacking from another plane of existence, nebulous makes sense. This business of magic being stolen from the very earth and hoarded by one or two mages: perhaps he, or they, are trying to rattle the nerves of all the paladins in the area and you caught the edge of the barrage."

She laughed mirthlessly. "If that was the edge, I'd hate to see what the center of the maelstrom looked like! At any rate, it was kindly done, both of you, and I thank you. I must thank him as well. And reassure him his spells are in safe hands."

He caught her as she made to rise and pulled her back down to him. "Not just yet, surely?" And he engulfed her tenderly. It was playful and affectionate rather than passionate, so neither was in any way prepared for the way the other's mind opened up like a sprawling vista bright with promise. There was a sweetness in the kiss that simply hadn't been there before, a poignancy, a sharper sense of connection. It was as if a barrier they never noticed had been removed, as if their hands had been gloved and now their fingers touched and they found delight in the sensation of skin meeting skin for the first time. Still, after a moment, they pulled apart abruptly panting.

"Oh, my gods!" gasped Mistra.

"I felt it, too," he breathed, simultaneously bewildered and delighted with the sensation. "What is it? Is it the *tal-yosha* rearing its head again?"

"No." She shook her head in disbelief. She was not displeased, only puzzled. "It's a kinship bond!" she said, still feeling around in her own mind to convince herself it was true. "It must have formed on its own in the night, when you two entered my mind to look after me. But that's—that's—"

"Unheard of?" he suggested. "More legend than history?"

A bemused nod. "Even on Caros, you only hear about a spontaneous formation in what would be fairy tales to Mosaia's people. It always happens after an act of great charity and self-sacrifice. I can undo it," she added hastily.

He turned his vision inward, struggling to find a way to express what he was thinking. "I know I didn't know, or ask, or—" He cut himself off, pursed his lips. "When we first met, you said it took no act of augury to tell that you and I would be great friends. I don't know that I would have been ready to invite this for a while yet, but... This feels like finding shelter in the middle of a blizzard, only what you took for a rude caretaker's hut turns out to be a prince's hunting lodge with a fire blazing in the hearth and warm, rich clothing, and a feast laid on the board."

She grinned. "So what you're saying is, you can live with it."

He solemnly nodded agreement, then gave her the smile he normally reserved for women he invited to his bed. "Is this what a consort bond feels like?"

She gave him an impish smile, but her eyes twinkled in the way she reserved for men she accepted. "A little. Except, well, er... not at all, in one way. Feel around the bond a little."

His eyes widened. "Great Phino in the Home of Homes! Mosaia's in my mind, too."

※

Mosaia woke from slumber with the sense that someone had turned on a radio several rooms away. He thought he heard some quiet chatter about focus and concentration, although he could only pick up about every third word. The first thing to come through loud and clear was someone trying much too hard (in his opinion) to sound scary saying, "Mosaia, you are dooooooooomed!" There followed by a sense of commotion as if someone were being slapped, some giggling, and a further admonition to concentrate. He had the odd feeling this last might be Mistra, although snatches of the first voice said, "...won't even hear... 're much better ... kidding."

There followed this a dialogue sequence, which oscillated in and out. At the beginning, the sound came through quietly and patchily, but as it went on and he learned to focus, it became more and more comprehensible. The strange thing was that the whole conversation seemed to be bypassing his ears and stimulating his auditory cortex directly.

"He won't hear anything unless we start trying to talk to *him* rather than each other." This definitely "sounded" like Mistra.

"He was in *your* mind. You try." This might have been Deneth. At least it sounded familiar and masculine.

"We were really all in each other's."

"No, the two of us were in *yours*. I just got him there."

A sigh of resignation. "Mosaia? Mosaia?" A beat or two of silence. "I don't know, I don't think I'm getting through. *You* try."

"Oh, all right. Mose? Ya there?" Further beats of silence. "This just doesn't come naturally to me like it does to you. I can't even feel any bounceback." This last was clearly directed to someone else.

"*I* can. I think he's just not sure what he's hearing. Telling him 'You are doooooooomed' probably didn't help him orient."

"It might have clued him in it was really me."

"That's for sure." He sensed a reorientation in approach. "Mosaia, you're not hallucinating—"

"—or possessed."

"Deneth, shush. It's me, Mistra."

"And Deneth."

"Mosaia, something extraordinary has happened."

"Yeah, Mistra agreed to—" He thought he caught a few words like "sleep," "mother," and "children," and got a definite auditory picture of active silencing and gentle, amicable combat.

Suddenly, it was his mind's eye rather than his mind's ear that was being affected. He saw a gift package, brightly wrapped and tied with a huge bow, gliding toward him. He considered a moment when it stopped, then focused his will. It took surprisingly little effort on his part to change the colors of the wrapping and bow and give the package a gentle push back the way it had come.

⚜

Mosaia looked up from his breakfast as the delinquent pair entered. Mistra forestalled him speaking by plunking a substantive illusion of the gift box in front of him. It resonated between the colors she had sent and those he had returned.

"It's called *shanora*," she said without preamble, planting herself next to him.

"You want out?" asked Deneth, flanking him on the other side.

He listened as Mistra gave him an abbreviated account of the Carotian kinship bonds and their several degrees: kin of the heart, soul, and soul's blood, or *shanora*, *sorle nahat*, and *kithana*. The first two could rarely arise spontaneously or morph spontaneously from one into the next. *Kithana* was considered as solemn a bonding as consortium or marriage and required a specific ritual. The first two could be dissolved; the latter could not.

"Not that anyone takes the step meaning ever to sever any of them," Mistra added, "but since there are rare cases of the first two arising spontaneously, the mechanism exists in case it was a step neither party truly felt prepared for."

"Is there more to it than the ease of communication?" he wanted to know.

He watched Mistra's face pucker a little: he suspected she was trying to frame an answer for someone who had neither mentalic communication nor this profound a degree of spiritual communion as a normal part of his culture. "It would be like, um..." She looked to Deneth for assistance, and he could actually feel a silly exchange between them: that her asking him for help to explain was like asking the lame to lead the blind.

For answer, Deneth tapped his temple. "Look inside here, Mosaia. Can't you feel a sense of Mistra and me lodged in there, like we're peering over your shoulder?"

He turned his vision inward, then smiled and wondered if that smile looked as silly or giddy as he suddenly felt. "Yes. Yes, I can."

"I'll dissolve it," Mistra suddenly decided, slapping her hands on the tabletop.

Guessing she was motivated to offer before he said no (or because he hadn't jumped on the idea quickly enough), he caught her hand as she lifted it to his brow. "Do I look that bad?"

"You suddenly looked like you'd overdosed on both wine and bright sunlight."

"Like a very happy drunk," Deneth added.

"But like you weren't quite sure how to react to it all."

Mosaia laughed at this description of himself. "Sorry. Just savoring this unique experience, I assure you." He looked thoughtful. "You would conceive of this as a gift of your gods? A Mystery?"

She nodded vigorously.

He frowned in thought. "Then it is not lightly to be thrown away."

"I just didn't want you to feel like you'd been bewitched."

"She's worried about those stories you've told us about magic on Falidia," said Deneth. "And don't worry—she worried about me feeling entrapped and unready, too. In Thalacian terms, I think she feels it's a little like forcing a man into, uh, well... into a shotgun wedding. Not that Thalacians ever, *ever* feel compelled to do the honorable thing." He only felt safe laughing at that one when he saw the other two chortle heartily.

"You—all of our good companions, but you two especially—are so mindful of my sensibilities," Mosaia went on. "I wish you could understand how remarkable I find that, and how kind. I will endure this bond, if only for the sake of the quest. I can foresee circumstances in which the ability to communicate this way could save our lives." *Ouch!* He felt a pang of sorrow from at least one of them that he could be so clinical. He found himself stumbling over the words as he tried to express what he felt. "And because I care for you both very dearly. In fact, I count it an honor to be bound in this sort of deep spiritual communion with you both." That got a rosy glow. "But wait a moment. Mistra has been mindful of both our sensibilities. Has either of us been mindful of hers?"

Mistra looked surprised that he would think to ask. "Mine?"

"Yes. It is not only men who can be entrapped by things like—shotgun weddings."

Now it was her turn to look introspective. "This is nothing I would ever have invited or asked you for—asked *anyone* for—on such short acquaintance. But after last night..." The look of introspection remained, but tears came to her eyes. She reached a hand to each of them and squeezed. "You're the two best friends anyone ever had. If love is what you *do* rather than just what you *feel*, then I feel loved more truly than Thalidis and Brisbee or any other lovers from the greatest myths and legends of our or anyone else's time or culture. But since I'm the only one who's benefitted, I didn't want to be the one to speak in favor of keeping it intact."

"You value yourself too little," he said kindly, then shot Deneth a sly grin. "Besides, there's the further benefit of having someone like me nestled in the back of Deneth's head."

"Yeah?" said Deneth. One eyebrow shot up. "Go on. I'll bite."

"It will keep your thoughts as pure, charitable and self-sacrificing as the act that initiated the bond."

"Me?" he protested. "What about her?" He cocked his head at Mistra, winking at her as they exchanged an amused glance.

Mosaia took in the look and tried very hard not to laugh. "You forget, Deneth. I was *with* you, but I saw into *her* mind. I think a human being could not be more pure and holy short of passing to the Other Side and transfiguring into an angel."

"Trust her, keep an eye on me, got it." They turned as one to Mistra.

She shook her head; her eyes rounded a little in amazement. "Boy, do I look good when I see myself through your eyes—all four of them. I'll do my best not to disappoint."

A surge of warmth, and he was laughing with them with childlike, joyous abandon that left a sense of euphoric peace in its wake and gave him a sense of being truly and uniquely blessed.

The three of them were still basking in the glow of their new-found link when the others came down. Habie greeted them with a cheery, "Well, did it turn into what I was thinking your note said it wasn't?" As an empath, she could hardly have missed that something had altered about their relationship, but other changes—the beasts said something had actually affected their scents, and Torreb swore he saw an aura embracing them—tipped the rest that something had happened during the night. Encouraged by Mistra's improved spirits, they lingered over breakfast while the trio explained about the nightmares, about Mosaia and Deneth's timely intervention, and about the spontaneous formation of the *shanora* bond. As Deneth could have predicted, Torreb looked desperately like he wanted to take notes, but the rest expressed unfettered delight at the turn events had taken for their friends.

The innkeeper had been merrily bustling around serving them, so they were astonished at the change in his attitude when he returned after they asked to have their horses made ready. He was a swarthy fellow, but his face paled till it looked like new cream.

"They have been stolen," he forced out after sputtering incoherently for a few seconds. "It *must* be, gone from their stables as they are, and such fine beasts I took extra care to have them stabled securely."

Mosaia pushed back from the table. "Let us look at these stables."

He, Alla, T'Cru, and Anthraticus made a circuit of the place aerially and on foot. Some hustle and bustle about the area had already obscured the markings on the ground, but Mosaia could see nothing to indicate that horses the size of the ones they rode had been led from the stables by any means. The beasts and Alla could smell nothing to indicate the animals had been frightened off. T'Cru sensed no fear, only bewilderment, and no human presence in the past few hours other than that of the grooms. Oddly, the stable doors were still locked. The horses might have turned to mist and dissipated with the morning fog.

"Likely enough," Mistra confirmed when he suggested this. "They were special beasts, maybe even divine in origin, and they served the purpose for which Minissa—or Whoever—sent them."

But the innkeeper refused to let them set out on foot, especially when Mistra pulled out the Portal Stone and indicated the direction their journey would take—into the hills to the west of the town, which were steeper and more heavily wooded than they had looked from the plain. He was an honest little soul, and enchantment did not, in his estimation, let him off the hook for the responsibility for *any* beasts disappearing while they were in his care. He gave them the best of his own stock, saying, "I won't have it said my security is poor or that I don't pay my debts, thank you!"

To this they agreed, though they tried to emphasize this would most likely be a short term loan. It turned out in the end that Minissa rewarded those wounded in her service, for, although their original mounts had indeed returned to serve the goddess in her own home, she saw to it that these more normal beasts returned to the inn, their cuts and bruises healed, and that they enjoyed superior health for the rest of their unusually long lives.

"Which way, Mistra?" asked Torreb as they mounted.

Mistra looked at the Stone again, frowned, and shook it as though it were a radio whose batteries were almost, but not quite, dead. "It shone fairly brightly before, but now the best I can get is that the Portal is still in the woods above the village. The signal's gone very indistinct." She turned her horse up a steeply inclined street whose cobbles ran out after less than a furlong. At that point, it turned into a game path that wound higher into the wooded hills.

They went in file at a leisurely pace for some minutes, wandering a little because the Portal Stone continued to give only a vague indication of where they should be going. When they went in the direction indicated by the Stone for any length of time, the signal changed to show they should go off in another direction entirely, and when they went in *that* direction, the Stone pointed to yet another. Eventually the new direction the Stone indicated led them back to a point where they had stood half an hour before.

"Swell," said Deneth. He made the simple word sound like the most vile curse imaginable.

"Is the Portal jumping around from place to place?" asked Habie.

Mistra shook her head. "The more likely explanation is that it's being magically obscured."

They pulled to a halt at her observation and looked stupidly at one another. "Comments?" Mosaia asked, falling back into his command mode.

"Yeah," Habie said in annoyance. "I *knew* it."

"Knew what?"

"That first adventure was too easy."

Torreb chuckled. He found Habie a very refreshing change from his fellow priests! "Are you saying that sweet Minissa lulled us into a false sense of security? The same Minissa who causes the trees to flower and the birds to fly?"

"Yes!"

"Look," said Deneth, "we must have circled it. Let's forget the Stone and just cut straight across—"

They never learned if his idea had merit because an explosion followed by a woman's piercing scream cut him off in mid-sentence. Both came from higher up the slope to their left. Mosaia cringed to think of this later, but they sprang as one up the hill toward the sounds with no plan and in no particular order, making what haphazard progress they could through the dense undergrowth. (But, even when he cringed, it warmed his heart that his new friends were so brave and eager they would go charging off to the rescue the way they did, with no notice, to help an unseen stranger.)

Soon enough, the smell of brimstone assailed their nostrils, and they became engulfed in a thick, clinging black smoke. Whorls and eddies in the darkness gave tantalizing glimpses of the forest around them, then blotted them out completely. "Here!" said T'Cru when the rest had begun to despair of finding their way. He had suddenly homed in on the scent of fear and the quiet sobbing of the young woman, and he led them without wavering when their human senses had failed them and their horses turned skittish.

Mosaia entered the clearing a step behind T'Cru. The air currents of the open space had dissipated the smoke somewhat, and he got his first clear view of the victim of this devilry: a small, fair, comely woman who had crumpled to the ground and buried her face in her hands. She whimpered so piteously the sound rent his heart. He dismounted and walked over to her as the others found their way into the clearing from various directions. Noting the clan symbol (his own) that she wore on a thick arm bracelet, he addressed her quietly in the private language of House Clear Water. Hoping it had not changed too much in the intervening years, he kept his tone civil, even gentle, in the belief that he could calm her after whatever shock she had endured. He was prepared for many responses from hysteria to fainting, but he was not prepared for the one he got.

The woman jumped to her feet, ran to him, vaulted the not inconsiderable distance necessary for her to throw her arms around his neck, and kissed him so ardently he had to use force to disengage her. He heard comments like "Gods, he has to beat 'em off with a stick!" "I'll have to take some of these paladin's vows if they have this effect," and "I've heard of a girl in every port, but one in every time period?" He glared at the offenders as he gently removed the young woman's arms from around his neck but got only theatrical smiles and fingers waggling back at him in return.

Disregarding these comments, she exclaimed, "Oh, it's you! It's you! I knew he would be unable to hurt either of us when our love is so pure and strong. And look, beloved," she went on, indicating the others. "Our friends are unharmed as well. Oh, this bodes ill for that black devil!"

Mosaia regarded the petite blonde levelly. She could have been his own sister Ruth. Her hair fell in loose curls to her waist; it was crowned by a circlet of flowers, as if in recognition of some festival. She was arrayed like a bride, in the purest white samite. A charm of silver dangled from a torque that encircled her slim throat. He recognized it as the quartered circle that was the symbol of his own faith. He did not recognize the embellishments he saw inscribed there, though: in each quadrant he saw a symbol inscribed, one for (he thought) each of the four elements. While he was taking all of this in, she drew near, took him in her slender arms, and laid her head upon his breast—a less impassioned gesture than the kiss, but one that still denoted a degree of ownership he was at a loss to explain. He floundered a moment, then, actually spurred to defiance by the fresh crop of grins this invited, put his arms around her in a firm but brotherly fashion.

She disengaged herself—he thought she was responding to the sense that his embrace was not that of ardent lover—and her angelic brow furrowed. She touched his face with a delicate hand. "Why, what is it, love? Oh, no! It is that cursed magician! He has deranged your memory!" She looked from one to the other of the company in a show of alarm. She seemed vexed when she saw there detached concern but no more.

Is she looking for recognition? he wondered. Sensing tension mounting toward panic, he gripped her shoulders and whirled her to face him, stooping a little so he could look into her eyes. "You are Gwynddolyn," he said with sudden conviction, "of the House of Clear Water."

She nodded enthusiastically, but her expression remained strained.

"Good. Now tell me who I am."

"But—"

"Tell me." He kept his voice gentle, but inflected it with a slight undertone of command. "If magic has forced the memory of you from my mind and those of our friends, it will be dispelled the more readily if you enumerate for me my true identity." He heard an echo of both Deneth's and Mistra's thoughts at that: *Good one, Mose! Why lie when you can misdirect?* from Deneth and *Where would you like me to start with the thousand or so things that are wrong with that one?* from Mistra, but both felt amused as well as appreciative. He noted peripherally (and with satisfaction) that the rest had settled down and were observing the scene with deepening interest.

She squared her shoulders. "You are Lord Gunthar Clear Water, my cousin and new-made husband."

His jaw dropped. "Lord *Gunthar* Clear Water," he murmured in amazement. It took but a moment for him to regain his sense of purpose. "And these, lady. Who are these?" He gestured towards his comrades.

She brightened a little, as if she liked this game. "Why, here are the good Father Eric [Torreb], who has just married us; his friend and mascot Prowl [T'Cru]; your harper Tallin [Deneth]; my best friend Ella [Alla]; my two handmaidens, Nura and Lucia [Habie and Mistra]; and I know not what manner of creature the little flying fellow [Anthraticus] is. He was not here a moment ago, but Lucia is always bringing home pets of the strangest sorts from the woodlands:

she has that way about her." Mosaia noted the way her comments were met with interest by all but Mistra, whose display of mild indignation forced Habie to comment in a stage whisper, "Boy, did you two get demoted in translation!" He caught an exchange between the little thief and the *aranyaka* mainly because he suspected she would go on to a second remark without waiting for a response to the first. What she said was, "You know that philosophical drivel you've been teaching me about figuring out what your face looked like before your parents were born?"

Alla, to his relief, did not take issue with the word "drivel" but only nodded in bemusement.

"And the stuff about the universe being a mirror and all of us mirroring all the rest of us?"

"Uh-huh."

"Is this what you meant?"

Alla, Mistra, and Anthraticus exchanged mystified glances and shrugged in unison.

The exchange finished, Mosaia persisted in his attempt to drive the logic of the situation home to Gwynddolyn. "A small ceremony for two of our standing, is it not?" he asked.

"But we *planned* it that way, for the safety of us all and our families and more besides. Oh, can't you remember?"

Mistra nudged her horse forward. "Lady Gwynddolyn, describe me to your husband." She had narrowed her eyes a little in a way that told Mosaia her brain had just shifted into high gear.

Gwynddolyn bristled—probably, he supposed, at the authority in Mistra's voice. From her perspective, this was her handmaiden addressing her as an equal! He saw Gwynddolyn force down a rush of both wounded pride and befuddlement as she said, "You are tall, slender—a little like a willow tree, I've always thought. Bright green eyes and terribly long hair, brown, but with auburn highlights any other lady would need henna to reproduce. I think that's why you were raised in the temple of Ignea, because when the priestesses found you, your coloring reminded them of the coloring of the fire nymphs."

"When they found me?"

"Yes, you were abandoned in the Sacred Grove as an infant. You were released from service as a vestal virgin in the temple of Ignea to come to serve me." She reacted to the sound of Deneth stifling a guffaw as if she wondered that a bard would be so rude and what she had said that was so funny. If she noticed the way her "handmaiden" poked "his" bard in the ribs, she gave no further sign.

"Ignea was a fire goddess in the days when we still believed in a multiplicity of gods," explained Mosaia, "before Our Lord taught us the reality of the One Creator. The chief deities at that time—at *this* time, I should say—related to the elements, as I understand it."

Gwynddolyn pointed at a spot on the breast of Mistra's garment. "Look. There is the medallion that betokens your consecration. Oh, please, won't someone remember? Gunthar has his that is like mine, and all the rest of you have your own. That is why Eric helped me to choose you, so all of our beloved gods would be represented."

Mosaia looked, as did the others. As Gwynddolyn had pointed out, all of them now wore medallions, each depicting one of the elemental symbols. From the artistic renderings on each, he guessed that, indeed, all four elements—earth, air, fire, and water—had their representatives in the persons of his friends. His medallion and Gwynddolyn's alone contained the quartered circle containing all four symbols. They fell this way: fire for Mistra and Habie, earth for Deneth and T'Cru, air for Torreb, and water for Alla. None advanced a suggestion about at what point the medallions had appeared; they certainly had not manifested before the companions left the inn this morning.

Deneth voiced what all of them were feeling, to read their expressions. "This is deeply weird."

"Can we possibly be duplicates of Lady Gwynddolyn's friends?" gasped Torreb.

"Oh, but you *are* my friends!" sobbed Gwynddolyn. "How can it be otherwise?" She looked appealingly at Mosaia.

"'Oft send the gods aid to imperilled lives,'" Mosaia quoted one of his forebears, a noted theologian: the only quote he knew that might have come from this period. At any rate, it was the only one he knew that mentioned 'gods' in the plural.

Her face lit up. "You know the words of my uncle Julian! All is not lost."

"No, it is not. Evidently God, er, the *gods* have indeed sent us to help you." He touched her shoulder. "Lady, I am not Lord Gunthar, but Lord *Mosaia* Clear Water, and I am not any contemporary of yours but a son many times removed. My friends and I have come across the fabric of time itself to right whatever wrongs have been visited on you and yours. We can offer you no proof except, perhaps, this." He drew from inside his tunic a rendering in gold and platinum of the cross within the circle and the elemental symbols. "It has been handed down father to son for many generations, but it may be that in your day it has not yet been forged."

Gwynddolyn's face became a study in wonder as she took the medallion. Her eyes widened as she turned it over. "It is my brother's inscription," she said, pointing to a rune stamped on the back. "How worn it is!" She looked Mosaia in the eye. "His son is but a child, and the medallion itself was forged not five years ago to replace the one desecrated by my brother's enemies when he was killed in battle. Is it possible? Is it—?" She regarded them each in turn again, paling. Then she swooned.

⁂

"Remind you of anyone?" asked Habie, referring to their experience with the archaeologist Sally Roarke and the succession of fainting spells to which she had fallen prey when they had first met her. "Are we going to go through this *every* time we announce ourselves? I swear, if any of you *guys* decide there's something cute and adorable about this, first I'm going to puke, then I'm going to disown you!"

But Torreb leapt, instantly and without comment, from his horse to attend the poor girl. She came around with little more than a brisk chafing of her hands. Torreb offered her wine from his skin, which she gratefully accepted, and they gathered around her to offer solace and encouragement.

At that point, Gwynddolyn seemed to have accepted that the questors were not her friends. "But I do believe the gods can do all things, and that they have sent you to me in my need. For in serving me, it is not my need alone you will serve, but the need of all Falidia."

Wondering a little at this statement, they bade her tell them her entire story.

"It is no secret," she began, "that my hand has been sought in marriage by Sigurd, a man of good birth but skilled in arts so black it makes my heart tremble to think of them. My dear Gunthar and I, knowing Sigurd would press his suit soon, chose to elope, to be married without the express, official consent of our parents. We knew Sigurd would first seek revenge on them if he knew they had given direct sanction for our union. My dear friend Eric, the only priest to whom we could turn in confidence, blessedly consented to solemnize our marriage, though it is our custom to prove the bride and groom's parents have approved the union before the ceremony can be held. He knew as we did that our parents approved the marriage in their hearts. Weddings among the nobility are grand affairs, splendid solemn rituals in which many take part, but Eric assured us the attendants could be kept to a minimum, as long as we observed the formality that each deity was represented by someone in his or her service. In this way, we hoped to keep the matter secret yet ward Sigurd off for legitimate cause when he at last forced my father's hand.

"Our own retinues provided that all four deities be represented, and we planned for the wedding to take place today. But Sigurd must have learned. He has many spies, and our own courts are not proof against them all, though most of the knights in the family have taken holy orders and our priests are many and true-hearted. But, believing we could not yet have been undone, we met here to be wed." Her small fist clenched. "We had repeated our vows, and my husband was just leaning over to kiss me. The moment our lips met, there came a terrible crash like thunder, and the glade lit up as though the sun itself had descended here. I threw my hands over my eyes. When I could see again, I found I was alone. Then you came riding into the glade, and I thought my friends were all safe. But now—oh, gods, what can have become of them all?"

She lowered her voice to a whisper. "There is talk, you know, of the great black magicians trying to seize power for themselves—not temporal power, though alliance with House Clear Water would give them that. They want to seize the power of magic itself and control it. Our house mage says that—" She broke off suddenly and clutched her heart. Stiffly, unseeing, in a daze, she rose and walked in a circle about them. Abruptly, she stopped, her finger stabbing the air. "There!" she whispered urgently. Her knees buckled then, but before she could tumble to the ground, she faded from view. She phased in, out, in, and out as they sprang to their feet. The last time she phased in, she choked out a single enigmatic sentence in a voice not her own: "That which was consumed has been returned to the material world, so that what was put wrong may be put right." Then, before they could act, she phased out for a last time and did not return.

While they stared helplessly at the spot where she had been standing just seconds ago, puzzling over the strange message, Habie suddenly exclaimed "Look!" There, roughly where Gwynddolyn had pointed, a rotting tree stump phased into view. While the others were still coming to grips with that and cautioning her against precipitate action, she had run up to it and begun to investigate. An inspection revealed a cleft in one side. In she reached. Inside, under a pile of leaf mould, she found a piece of cloth loomed in many colors and decorated with characters sewn in threads of silver and gold. With its shape irregular and its edges frayed, it looked as if it had been torn from a larger work, and not carefully. Embroidered on it was a small crown; beneath the crown sat a shallow depression about the size and shape of the medallions they had inexplicably found themselves wearing.

"I hope you're not thinking of pocketing that," Deneth said as they crowded round.

"And why not?" she protested. "I found it."

"Or, it found us," Mistra theorized. She held her hand over it. The cloth shone briefly with a golden light.

"Magical?" asked Torreb.

"Uh-huh. I wonder..." She ran her index finger along one of the frayed edges of cloth. Little sparks like those generated by static electricity shot out in the wake of her finger's passage. "This may be some part of an elaborate piece of physical magic. If Gwynddolyn has any facility at all, she might have been trying to put us on the right track just before she faded."

T'Cru sniffed at the tapestry, then snorted. "This has recently been held by someone of malevolent disposition, or I am no judge of human scent. Malevolent, and, hmm... triumphant."

"Are you proposing" Mosaia asked, "that this Sigurd person is really responsible for the disappearance of Gwynddolyn and her friends? Is it possible for one person to have such power?"

"Certainly," replied Mistra, "especially if his lair is well established and nearby. It would take some preparation, of course."

"Thank God!"

"Don't thank God too quickly," laughed Deneth. "I'm sure Mistra here could do as much on the fly with half her grey matter tied behind her back."

"And get the sanction of all sanctions for my temerity," she said with a smile that became suddenly thoughtful. "My guess would be that this hank of cloth is part of a larger tapestry, as are these medallions, and that the shredding of the tapestry activated the spell. And yet..."

"What?" Deneth prompted.

"Well, why use such an elaborate physical trapping in a way that allows its component parts to disperse unharmed?" She took the cloth from Habie and rubbed it between her fingers. "This cloth itself was never made by magic, and if it was made *manually*, it was not made overnight. The rumors we've heard of magical power being, well, stolen and harnessed reminds me that there are ways to make great repositories for power. They needn't be made with a specific purpose in mind, they can be imbued with purpose later."

"You mean mages can kind of save bits of their power for a rainy day?" asked a skeptical Habie. "The way you might put your spare change in a bank and let it accumulate?"

"In effect, yes. It's more typical among those without the genetic access to the Art Carotians have, of course. I was wondering if this tapestry was such a repository, imbued with great power at some time in the past, then consecrated—*desecrated*, I should say—to this specific use when Sigurd learned all the details he needed."

"But like you said, why go to all that trouble if the pieces were just going to reappear so any fool could come along and put the thing back together? Isn't that what you're thinking, that reassembling it will bring Gwynddolyn's friends back?"

She nodded. "And I don't know the answer." She gave them a crooked smile. "Of course, this is just one small piece."

"Maybe they have a trickster god, or a god of humor like Strephel," suggested Torreb, "who's trying to help us, but not too much." He donned a crooked smile much like Mistra's.

So did Habie. "Yeah," she guffawed. "Why make it a breeze when you can torture us? I mean, whatever gods are around must know we've got to follow this through to the bitter end, right? *If* we ever want to get out of here."

"And Gwynddolyn?" asked Mosaia. "What's happened to her?"

"Use your imagination, mate," said Deneth. "If I were a powerful enough mage who lacked merit in the eyes of the woman I wanted, I'd use my talents to spirit her off to the love nest I had prepared and zap her with a love spell. Trust me, we find his lair, we'll find his lady love—excuse me, Torreb, his lady *lust*."

"Lady lust?" asked the priest with a befuddled look.

"Well, if you extrapolate from your idea that love and evil can't exist in the same heart, what else is left?"

"The 'love nest'—*lust* nest—being where?" Mosaia said loudly enough to get them back on track.

Surprised that Mosaia had taken him seriously, Deneth replied, "Dunno. She pointed that way." He nodded in the direction of the stump just in time to see it vanish. He gave a low whistle.

Mistra whipped out the Portal Stone. It glowed more brightly than it had since they had left the inn courtyard but still gave no clear sense of direction. Had it glowed a few foot-candles more brightly, she would have said they were standing virtually on top of the Portal. She shrugged, made a little moue, and shook her head.

Meanwhile, Mosaia, in a sudden fit of inspiration, removed his medallion and touched it to the depression in the piece of tapestry. The instant metal touched cloth, the two began to fuse as if invisible fingers and threads were weaving the medallion into the pattern of the cloth. Then, at the last possible second before it became part of the cloth, the medallion disengaged itself. He had the silliest feeling that the tapestry had gotten excited at the touch of what it perceived as a missing part of itself, had thrilled at the sense of reunion; then, at the last instant, had identified the medallion as "other" rather than "self" and rejected it disconsolately. He fancied he could hear a dejected sigh.

"It was a good thought, Mosaia," Mistra said, putting a gentle hand on his arm.

"You're starting to put the magical pieces together like a pro," Deneth seconded. "None of us gets it right the first time every time."

"I have this sinking feeling," said Habie.

"Like we have to rescue Gwynddolyn and her friends before we even *find* the Portal?" Deneth suggested.

"Uh-huh."

"And *I* have the sinking feeling," Mistra added, "that the gods—theirs, ours, Mosaia's—are having a jolly good laugh at our expense."

No one could think of a better direction in which to set out than the one Gwynddolyn had indicated, so they remounted and set off what turned out to be due west and slightly uphill. They rode for about an hour in silence. The wood, though no longer dense, became more and more oppressive. No bird sang, no creature stirred in the undergrowth. The sound of their horses' hooves treading the woodland floor reverberated in their ears. To Mistra, whose ability to commune was effectively superhuman, and to Alla, the place seemed not so much silent as empty, totally devoid of any life forms that had been capable of departing an area they did not find wholesome. "As if the dryads themselves have deserted their trees," Alla thought.

The sense of oppressiveness deepened from vague dread to a palpable physical pressure beating upon the brow. A sentient will or other force resisted them, daring them to go forward, waiting to pounce if they had the temerity to breach the area it had circumscribed as its own. Habie suddenly squealed and threw her arms across her face. The others pulled up, startled.

"What is it?" asked Mosaia.

"I can't do it," she panted. "I can't go on like this."

T'Cru sighed. "The young lady has spared my dignity. I was about to express the same sentiment. This place is so unnatural as to offend my sensibilities."

Mosaia nodded. "And mine, mundane and prosaic man that I am. It's like trying to push through a force shield a kilometer thick, one that permits entry but opposes progress on every hand. It is a great weariness to the body and the spirit."

T'Cru sniffed the air. "Nay, my good knight, no force shield this. Such devices lack the sense of un-nature I sense here, of malevolent purpose."

Mosaia turned to the others. "Who among us is able to go on?"

"I am," Alla volunteered with an effort, "for the moment. But it's becoming more difficult."

Mistra, frowning thoughtfully, touched her horse's brow. "Odd. The horses don't seem to perceive it. Must be some kind of spell aimed at sentient creatures."

"Here," said Torreb. He pulled out the Balance. "I may not be able to counter the exact spell, but I can make one of my own that should strengthen our will to endure it." He touched the symbol to the brows of each of them in turn, muttering words of blessing as he did so.

Deneth, watching him work, brightened as if in inspiration. He plucked the lute from its case, disturbing Anthraticus, who had retired once again to his backpack. The spragon hopped into the hood of Deneth's cloak and curled up in it as if it were a hammock. While Torreb completed his work, Deneth launched into a song—a formal anthem about the essential harmony of the universe, the elegant pattern upon which the godhead had structured it, and the deep and abiding primal love that had caused the One to give them birth on the Day of Creation.

His friends sat enraptured. Anthraticus even poked one eye out of Deneth's hood. They wove together, priest and bard, a spell greater than any either of them could have produced alone. It may have been that Torreb's counterspell gave his friends heart to withstand that psychic pressure while Deneth's melody opened for them a tunnel in the wall of force that sought to deny them passage, the evil will that had erected it bending before a beauty too piercing and pure for it to bear. Or it may have been that the beauty of Deneth's music heartened them while Torreb's application of the Balance made the tunnel, its dweomer and the purity of the priest's spirit being too much light for the dark to withstand without crumbling. Whatever the mechanism, the pressure suddenly abated, and they found themselves free to move ahead, though none doubted that if they strayed but little to the left or right the pressure would again assail them.

CHAPTER 4

A Gate and A Guardian

"They say the quality of mercy is not strained. Around here
we drink it, twigs, leaves, roots, and all. It's a man's drink."
—Deneth bent Elias, of life in the streets of post-war Thalas City

THE EDGE OF THE forest loomed ahead. Deneth, who had taken the lead, stopped playing and beckoned the others ahead; Torreb, the first to draw level with him, stopped his chanting and lowered the Balance. As the rest came up beside them, they saw they must have passed the edge of the barrier, for all sense of the oppressive weight had vanished even in the absence of the two spells. The normal woodland sounds were still absent, but the questors no longer felt beaten back by an opposing will.

They had come to a grassy upland, a broad sward that reached, after many meters, a blank cliff wall that rose to unguessed heights. In the center of the upland sat two thatched cottages. Between the edge of the forest and the cottages were numerous weathered rock formations, the largest being about Mosaia's height.

As one, the companions dismounted and hobbled their horses. They had no need to confer aloud; they knew this was not an area they could go charging into blindly. They had to scout carefully, and they had to do their scouting as a team and on foot.

They skirted the eaves of the forest, going from one rock formation to the next. They had been creeping among those formations for some minutes before anyone began to be bothered by their sheer number, or by the details that suggested they were not natural. They looked more like worn statues than like the termite hills or rocks carried along by ancient lava flows the travelers initially assumed them to be. Whatever they were, they were useful for cover, and the companions began to flit from one to the next in an effort to cross the upland.

Mosaia drew them to a halt in the shadow of one of the broader formations about a third of the way across the sward. Narrowing his eyes, he observed the area around the cottages a moment, then nudged T'Cru. "Do you see something just there?" He pointed to a spot midway between the cottages.

They all looked. None of them needed the Tigroid's senses to see the shimmering red spot that was phasing in and out repeatedly. When it was visible, they fancied they could see the outline of a beast of immense proportion: large, reptilian, and multi-legged.

"Another dimensional gate?" Mistra suggested.

"With something big and mean behind it," Deneth added. "I think we've found Sigurd's front door. Anybody get a projectile weapon with his gear this time?" Lots of heads shaking. "Anybody think to pick one up in town?" More of the same. "This is the result of poor planning, folks."

"What about you?" asked Torreb.

"What about me?"

"The lute. It moved the earth. Perhaps it would have some effect over the elements." He gestured to indicate that by "elements," he meant weather and wind rather than earth, air, fire and water.

"What do you want me to do—give it a sunburn?"

Torreb cuffed him. "No, you clown. I was thinking of something more potentially damaging, like a snowstorm."

"Of course!" chirped Anthraticus. "If it *is* reptilian, it is likely to be cold-blooded, and the chill would slow it down, if not send it into hibernation outright."

"Oh. Right." He looked abashed at not having thought of it first.

"Just—have a care where you aim it," T'Cru cautioned, ruffling his coat at the thought of an inadvertent soaking with icy water.

"Please, I'm not completely dim," he groused as he unslung the lute. He frowned thoughtfully, then set about plucking the strings. Immediately, though the day had turned fine and clear, an ominous black cloud formed above the suspicious area between the cottages. They gasped collectively as, without further warning, hail, sleet, and finally snow began to pour from the clouds in torrents. Oddly, only about half of it reached the ground. The rest vanished through the "gate"—or so they assumed. Whatever the cause, it simply disappeared from view.

And wherever it went, it provoked an immediate response. The sketchy image of that reptilian shape suddenly gave way to a monstrosity that made eyes pop and hands fly to weapons. The beast that materialized stood easily twelve feet high and measured nearly twice that from snout to tail. Fortunately (for the creature, not for the party) it had eight legs to support its great bulk. Each ended in thick talons; teeth edged like razors filled its maw. The creature was as close to soaking wet as a reptile could possibly get, and it looked not at all pleased about being doused unexpectedly with freezing water. Neither did it look particularly torpid, although ice crystals clung to its hide. Doubtless it possessed a brain the size of a walnut, but it had enough acumen to focus on the group of adventurers as the cause of its current miseries. With a bellow, it lumbered toward them.

"Good thinking, fellas," Mistra said sourly.

❦

Habie, drawing sword rather than daggers, yelled, "Come on, you guys!" Before anyone could caution or stop her or make an effort to deploy the party intelligently, she sprang toward the creature.

Something clicked in Mistra's brain just then regarding the creature, the gate, and the jumble of stones. "Habie!" she screamed. "Don't! It's a basilisk!" Then she, too, was off and running, hoping her own skills would serve to avert disaster before it struck her friend.

"A what?" she called cheerily, not breaking her stride.

"The stones! They're people!"

That *would* have brought her up short, but she was about two meters shy of the basilisk's great forelegs at that point—not the best place to stop! She vaulted forward, somersaulting through the creature's legs. The basilisk, by virtue of being slow and nearsighted as well as stupid, did not react immediately. Its poor reflexes gave both women a precious extra few seconds in which to act. When it did react, it did not strike at either of them immediately but tried to bend its thick neck so it could see what manner of creature had just plunged under its belly and whether it might be good to eat (and therefore not worth turning to stone).

"Don't look into its eyes!" Mistra yelled, stooping to grab a handful of rocks, then lobbing them at the creature to distract it. She tried not to think of what part of some unfortunate adventurer's anatomy she was using as ammunition.

"Yeah, OK!" She pivoted. Averting her eyes, she stabbed in the general direction of the basilisk's descending face. A lucky shot! She felt the blade connect, then sink in up to its quillions. She had struck an eye—its left, as it turned out. "One down!" she called in triumph.

But Mistra's warning had prepared none of them for the possibility the beast had other weapons. Now, instead of biting or mauling, it exhaled forcibly through its mouth. A bilious green vapor billowed forth, blossoming into a cloud large enough to engulf both women. Mistra danced nimbly out of the way as the others closed, reorienting to avoid the noxious cloud, but Habie could do no more than stagger out from under the monstrosity's belly, swooning. The creature's exhalations must be toxic! Regrouping, Mistra launched herself toward Habie with the intention of grabbing her and guiding her away from harm. The creature, seeing two targets within easy striking distance, raised two of its legs as if it would maul them, but before it could land the blow, the rest of the party came bounding up, hurling impromptu projectiles—everything from more rocks to Torreb's mace—even as they ran. They attacked with such vigor they forced the brute to abort its own assault and turn its thoughts to defending itself.

Before the rest of the party even came within range to engage the creature hand to claw, their attack had inflicted many small wounds. No one bloody gash represented a serious injury, but taken as a group they had damaged it enough to begin sapping it of its strength. Those tiny wounds had stung, though—the creature was becoming more and more enraged with each attack. By the time the last rock struck home, its mood had escalated to one of murderous frenzy. Its limited ability to think had been completely compromised by the rage, so it could not mount any sort of organized attack. It strength and speed, however, were both augmented, and it laid about itself with talons and maw like a thing possessed. In seconds, every single member of the party had been variously raked, chomped, swatted, thrown, or breathed upon. Any hope of baiting it or slipping past it had evaporated now that it had tasted blood: they would have to kill it, or it would kill them.

T'Cru was the first to realize their best alternative was to come at the creature from above and behind its massive head. With a mighty effort, he (and Alla, who caught his drift and shape-shifted) leaped onto the creature's back. Even little Anthraticus saw the sense in this. Avoiding the basilisk's remaining good eye, he connected with the Ether and threw the cantrip that had caused Deneth and Mistra so much trouble at their first meeting. The spell did little more than disorient the creature, but it depressed its perceptions enough that for a few minutes it perceived the wicked slashes of claws and the thrusts of swords as little more than annoying scratches: sensations to be shrugged off rather than actively guarded against. The murderous rage quit escalating, then began to ebb. For a few minutes, the companions were able to slash in earnest without fear of retaliation: they had the monster bleeding from a number of serious wounds before it had any further thought of defending itself.

Of course, when the pain of its wounds seeped its way into the basilisk's walnut-sized brain and it decided to fight back, it did so with a vengeance. It swung one massive foreclaw and sent Deneth flying, then tried to catch Mistra with the backswing. The sorceress put a deep gash in the beast's foreleg as it walloped Deneth, then somersaulted out of the way before the backswing could connect. Torreb circled, then waded in from behind, seeking to climb the beast's back by using its tail as a stairway. He got thrown for his efforts, but not before he had landed several solid blows to the base of the creature's spine.

Mosaia pulled back to survey the damage he and his friends were inflicting and saw it would not be enough to fell the creature. What it would take, he thought, was a deep gash, one that cut to the abomination's vitals. He had learned from their friend Postumus that the stories about dragons having a softer underbelly were true: perhaps a basilisk would be equally vulnerable from beneath. Pulling the Retributor, he rolled under the basilisk, slashing with all his God-given strength at its belly, then striking to impale through the rent he had made in the creature's flesh. He placed his stroke well. He felt the Retributor first bite then cleave through layers of reptilian flesh. Slime oozed from the wound and burned his exposed hands as he rolled away. He shrank against the side of one of the cottages, trying to block the searing pain from his mind.

"Hurl me at that abomination!" the sword urged. "I can cut it to its black heart!"

"I can't," Mosaia gasped. "My hands..." He tried to clench and unclench them, but the burns had frozen his fingers into a claw-like posture: he could not grip the sword's pommel well enough to manipulate it. He looked up. He had dived to the beast's left, so its maimed eye rather than its good would be aimed at him—but its great head was turning in his direction! He sought out his companions. Habie lay to his right, still swooning. Deneth lay on the beast's other side, alert but unable to move without inviting its notice. The cats were mauling the creature's neck and sides for all they were worth: their efforts were the one thing that was saving him from an immediate reprisal for the wound he had inflicted. Suddenly, the beast reared, roaring, on its four hind legs and sent the felines catapulting from its back with a force that threw them across the clearing. Mosaia had little trouble reading both his death and Habie's in the creature's maimed eye as it lowered the bulk of its forward half in their direction. He saw Mistra spring into the gap between them and the beast; he opened his mouth to cry out to her to save herself but *whop!* Torreb regrouped and landed his mace with bone-shattering force on one of the creature's hind feet. With a shriek, it began to back not toward Torreb, but toward the nothingness from which it had appeared.

⚜

"Don't let it get through the gate!" cried Alla. The position in which she had landed allowed her to grasp before the others that the beast was about to disappear back the way it had come.

The basilisk stopped at the sound of Alla's voice. Mistra, who had been set to pursue, skidded to a halt, her sword raised. She and the beast regarded each other, summing up, Mistra avoiding the gaze of its one good eye but otherwise posturing in a way that meant serious challenge to most woodland creatures.

She was vaguely aware of Anthraticus fluttering around the basilisk's face. She had just decided to move forward and attack, suicidal though it sounded, when she heard Mosaia choke. Sparing him a glance, she saw the look on his face change to one of hopeless desperation. He was regarding a shadow that stretched out before him. She looked at the shadow, then raised her eyes slowly, seeing from her vantage point what Mosaia was missing from his—the source of the shadow. She gulped. She wished she had not looked.

There, towering above the cottage that provided partial shelter to Mosaia and Habie, stood another basilisk. This one was smaller, and its grey skin bore a pinkish cast. The newcomer was regarding the first basilisk rather than the adventurers. Mistra swore she saw long, thick eyelashes on the creature, and took in the way it—*she*—was batting them daintily at their foe. As she digested that, she noticed the first basilisk had lost all interest in them. It oriented on the second creature and, looking a bit like it wished it had a bouquet of flowers and a box of chocolates to hand, strode in the female basilisk's direction.

Mosaia let an oath escape his lips. So did the Retributor! The beast's path led over the cottage and, hence, over both the paladin and the sword. With a supreme effort of will, Mosaia braced himself against the cottage and held the Retributor securely enough with his wrists and forearms and torso that the basilisk unwittingly impaled itself as it barreled toward the newcomer. With the help of the beast's own momentum, Mosaia drove the sword deeply into its chest, where it quickly ferreted out the creature's heart and pierced it.

Mistra, Torreb, and the cats had anticipated both Mosaia's actions and the need to get him—and Habie—to safety the minute the paladin drove the Retributor home. They were in time to get the pair out from under the beast's thrashing legs before they were harmed, but just barely. The basilisk's death throes decimated both cottages and much of the ground in between them. T'Cru risked his own life to retrieve the Retributor before the beast's thrashing broke its blade off at the hilts or otherwise damaged it: the sword had lodged deep in the basilisk's rib cage, and the creature was making random swats with its poisoned claws at anything that moved.

Once they had guided the wounded to safety, the five of them who were still capable of fighting turned to face the new threat. They found, to their surprise, that they were now alone in the clearing: the second basilisk had simply vanished. Deneth actually faltered at that moment, as if without the fear of death to rally him, his legs decided on their own authority to give out. Anthraticus was suddenly there, latching on to his jerkin and lowering him gently to the ground. His fluttering slowed as he felt their collective gaze pin him.

"More of your cantrips?" Mosaia guessed wearily.

Anthraticus' cheeks went from azure to indigo: his equivalent of a blush. "Reptiles," he began, stammering a little, "well, *all* beasts, I suppose—well, *many* of us are open to the suggestion of certain—well—*drives* in other creatures of their own kind. The second basilisk was a phantasm, an illusion of my own creation—a female in season. That, the illusion of some pheromones, and a bit of suggestion made the first basilisk—a male in his prime—forget both his wounds and his ideas about retreating." He shrugged diffidently.

"Well done!" chuckled Torreb. "A very creative application of your magic."

"Yeah," Deneth agreed, dabbing at his wounds with his cloak. "I thought we were all about to become lunch."

Torreb looked from Deneth to Mosaia and back. He had his work cut out for him here! "Gods, which of you do I see to first?"

"Deneth," Mosaia directed. "The burns hurt, but Deneth's wound appears to be festering."

Torreb nodded and set to work, looking to Mistra in mute appeal. She knelt next to Mosaia. "My power to heal is limited, but I may be able to get this under sufficient control you can manage the rest yourself." She waited for him to nod permission before she rested one hand on his arm above the burn and the other on his brow. Immediately, he felt like a victim of heat prostration who has just been given a cool drink and had a number of iced cloths pressed to his skin: a most delicious sensation. Stranger and more wonderful, he felt her mind touch his; if he wished, he could communicate directly with her.

Don't be afraid, he heard in his mind. He recognized the voice as Mistra's. He thought back to her that there was nothing in this to be "afraid" of, that it seemed more reward than penalty to be so linked with so gentle and gifted a creature. That got him the mentalic equivalent of a gracious smile. The next moment, without his having asked specifically, he felt her stepping aside so he could, if he wished, explore her mind. She must trust him to know the bounds of propriety: odd, since he had inadvertently overstepped them the first time he entered her mind. On the other hand, he realized *his* mind lay very open to *hers*: perhaps she had seen there all she needed to tell her she *could* trust his discretion. Beyond that, he thought she was making an effort to help him accustom himself to the way the barriers between them had simply vanished.

He did not understand everything he gleaned, but he learned enough to sort out forever the strange mixture of misgiving, awe, and curiosity with which he had till now regarded Carotian magic. While he thought of Mistra as nothing less than virtuous now that he knew her, he had till now doubted he could apply that trust to the Carotian Union in general. Now he learned of something called the Disciplines and something else called The Ethic, which, combined with a profound respect for privacy and the rights of the individual, allowed the Carotians and their brethren to survive what he had thought of as the curse of their mentalic gifts. The Disciplines taught them control, the Ethic taught them application, what constituted use, misuse, and abuse of their gifts. On a world where Law as he knew the use of the term barely existed, where a single creature could be born with the power to lay waste to entire civilizations, crime was practically unknown. More, he got the impression that here was a people who, as a rule, were incapable of forming criminal intent except as an intellectual exercise that might lead them to a higher understanding of The Ethic. Lastly, he heard an echo of a passage he knew Mistra conceived of as being the voice of the One saying, "I loved thy creation. Hence, I created thee, and filled thy soul with the spirit of light..." It came as a revelation. *We do not believe so differently,* he thought.

He met Mistra's eyes as she withdrew from the contact and saw she had followed his train of thought when he had gone exploring. He grasped her hand when she would have turned her attention to other things: he needed to know not only that she had followed, but that she had seen through his eyes. The answer she gave was more than he felt he had a right to! Not only did she smile brilliantly, she reached out mentally with a caress as gentle and sweet as the first breeze of spring. When he looked down at his hands, he was not surprised to see the burn completely healed.

"You are too modest about your skills, lady," he said with a fond grin. "I could have done no better."

Her eyes widened a little at the praise. "I wasn't being modest. That really must be the bond helping." She squeezed his hand, then turned to help the rest of the company with the injuries that remained.

The sun was nearing its zenith before the whole party felt well enough to set off again. They had rested—even the healers had needed time to recuperate—and eaten, and Torreb, Mosaia, and Alla had offered various invocations and blessings. It remained, then, to determine how the gate might be breached.

"Why don't we just try walking through?" Habie suggested.

"Because you stand a good chance of being zapped or dropped into a bottomless pit or ending up in the Abyss or something," explained Deneth, not at his most patient.

"Even with that– that—" She indicated the dead basilisk with a shudder.

"Thing," she finished lamely.

"I would agree that precautions are in order," said Mosaia, "even with our having defeated 'that, that thing.'" He patted Habie on the knee and smiled fondly at her, pleased to see her brighten.

The others agreed, but the breadth of suggestions they made as precautionary measures made a list a kilometer long. After some discussion, they settled on securing one of the larger gems from their previous adventure with a rope and tossing it in the direction from which the basilisk had come. Torreb volunteered to throw it for no better reason than that he felt lucky and had come through the fight relatively unscathed. He joked that Ereb must have protected him and would undoubtedly continue to do so, but the others brought their weapons to hand and followed him closely.

The gem vanished in mid-air just at the tip of the basilisk's tail—literally in mid-air: the rope remained suspended at about waist height. A collective thoughtful "Hmph" from the others. A frown from Torreb. "It feels weighted," he said, "as though it were dangling over the edge of a table top or something." Cautiously, he drew the gem back. Neither rope nor gem had changed detectably. Still, none of the questors looked too willing to make the trip himself.

"Oh, bother," Anthraticus sputtered after a moment, "I'll go through the gate. I can hover or fly if there's a drop-off, and I do have my magic."

The others agreed, but insisted he fasten the rope around his abdomen. "Just in case," they said, though no one elaborated on what the measure might be in case of.

"We shouldn't be letting him go," Mistra protested as he faded from view. "It's not his quest, after all."

"I think rescuing the fair Gwynddolyn concerns us all," disagreed Mosaia, who was paying out the rope. "And *that,* we must do in a timely manner." He flashed her a smile in the hope she would understand he meant no disrespect to her opinion.

"What he means to say," Deneth explained, "is we'd stand a much better chance in a fight if we went back to the inn, ate well, and got a few good nights' sleep. But by that time, 'the fair Gwynddolyn' could be dead or turned into a frog or—I don't know, whatever it was Sigurd had in mind for her to begin with. What do you think, Mistra? What would you do if you were Sigurd? Not talking Carotian ethics, just magical possibilities."

"Well, love enchantments do exist, as you know, although..." She looked thoughtful.

"What?"

"They do have a tendency to rebound on the caster." She pursed her lips. "If I were *vengeful...*" She seemed to be choosing her words carefully at this juncture.

"It might be gratifying just to find a flamboyant way to display my power."

"So not a quick, clean death?"

She gave an involuntary shiver. "This is nothing it's easy for a Carotain to frame, but... There are spells that can result in involuntary incarceration or removal of the will in a way that leaves the victim aware of his actions."

The seven of them lapsed into a thoughtful and somewhat disturbed silence, happy to have it broken when Anthraticus came fluttering back a few minutes later. "I've good news and strange," he said. "I had no sensation of flying downward, yet, as I passed the gate, I found myself dangling, as though the rope hung from the ceiling at the crossing of two halls, both lit from an unseen source. Doors I could descry, but not a creature did I hear or see or feel disturbing the Ether. Still, my senses aren't what they were a hundred years ago."

"Sounds good enough for me," said Deneth, already spoiling for more action. "Let's go."

"A moment," cautioned Mosaia. He pulled a wooden stake from his pack and pounded it into the ground. To this he secured his end of the rope. Mistra, catching his drift, held her hands out first over the assembly and then over the basilisk corpse till each glowed briefly with a soft light. The light throbbed several times before blinking out. "To ward off unfriendly eyes," she explained.

"Good thinking, Mistra," said Torreb.

"Yeah," said Deneth, "we'll have a nice mundane means of escape if our magicks all go kaphlooie and we have to beat a hasty retreat." He sounded less than enthusiastic.

Torreb knew his friends had nervous energy to dissipate and were champing at the bit to get moving; still, he halted them and ventured, "Would anyone care to say a blessing?"

Deneth's tone was utterly flat. "Yeah, I've got one. May we all be drinking in the Home of Homes an hour before Ahriman hears we've shuffled off the mortal coil. Now can we get on with it?"

That got everything from a mortified stare to eyeballs rolling heavenward to outright belly laughs, but it did have a bracing effect on the party. Off they went.

Following Anthraticus and going in file, they entered the gate, grasping the rope for support. As Anthraticus had suggested, they had no sensation of sliding down the rope or of falling or of gravity reorienting itself. Yet, when they reached the floor of the magician's lair, there stood the rope, as perpendicular to the floor as if it had been part of a circus charlatan's rope trick.

"And only *we* can see it?" Habie asked Mistra. She cast a suspicious glance at the very solid looking piece of hemp.

"Yes," replied Mistra. "At least without a counterspell."

Mosaia shuddered. "It is an evil place."

"Yeah, thanks for the news flash," Deneth muttered, but the Retributor jumped in with, "Verily." It (or Mosaia) pointed up the southern hall. "There is the source. Shall we advance upon it and give battle?" It was not exactly asking permission; it was, in fact, demonstrating the rhetorical nature of the remark by tugging at Mosaia's arm.

"I think the place bears investigation first. If this master spell does use the physical magic of the tapestry about which we have been speculating, securing it may be necessary to negate Sigurd's power over Gwynddolyn and her friends. You wouldn't want your own best efforts to prove futile, would you?"

"Oh." The Retributor obviously saw it as a valid, if novel concept. "No."

"You know how it is with cocky evil magicians," Mistra pointed out with a twinkle in her eye. "Sigurd may have inadvertently left some clues lying about for us."

"Oh." The attempt at levity was lost on the blade, or else it refused to give a lady the lie to her face. "Yes, I see." It obviously didn't.

"How much of a threat do you sense, Mosaia? Can we risk splitting up?"

"Didn't seem to hurt last time," Habie offered.

"Those were mere pirates we were dealing with then," Alla observed. She found herself shivering involuntarily; she was glad when Torreb cast an arm over her shoulders. "Here there is something deadlier trying to stop us. It feels like—like—"

"Syndycyr?" Torreb suggested.

"Yes, though not as strong."

Only Anthraticus, who was thoroughly enjoying his new-found life as an adventurer, did a little somersault and cackled, "Who knows? The Powers may split us apart in despite of our own efforts!"

"Fine," muttered Deneth. "You're a big help. Here." He pulled out a coin from his pocket and knelt on the floor. "Marvelous coins these. Perfectly balanced." He set it spinning on end. "Thalacian craftsmen make them specifically for gaming."

"And they're not two-headed?" Mistra asked drily.

"Nope. They're legal tender as well. I say heads we go west, tails east, and north if it stays upright." Being able to offer no better alternative, the others agreed. Presently, the coin tipped to one side, landing heads up. Deneth snatched the coin back and, sword drawn, started off into the western passage. Habie was just getting ready to mention her usefulness as a scout when Mistra reeled as if she had been struck. Mosaia caught her before she completely lost her balance and was rewarded with a grateful smile once her disorientation passed.

"He's feeling us out," she managed, still leaning on Mosaia. "I had just time to throw a mind screen up. I think I got us all covered, at least to the extent that he won't know our capabilities. Our numbers he may have guessed at already."

"Wouldn't such a spell indicate to him—well—abundant power on your part?" asked T'Cru.

She flashed him a wry grin. "Maybe not. I aimed at making us seem as rustic and unschooled as possible. He must have bought it. I think I felt a thrill of amusement from him, like we weren't worth the bother, or even if we were, he'd enjoy sitting back and letting us fry ourselves in our own skillet."

"Marginally comforting, that," Torreb chuckled. "Come on, then."

They assembled themselves into a defensible marching order and continued up the western passage. Habie modified her usual scamper to a respectable show of stealth while Anthraticus flew above her, he checking for doors and traps from above, she from below. Alla, having found the feline shape useful for adventuring in that it was lithe as well as powerful, had shifted again. She and T'Cru served as rearguards while the others spaced themselves out evenly in between, weapons in hand.

The first openings they came to were two large doors flanking the hall, one to the north, one to the south. They were initially drawn to the one on the north wall (or repelled from the one on the south wall: it was a difficult feeling to define). To Habie's disappointment, it turned out to be unlocked. They entered cautiously and found to their surprise that the place was filled with animal fodder.

T'Cru sniffed the air. "Curious," he said. "I would have mentioned it earlier, but I thought perhaps I was hallucinating or ensorcelled. I'd been noticing the smell of a host of livestock of various sorts."

Mosaia shrugged. "Well, if he has intended this place as a fortress, he would be prudent to have seen to the physical necessities like a source of meat."

"I hope he's not looking to your kinswoman to supply one of those necessities," said Deneth, a crooked grin on his lips.

T'Cru emitted the barest hint of a growl and flicked him across the thigh with his tail. "Friend Deneth, *do* try to limit your tasteless remarks while the young lady's life and honor are still at stake." He cast a glance at Mosaia, who looked supremely thankful someone else had voiced his own sentiments— indeed, that someone else appeared to *share* his sentiments. He had begun to feel lonely in them!

Deneth nodded with a kind of grudging contriteness; any attempt at working out atonement took the shape of poking through the piles of fodder.

Even focusing on the task and working for some minutes in silence, they could find nothing of interest: piles of hay and sacks of various grains and flours and the compressed pellets one feeds to smaller animals. Of one thing only did they notice a dearth: straw. They found but one tiny pile of it lying in a corner. Mistra alone had a vague feeling she saw something in this worth remarking upon, but she felt it was too far-fetched a notion for her to bother bringing up just yet.

They were about to leave when Habie's nimble fingers detected a concealed hinge behind a large pile of bales of hay. She looked to the others for confirmation. No one seemed particularly impressed by a sense of immediate danger or evil, so she set about finding and springing the lock. She found no trap on the lock of the smallish door, set to work on the lock, and felt the tumblers fall easily into place. The door swung inward.

Their surprise at finding the feed room was as nothing compared to their reaction to what lay before them now: a massive hall, whose dimensions exceeded anything any of them had seen short of a Dantonian Ultra Polo stadium. It extended outward in all directions from their point of entry. Rows of Corinthian columns that marched to the edge of vision supported the ceiling. The floor was intricately tiled in browns and tans and in earthy shades of greens, rusts, and ochres. The tiles were cut in odd angular shapes but fit together perfectly like pieces of a jigsaw puzzle, so no mortar and very few seams were visible. The overall effect was that of a woodland glade.

For a moment, the companions just stood with their mouths hanging open. If this was not the last thing they expected, it came pretty far down the list. The first of them to cast off the glamor and move again was Mistra. On a whim, she set down her pack, executed a few waltz steps, and then launched into a small balletic *enchaînement*. She ended with a clean quadruple pirouette!

"What a ballroom this would have made," she sighed wistfully, then, realizing how out of place this must have looked, returned to her friends with a diffident smile. Deneth patted her head as if in approbation at the antics of a child of limited intelligence.

At Mosaia's nod of confirmation that the place was relatively safe, they fanned out. Still a bit bemused by finding what could have served as a ballroom in this strange place, she took the opportunity to investigate a spot that had caught her eye: a perfectly circular area about a meter across. It stood as close to the exact center of the irregularly shaped room as made no odds: she could see only a shallow, leveled patch of planed earth a few centimeters below the level of the floor. She could tell only that those few centimeters represented the thickness of the tiles surrounding the depression and could only surmise that a largish round tile had once rested here. She could gain no sense of whether the tile had been removed or never laid in the first place, or whether the spot had been occupied by one great decorative tile or many small ones. The disc itself seemed an oddity in this place where the other tiles had been shaped into angle after irregular angle.

The others, meanwhile, determined the room did have a regular shape of sorts. It appeared to be a section of a hemisphere: almost a perfect quarter of one, in fact, except for the few irregularities that now proved to be symmetrical. The storage room had an analogue protruding from the east wall, in which Habie found a second concealed door. Two more room-sized protrusions, one farther west and an analogue farther north, were identical in shape and size but inaccessible from this chamber.

T'Cru and Alla wriggled their noses curiously at the bare patch when Mistra called it to their attention. "It has an earthy smell," T'Cru declared.

"Of *course* it has a draffing earthy smell," remarked Deneth. "It's dirt."

"Oh, Deneth, you *can* be tiresome," T'Cru said with more showmanship than rancor.

"Patience, T'Cru," Alla counseled. "Even *I* haven't your keen senses in my human form." She turned to the others.

"I can barely explain it. It's as if, if the element of earth had an *essence*, it would smell like this."

"He's right," Alla agreed. "It's not just the smell of dirt such as I might find in my garden at home. It's the scent of newly turned earth in spring, of moss and wildflowers and freshly scythed grass."

Torreb smiled at her. "How very poetic." Then he looked discomfited. "I wish I knew what it meant. I think we must push on if we're to learn the truth of the matter. Where to from here, then?"

"Back to the hall, I would say," advised Anthraticus. "You youngsters may like to take off as opportunities arise, but my wisdom says we should stick to our original, orderly plan." He made for the feed room as if the matter were settled.

"Wisdom or no," Deneth commented in aside to Mistra and Mosaia, "I bet we youngsters rescue his ageless rump before the day's out."

They followed the spragon back through the feed room and into the hall. But where he gaily fluttered in front of the door opposite, waiting for Habie to try her luck with the lock, the others held back. Deneth followed Habie, as did T'Cru, but Deneth stepped warily and Tigroid's hackles had risen. Something about the door drew Torreb forward, his face that of a man at once fascinated and horrified by the thing that confronts him. Mistra and Alla actually recoiled, as if they had struck at a point midway between the two doors an invisible barrier whose very touch befouled them. Mosaia had the same initial reaction, after which the suggestion of threat braced him. Where the basilisk had been a poor dumb beast, the threat before him came from a malign will. With women and weaker folk to protect and a source of conscious evil before him, he was in his element!

"There's something horrible behind that door," Alla whispered, pressing a little closer to Torreb.

"Well, then," blustered the Retributor, "let us go forward and deal with it."

"It *is* totally malign" Mosaia pronounced. "Yet I feel a restraint about it. It has not unbridled power." He squared his shoulders. "*I —we—*" he added in deference to a little tug of indignation from the Retributor, "will see what lies in wait for us." He strode forward, waiting only for Habie to move aside from the door before he turned the knob and flung it open.

"No," Mistra said when Habie hesitated and looked to her for direction. Though she still felt a sense of revulsion, she had regained her composure and her sense of duty the minute Mosaia had plunged ahead. She could hardly allow a mundane, even a paladin armed with a Holy Retributor, to enter such a lair alone. She followed up the single word of abjuration quickly, lest any of them think she doubted Mosaia's resolve or courage. "We will all go, or none of us, for no one of us can deal with it alone—not even you, Mosaia, not even me. Not even, I think, Torreb or Anthraticus."

Torreb nodded agreement. "If I have the strength, it has not yet been tested. If it is some creature of the nether planes, it may require all of our skills— clerical, magical, and combat." He smiled pleasantly at Habie. "And—who knows?—the skills and good common sense of our little thief."

"And the wisdom and valor of a Tigroid," Alla added as she phased back to her human shape. While she fought better as a beast, she thought faster as a human, and something told her what they were about to confront would require intellect rather than brute strength.

As if to save them the trouble of planning their entry and attack, the door at that moment swung inward of its own accord. "Now that you have finished lauding one another," a deep voice boomed, "come forward! Come in and know me better! For I know *you!*"

The voice chuckled, a grating sound plucked from and tinged with the screams of the damned from the lowest levels of the Abyss.

CHAPTER 5

Guardians of Things Various

"When bargaining with a devil, never underestimate the value of a consecrated weapon, a liter of holy water, and a really good attorney."
— Ariane bas Carthanas, on dealing with nether creatures

THEY LOOKED INSIDE WITH deep misgivings. Utter blackness confronted them. It was black not as a stormy night is black, nor was it black as a point that absorbs light is black. It was as though this were a spot that rejected light utterly—or, perhaps, it was an extension into this universe of a place in which visible light held no meaning. Mosaia pulled out a torch, lit it, and thrust it through the doorway. They thought it had been extinguished, for the instant it passed the lintel, it ceased to give light. When he drew it back, however, it still flamed. The demonic chuckle resumed.

"Uh-huh," Torreb grunted. Some say fear and anger cannot exist in the same heart and, for this reason, the best way to drive out a fear of something is to become angry at it. This is rot. Annoyance works just as well and has the added feature of bracing one's ability to reason, while anger will make many people lose all sense of perspective in an effort to eradicate the thing that formerly terrified them. Many a ravening chimaera has gotten an easy lunch this way, employing the mind trick of engendering anger rather than fear so that its quarry rushes in to attack it with no regard for the inadequacy of its own weapons.

All this is to say that, when Torreb grunted, he was indicating annoyance. He looked at Mistra, as if to ask which of them should make the next move, and saw she looked like a hound on a fresh scent, if such can be said of a logician seeing a problem that intrigues her. She nodded to him, the light of distracted calculation in her eyes. With a shrug, he pulled the Balance of Ereb from his belt and held it aloft. Murmuring softly, he entered the room. A gentle light issued from the symbol so that, even in that room of un-light, he remained illumined. He hugged the wall, cautioning the others to do the same as they entered.

A well-placed caution! For, by the light of the Balance, they could now see inscribed in the floor a thaumaturgic circle so large it nearly touched the side walls of the oblong room. Nearly, but not quite. A small gap lay on either side, agonizingly tempting for the glint of gold that was reflected from the cache that lay against the far wall. Chests, sacks, and loose heaps of gems and coins rose almost to the ceiling. If Habie had been a cartoon character, her eyeballs would have been replaced by credits signs for a panel or two.

But, as a single, unset, perfect diamond will outshine the largest pile of costume jewelry, so the lone denizen of the room completely eclipsed the splendor of even so massive a treasure: a huge, shadowy creature, a humanoid male with wings pinioned to his sides by the magical wall of force that bounded the circle. His eyes smoldered like rubies, his fangs had the nacreous quality of pearls. Glints here and there told of bits of jewelry with which he had adorned himself. His head nearly brushed the ceiling, a good ten meters above them. He possessed just two (massive) arms, but his lower torso shaded away to smoke, so the number and, in fact, the existence of lower limbs became matters for conjecture.

They saw him follow their gaze from the treasure to him and back. A smile came to his lips—the sort of smile all of them had seen on the faces of traders in their local markets whose goods were of such dubious quality they knew their only chance to move them was to talk fast and sell quick. In a trice, he went from towering above them to hovering just above eye level for the taller men. It was a very smooth transition, but his form remained so vague they could not have said if he managed this reorientation by kneeling or sinking into the floor or somehow compressing his entire body, the better to fit the space of his confinement. He took a moment then to scrutinize them before he spoke.

"Well, my little friends," he said at last, bellowing and rubbing his hands together. He put the emphasis on "little," and, although none of them could really guess his exact size, they all suddenly felt very tiny and completely insignificant. "I see you've noticed my hoard." He gestured. "Come," he said with a show of expansive benevolence. "Examine it more closely. Help yourself to some souvenirs." A further bellow, this time of laughter. "I am no dragon who sits covetously on his hoard, menacing all who would come near to steal his treasure!"

Habie, her eyes ablaze with lust for the shiny, sparkly goodies, started forward at the invitation. Mistra's hand shot out just in time to restrain her.

The demon made an indignant little grunt. "You *dare* to restrain one who wishes to avail herself of my hospitality?" The threat of a growl underpinned that simple indignation.

"Yeah," Habie snapped, shaking free of Mistra's grasp.

"Don't be a fool, Habie," Deneth hissed.

The demon chuckled. "Can it be the bard is learning some self-restraint? Or are women and wealth no longer the way to his heart? Hah! At least the little thief is honest about her desires. For, which of you does not feel in your heart the burden of the lust for a thing you dare not crave? Who knows what fantasies lie buried in the hearts of the purest among you—of priests, of paladins, of those who hide behind a crown, or behind the love of all creatures that walk free upon the earth? Power—is that what you wish? Or the man or woman who haunts your most closely-guarded dreams? Glory? Fame? Ha ha! All have a dark side that will play you false in the end unless you possess the ability to see *all* ends. But here is something safe: wealth, freely given and to spare. Come! Avail yourselves of it!"

At that, Habie started forward again, but Deneth's foot wandered into her path. She tripped and landed face down at the very edge of the circle. She looked up. Power of some sort emanated from the inscription before her—she could feel it. Worse, far above her, the demon's eyes had taken on a dangerous cast, as if they were now full of malevolent glee. Much to her surprise, she began to tremble all over: as involuntary a reaction as the chattering of one's teeth during the throes of a high fever, and as impossible to control. She hated herself for it.

Deneth stepped in, adroitly calling attention away from his friend and her discomfited state. "Before my friend wanders into your domain," he suggested affably, "why don't you point out some of the, um, goodies you might allow us to take?" His voice and manner remained affable, but a malicious glint came to his eye.

"Yes," Mistra played along. "Toss us a sample of something you'd consider, you know, not too presumptuous. A ring, a small enchanted weapon, the tiniest strongbox full of the least consequential treasure in your hoard..." Her family had a history of attracting the notice of demonkind, and she had picked up a thing or two about how they operated. His taunts so far had been general, really the sorts of taunts any demon might hurl at any band of adventurers who had a goodly purpose as their aim. She did not like the way these gibes seemed to be affecting her friends—Habie's interest in the treasure and the torpor or unwillingness to act evinced by most of the others seemed to be out of all proportion to these mere opening gambits. She thanked every god in the Pantheon that Deneth had stepped up to the plate to show the demon's greatest weakness up for what it was.

The demon shot the two of them a glance that said, had he been at liberty, he would have incinerated them both on the spot, and Mistra was forced to smile—they had just scored, and, however minor the victory, the hit had a bracing effect on the rest of the party. All around her, her friends were suddenly shaking their heads as if rousing from a daze.

"You see, Habie," said Torreb, who had also caught on, "he can't go outside the confines of the circle. Unless, of course, it's broken *from the outside*." He knelt to help her up.

"Oh," Habie replied in a very small voice. With Torreb's help she scooted back, still on all fours, till she had put enough distance between herself and the circle to stand safely. She was still shaking so she dared not be cavalier about even that simple an act. For the first time, she was truly glad of the priest's touch, and for the small cantrip she felt him cast unasked to soothe her ruffled psyche.

"A magician would have to be very powerful to entrap such a lordly creature," Mistra purred, turning on more charm than Deneth could normally manage without the aid of his music. "Usually, he must protect himself by placing *himself* inside the inscription. Certainly he did so the first time he summoned you. How it must rankle to have your positions reversed." She let that sink in for a beat, then turned back toward the door. "Come on, ladies, gentlemen, there's nothing here of interest to us."

The demon glowered. "It rankles, little sorceress, but no more than it rankles to be forced to abandon the man you desired mere days before the *tal-yosha* took you in its grip, or to be unable to fulfill that most basic of drives when men whose attentions you crave are so close to hand."

That stung! "Out," she hissed. "Get out of my mind NOW!" It came out partially as a bark and partially as a growl, and was less reaction to his words than to the way she now noticed tendrils of his thought insinuating themselves into her consciousness. There must be limitations to the restrictions the thaumaturgic circle imposed. She wondered how she missed the first pass that let him into her mind, and how the others were faring.

She blocked him with an effect that should have left him smarting as if he had gotten his fingertips caught in a guillotine, then reached out in an effort to ward the minds of her companions from intrusion. In both cases, she moved a hair too slowly: he had withdrawn from her own mind before the effect could manifest, but he got to the rest an instant before she could connect. She pounded the air in frustration.

Encouraged by Mistra's reaction, the demon went on smoothly, "And why should I struggle when there are minds far easier to enter than yours close to hand? Let us leave off the generalities and get down to all the specifics. What about you, holy knight—what stirs in *your* heart? Curiosity at the yearning there caused by women not even of your own race? Jealousy at the prowess and appeal of men whose better you deem yourself to be? Fear that that One you seek will wear a veil of poverty so you will disdain to serve Him? And you, Tigroid? What would you give to have that blemish eradicated from your coat so you will no longer be outcast when you return to the people you would one day rule? But I was forgetting! That might offend that goodly deity who so marked you. Curious how the Carotian Pantheon honors its favorites by marking them for

tortures of the heart—oh, yes, I recognize your worlds of origin, even those of
the knight who is a stranger to the rest of you and the little coatl who was not a
member of your company in the beginning—even the bard from the world that
would serve as willing overlord but balks at the idea of confederation."

"Look," Deneth grumbled before he went any farther, "I'm sure you could
solve all of our problems for us." His voice dripped irony. Like Mistra, he saw
he was standing up to the barrage better than most of the others—even Torreb
had seemed to shrink before the might of the demon as he had explained the
prison to Habie—and he meant to put the observation to work for him. He let
a suggestion of willingness to deal seep into his posture. "And we'd like nothing
better than to let you—*if only you'll shut up about it.*" All sense of wheedling left
his posture; he turned to go with a chuff of disgust. "Mistra's right: this clown
can't do anything for us. Let's get out of here."

"I *could* help you with your present task," the demon said. He spoke hastily,
but his tone was shrewd and nonchalant rather than flustered. "There *are* things
in my hoard—small things, things my master might never notice were they to
go missing—that could help you in your quest to defeat him."

Mistra rolled her eyes. "Here we go," she said under her breath.

"For but a small price, no doubt," Mosaia said drily.

"Oh, the smallest," the demon assured them. "Only free me, that I may
revenge myself on the magician who thrust the indignity of capture upon me."

At that, Mistra sat up and took notice: she gave every appearance that she
was considering the suggestion. "You know," she said so she seemed to be
speaking to her companions alone while she pitched her voice to carry to the
demon as well, "from the read I have on this Sigurd's personality—you know, a
megalomaniacal egotist with a flare for showmanship—I wonder if this demon
hasn't been set here to guard something he knew could destroy him, perhaps
something easy to conceal in a hoard of riches." She had been speaking to her
companions but not caring particularly if the demon heard. Now she turned
to him specifically, said, "A moment," and gathered her friends into a huddle.
A ripple in the Ether told the rest she had set up around them some sort of
magical barrier to eavesdropping. "Someone tiny like Habie could get back
there and sneak out something small—a scroll, for instance, or an amulet."

"You think it'll be that simple to find something Sigurd knows could destroy
him?" Habie hissed.

"Oh, I said that mainly for show. My real thought was that the demon knows
of some other item that could blindside Sigurd and that Sigurd may not have
known about or may have discounted entirely."

"It takes not size on the part of *anything* magical," posited Anthraticus, "to have the capacity to devastate. It takes but clever usage." He cackled and did a little aerial somersault. "'Tis true of both beasts and artifacts!"

"Is it worth a try?" asked Torreb.

"I can do it!" Habie volunteered. The trembling had stopped in the wake of Torreb's spell, and she wanted at least to appear eager to show them all (including herself) that her little spate of terror had had no lasting effects. "I wouldn't know what to look for, though."

"Me?" Mistra offered.

"Only if you go sideways and turned out and—" She made a show of looking from Mistra to the space between the wall and the circle and back as the huddle broke up. "Well, it's a good thing you're built athletically. Alla would never make it."

"Something else I could remedy," called the demon.

"Yeah," Mistra laughed, "like a dancer has any wish to be so generously endowed she comes spilling out of her tutu!" She had rejoindered an instant before she realized her spell had unraveled far before the time she had set for it to dispel.

"It must be the desires of the men I'm interpreting," he chuckled. "To many, a comely face is as nothing without a full bosom to complement it!" As all the men tried to protest this idea, he rotated 90o to the horizontal so he appeared to be bobbing up and down on some sort of buoyant couch. "I begin to like you, mortals. I will make you a bargain."

"Oh?"

"Alone, unaided, you could barely defeat me. You stand little chance of defeating *him*, especially if he orders me to attack you directly. But you know we demons are never willing servants. You're on the right track with your guess and your reading of the heart of my current master. There is in my hoard a specific item that will help you defeat Sigurd (which would then permit me to carry him back uncontested to the Abyss as my slave). It is not as specific an artifact as a phylactery that bears his soul, but, as the coatl says, a small thing in the hands of the cunning can work great deeds. Get as far as my hoard without violating the thaumaturgic circle that binds me, and I will offer you three hints to steer you in the direction of the useful item."

"And while one of us sneaks back there, you'll—what?" asked Deneth, skepticism in his very posture. "Just stand back and do nothing to interfere?"

"Well, I do have my professional pride." His smile was the unctuous, greedy one of—well, only Habie had the right frame of reference to describe such a smile, and she said to herself, "If he had to make a dishonest living, he'd do it by selling home-brewed snake oil."

Habie looked the area over. "There's only a meter or so where it's at all touch and go, and then more for you than me," she said to Mistra. "I say let's do it." She grinned. "Long as you're game to try and can hold your turnout for that long."

"Wait a bit," said Mistra. She put a hand to her brow. A short silence, then poof! In a puff of violet smoke she shrank to a tithe of her size: now she barely crested Habie's boot top. She looked herself over as if to ascertain that all the bits were still present and in working order. "Well, this is a *bit* more extreme than I had intended. Oh, well." She held a tiny hand up to Habie, who grabbed and planted the sorceress squarely on her head.

"Secure?"

"Uh-huh."

She cracked a broad grin. "This is a treat, not being littlest." She exchanged a glance with Anthraticus, who suddenly looked cross. "Well, the littlest humanoid, anyway."

"Have an eye on your friend there," Torreb cautioned, nodding toward the demon and holding the Balance aloft. "He says less than half he means and means less than half he says."

The demon roared with laughter. "You expect me to play you false?"

"Yes!" said Habie, Mistra, and Torreb together.

⁂

Habie squared her shoulders and began to edge her way around the thaumaturgic circle. The closer those arcane figures came, the more she had to fight the urge to bolt—either back to the safety zone at the front of the room or into the circle itself. "Actually," she heard Mistra whisper to her, "he, or something around here, is beginning to play us false already. The spell I cast should have left me about your height. No worries—just be on your guard."

She merely nodded. Edging through such a small space with a leering demon towering over her unnerved her more than she had expected it to. It was requiring more of her concentration than she could have imagined not to run screaming into the circle.

"Have a care to watch your posture, little thief," taunted the demon as she advanced. "You need only break the *space* above the circle to free me." She risked a glance upward—he had flipped over another 90o, this time horizontally so he lay on his belly, his chin propped on his fists. His eyes as they followed her were like windows into the Void, or into some other lightless place where souls writhed forever in torment. She wished she had not looked up.

Habie's steps slowed as she reached the narrowest part of the passage, and she pressed her back into the wall behind her. She thought keeping her eyes fixed on the circle before her might help by allowing her to orient on a fixed landmark, but this turned out to be a mistake. Before her startled eyes, the inscription began to buck and swim. She held her breath and stopped moving altogether, unsure if her next step would fall inside the circle or in the area outside. *What ego trip was I on that I thought I could do this?* she raged at herself. She heard herself emit a tiny shriek: the magical characters were writhing now, snaking out to touch her with their unclean grip. They would trip her or push her or yank her forward into the circle if they must; they would force her to interrupt the integrity of the circle no matter what she did. She had no hope of—

"Don't look," she heard Mistra hiss in her ear. "It's just an illusion. It can't hurt you."

"I can't help it," she whimpered. "They're awful." She recoiled and, finding she could retreat no further, felt clammy fingers of panic groping for her mind.

"Shut your eyes," came a gentle command. Two small hands crept into her field of vision before she had done so, then withdrew, tracing small designs in the fur above her brow as they moved. She saw a stream like tiny particles of stardust arise in their wake. They swirled like snowflakes in a storm, periodically coalescing into an image in which she took comfort: the first flowers of spring, the books from which she had learned reading and maths, a finely wrought brooch of gold and sapphire she had purloined and then given to an orphan less fortunate even than she. She blinked and saw that, unlike the vision of the writhing tentacles, this effect persisted even when she closed her eyes. It was so beautiful she wondered if her friend had ever toyed with the idea of becoming a visual artist before dancing had claimed her heart. "Shut it all out," she said soothingly. "Let me see it for you. Let *me* be your eyes."

"O–OK," she said nervously, realizing what Mistra was really asking her for was the one thing she had trouble rendering to any sentient being, asked or unasked—her trust. She knew it not rational, what with the art of thieving being one that relied on many senses besides sight, but asking her not to see, or to see through someone else's eyes, was unexpectedly difficult in exactly the same way. With a massive effort of will, she yielded. She shut her eyes. She stroked the wall behind her, and it still felt solid enough. She sensed the air before her, and it seemed totally free of the obstructions she had been sure had arisen from the circle. She took another step and suddenly realized she was seeing *something*. Mistra had not been speaking metaphorically. She was seeing as the sorceress must see from time to time, not seeing the material world but somehow perceiving the spiritual realities before her. Her friends were there as shining lights, the demon as an inky silhouette. She could see the energy signature of the thaumaturgic circle, but there were no tentacles, no baneful runes bent on her destruction...

This is pretty cool, she thought, but if the sense of peace Mistra had given her was a still pool, the demon cast a rather large rock into it. "And what will she see?" he asked in a silky stage whisper. For a moment, she thought she heard him with her mind rather than her ears. When no one seemed to react, she was sure. He issued this private torment for her benefit alone. "Perhaps her home? Perhaps the scourge with which she was beaten often enough? Perhaps—yes, perhaps those clan colors a fatherless orphan never develops?"

Well, at least Mistra could hear, because she felt a struggle begin between the sorceress and the demon. She did what she could to help Mistra keep this monstrosity out of her mind: she spurned the images that, despite Mistra's strength of will, were forming there. But they were etched too firmly in her memory not to be easily evoked. They did not precisely drive away the soothing swirls of color Mistra had put before her eyes. But now the two sets of images existed side by side, an unholy pairing of the sacred and the profane.

And what finally won out was the profane. She "heard" Mistra swear in her mind's ear, but her friend's anger seemed suddenly a distant thing. It was as if the demon had somehow evicted Mistra from her mind and taken up residence. She did not will her arm to go up to avoid the illusory blow, but she knew it moved. She felt Mistra lurch, heard her shriek out a warning—the involuntary motion must have come close to breaching the integrity of the circle. But the demon bombarded her to such an extent with images drawn from her own worst memories that she could not pull herself free of the maelstrom. The stroke that had caused her to react fell again and again, each time evoking the pain of the blow from her memory.

When she had received this most brutal of beatings, defiance had kept her strong—she had felt the pain but refused to give her tormentors the satisfaction of hearing her cry out. The demon plucked from that vision only the pain and the inexorability of the blows, undercutting her ability to resist, and she simply could not find the strength to rally. She felt her knees start to tremble. Much more pain, and they would buckle; she would spill them both into the circle and free the demon. She felt Mistra try to break through, heard her friend try to rouse her, but her voice turned to the taunting of her assailants. They were so loud, so real, that the last vestige of Mistra's peaceful words were drowned out.

Crack! and she heard "Fatherless whelp!"

Crack! and she heard "Thief!"

Crack! and she heard "Spawn of evil!"

Crack! and she heard—

Deneth.

Deneth?

Deneth. "You drekking bastard," he fumed at the demon, and now she knew that the others had heard, or guessed, the source of her agony. "That's low, even for your kind. We all struggle with temptation: with lust, with violence, with what's in our hearts that just shouldn't be there. Bring that up, yeh, that's a fair cop." She heard the rustle of cloth: he must have been gesturing furiously at this point. "But even a fiend like you should have the sense of place—hell, the sense of style—to let alone my friend's life of virtual slavery. What control did she have over that? How did she invite it? How did she *deserve* it? You think it's her fault her father was killed in the war and her mother died of grief, her fault that the Lemurian elders are a pack of blithering, short-sighted old gits who have no more idea how to see an orphan brought up right than you do how to consecrate a temple to one of the Pantheon? Listen closely while I say this, 'cuz I'm gonna say it once and then my sword flies on its own: you bring up my friend's life of slavery, of hell, one more time and try to torture her with it, and you won't have to worry about tricking her into breaking into your circle. I'll do it myself and give you a taste of this!" More rustling and some steel rattling; he must have been bringing his sword into play about now, and, knowing him, making obscene gestures as he did so. Despite her blind terror, she was struck suddenly silly by the thought. She braved opening one eye to see if reality matched the image in her mind. It did. She had to bite her lip to keep from bursting out laughing. Good old Deneth! If she had been human, she would have been begging him to let her be the mother of his children!

The demon, amused rather than enraged, had turned his eye to Deneth. "Well, go on," he invited, flipping up on his side, propping himself on an elbow and drumming the fingers of the other hand as if in boredom. "Tell me to pick on someone my own size, why don't you?" He chuckled malevolently. "Foolish bard! Go on raving at me—or fall silent. It matters little to me if I decide to invade your mind. Are you brave enough to stand up to that? Like to take your friend's place, would you, as the subject of my mental anguish?" He paused briefly, giving her the impression he was uploading data the way a computer might. "How much have you told this lordly assemblage of life in the streets of post-war Thalas City," he went on after a moment, "of the true measure of a man who professes only to want to attend to his studies? Shall I tell them, perhaps, how you came by not only your weapon but by the skill with which you wield it? Do you trust in the love the little thief bears you—that *any* of your companions bear you—to the extent that you will test whether they will rally to defend *you* if once they know your secrets?"

"Go, Habie!" she heard Mistra urge her. The spell on her mind had lifted at Deneth's first words. Now, with the demon's attention completely diverted, she found she could move. When she opened her eyes, things were no more than they had seemed originally: the phantasms that had threatened to ensnare her had vanished. She would have preferred to stay put and watch Deneth—the more the demon taunted, the more defiant the bard's stance became—but she knew Mistra was right. She went. Three more steps, and she had squeezed past the narrowest part of the passage. Six more, and she was through! The treasure hoard loomed before her, towering over her head and spreading out endlessly in all directions. She clapped her hands and capered about, almost dislodging Mistra in the process.

The demon turned, swore, turned back, and stabbed a finger at Deneth. He righted himself, and all signs of lassitude vanished. "You should have my undying anger for disrupting my illusions: they are among the few powers I can manipulate from within my prison. Were I to be released this moment, I should avenge myself on you for interfering."

Deneth trotted out a little trick the others had never seen. A few chanted words, and a small sphere of crystal appeared in his hands. He extended it toward the demon. "Here's a crystal ball," he said calmly. "Why don't you use it to contact SOMEONE WHO CARES??" He raised his voice on the last three words more as a display of histrionics than a show of anger.

The demon for a moment looked so torn between fury and disbelief at the show of bravado that he looked like he might split in two. Such menace had come to his posture that all around Deneth, hands were tightening on weapons (the beasts were clearly gearing up to spring) just in case. He held his menacing pose for a moment, then postured down suddenly and bellowed again with laughter. "Ah, well," he said, addressing his foes on both sides of the circle. "We set no rules to our game, so there were none to violate. You beat down my magic with nought but misdirection and the fury in your hearts, and that I must admire. To tell you the truth, it gets boring floating here guarding this treasure, and I have little to do but work out creative ways to apply the few powers the thaumaturgic circle and its constrains allow me to use, which are not much more than illusion and psychology and the ability to probe minds. Nothing personal, eh?"

"Not if you stick to your end of the bargain," said Mistra, who had to shout to get her voice to carry.

"Yeah," agreed Habie, now much recovered and ready to be defiant again. "Where's our three hints?"

"Right you are, little thief." Back to the used home-brewed panacea salesman approach. "Three hints, let me see..." He chose his next words carefully. "One:

all that is of value does not have the glitter of gold. Two: the best weapons to use against your enemy are ones of his own devising. Three: unravel the first two clues, and you'll have the case all rolled up." He broke out laughing then, presumably at his own cleverness.

Mistra's tiny face looked thoughtful. "He's telling the truth, or I'm no judge," she said to Habie. "Not that anything stated that cryptically isn't open to misinterpretation."

Habie sighed wistfully as she took in the mountains of wealth piled all around her. She looked over at the narrow space she had just passed through, then back at the piles of coins and gems and oddments, then up at the demon. Then over. Then back. Then up. And so on. Finally, aware she was giving the impression she might actually be calculating how the treasure might be most efficiently (and completely) moved past its guardian (this was, in fact, precisely what she was calculating), she muttered, "I know, I know: Habie, don't even think about it," and set to work. "There's no hope—?" she began as she set Mistra down on a huge strongbox midway up one of the piles. There was no harm in *asking*, after all!

"*No*," Mistra replied firmly before Habie could voice the hope that the riddles somehow added up to a quest for lots of loot or meant they had to remove the whole hoard bit by bit. "In fact, I'd say that last remark sounded extraordinarily like a bad pun. I reckon we're looking for a scroll of some sort."

"Huh. So the first two mean it's a good bet whatever we're looking for looks scruffy and is—what?—magical?"

"A weapon of Sigurd's own devising? That's how I'd interpret it."

Habie whistled. "This sure is a mess of stuff to look through. Can you tell what's magical and what isn't?"

She nodded. "It won't be easy this close to a thaumaturgic circle, but..." With a little "here goes nothing" sort of shrug, she steepled her fingers, closed her eyes, and concentrated. She turned slowly, using her fingers as a natural divining rod. When she felt the pull from a spot deeper in the mountain of treasure, she let it draw her forward—a mistake, considering she still perched atop the strongbox. It was large enough that, at her present size, it would have served her as a polo field with room left over to stable the horses, but it was still a finite space. She shrieked as she went tottering over the edge and slid down a pile of golden scree. Coins slid from under her feet and went arcing over her head, burying her and plunging her into utter, encroaching darkness. For a few seconds, she lay panting, not daring to move for fear of being sucked deeper into the pile. She was so disoriented, she nearly drove her sword into the hand that came in search of her.

"You OK?" Habie asked. She picked Mistra up by the collar, the easier to avoid the small but deadly sword. It saved her hand from being stabbed, bitten, or clawed, but it put Mistra in a foul temper, which worsened when Habie held her so they were eye to eye. "You know that was real dumb? You know you shouldn't have—oh!" Even though Mistra's body blocked most of Habie's field of vision—the more so since she was kicking and wiggling and swinging her sword wildly from side to side in a vain attempt to extricate herself—the flicker caught her eye. At home, other accomplished thieves had credited Habie with being able to see the glint of gold through three meters of marble on the other side of the world. So, what with her having only Mistra to obscure her view, her gaze went instantly to that lovely, pale, yellow radiance, and she lost all interest in reprimanding her friend. In fact, so completely distracted was she by the sight that she nearly dropped Mistra on her head.

Apologizing, she set Mistra carefully back on the strongbox and reached for the source of the light. It was partially buried under the loose coins and gems. She outlined the object with one hand before she attempted to prise it loose. It felt like no statuette or block of bouillon or any other object she would have associated with the phrase "solid gold." It had the resiliency that suggested fine wood; she could feel many designs carved into its surface. When she had worked it free, she found she was holding a long, slender cylinder. The golden glow that had suggested the presence of precious metal had nothing whatsoever to do with its composition. What she was seeing was, rather, an aura, a soft radiance that spoke more of magic than of metal. She was surprised by her own lack of disappointment.

"Is this it?" she asked Mistra, whose ire had quickly faded in the face of the discovery.

"It should be."

"Did your magic do this?"

"Uh-huh. Open it." She leaned forward eagerly.

Mistra hopped up on to Habie's shoulder so she could watch her open the scroll case. Once Mistra dispelled the charm that had identified the case, the glow winked out so the case's true appearance manifested. It must have been a fine thing at one time, and a beautiful. Now, however, Habie's "scruffy" was about the kindest descriptor either of them could come up with. Taking care that the fragile wood did not splinter in her hands, Habie gingerly opened the case. Inside sat a sheet of creamy vellum, the paper in perfect condition, the lettering bold. Despite the condition of the case, the scroll might have been created in the last few hours.

Mistra arched an eyebrow. "Temporal stasis," she mused. "Now there's something we could put to good use." She reached over and touched a finger to the vellum. "And, again, I believe our nemesis here is telling the truth."

"*I* could have guessed at that. I mean, it's lettered in Common and I can read it."

"I will tell you," said the demon in a conversational voice, and he leaned over so he actually seemed to be peering with interest over Habie's shoulder, "since you unraveled my riddle, that scribed on that scroll is a spell usable by *anyone*. Do you understand? Anyone, even one who is from a world that abjures the very mention of the word magic."

The two women looked up; Mistra nodded a grudging thanks for the extra tidbit of information.

Habie rolled the scroll up and slipped it back into the case. "Just a few little jewels?" she whispered to Mistra, this time taking care not to look too greedily at the treasure.

Mistra had not taken her eyes from the demon, so she had seen the change in his aspect: he was now looking at them with all the subtlety of a cat watching a mousehole. "Don't push your luck, munchkin. Remember your own story of how my sister and brother-in-law came to lay hands on you in the market. An extra bauble may void the spell on the thaumaturgic circle altogether!" She ruffled the fur behind one of Habie's ears. "So far, you're doing very well for your first encounter with a nether creature."

But Mistra learned *she* was not when, once they had returned to the other side of the circle, she found herself unable to resume her normal size. "Here," she accused the demon. "Is this your doing?"

He chuckled. "No, it is the doing of this place. Your magic will always have *some* effect, but it's anyone's guess whether the effect produced will be the one you were after in the first place. You are, after all, in the territory of a powerful mage who is your foe and inimical to your various ethoi. You ought to know what sort of force it would take to oppose a hostile will in its own lair."

"Let me try," offered Torreb.

"Oh, it's OK," said Mistra. "Who knows—it may have its advantages."

"Unless the spell wears off while we're trying to sneak you through a keyhole or something," Deneth said agreeably.

"Let us thank the demon and be on our way," suggested Mosaia, wisely wondering if it were the room rather than the entire lair that was affecting Mistra.

"Thanks from a holy knight!" the demon roared with laughter. "What am I coming to? And what would my true lord Ahriman say?"

"Not a bad chap for a demon, eh?" Anthraticus asked with his unquenchable cheer as they proceeded up the hall.

"Oh, shut up," replied a sullen Mistra, who had taken to riding on his back.

"Well, even our good paladin thanked him."

"He assisted us, against the nature of his kind," Mosaia returned mildly.

Torreb chuckled. "On the Falidia of Mosaia's day, I think you would say we gambled with the Fiend and won, which is remarkable. Don't worry! His amity and good will will last just as long as it takes Sigurd to release him and order him to attack us."

"That was some show, Deneth!" Habie said, capering a little to show her approbation. "You must have, uh–" She pulled herself up short on the descriptive anatomical reference she had been about to voice, not sure how it would go over with the holier or more formal party members.

"I think the substance I've heard mentioned is either cast iron or stainless steel," T'Cru said with a straight face. "And, er, I've often heard humans append the term 'industrial strength.'" A grin tugged at the corners of his mouth with this last.

"Yeah," she agreed with a sheepish grin. "Those."

"To say truth, I surprised myself," said the bard.

"Ah," said Mistra, "humble as well as brave."

"I mean," he went on pointedly, "that I'm surprised I could stand up to him. The showmanship and bombast and righteous indignation—yeah, that's me, right? But I was expecting my knees to start wobbling or him to blast me to a cinder, thaumaturgic circle and all!"

"Yet you kept going," remarked Alla. "It was an act of extraordinary compassion for Habie, and one of great bravery."

"Well, the odd thing is—you know how we told you about the *shanora* bond? I don't know if they meant it consciously, but it was like when the demon turned on me and I felt him try to invade my mind, I felt Mistra and Mosaia there beside me. It was as if they were closing ranks in front of me and making a wall he just couldn't get through. I think I would have been protected even if the circle hadn't held and he tried to incinerate me." He turned a querying eye to his bondmates.

Mosaia's brow puckered. "I wouldn't have said I did anything purposeful, but I'm so new at this! I felt only an overwhelming admiration and a wish to protect you—with my life, if necessary." A shy smile, and a warm glow suffused the entire party.

They had reached the end of the hall. There they found two more doors, one on either side of the corridor. "Think this is the other irregularity in the wall of that chamber?" asked Deneth. He jerked his head toward the cavernous hall they had explored.

Alla looked at the symbol on the chain at her throat. "I wonder..." she speculated. She glanced at the one Mosaia wore, then, first looking to him for permission, lifted it from his breast. "How symmetrical everything in here is. Could it be the whole place is as symmetrical as this symbol? Designed on it maybe?"

"If that were true," replied T'Cru, "why couldn't the designer have added in all of these little rooms?" He pawed at the door in the north wall. "Hmm. It feels cold, as if Deneth's ice storm had retreated here."

"If they keep fodder," said Deneth, "maybe they also keep a meat locker." He tried the door. It opened easily enough, but they were nearly frozen stiff by the blast of cold air that met them.

They stood peering stupidly through the doorway for a moment. Around the perimeter of the room and about a meter off the floor, the wall turned on itself to form a shelf from which seethed some gaseous material. It exuded no noxious smell to suggest poison, nor did it emmit the subliminal hum that suggested powerful magic or the presence of evil. It was just profoundly cold. Deneth endured the blast till his teeth started chattering, then reached in and shut the door. "Well, that was fun," he remarked.

Alla frowned. "That's odd. I think I judge distances and shapes well enough, and I would say that, if this room *is* one of the irregularities in the great hall, it seemed much smaller from that side than from this." She shrugged off the thought. Without waiting for counsel, she crossed the hall and opened the south door. Her jaw dropped. "I wonder what *this* one looks like from the other side."

They looked past her, as mystified as she was. On the other side of the door—it could not accurately have been called a room—lay a huge desert oasis. About ten meters from the door sat a small, perfectly round well made of stone. It arose from a broad expanse of packed earth around whose periphery grew palm, olive, and date trees. Above lay cloudless blue sky. The trees clustered so tightly about the edge of the oasis they could get little sense of the depth of either the belt of trees or the "room" itself. No one doubted that *this* room, at least, was larger inside than out.

"This is deeply weird," Deneth said after they had stared for a full minute. He got no argument!

"At least it's a little balmier," was the best Alla could come up with in the way of a suggestion that they enter.

"Seem evil to you, Mose?"

"No," said the paladin, "just very peculiar." He gave a helpless shrug. Falidia was not like this in his day. At least, he thought, it wouldn't be!

"Come on, Anthraticus," said Mistra. "I'm game if you are."

"I am, as always, at the service of a lady," the dragon replied gallantly. Together, they led the party into the oasis. Once inside, Habie stopped to look back the way they had come. Behind her lay the door and, beyond it, the hallway. Both looked ridiculously incongruous sitting in the middle of an oasis. More disorienting still was the way the oasis stretched out in all directions. The door and hall should have bounded the place on that side, but arching over the doorway from the side opposite them stood a tall palm; behind the palm and marching to the horizon lay a sea of sand dunes.

Anthraticus flew first to the well, where he hovered, peering curiously into the water. "Magical, lady, or I am no judge."

T'Cru leaned his paws on the side of the well and considered the azure water. It sat high enough in the well that the Tigroid could easily make out his own reflection. "And what might its enchantment be, do you suppose?"

Deneth held up a dipper he had found lying in a bowl on the side of the well opposite the door. Both were simply but beautifully crafted of heavy silver. They appeared to be courteous invitation rather than lure. "Anyone feel brave enough to give them a try?" he asked. "Mistra?" he added with a wicked gleam in his eye.

Mosaia felt an acerbic reply coming from Mistra and cut her off with his own assertion: "I still warrant there is no evil will here." He half drew the Retributor, which he had sheathed after the encounter with the demon. "What say you?"

"By Ereb," said the sword, "not evil, but it has the feel of– of– how shall I say it?"

"You'll think of a way," he muttered.

"It's the way I can detect inclines too subtle for you mobile creatures to notice. It has that feeling of subtle difference—*in* this world, yet not *of* this world, is what I would say, if you take my meaning."

"Surprisingly, I do. There is something in Scripture that advises us thus, an admonition I've always been rather fond of."

"I will brave the magic," Torreb offered. "At least, I'll draw a dipper or two of the water and see if I'm struck by lightning or anything." Before any of them had pointed out that he alone had the power to resurrect any of them who dropped (and so perhaps another should be taking the chance), the young priest had retrieved both the bowl and the dipper and ladled out several dippers full of water from the well. It retained some of its lovely azure tint after he had poured it into the bowl. Beneath the water, the bowl sparkled in the room's inexplicable bright sunlight. The azure, gold, and silver made a beautiful picture, one that would have woven enchantment even in the absence of magic. Torreb, not letting artistic appreciation stand in the way of practicality, considered the bowl and its contents a moment, then did some serious evaluating. He went so far as to dip his fingertips into the water, rub the liquid between his fingers, sniff it and, finally, taste it. He looked disappointed. "I don't know," he said with a helpless shrug. "It seems to be water. Mistra?"

Anthraticus landed beside the basin so Mistra could take a palmful of the fluid. She, too, inspected it and came up nearly as empty as Torreb. "It doesn't remind me of any potions I've ever known of. It does behave like water, except that it feels like, well, like it has a Special Purpose of some sort, like it would do everything normal water would do unless it encountered the place or the situation for which it was purposed. Then..." And she, too, shrugged as she screwed up her comely face in thought over what the significance of this impression might be.

Deneth shrugged as well, just to be companionable. "Should we just take it along till we figure out what that Special Purpose is?" He sounded skeptical about the water having any such purpose but was unwilling to give Mistra the lie to her face.

"But—" Habie protested, then quieted.

"What?"

"Well,-er..." She watched her toe drawing designs in the earth as if the process were truly fascinating. "Mightn't it sort of be, er... stealing?" She looked up as she spoke the last word, just so anyone who didn't believe his ears might read her lips.

"Blessed Arayne!" exclaimed the Retributor. "The child has seen the light!"

"And well she might ask!" boomed a voice from the edge of the trees: a deep voice and a strong, but, where the demon's voice had made everyone's skin crawl, the new voice braced them like a cool sea breeze. Although the words were harsh, the voice itself sounded amused rather than angry.

They looked up to see a swart male, human in form, bald save for a small topknot. The open vest and flowing breeches he wore revealed sculpted muscles that rippled with vigor as he moved. But one thing drew their eyes more than than his person or his clothing: they could see another piece of the tapestry appliquéd to his vest. Upon it was embroidered the Balance of Ereb.

Anthraticus recovered first from the shock of their having been discovered almost *in flagrante*. Disregarding Mistra's tiny shriek as he took to the air, he hovered before the creature, looked him fearlessly in the eye, and said, "Greetings. I am a spritely dragon—really a breed of coatl. What manner of creature are you?"

The creature laughed—a sound deep as the earth and broad as the ocean as warm and merry a sound as the demon's laughter had been chill. "I am a marid, little friend," he responded amiably. "I am the guardian of yonder well and the safe haven that surrounds it."

"A marid!" breathed Alla. Wide-eyed, she came closer. "No wonder the Retributor felt this place was otherworldly. Are your folk not of the elemental planes?"

"Yes, good lady—my kind are of the plane of water, for which reason that well is my charge. You are not on the plane itself, but in that shadow region that joins my world to yours."

"A spatial interface," said an amazed Mistra.

The marid had to look from one to the other of them before he could identify who had spoken, and Mistra got a taste of life as a Lemurian among humans! "Why, what have we here?" he asked when he had located her. He moved in for a closer look, his grin widening. "It looks like a tiny fairy princess, but it speaks with the language of what men will one day call science." He gave her a friendly poke in the ribs, almost dislodging her, then offered his hand to help her dismount. She did so, pirouetting on his palm so he could get a good look at her, then curtsying gracefully.

"*May* we take the water?" Torreb asked respectfully.

The marid's laugh was jovial. "How am I to refuse a priest of Ereb and holy questors who bear the blessing of Minissa, sister of Thalas, she to whom we owe allegiance in any one of her many aspects? Do not look so surprised! Yes—I know of your quest and will aid you if I can. The water is yours, if you will only be so kind as to leave me my ladle and bowl."

"Oh. Oh, of course. Um–" He rummaged in his pack for some other vessel. He failed to find anything there, but his eyes fastened on his wineskin. "There's this, I guess. Of course, it's full of wine."

"Oh?" The marid's eyes lit up like two firecrackers.

"Perhaps," Deneth said slowly, "such a diligent, learned being would have the, um, palate to determine the quality of the wine Torreb's carrying?"

The marid's entire face brightened, feature after feature now lighting up like an entire fireworks display on High Summer's Eve.

Half an hour and several wineskins later, the questors had a very happy marid on their hands. If he had been well disposed to them before, now he positively brimmed with camaraderie and good will. At first, they had stayed merely for the sake of courtesy, but he had bidden them sit on the hordes of satin pillows he conjured and join him. A festal board appeared at his command. On it were the many sweetmeats his own land held dear: the freshest fruits, the coldest iced sherbets. As he served them and saw to their comfort, he regaled them with tales of his home, a wondrous, magical place, by all his accounts. As he went on at length and displayed a remarkable fund of both lore and wisdom, it came to Deneth's mind the marid might know something of this place, something that might prove useful to them. At his next full stop (these were few and far between, as the marid was as adept a storyteller as the bard and twice the ham), he asked.

"Ah, full of magic this place is, too," the marid replied. "Most of it has become the abode of evil, thoroughly corrupt and malign, since Sigurd took it over. So I keep to myself, as do the other elementals about the place, unless we're disturbed..."

"*Other* elementals?" asked Alla, fascinated.

"Oh, yes. There's one interface with each major plane, though if the gods know what sort of guardian the other three have, I do not. I suspect if you run into the others, they'll not prove as hospitable as I, especially if you try to take what is theirs."

"Theirs?" they chorused.

Knowing he had hooked his audience, he went on with relish. "Yes. Well, theirs as the water is mine." He leaned in closer and lowered his voice. "Sigurd's lair, did I say? I misspoke! This is an ancient place, a shrine dedicated many lifetimes of men ago to the elemental powers. The people of this world deified the elements in ages past. They still worship those gods, so, although this shrine first fell into disuse and then was taken over by an evil power, those gods still possess the force to keep it sound and work their will in some measure. It was always a place where a mystical balance hung about everything, and Sigurd was unable to alter that one aspect of it: the shrine looks after itself, and in a way that that black-hearted villain can neither predict nor understand. A powerful destructive spell on his part might, for instance, provoke an equally powerful creation magic, one that would be cast not by the gods but by the shrine itself in order that the two extremes would cancel each other out.

"When Sigurd took the shrine over, he used powerful spells to create a very few artifacts of enormous potency. They are repositories of power, these artifacts: they may absorb all the magical force with which a region or a person is endowed, or they may be destroyed to release power for a spell no one being could normally work alone. I felt the energy issue from one such early this morning—a fabulous tapestry consumed in the unleashing of that power. I spied on him as he crafted it bit by bit over the course of one of your mortal years. He had already drawn much of the magic out of the earth and waters of the surrounding district; the depletion forced him to turn to the magic of the shrine itself to complete his design, to draw on it as his only source apart from his artifacts and his own great self, with which he daren't tamper!" He scoffed at the mage as at a coward best pleased when he plotted well but let others carry out the dangerous parts of his schemes. "And to do *that*, he had to destroy a part of the place, the way you might crush an amulet to release *its* power."

Deneth gasped. "You don't mean the hole blasted in the great hall across the way?"

"I do, and not only that one. There are four of those halls. Very symmetrical is this place, very symmetrical." He nodded toward Mosaia's medallion. "If you could see it from above, it would look something like that token you bear, or it would if Sigurd had never tampered with the place. When his spell destroyed the tapestry and released that tremendous energy, I felt the jolt, especially when the wave of power damaged the floor in the room dedicated to the plane of water, I can tell you! But then a curious thing happened to my well. The water was, as you say, other-worldly, but it had no special properties. Soon after that jolt, it suddenly began to radiate magic. I know not the meaning of it."

"I think I do," said Mistra. "If what you said is true about balance, is it possible the shrine itself may be providing the means to undo what was done without the leave of your gods?"

He raised an eyebrow in query.

"I mean," she went on, "if Sigurd took this place over and desecrated what was once a temple consecrated to your gods and then had the temerity to use the shrine's own power to construct this tapestry, and then destroyed the tapestry in order to release its power, mightn't the magic of the shrine bring back the tapestry's component pieces?"

"So they could be reassembled and Sigurd defeated with his own tool?" He frowned and scratched his chin. "It is an interesting theory. It would be good to have something tangible to support your idea."

"But I think we do! See?" She motioned to Habie to pull forth the section of tapestry they had found in the wake of Gwynddolyn's disappearance. "We've found a piece of something *like* the tapestry you describe. I can't imagine there are two of them."

The marid cocked his head and examined with interest the piece of cloth Habie proffered. "The shrine has begun to assert its power already!" he gasped in hushed, reverent tones.

"What about that bit of tapestry on your vest, mate?" asked Deneth. "I don't imagine Sigurd gave it to you as a birthday present, or for safekeeping."

"Hmm?" he asked distractedly. "What bit of tapestry?" He had to cross his eyes to focus on the spot Deneth indicated. This took some doing, as, with the quantity of wine he had consumed, he was already seeing many things double and having trouble seeing objects in the middle distance with any degree of clarity. It has never been posited that Carotian blood runs in that of any of the elemental species, but he could have benefitted from a drop or two of Mistra's just then! "Curious," he said when he had finally succeeded in sighting on the object on his breast. "It can not but have appeared when I felt the power of the tapestry released."

"'That which was consumed has been returned to the material world,'" Mosaia murmured, quoting Gwynddolyn, "'so that what was put wrong may be put right.'" They had explained a little about Gwynddolyn and the aborted wedding, but now he launched into a short account of the disappearance of the guests, and of the curious resemblance the questors bore to the groom and the members of the wedding party.

"Suppose," Mistra went on, warming to her subject, "once he learned about the wedding, Sigurd manipulated the tapestry so he had one of these pieces for each member of the wedding party—that might be why the ones we've seen so far, and probably all of them, are marked with some sort of icon. And the physical action that made everyone disappear was the destruction of the tapestry. Then, by your explanation of the balance of things and the way it's preserved here, the shrine itself caused Gwynddolyn to linger in realspace long enough that she could communicate her story to us."

"And you think the pieces of the tapestry were dispersed rather than destroyed, or destroyed and then brought back into being piecemeal, so there would be a means of reversing the spell if someone happened along who was brave and astute enough to collect the pieces and reunite them?"

She nodded and looked hopefully to the others for confirmation.

"By reunite, you mean sew them back together?" ventured Deneth.

"Uh-huh."

"'Twould fit, little fairy princess," said the marid. "Is that what you intend?"

"It is why we came to this place," announced Mosaia, with both conviction and a sudden fierce show of pride in their mission.

"Then here," urged the marid. "Take it, by all means." He slid his finger around the edge of the cloth, detached it, and handed it to Mosaia. Once Mosaia had examined it and stowed it in his pack, the marid waved his arm above them. They took it as no more than a gesture of blessing, but above them the sky began to fade with slow majesty. The marid himself was as suddenly being much less merry and much more solemn.

"In this time," he intoned, "your forebears, Lord Clear Water, worship a tetra-partite god, yet even in this day, those of discernment know the Four are but an aspect of the One Above All, a way of describing that which cannot be described. Look in your hearts, or at the grandeur of nature all around you, even here in the stark desert. There is the One! He it is Who cleaves out the morning, and makes of the night a repose." As if the marid had bidden them forth with a second gesture, the stars blazed forth like brilliant jewels in the firmament above. "He it is who made for you stars that ye might be guided thereby in the darkness of the land and of the sea," the marid continued. "He it is who made you spring from one soul; clear has He made His signs for men of insight. Do you fear to go on? The One is your Protector—the Best to protect and the Best to help." He let the stars linger a moment longer, then waved his arm again and allowed daylight to re-suffuse the vista.

CHAPTER 6

A Disturbance in the Elements

"Be ye on your guard and ever wakeful! Quick-witted and keen of intellect are the faithful, and firm and steadfast are the assured."
—The Book of Life

THEY STOOD OUTSIDE IN the corridor for some minutes marveling the unusual benediction the marid had offered them and pondering their next move.

"I don't get it," said Deneth. "If *that* was an interface with the elemental plane of water, then what was the room with all the mist?"

"I know little of such things," T'Cru said as he groomed himself. The moisture in the oasis in the Water Room had made his fur frizz in a way he was certain was most unbecoming. "But is there such a place as a plane of mist?"

"No," Alla replied. "The primary elemental planes relate to the primary elements of earth, air, fire, and water. I agree, Deneth: mist is something I would have associated with the plane of water."

"Bit *cold* for mist, wasn't it?" Torreb wondered.

T'Cru stopped licking his paws and looked up sharply. "Yes. Yes, it was. I've only been in the far north of Caros once, but I seem to recall that, at the sorts of freezing temperatures one finds in such places, the ambient moisture presents as something liquid, or even solid. Even the rain is crystalline there."

"That's right. Now I think about it, it was so cold it seems odd a blizzard didn't come whipping out that door the minute we opened it."

"So what are you suggesting?" Habie asked, impatient to be on the move and thinking this sort of theorizing was for the birds. "An elemental plane of snow?"

Deneth whacked her amiably on the head, but Mistra groaned in recognition. "Of course! I should have thought of it sooner. It can't be fire or earth, and we've found the interface with the plane of water. It's the plane of *air*. The mist isn't water vapor at all: it's air cooled almost to absolute zero. *Liquid* air."

"Oh, swell," said Deneth. "If we need to collect it and tote it around the way we're doing with the well water, how are we going to keep it from freezing our skin off?"

"If the gods of this time have decreed we find a way to undo Sigurd's plots," reasoned Mosaia, "then the means of that undoing must be somewhere to hand. I suggest we continue our explorations."

To this they all agreed. Habie bounded ahead as they returned to the junction. She meant to lead them into the eastern passageway, but Mosaia bade them halt. A curious frown had come to his face. He made to point toward the south with the Retributor, just to indicate his interest in exploring that passage next, but the sword pointed with such conviction it nearly yanked the paladin off his feet. It seemed to be making the point that *it* and not Mosaia had had the idea first. "Humor an old soldier," said Mosaia, regaining his balance and composure and glaring a little at the sword. "*I* greatly desire to see what lies down this corridor now we have made some inroads into the solution of this problem." Something in his tone of voice made the Retributor forbear to mention his own thoughts on the matter.

T'Cru twitched his tail. "Do you really think that's wise? Was it not you who felt that down this passage lies the source of al the evil in this place?"

"Yeah, Mose," Habie agreed. "And don't you get the feeling there's a few more things we need to collect first?"

"Yes, but..." He shrugged. "I feel no present danger—I'm sure our good beasts will bear me out on that point. What I *do* feel is there is something yonder that it would be well to be apprised of." He looked the smallest bit abashed. "Granted, it is a hunch, not a deduction."

"That's the first time I've heard you admit to *that*," Deneth said with a wry grin. "Makes me feel we should either disregard it completely or snap to attention and take orders."

Rather than gainsay Mosaia's leap of intuition, they proceeded cautiously as a group down the southbound corridor.

"I have read," said Torreb as they scouted in support of the knight's intuitive leap, "that battle lords first prove themselves with logic and strategy, but that *great* battle lords are either blessed by their gods with intuition or process information at such a rate that what is really systematic thought appears as hunches. In either case, having hunches and knowing when to play them are what distinguish the great from the common." He bowed a little in Mosaia's direction. Mosaia acknowledged the sentiment but merely looked thoughtful.

Precisely where the corresponding larger rooms had been in the western corridor were two more doors. A cursory inspection showed them both to be places where livestock were kept. They continued on, expecting to find two more doors leading to two more "elemental" rooms but found none. Rather, about fifteen meters beyond the livestock rooms they found their progress halted by a rent in the floor. It looked as though it had been cleft by a lightning strike: jagged and gaping and even smoking a bit around the edges. It measured at least ten meters across at its narrowest point. They could only guess at the bubbling of a subterranean stream farther below than any of them cared to reckon; the rent was, for all practical purposes, bottomless. Anthraticus offered to brave the crossing, but, even relieved of Mistra's weight, he was buffeted and repulsed by the chasm's treacherous updrafts.

Agonizingly, they could see that, beyond the chasm, the corridor terminated not in a blank wall, as had the other, but in a majestically arching doorway. Runes of power had been inscribed around it, though none of the party could guess at their exact meaning from this distance. It took neither magical powers nor the innate ability to recognize evil to know that beyond the door lay the spring from which all the black magic in the complex issued: the doorway might have been lit up with neon signs that said "Abandon Hope, All Ye Who Enter Here". Neither did it take much effort for the spellcasters to determine that the walls, floor, and ceiling, along with the intervening air space, were set with cunning spells all the way from the far side of the chasm to the archway. To allow Habie or Deneth to try to use their thieving skills to cross that stretch of ground would be tantamount to murder.

"Well, this has been educational," Deneth remarked.

Mosaia clucked his tongue. "'Tis always best to know the full strength of your enemy before you lay your plans."

"Yes," Mistra agreed, but she was grumbling, "and I don't think we do yet."

They had purposed to return to the junction, but Habie persuaded them to examine the livestock rooms more closely, saying, "I bet there are doors here like there were in the feed room." It seemed reasonable, and it turned out that she was right. What was more, both doors led to chambers that were mirror images of the immense one they had found behind the feed room. To the west lay one whose chiseled area had (according to Anthraticus) the tang of a sea breeze, and to the east lay one whose corresponding area reminded Alla of a mountain stream.

"'Twould make sense," Mosaia informed them as he examined his own locket from their vantage point in the great chamber to the southeast of the junction. "The symbols for water and air are in the corresponding quadrants of the cross if I hold it so the top is facing north."

"So what do we do?" puzzled Deneth.

"Try pouring the water from the marid's well into the bare spot," Mistra suggested.

Torreb, thinking this sounded reasonable, was about to comply when Mosaia stayed his hand. "Will there be some sort of effect, do you think?" he asked Mistra. "An aftershock, for instance?"

Her brow furrowed. "I don't know," she said in all honesty. "Are you thinking one of us should pour the water while the rest of us clear out?"

"I think the idea has merit, yes." He looked thankful she had proposed the idea first. He had not known how to phrase it without sounding either presumptuous—as if he were putting himself forward as the only person of merit in the group—or cowardly—as if he were thrusting a dangerous task on another while seeing to his own safety.

They mulled that over for a minute, even Habie, who was otherwise still champing at the bit for action—she had never yet released the tension she had let build during their encounter with the guardian demon. Presently, Torreb spoke up. "I see two problems with that."

"Only two?" Deneth muttered. He said it just loud enough that Anthraticus, perched on his shoulder, and Mistra, perched on Anthraticus' back, heard and chortled.

"How do we pick who does the honors? And what if the one who does is injured or attacked or somehow compromised so it would have made a difference if the rest of us had been nearby? I don't know about the rest of you, but I could never live with that."

"And I could not live with seeing the rest of you come to harm for a task one person could easily assume," Mosaia responded with surprising earnestness. He took the wineskin from Torreb: a peremptory gesture! "I shall take this responsibility on myself and absolve you of yours."

Torreb made as if to protest, but the sound died in his throat at the solemn authority in Mosaia's eyes. Habie, however, was not so easily daunted. Someone was finally taking action, and that someone was not she! She had to stand on tiptoe and reach well above her head to poke the paladin in the abdomen, but she did so, with what she hoped was some degree of command.

"I don't care if you *do* say we're not responsible," she fumed. "We started out together, and we can't run off and abandon each other the first time things look dangerous."

Mosaia smiled warmly in spite of himself. Deneth had upbraided him in the inn last night, and now Habie was actually crossing him! It was not at all a bad feeling to be treated this way—at least, not by creatures so worthy! What he said was, "The *first* time things look dangerous, is it? Well, Habadiah, I give you ten out of ten for loyalty and minus several thousand for discipline."

"What's that mean?"

"It means if you said that to me in the field, I might be forced to clap you in irons for the danger you presented by disobeying a direct order. Such a display could easily cost many lives."

Deneth intervened before Habie could either retort or deflate in response to the dressing down, congenial though it had been. "Well, that wasn't exactly a direct order," he said, "and no one died and left Mosaia—or anyone else—in charge."

Mistra took over, thus putting a stop to the look of smug satisfaction Deneth's assessment had brought to Habie's face. "You know, direct order or not, I'm not so sure Mosaia's doing this is a bad decision. After all, this is a very magical place, and his going means he leaves those of us with the higher order magical skills free to operate."

"And bail his carcass out if something bad happens."

"Of course, if *I* were in charge, I would delegate, and I might give a thought to keeping the magical skills balanced between the person who does the deed and those who back away." She looked expectantly at Mosaia, who burst out laughing.

"If you mean *you*, my little fairy princess, in your present condition you couldn't lift the wineskin, let alone the water inside, and I deem you've suffered enough consequences for a bit. No, I'll do it, if you will all oblige me and move further off. Though, if any of you would care to invoke your gods on my behalf, I, um, would be grateful."

"If people are going to keep calling me that," Mistra said sourly as she prodded Anthraticus back in the direction of the stock room, "one of us ought to see about getting me a pair of wings."

The others followed. Mistra and Torreb pulled out their respective holy symbols; even Deneth and Habie were murmuring benedictions under their breaths. Still, by unspoken mutual consent, they stopped short of the door and turned. Mosaia's stood with his back to them. He was already lifting the wineskin in a ritual asking the blessings of the Almighty, so they imagined it could make little difference to him in his state of absorption whether they actually left the room. They watched him pray and gesture reverently a few times. When he seemed satisfied, he uncorked the skin and poured its contents onto the bare spot on the floor.

There came a rumble followed by a blinding flash. When they could see again in the subdued light, they saw the bare spot had been completely filled in: colorful tiles showed the pattern of wavy lines that comprised the symbol for water. On the newly tiled area lay a third piece of the tapestry, this one depicting a jeweled collar.

But Mosaia was nowhere to be seen.

Deneth swore, but it was more in the nature of a gasp than a vehement oath. As the others looked helplessly around, he plucked Anthraticus by the neck from mid-air and touched a finger to Mistra's temple. She yielded once she understood his intention to search out Mosaia's consciousness and learn what had befallen him. Anthraticus had the sense to hush the others when he saw what they were doing. At least, what he said came out as a "shush"ing noise, whatever he had intended, as Deneth's grip effectively precluded use of his vocal cords. He looked like, while he understood Deneth's intent, he was struggling to put down a show of indignation.

"Well?" Alla prompted after a moment. She could not have explained how she grasped what they were doing: she would have said she saw it in the Ether.

"Unharmed..." Deneth whispered, still probing, sounding like he was summarizing the first chapter of a book he had not yet finished reading.

"Someplace dark... unfamiliar...alone," Mistra went on in the same sing-song voice.

Deneth frowned, then shook himself out of the altered state. He looked at the hand clutching Anthraticus's neck as if it belonged to someone else, then loosed his grip with an apologetic grin. "In the complex still, I think, huh, Mistra?" he said more decisively.

She nodded.

"That was excellent information for a mentalic contact made at distance," said Torreb, a bemused frown on his face. He looked like he was resisting the urge to rifle in his pack for his notebook.

Habie's eyes had widened at the display, and she was looking at her friends as if she had suddenly learned she had been traveling with two demi-gods who had till now kept their splendor concealed. T'Cru made an odd sort of growling noise in the back of his throat. Alla rested her hand on his head in a comforting sort of way and cocked her head thoughtfully. Mistra and Deneth exchanged a glance that made them look like two junior clerks caught with their hands in the till.

Alla saw that and took the initiative. "Don't look like that, you two!" she admonished. "You did a good and brave thing. But we must get on with things quickly, since we have one more person to rescue now." She scooped up the new piece of the tapestry and motioned to Torreb and Habie to pull out the two they carried. "You know, when Mosaia set his medallion into the piece of the tapestry that Gwynddolyn led us to, I wonder if we just gave up too easily. Look here, and here. Mistra, you said you thought there might be one piece of tapestry for each person in the wedding party. I think, as you suggested, these symbols are meant to be clues of some sort about which of Gwynddolyn's friends relates to which piece of the tapestry. But it also looks like there's an area here on each of them where something else should go. There's a depression like the one Mosaia noticed in all three pieces. Remember how Mosaia's *almost* fit the first one we found?"

"And we said, 'Close, but no cigar on this one,'" said Deneth.

"But how could they have anything to do with us?" asked Habie. "I mean, we're not the people Sigurd had in mind when he activated the spell that made Gwynddolyn and her friends disappear who-knows-where."

"No," agreed T'Cru, "but Gwynddolyn told us who we were, or who she *thought* we were, and many of our callings are similar to those of her friends. Torreb's, for example, and Deneth's. Only Mistra's was *very* different."

"And my alter ego was a consecrated priestess before she became a handmaiden," said Mistra, "so even I didn't change all that much in translation."

Torreb touched the piece of cloth he had obtained from the marid. "And this rendering of the Balance," he said of the design stitched into it, "if they don't call it the Balance of Ereb here, I'm certain it's still some sort of holy symbol, some representation of the idea of justice. Justice *is*, after all, a basic attribute of any goodly deity or pantheon." He unclasped his locket and set it into the small depression in face of the cloth while the others puzzled over the design on the new piece and what it might be.

"A collar?" Deneth wondered. "If it were meant for T'Cru's alter ego, it might not mean much, but if it's meant for a human, it might indicate some lower status, don't you think? The way a slave bracelet might where slavery is accepted?"

"Slaves—or handmaidens," Mistra said pointedly. "Whether they were priestesses in a former life or no."

"Here," said T'Cru, "since I am less offended by the role of feline companion than Mistra is by that of handmaiden, let us try my locket first."

Both Torreb and T'Cru proved to have been on the right track. The instant Torreb fit his locket into the tapestry piece bearing the Balance of Ereb, the two fused. The same thing happened when they set T'Cru's locket into the piece bearing the representation of the collar. The lockets fused so completely with their proper pieces of cloth, in fact, that there was soon no sign they had ever existed as discrete objects. They could see no telltale ridge, no spot where the cloth suddenly became less flexible as if a coin had been sewn into it, no suggestion the cloth itself had been woven in any other way than with the elemental sigil set in gold thread below the personal symbol. The stitches used in both designs matched; they might even have been set by the same hand. Additionally, this melding produced a subtle change in the psychic "feel" of the tapestry pieces. Now even the most mundane of them could sense the magic emanating from them. The only disappointment in all this was that they could find no locket that would set itself into the receptacle on the piece of cloth they had found before entering Sigurd's lair.

"I wonder..." said Mistra.

"What?" Deneth prompted.

"Well, we don't wear really elaborate crowns at home, but from what little experience I have with imperial headgear, I'd say this looks, well, *dainty*."

"And there would have been two royal people involved in the wedding," T'Cru extrapolated. "Gunthar—*Mosaia*, I should say—and Gwynddolyn." He emitted a low growl from the back of his throat.

"Hooooo, boy," Habie said without much rancor. "We have to rescue the bride to have a hope of saving the groom, then. Great."

With that grim bit of reasoning voiced, they turned their attentions to the analogue of the stock room that sat in the north wall.

⚜

Mosaia came to himself with the sensation of having not so much been rendered unconscious as pulled, inside out and backwards, through a time warp. Patting himself down, he was relieved to find his gear still intact. He drew the Retributor more as a reflex than from any sense of imminent danger. He became less relieved when it started to chatter.

"What happened?" it demanded. "I really wish you wouldn't sheath me every chance you get. I could warn you about things like this. I could protect you. I don't ask much, you know—just to be of service now and again—"

"Then be of service now," he snapped. The relief that he was not alone and the sword not un-magicked passed quickly once the blade started prattling. "Floor?" Mosaia thought himself fortunate right then that sentient blades have few feelings that can be hurt and can make sense of their master's words even when they leave out crucial verbs.

"Perfectly level."

"Moving?"

"Stationary."

"Minds?"

"One evil one is bent on you just now, and—hmm..." It paused, listening—or whatever it did to get its impressions. "Why, how exasperating!" it blustered suddenly. "It's that Sigurd person, and I do believe he's *laughing* at us. Of all the nerve."

"Well, I can't deny him his laughter when he took me unawares. I expected an assault, but this magical entrapment was not what I had in mind. Wait a minute—you sense only Sigurd?"

"Unequivocally. Have I erred?"

"I think not. No, it was nothing," he decided. But for a moment, washing over him like a gentle wave, he had felt a sense of being sought and troubled over by another mind—one, or more than one. It (or they) had withdrawn after lingering for mere seconds, satisfied to have found him alive and uninjured. He would have written it off as an hallucination had it not been so strongly reminiscent of the experience he had had joining minds with Mistra and Deneth. In fact, the more he thought about it, the more he knew he had felt what he would come to think of as their mental signatures. It reassured him, in an oblique way; if Deneth and Mistra were alive and had leisure to expend the energy to divine concerning his fate, that gave him every reason to suppose they and the rest of the company were still safe.

"Light would help," Mosaia said next. "Of course, that's of no use to you, is it?"

"No. I neither see nor hear in the sense you do. I merely perceive. But I can oblige your desire." The sword shuddered; instantly, a soft radiance began to emanate from its shaft.

"Thank you! And please tell me if you *feel* anything I might want to know about while I'm occupied here." Setting the Retributor against the wall, he rummaged in his pack till he found a torch and tinderbox. "You're not really a bad, er, fellow to have by one's side in a pinch, you know," he went on as he lit the torch. "You're a little impulsive, but your heart is in the right place, er, so to speak."

"Heart?" It rolled the sound around in its vocal apparatus as if it were a word from a foreign language. "That is the muscle that pumps blood around the bodies of your kind? I do not understand the reference."

Mosaia held the torch aloft, the better to inspect the chamber. He should have seen *that* one coming. "It means you do things for the right reasons, even if they're not always the right things. Which, I suppose, is philosophically more tenable than doing the right things for the wrong reasons." He got the impression the sword was thinking deeply about this before it replied.

"Oh. Oh, yes, I see. But it would be best to do the right things for the right reasons. But—"

"What?" He surveyed the place: an oblong cell of dressed stone perhaps fifteen by thirty feet with a door in the far wall. It was completely bare save for a large pile of straw in one corner. He supposed this might be rearranged somewhat to form bedding if circumstances forced him to stay for any length of time. He noticed one sconce; in this he set the torch. The two sources of light coming from opposite ends of the chamber provided him with tolerable ambient lighting.

"But isn't it justice to rid the world of evil creatures?" the sword pursued.

Mosaia went to inspect the door again, now that he had both hands free. Really, the sword echoed his own sentiments, but just now the speech and mental exertion of playing Fiend's Advocate were serving to calm and orient him. So he took issue with the sword's perspective. "If justice were the be all and end all of the Carotian way, why do you have a deity of mercy as well as one of justice?"

"Hmm. I must consider that point of view a moment before I can make an intelligent reply."

Mosaia smiled to himself. "You do that." He peered through the small barred window on the door and gave a low whistle. On the other side, currently lit only by his torch, lay what could have only been the wizard's workshop.

⁂

The party of adventurers nearly laughed in relief when they opened the door to the next room. They had all drawn their weapons in preparation for what they might meet here. After all, if their ideas about the complete symmetry of the place were correct, this room corresponded to the one in which they had met the demon. But the room was filled not with otherworldly creatures, but with spinning wheels!

"How very curious," said T'Cru, who, they were learning, had a positive gift for understatement as Deneth had one for sarcasm.

"You, uh, don't suppose they change into undead warriors or something if we go in?" Deneth wondered.

"I doubt it," replied Mistra, encouraged by the pained look Anthraticus gave her at his suggestion. "Still, we're the worst targets in the group," she said of herself and the dragon.

"And the best magicians!" he cackled. "Shall we scout, my dear?" Without waiting for an explicit reply, he fluttered ahead into the room. The pair readied a half dozen spells both offensive and defensive in case Deneth's suggestion turned out to have merit.

It didn't.

The spinning wheels, set in two neat rows that ran the length of the room, were just what they had seemed from the doorway. Anthraticus had reached the far wall and started back when he felt a prickling sensation run down his spine, at which he wondered if he had misjudged. He craned his neck around to look in query at Mistra, who nodded.

"I feel it, too," she said. "Weak, but present."

"Weak," he postulated, "because only one thing here is magical, do you think?" He circled till they narrowed their search to three of the spinning wheels, then went from one to the other, considering, till they agreed on one, over which he hovered. He had selected a completely nondescript wheel, easily the smallest and plainest of the entire field, and it sat far back in one corner so it would not easily have drawn anyone's attention. But it was definitely the source of the magical emanations.

"Whatcha got?" asked Deneth as the rest of the company joined them.

"This one's magical," Anthraticus announced.

Alla ran an appreciative hand over it. She had spun and loomed time out of mind, and she recognized in this machine, humble and unadorned though it was, quality craftsmanship. Even if it had not been magical, it would have spun a superior thread. "What does a magical spinning wheel do?" she mused. "Spin faster, or spin a finer thread?"

"Maybe it makes magical thread," Habie suggested with the note of sarcasm she had picked up from Deneth.

The others laughed at the jest save for T'Cru, who said soberly, "But isn't magical thread just what one would need to sew a magical tapestry back together?"

That cut the laughter short! Now all but Habie became serious as they considered the point and how to apply it. "And what would you get that from?" she retorted, irritated at having her joke spoiled. "Magic sheep?" She was completely discomfited when they took this suggestion, too, seriously, and looked as one back at the stock rooms.

"Keep them coming, munchkin," laughed Deneth.

"Yes," agreed Torreb. "Your jokes have more clarity of thought to them than logic from the rest of us."

"I do not think the sheep were other than they appeared," said Anthraticus.

"But—" Mistra began, then stopped, looking diffident. Something in her memory had just clicked, but it made less sense when she tried to say it out loud than when she had turned it over in her mind.

"Well, out with it," demanded Anthraticus. He was more aware of her reticence than the others, as he could feel her squirm and re-posture on his back as her ideas struck her as alternately brilliant and idiotic.

"It's just that—no, that's crazy."

"What?!" screeched Anthraticus, Deneth, and Habie in unison.

"Go on," Torreb encouraged diplomatically. "With as many unusual things as we've seen on this quest so far, one more crazy idea will feel right at home."

"In fact," added T'Cru, "I think the crazier it sounds on the face of it, as in the Undercity on Astra, the more likely it is to be the solution. There *is* that to be said for this place—it is nothing if not consistent." He would remember later that, while this was one of the first times any of them commented on this aspect of their adventures, it was not the last.

"OK," Mistra replied, taking a deep breath as if she were about to dive into unknown waters that were almost certain to contain unpredictable currents. "Here goes. The straw in the feed room, the *only* straw in all that fodder. I remember a folk tale from my sojourn on Earth about this maiden whose skill at spinning was so fine her family boasted she could spin straw into gold." She shrugged. "There was something different about that pile of straw beyond its being so singular, but I couldn't put my finger on it when we were there. That's all. I told you it was silly."

"So you're saying," Habie reasoned, "we should try feeding the pile of straw into this magical spinning wheel—and see what comes out the other end?"

She nodded, then shrugged and looked diffident.

"Well, *I* think it's worth a try," Torreb said a shade too brightly when the others showed no immediate signs of acting on her suggestion. "I shall even go and retrieve it."

"Hold on," Deneth said. He flashed a resigned smile at Mistra, a belated show of support for her sanity if not for her logic. "I'll ride shotgun. Your arms'll be full."

Alla nodded. "I'll get to work on the spinning wheel." She smiled back at Mistra, whose face lit up as they fell in line behind her idea.

Torreb and Deneth retrieved the straw without incident. To her genuine surprise, Alla found as she fed handfuls of straw onto the flyer, they caught as easily as the best wool and produced a thick, supple thread of pure gold.

"I'll lay odds we need a magical scissors to cut it and a magical needle to stitch anything with it," Deneth commented as he handled it. His voice was amiable, his expression bemused. "It's beautiful, isn't it?"

Their confidence bolstered, they exited the room into the east hallway and crossed to the corresponding door in the north wall. They entered and found that its contents, too, fit the bizarre logic of the place. The room was stacked as deeply with yarn as the feed room had been with feed. There were also racks of knitting needles and crochet hooks. In a compartment in one of the racks sat the magical scissors whose existence Deneth had postulated, but they could find no sign of a tapestry needle, magical or otherwise.

Farther to the east were two smaller doors, one on either side of the hall, that corresponded to the "elemental" rooms in the west hallway. Unlike the last two doors, these two gave them pause. The marid had been friendly enough, but he had indicated the other elementals might not welcome them as congenially as he, and they had never come in contact with the elemental in the "air" room to test his hypothesis.

They decided to hazard a peek only into each room before they committed themselves. No one had any doubt they must face all four creatures, and possibly worse, to obtain all the pieces of the tapestry and break the spell, but they saw no reason to go charging headlong into danger, especially with their strongest warrior missing. The chamber beyond the south door struck them immediately as oppressive—ominously so. It was dark, but, like the oasis, it gave the impression it, too, extended off into infinity. A breeze like the blast from a distant furnace supported this perception. About five meters from the door stood an ornately carved pedestal. In a sconce atop it sat an ivory torch. It, too, was ornately carved; in the red light it gave, the carvings themselves seemed to take on a sinister meaning.

They deferred more thorough explanation of the Torch Room in favor of checking out its analogue on the north wall. This door opened on a chamber that showed a bit more promise. Four bare stone walls defined a finite space about ten meters on a side. At its far end, spanning one entire wall, sat transparent bins filled with gems of every description.

"This looks hopeful," said Habie, her eyes catching fire at the sight of the gemstones. The more astute of the party eventually learned to read the look on her face as "Charge!" or "Geronimo!" or some other precursor to precipitate action—and to restrain her before she attempted anything suicidal. As things stood now, she had crossed half the room in several spritely bounds before any of them reacted. They tumbled into the room, weapons ready, looking for a hidden guardian that, to their collective relief, did not manifest.

Habie, her sword now held up more for show than utility, was by this time pawing madly through the bins. Her movements became less frenetic as she went from bin to bin. She removed nothing; at last, her little shoulders drooped. "Worthless," she muttered. She kicked the last of the bins as if the valueless stones it contained were somehow its own fault. "What a lousy thing to do—getting a poor little street kid's hopes up with stones that look all pretty and shiny like diamonds and rubies, then when you get up close they're nothing but stuff like quartz and agate."

Torreb and Alla joined her, Alla draping a sympathetic arm across her shoulders. "Perhaps Dorlas in her wisdom has decreed that we've had our fill of *precious* stones this trip," Torreb conjectured. The glitter of jewels and precious metals held little interest for him: his chief interest lay in why bins of gems that had turned out to be mere trinkets took up so much of the space. He plucked a piece of agate from one of the bins. "Pretty, though, in their own way."

"Pretty and five credits gets you a cup of coffee in the bazaar in Caros City," Habie groused.

"The point of this quest isn't to make ourselves rich," Alla reminded her as she examined a piece of rose quartz.

"Speak for yourself," Habie said under her breath.

If she heard the remark, Alla chose to disregard it. She turned to the Tigroid, who was pawing through one of the bins with a curiosity similar to Torreb's. "Remember, T'Cru, how you said the one room had such an earthy smell?"

He stopped, resting his forepaws on the rim of one of the bins. "Are you thinking we must take a small quantity of these gems and place them in that empty space, as Mosaia did with the well water?" He snuffled a little at the gems. "Yes. I've not the supernatural talents some of you possess, but I must admit that these—well, er, it's not exactly that they *smell*, is it?" He looked up at her. "They *feel*—that's it—they feel the same as the bare spot in the one chamber. No question about it. It's as if the one will be forever incomplete without the touch of the other, or like they were made from the same substance."

Deneth looked around, his suspicions aroused. "Where's the guardian, then, eh? Out on his lunch break?"

"You might note," said Anthraticus, "that the good marid did not manifest until *after* we tried to remove the water from his well. Perhaps we can come and go as we like in any of the rooms—till we try to remove something from them."

"Good thought! Well, anyone in need of refreshment before we make a run for it? No? Good." He did not truly wait for a reply before he dropped his pack. He then drew his sword with one hand and scooped up with the other a small handful of each type of gem: these he stashed quickly in his pack before once again shouldering it. He moved with the speed and grace of a cheetah: no one watching could have doubted that, had music not been such a part of his soul, he could by now have retired on the proceeds of a lucrative career as a cat burglar.

"OK, folks, let's do it," he said. He started toward the door. He was not precisely making a run for it, but he was moving at a good clip, so he had good cause to thank Strephel for the briskness of his reflexes when a most strange creature emerged from the floor just in front of him and attacked. He pulled up short, thus avoiding the thrust of the creature's snout, and had taken a swing at it before he had a chance to fathom its nature. Two things only registered in that first instant of engagement: his sword arm had gone numb and his blade came away nicked. He was just springing back to regroup when Habie shot past him and threw herself underneath the creature, hoping for a shot at its belly.

If it *was* a belly. The creature's body was made not of flesh, but of crystals of all shapes and sizes. It looked as if it had been made by the child of an earth god who had been given a room full of gem-shaped building blocks and told to fashion a pet. The resulting creature looked like a rackless elk, created of transparent blocks shaded in pastel blues and greens. In and of itself it angular body could not threaten, but its snout ended in a wicked point where five cleavage planes met. It had no joints in the conventional sense but was able to twist and slide the various parts of its body wherever they articulated one with the next: it could kick or strike outwards to a limited degree with its "legs." Habie had stumbled on the one place it could not attack; try as it might, it could not maneuver its stiff neck so it could strike at something lodged beneath it.

If it could not harm Habie, neither could she do it any damage with her small sword. Striking the creature was like trying to drive a blunt paring knife through a hundred carat diamond: on one particularly vicious strike, her blade almost snapped. Where Deneth's had been nicked, hers remained bent and practically useless. More infuriating, inside the creature's "gut," she could see not only a number of valuable gems but another piece of the tapestry.

Torreb waded in with his mace and landed a blow that would have felled a charging elephant. He could not dodge quickly enough to avoid a stab to his leg from the creature's snout, but he saw its back flake where he had struck. "Look!" he cried. "Don't slash at it. It needs blunt force!"

"Now he tells us," Habie and Deneth muttered almost in unison as they looked at their damaged weapons.

They found the advice, though sound, difficult to act on. As they had few distance weapons, they had few weapons or implements capable of dealing a crushing blow. The flat of a blade did little damage, as did a torch used as a club or a utility hammer. Mistra, trying to avail herself of the small arsenal in her wristband, learned the spell that was keeping her shrunk to the size of a dragonfly with an overactive thyroid was also affecting the weapons she stored: she could turn spare sword to club and blaster into morning star, but both remained no larger than the cups and spoons with which she had served tea to her dolls in the days of her childhood. Meanwhile, her friends waded in, clobbered with what force and weapons they could, and suffered the infliction of puncture after puncture from that strange snout.

Shortly, all of the party save Mistra, Anthraticus, and Habie were nursing injuries. And Habie was effectively pinned, as she could not get up the momentum to escape from her position under the creature with enough speed to guarantee it would miss her when it lashed out. The other two, tiny though they were, tried to distract the crystal creature while the party regrouped. Anthraticus fired at point blank range the cantrip with which he had first ensnared Mistra and Deneth, and Mistra got off a generic energy bolt, but the creature had no fluids in its makeup capable of fermentation, and the energy strike affected it about the way a mosquito bite might affect a human.

They reached a standoff. When the creature remained still, they could see chips in its body where it had been wounded and trickles of something that looked like sap that must have served as its blood, but it was nowhere near being cowed. As the eyeless face considered them, Deneth, suddenly inspired, dropped his sword and pulled out the lute. Torreb said something about that not being what he had in mind when he told them to use blunt weapons, but Deneth disregarded the gibe and began to play.

Slowly, looking as confused as a creature with no face can look, it rose into the air and began to circle. It lay about itself with great ferocity, almost skewering Habie at one point, and almost shooting Anthraticus and Mistra out of the air when it launched a barrage of small crystals from its snout. If it had a second volley to throw, though, the creature got no chance to fire it. Under the influence of Deneth's spell, it circled faster and faster above their heads till its movement became too dizzying for any of them but Deneth to watch. A final dissonant chord, and it went sailing out of its orbit to crash into the far wall.

Down it slid, in two pieces. The impact had shattered its midsection. Out fell a number of jacinths and opals and the piece of the tapestry. Habie hastily retrieved the lot, and the creature made no move to stop her. She paused next to it, out of reach of the snout, and raised her sword as if contemplating a further attack.

Alla touched her sword hand. "No, Habie," she said quietly. "If it will let us go in peace, we have no need to harm it more. We have what we came here for."

"Isn't it crueller to leave it half dead?" asked Mistra, truly unsure of her reasoning.

"But it isn't harmed beyond help. It will mend, the faster if we leave it some of the gemstones. It is, after all, only a poor, dumb beast protecting its territory and its food supply." She took an armload of stones from the bins and set them within reach of the creature. Habie even set one of the larger jacinths on the pile. The creature turned in their direction, uncertain for a moment what to make of the gesture. Then it began to munch on the gems. It took no further interest in the questors.

Once outside, they breathed a collective sigh of relief. None of them had any experience with beings from the elemental planes, and they were finding the creatures' range of attributes and capabilities one step beyond their ability to anticipate. Habie alone was enthusiastic about tackling the next room right away. Her fortunes had changed so much in the short time since she had left Caros that she viewed any danger as a challenge to be met and enjoyed rather than an obstacle to be avoided. But Torreb, himself wounded, overruled her in his eagerness to get his friends back in good repair before they entered the forbidding torch room. He beckoned them into the knitting room for a brief respite. There, he, Alla, and Mistra set to work to mend the worst of the injuries.

"Anything anybody can do about this?" Habie asked, holding up her bent blade. She and Deneth both seemed to think of the same anatomical reference at the same time, then both seemed to bite their tongues in light of the company they were in, and then both stifled a simultaneous outburst of crude laughter.

"Deneth's the one with the dominion over earth-y things," said Mistra when the others turned to her and Anthraticus. She, too, was stifling a laugh, as were most of the company.

"Tut, tut," said Anthraticus. "I have a spell or two that might serve, though I'd have them looked at by a weaponsmith if ever we finish here. Let Deneth save his energies for creative applications in combat!"

And, in two trices, the blades looked much as they ever had.

When they again entered the Torch Room, it was deathly quiet. The outrushing of wind had stilled; where before it had felt like the heat of a blast furnace whipping forward from the unguessed depths of the chamber, now its fury would have made a welcome contrast to the eerie silence. The wind had seemed a generic menace, an indiscriminate barrier meant to deter all who entered. The silence felt aimed at the seven of them specifically, an uncanny sensation that provoked in all of them at least a fleeting wish to do an about-face and march back to the inn. In the blackness beyond the pool of light cast by the torch, they sensed a watchfulness, an evil will biding its time, holding its hand till the time came when it could cause the most damage to those who dared intrude.

"I got the gems," Deneth whispered in an attempt to lighten the mood. "It's somebody else's turn."

"I'll get it," Torreb volunteered, displaying many times the confidence he actually felt, which was almost none. He felt the draft start up again as he approached the pedestal, but now it felt less like the heat of a blast furnace and more like the unleashed wrath of the Seven Hells. He mopped his brow with his sleeve and peered into the blackness, which no longer seemed like the mere absence of light. In combination with the intense heat, he actually had the impression he was staring into the thick smoke of a blaze gone wildfire. It stung his eyes so they burned and teared, so, at first, he wrote off the tiny specks of flame he saw as illusions. It was not until he had removed the torch and turned to see the horrified expression on the faces of his companions that he realized they were no hallucination.

An oath escaped his lips as he caught sight of a huge bat-like shape out of the corner of his eye. He fought his first inclination: to freeze in the hope the beast would not notice him or, better, would simply sonar its way around him. He had just time to grip his mace and swing, albeit wildly, before the bat attacked. He could not tell if the thing were made of fire or if it were flesh that could self-immolate without being destroyed, and he had no time to reason it out.

Close on the heels of this one were another score of the creatures, who wheeled in, bent on (he supposed) barbecuing them. As he set his mace in motion again, he realized the bats were attacking in an organized manner, like the smartest of hunting pack animals—dividing into attack squads, some of which dived directly at the questors and others of which flanked the party, cutting them off from the door and herding them toward the suffocating darkness. Simple arithmetic and the evidence of his eyes told him he had not one opponent to deal with, but several, and that the odds would worsen considerably if even one of his comrades fell.

The bats arrayed themselves so a squad of at least two harried each of the intruders. Their size permitted three to attack each of their larger opponents; only two could crowd in around Habie and around the small package represented by Mistra and Anthraticus. The rest circled and herded and nipped in for a quick attack wherever one of the intruders dropped his guard; whenever one bat fell to the assault, another instantly scooted in to take his place.

They were formidable opponents! A mere brush of their wings seared exposed flesh. Their bites penetrated with the feel of a myriad needles of molten lead. They flitted with the agility of far smaller creatures; the very margins of their bodies were difficult for their opponents to define once flames enveloped them, so they made poor targets indeed.

And they made it clear from the outset that the battle would be decided in this room: there would be no question of retreat for the questors while one of the creatures lived and drew breath.

Seconds before the bats attacked her, Alla shape-shifted to a feline form, a large and supple one with a very sparse coat: flesh would be harder than fur to immolate, and the minimal insulation should help keep her from stifling in the already sweltering room. The sight of her preparations to make a brave stand rallied T'Cru. The heat was unbearable for all of them, but it was worst for the Tigroid with his thick coat. He saw early on that if he could swat them from the air, impact with the ground would douse their flames and make them easier opponents. A minute of springing and swatting at the creatures' wings, however, of connecting with them as often as not only to have his paws seared and his claws blackened, and he found himself on the point of being overcome by heat exhaustion. Only his honor and the loyalty of his great heart kept him fighting while his friends were still in danger.

Now, he closed with his shape-shifted friend and fell to the attack with renewed vigor. Together, the pair made a better defensive force with their claws than did the others with their extraneous weapons. Although such maneuvering singed their fur, the two of them continued T'Cru's strategy of clawing vigorously at the bats' wings, going so far as to spring into mid-air to engage them. When T'Cru leapt and swatted at one of their attackers, Alla remained close to the ground to pounce on it as it fell; when Alla landed a glancing blow by pulling up on her hind legs, T'Cru was there to net the dazed creature and grind it beneath his paws. Eight eventually came within range of their integrated attack. Three were soon limping pathetically off into the darkness from which they had come; the other five trembled feebly then moved no more.

Habie was finding her sword to be of little use. By three minutes into the fight, the best she had been able to do was to fend the bats off by swatting at them. Try as she might, she could not get a blow to connect. She dropped her guard for the barest fraction of a second when one of the two bats engaging her flew off to attack Alla and T'Cru, then saw too late that the evasive maneuver was a feint. She had not even lowered her sword; she merely allowed her gaze to be diverted. It was enough. The second bat swooped in from behind and buried its fangs in her shoulder.

She screamed in rage and pain—she who had endured the most severe of beatings with barely a whimper. Somewhat irrationally, her first response was to try to shake the bat off. It took her a moment to recognize it had sunk its claws firmly through her tunic—and into the flesh beneath—and was contentedly sucking her blood. She made an awful face and squeaked out a little "Ew!" at the realization that they were a breed of vampire. Her second thought was both pleasant and practical. Although as a vampiric race, their bite was tenacious and their fangs would, she supposed, suck the life out of any opponent too weak to cast them off in the first few seconds, her enemy had now come within striking range and was holding quite still. So her second response was to hack gleefully away at its wings, muttering, "I hope Lemurian blood gives you the pox!" The bat had drunk nowhere near its fill when it saw that, in the interest of self-preservation, it had better move on from dining on Habie to getting its dessert from someone else. It screeched as it detached itself—a signal to the rest to reshuffle and redivide themselves to keep Habie from going to anyone else's aid.

Mistra and Anthraticus quickly found themselves in circumstances almost as hopeless as T'Cru's before the sight of Alla had rallied him. The two of them together were barely the size of the smallest bat; airborne, they made the most engageable target for the creatures, and their diminutive statures made them easy prey for the effects of heat prostration. They, too, sensed the cunning in these creatures that had struck Torreb: they knew mere brute force would not allow them to triumph. Two bats hovered near them, and it took little imagination to read in the bats' eyes debate over whether they should attack their prey as a unit or power dive so one of them could grab Mistra and the other Anthraticus. There was, after all, only so much surface area to these small but certainly delectable creatures...

It is no easy matter to get off a destructive spell when one is engaged in pitched battle. After about half a minute, Anthraticus gave up trying and simply snapped and raked at the first bat to attack him directly. His small teeth could gain little purchase, but he did let go his fermentation cantrip as the bat swooped away. The creature did not stagger but did begin to look disoriented. It was a start.

Mistra loosed her grip on Anthraticus' neck; a deliberate move so she could free her hands. A good rider, she held on with her knees, and, if she had never ridden a dragon bareback before, she knew enough about staying on a horse that she could apply those same principles. Her sword would do her no more good than a sewing needle in this situation, so she tucked it away. Where Anthraticus had a few natural weapons, she had none in this state and so turned her thoughts to spellcasting. A ripple in the Ether, and a small bow and quiver appeared in her hands. If her sword had been likely to do no more good than a sewing needle, the arrows would have looked like so many sewing pins to an observer in the moment she conjured them, but she never bent the Ether without a logical purpose. Out came an arrow, up went the bow, and off zinged a tiny arrow past Anthraticus' head. It froze solid in mid-flight, the small enchantment allowing it to sink deeply into the second bat's obscenely swollen body.

The hit turned out to be a mixed blessing. She wounded the bat, though not mortally, but the appearance of an arrow protruding from its middle irked it enough that it reconsidered its cautious approach. It swooped down and plucked Mistra neatly from Anthraticus' back. It started toward the hidden recesses of the chamber, and it might have succeeded in carting Mistra off to its larder if it had not flown over the pedestal.

Anthraticus, pursuing, saw this scene unfold. He sensed the splash in the Ether that told him that, with a sense of goodly magic looking out for its own, the pedestal somehow recognized Mistra as kin. Torreb was holding his position right next to the pedestal. Whatever was at work—luck or skill or the hand of the Minissa, or the magic inherent in the pedestal itself—Torreb's next blow went wide of his own mark but landed so it perfectly occupied the space that Mistra's bat was about to enter. Torreb caught the bat squarely across its middle, winding it and forcing it to release the princess. It screamed—a horrible, piercing cry— and went careening into the bat for which Torreb had actually been aiming. The impact extinguished what little life was left in both of them, and they exploded in a small fireball. Mistra landed in a heap on the pedestal and lay there winded and barely able to move. Being carried in the bat's talons had subjected her to a veritable bath of flame; only the operation of her personal shield had kept her from being roasted alive. Burns of one sort or another covered every square centimeter of her body now. She could hear, but her vision had been severely impaired by the burns. What she heard told her the battle had not yet been won. If only seconds of consciousness—of life itself—were left to her, she must strike out in a way that counted. Her brain at least had not been fried, and she thought furiously even as she husbanded her failing strength.

Anthraticus turned then and grappled their second foe in earnest. Anger over seeing the bat's counterpart pluck Mistra from his back and nearly cart her off to its lair fueled his attack. His scales did not singe easily, and the creature was close enough to his own size that, in his fury, even his small claws and fangs inflicted substantial injury. The bat barely thought to retaliate—it had remained bewildered from Anthraticus' cantrip. Down it went. Once he put his foe out of commission, Anthraticus fluttered over to Mistra and hovered protectively above her, but none of the remaining bats seemed inclined to approach. It was as if the creatures regarded the small area of the pedestal as sanctuary they were debarred from attacking.

"I wonder," Anthraticus said to himself, "can I shrink everyone and get them teleported here so they can heal before the bats attack again..." Lost in thought, he neither noticed the motion on the pedestal below him nor recognized its import.

After the collision near the pedestal, the bats rearranged themselves again as though they were involved in some sort of macabre dance. There were only nine left now, two each attacking Deneth, Torreb, T'Cru, and Alla, and one zeroing in on Habie. Deneth's were by far the most aggressive; they attacked as if they knew how sweet the blood of a bard would be. And Deneth, who had held them off them since the fight began, was finally beginning to tire.

He had at last succeeded in clipping one who had come too close and moved away too slowly, but the two who remained harried him like hounds nipping at the heels of a deer. One would swoop in to rake his face; as he lashed out at the one, the other would close on a body part he could not simultaneously protect. Neither had attached itself as the one had done to Habie, but each had gotten in a half dozen juicy bites, and Deneth was now bleeding from a dozen small but painful punctures. Like Anthraticus, he did not notice Mistra struggle to her knees atop the pedestal and hold her hand aloft, nor could he have spared the attention to observe if he had seen.

But he could not miss the result! From her outspread fingers, a barrage of icicles flew—small, but dangerous for a fire-based creature, colored delicately to resemble the aurora borealis. Her every physical faculty might be impaired, but Mistra still had her access to the Art. She did not fire blindly—not quite. She could make out an imprint of Deneth in the Ether through the aegis of the *sha-nora* bond and could extrapolate the position of the creatures that harried him. A score of the tiny needles split and impaled the two bats harassing the bard. Weakened and dazed from the fall, she could not put enough power into the barrage to make it kill, but the volley sufficed to extinguish the bats' flame. Both bats paused in mid-air, knowing something untoward had just happened to them but unable to figure out what. Still puzzling over the effect, neither seemed to notice when Deneth sliced them neatly in two with one smooth stroke.

"Oh, what fun!" cackled Anthraticus, who had taken till now to understand Mistra's general plan. "I get the picture. Let's see what *this* does. Torreb! Mind that torch!" He pronounced a few words in his native tongue. Directly, it began to storm—mushy particles like frozen rain or partially melted hail spattered everyone in the room. In seconds, his friends were soaked—but so were the bats. Bewildered, waterlogged, and no longer aflame, they became easy prey. Habie jabbed and Deneth stabbed and Torreb walloped; the felines raked; all five felt the satisfying crunch of bone and sinew. And that was the end of the barrage of bats. The questors faced the darkness and waited for the attack to be renewed, but no creatures came to take the place of the fallen. They breathed a collective sigh of relief and postured down.

Once they dispatched the last bat and assured themselves none would come to resume the attack, Torreb did his best to coax the dwindling flame of the torch back to life. He had protected it as much as he could with his robes and body during the brief downpour without immolating himself, but it had begun to sputter. He dashed out of the room in search of the drier, warmer air of the corridor. A quick prayer to Ereb and it blazed back to life. The joy in his victory was short-lived, though. In the heat of the battle, he had not seen how severe some of his companions' injuries were. T'Cru and Alla could barely walk, their paws were so singed; Deneth looked like he had been mauled by a pack of wild dogs; Habie had lost enough blood he could see the pallor even through her fur. Anthraticus, himself relatively unscathed, was flying very erratically—the spragon bore Mistra as well as he could, but it was clear she was keeping from a complete swoon only by main force of will.

"Would that Mosaia were here," he sighed as he settled them back in the knitting room. "He, too, has the hands of a healer, and I am already weary. These wounds may be beyond my skill to heal."

Anthraticus somersaulted once in the air before him. "Silly priest," he chided, "Is your skill only in the laying on of hands? Is it not in the knowledge you own as well, in the concoction of unguents and teas and such?"

"Yes, but my supplies are so limited. Mistra, I'm sure could conjure for me, or *you* could, but the effect—oh! I'd forgotten about the medicines we made to cure the dragons. I wonder... Habie, come here." He removed the blood elixir from his pack and dabbed it carefully over the fang marks on her shoulder. They stopped bleeding instantly. On a guess, he applied some on the burns around the two punctures. They, too, began to look better immediately. He tried the tiniest drop on Mistra's burns, which were far more extensive, with results that surpassed his precarious hopes.

Deneth, once Torreb saw to his bites and burns, occupied himself with his lute. He had been rather put out at being drenched to the skin, indoors and without his leave, even if the impromptu shower had spelled the defeat of the bats: the unguents had done nothing to dry out his clothes or skin. So, while Torreb continued to ply his craft, he plucked out a tune intended to control the movement of air in the room. It took several tries, but in the end he produced the effect he was after.

Several small vortices of warm air sprang into existence. These proved far better for drying them off than a fire of any size could have done, for they could step into the vortices and let the warm air swirl around them till they got dry—a supremely pleasant sensation. The only one dissatisfied with this arrangement was Anthraticus, who got caught in one of the small whirlwinds. Around and around he went until, forcing himself free, he went sailing into the nearest wall. He was unharmed, but his pride suffered enormously at the humor the others found in the episode. Although Deneth looked at the incident as a form of poetic justice, it was some time before the spragon managed to be civil to any of them.

CHAPTER 7

Sigurd's Collection Waxes Great

The fruit of purity is true and sweet; the fruit of lusts is
pain and toil; the fruit of ignorance is deeper darkness.
—The Book of Wisdom

MISTRA LAY CURLED UP on T'Cru's back. She stretched from time to time, sensing the warmth of Torreb's magic surging through her and strengthening her, languishing in the feeling that she lay wrapped in a rug of the deepest, softest fur before a roaring fire. It lacked only the presence of her lost consort to make it complete, she mused as she drifted in and out of the strange twilight sleep that rapid magical healing often induced.

She thought for a moment her wish had come true, for, in that place where dreams and reality flow together, she thought she heard the voice she loved best in the world call to her. At first, it sounded like the voice of her father, with whom she had always been close; then of her brother Philo, whom she adored; then of Isildin, who had been lost to death; then of Pezheska, who believed her dead and gone. Finally the four blended into a music made of the voices of father and brother and consorts all rolled into one, till it sang, and then it was Deneth, and when it whispered endearments, it might even have been Mosaia...

Opening one reluctant eye and wondering where that last thought had come from, she saw someone looming over her. She started and gave a tiny yelp in the moment between her eyes telling her she was regarding a fearsome giant and her brain telling her it was only Torreb and that she remained smaller than the average house cat. "Do you feel well enough to push on, Mistra?" he asked. His voice was kind, and she suddenly understood why a wise and ageless creature like Alla might be drawn to him. Then she wondered where that thought came from as well. Was it from fevered imagination or true contact with the Ether when her mind had been freed while she healed?

"What?" she murmured. "Oh. Oh, yeah, sure." She sat up and stretched.

"Because we've been discussing what to do next, and, of course, we need your opinion."

"I say try our luck with either the torch or the gems." She yawned. She was never at her most courteous or lucid upon waking.

"Yes," said T'Cru, nuzzling her as he might a cub. "We'd thought of that. We'd also thought of Mosaia's disappearance when he, er, 'tried his luck' with the water."

"Oh, that." She tried to avoid his ministrations by burying herself in his fur, but only partially succeeded. "M'll oo urch."

"What?"

She raised her head and said clearly, "I'll do it," as if that settled the question.

Deneth chortled. "And which do you think you're going to lift, the flaming torch or the kilo of gems?"

She glared at him, the impact of the look not having diminished in proportion to her size at all. "Did you think my magic deserted me when I shrank?"

"You're telling me size doesn't make a difference?" he replied with a wicked grin.

It was a remark only Deneth could have gotten away with making without offending the rest, and Mistra laughed as heartily as anyone. Even Torreb chortled through his blush at the ribald play on words—more than any of them, he welcomed the display of humor that defused the tensions that had built over the course of the past hour. "I suspect I can resist the teleportation spell better than any of you," she went on in a better temper, "except maybe for Anthraticus. I'm willing to give it a whirl, at least."

Alla sighed. "That's very brave, Mistra. Well, we have to get to it some time, I suppose, and Deneth would still have this mentalic link with you so we'd know if you got into too much trouble. I can't think of anything much safer."

"That's assuming she ends up in the same cell as Mosaia," Deneth protested. "Suppose one of them is trapped to land you in quicksand or a dragon's lair or something."

"No," Mistra rebutted with surprising earnestness. "If what the marid said is right, I think Sigurd might not even know the elements of the tapestry have rematerialized around his lair. I don't think he can have prepared for us specifically. I'm not even sure Mosaia's disappearance was necessarily triggered by something Sigurd did."

"You think this is the way a temple consecrated to a bunch of nice deities rewards us for putting their puzzle to good use?"

"No, I think it's more like the law of the conservation of energy and matter. We're forcing some elements of the puzzle to manifest, so whatever magic is allowing them to reappear is sort of reshuffling matter."

"Balance," Alla murmured.

"What?" asked Deneth.

"Everything in balance. It *is* like the marid said."

"What?" The bard directed this query at Torreb, who wore a thoughtful frown.

"What?" He shook his head as if clearing it of cobwebs. "Oh, I was just thinking about something the demon said. Something about seeing all ends. I was thinking about that cleft in the floor. If Sigurd's over there and his dungeons are over there and whoever places the material elements in these holes in the floor ends up over there, the balance of this place or the elemental gods or whoever is teleporting people may really be doing us a favor." Interpreting Deneth's skeptical look as a slight on his sanity, he smiled wanly. "I mean, Mosaia may be in a dungeon, but teleporting did get our most powerful warrior and his enchanted sword to Sigurd's side of the chasm."

Mistra jumped in before Deneth could argue. "For my money, the real danger won't come till we've filled in all of the bare spots and collected everything necessary to complete the tapestry." She thought a moment. "And, of course, gotten the four of you who won't be teleporting safely across the chasm and through those traps."

"So what you're saying," Habie grumbled, "is that the better we are, the more trouble we're gonna get into."

Alla smiled fondly. "I think, my dear little thief, that is true of all of life."

Mistra flashed a theatrical smile. "If we do it all quickly enough, he'll never put it all together in time, and we'll trounce him soundly and be home in time for tea."

They packed up and proceeded cautiously back to the Earth Room. Mistra slipped from T'Cru's back and bade Deneth place the pouch of jewels at the edge of the circle. She waved the others back, but Deneth knelt beside her and took her small hand in his as well as he could.

"Are you sure?" he whispered.

She nodded.

"Be careful."

She tapped her temple and smiled. "I'll keep in touch."

He backed off, nodding in what he hoped was an encouraging—or, at least, understanding—way. He was feeling less confident about this approach by the minute. Losing Mistra would weaken the party and their chances of getting through to Sigurd, or so he rationalized. But that reasoning did not account for the tightness he felt in his chest as he watched her prepare to cast her spell.

Mistra steepled her fingers and focused her will. Before she tried to levitate the bag of gems, she took a moment to put up the best defenses she could against a spell whose parameters she would never fathom. *Let's see*, she thought, *mage on his own turf, ethos opposed to mine, probably diametrically, has at his disposal the mana drawn from the earth and waters of an entire province. Right. I'll be doing well just to keep my synapses from getting fried.*

"OK," she murmured when she supposed she was as ready as she was going to get. "OK, Mistra, let's do it." She pointed an outstretched hand at the bag of jewels and drew it into the air and out over the circle. A second motion and the bag inverted and dumped its contents onto the bare earth.

For the second time, there came a rumble and a blinding flash. This time these were accompanied by clouds of thick, grey smoke that smelled faintly of brimstone. When the smoke cleared, they could see the circle had been filled in with the tiled rendering of a mountain. Sitting atop the design was another piece of the tapestry.

Mistra, however, had vanished.

Mosaia had tried every trick of what he admitted was a limited repertory to get the cell door open, all to no avail. With its consent, he had even used the Retributor to try to bash his way out. Both paladin and sword had gotten jarred badly when the door turned out to be not only very solid but ensorcelled. Mosaia was forced to take a moment to soothe the sword's keening wails before he turned his healing energies on himself for the damage the attempt had netted him.

He finally forced himself to be content with gazing longingly through the small, barred window at Sigurd's workshop. Perhaps, he reasoned, he could learn something by observing the place. The room itself was spacious. A grand ball could have been held there without crowding either the guests or the musicians. To his left lay an ornate archway; he could see little of what lay beyond because of the angle from which he was viewing it. Opposite him was a cell door he supposed looked much like his own. Far to his right, at the very end of the workshop, sat a curtained alcove: he suspected that this must be the entrance to Sigurd's living quarters. The floor of the workshop from arch to just to the right of the cell doors was as smooth as glass. Either it had been planed and polished, or else cut from a crystal so huge the entire floor represented a single facet. He thought he made out the black of ebony, but the surface was so reflective he found it difficult to determine the color. Here and there, thaumaturgic circles and pentagrams of various sizes had been drawn; characters and figures strange to him had been inscribed within and around the borders of each.

Strange, yes, he thought, *yet even I can tell that not a one means me and my sort well.* To his right, beyond that part of the floor, sat lines and lines of lab benches much like the ones his chemist and alchemist friends used. Retorts and jars, reagent bottles and dead animals (mostly rodents and reptiles), and bits of apparatus were scattered along the length of the benches; on the most central bench stood a huge gazing crystal. The walls were set with more mysterious symbols. Most were drawn in vibrant colors, but a few had a sheen as though they had been traced with some precious metal. They were beautiful in the way a minion of the Fiend might be beautiful; it took no familiarity with the language of magic for him to know these were things baneful and forbidden. Although Deneth had indicated Mistra could, if she needed to, use physical trappings like this, he knew she would cut off her own hand before she would trace out abominations like these.

He wondered absently what the others were up to.

As if in response to his thought, there came a deafening rumble. Thunder was his first thought. An earthquake was his second. He whipped around. A figure appeared so suddenly he could not have said whether it had materialized or dropped through a trap in the roof. It was huge, easily as large as the largest giants he had ever seen. Its booted foot narrowly missed crushing him. It had landed sitting, legs outstretched, its head almost brushing the ceiling. It grunted as though the fall (or the teleport) had winded it. Although it seemed in too much of a daze to harm him purposely, he made a dive for the Retributor.

Then, as suddenly as it had appeared, it began to shrink. As it passed through human size, he recognized several familiar features, notably the deep auburn hair and the wristband. When it had shrunk to roughly thirty centimeters in height, he realized it was Mistra. He started across the room to help her, but no sooner had he reached her than she began to grow again. The strange effect forced him to press back into the corner near the door, watching in fascination and horror, lest he be flattened.

She shrank and grew many times like a sound wave whose amplitude was narrowing toward extinction: he would have said she appeared to be resonating. With each change, Mistra grew or shrank to a size slightly less extreme than the one before till, at last, after many minutes, she reached and maintained her normal size. Muttering an oath strong yet fraught with relief, she got shakily to her feet. She looked up, recognized him, smiled, and lifted a hand to wave. Then her knees buckled and she collapsed with a groan.

He strode to her side, ready to practice his healing skills, but she had no need of them: her problem was exhaustion rather than injury. She looked up and flashed him a wan smile.

"What happened?" he asked, his face as full of concern as his voice. He helped her over to the pile of straw, thinking it would be more comfortable for her than the hard stone floor, then sat beside her and chafed her hand.

"Rebound," she replied weakly. "My diminution spell must have snapped rather suddenly when I teleported. In fact, I think every magick active on my body or mind got stripped. It happens sometimes when you're resisting a spell and suddenly there's nothing to resist, like having the other team drop the rope when you're playing tug-o'-war. Whew." She lay back in his arms and closed her eyes. He thought she had dropped off from the effects of her exertions and was just beginning to feel awkward—how often had he held a sleeping woman in his arms?—when she began to shiver violently.

"Cold," she murmured, still only half-awake. "I'm so cold."

He unfastened his cloak and tucked it snugly around her shoulders. Then, shrugging off his self-consciousness, he drew her into his arms, holding her tightly and quieting her as he might a child or an ill comrade. He felt her nestle against him then release all the tension as she drifted off to sleep.

He leaned his chin on her head, considering what further he could do for her. "Ah, Mistra," he whispered. "What small magic of mine might serve to help a Carotian? And what do you need?" He probed her mind gently. He cocked his head as if listening, then suppressed a fit of laughter. "Why, it feels very like a hangover. I didn't know one could overdose on magic! I know," he ended decisively. And he began to chant a lullaby into which he wove the thought patterns he knew soothed overstimulation by drug, alcohol, and general overindulgence.

⚜

As he finished, Mistra inhaled deeply. The unendurable cold had dissipated leaving in its wake a delicious warmth. She felt as though she were in a field of fragrant wildflowers, basking in the sun. Floating on the breeze that ruffled her hair was a deep, rich baritone that simultaneously sang away the last vestiges of the cold and painted the petals of the flowers. It was wonderful. She opened her eyes and shook her head, disappointed to find that she was in a dark cell rather than a meadow. Otherwise, the daydream persisted: the feeling of well-being remained, as did the voice. She looked up and took in Mosaia singing away the aftereffects of her spell. She smiled up at him. His embrace was incredibly comforting.

He looked down and smiled, no longer uncomfortable with her nearness. "Better?"

"Oh, yes, much," she replied. She stretched, then settled back in his arms. "Did you miss us?"

"Very much."

"Oh?" She looked hopeful.

"Yes. We're locked in, you see, and it's beyond my skill to open a door that's been enchanted shut." It came out with practiced innocence.

She let her shoulders droop just a little. "Oh."

"Well, I was a bit lonely, too, if that's what you meant."

She pouted in a way she knew men found attractive, thinking that, for a man who knew so little of women, he had learned to flirt and bait in a hurry. *No, that's not fair,* she thought. *I can feel through the bond that he's teasing me, but there's dimension to it, and even a little charm.* "Oh, very good," she said aloud. "That's intensely romantic."

He chuckled. "Oh, all right. I missed you especially. I suppose if I were Deneth, I'd think of a poetic way of saying it and mentioning how fair and brave and wise you are."

She gave him a sidelong glance. "Hah. If you were Deneth, you'd find a way of *showing* me."

"Would I? Yes, I suppose I would."

She watched the interplay of thoughts on his face, felt them in her mind. *But I'm not Deneth,* he seemed to be protesting. She felt, to her surprise, a small pang of sorrow associated with the comparison. She turned to face him, searched his eyes intent on finding a way to communicate that she knew she had gone too far, that she hadn't really meant it as any sort of affront, that he was perfect just the way he was. But she looked too long and too deeply and suddenly found herself ensnared. *Oh, this was a mistake,* she thought as a sense of decisiveness came to his posture and he leaned over and kissed her. *Or not...*

She flashed on the day in Tuhl's wood when she and Deneth had fallen mindlessly into each other's arms, experienced a moment of panic, then saw where that had been violent undertow, this was gentle current. At first offering no more than a tentative brush of his mouth against hers, he followed that up with a number of other passes, each lengthier and a bit more purposeful than the last. The sense of them meeting in the mindscape drew her in. She had visions of the same bright meadow, but now a myriad dancing butterflies filled it, and the sky was a more vivid shade of blue. She suddenly forced herself to stifle a giggle: she got a keen sense of him making a comparison between kissing her and eating the richest of desserts—one made of all his favorite flavors, textures, and colors. The bond they shared was fresh, yet his thoughts came through to her with startling clarity: the increasing warmth of her response came to him as a welcome surprise, and he allowed it to drive and guide him. If she backed away, he would not take offense; if her reception continued to be hospitable, he would continue to make good use of the time without seeking to take advantage.

If he has no experience of women, he has instincts I would not have put together with such sobriety of bearing—superb instincts! Drifted lazily through her mind, followed by, *And no reservations about yielding to them.* She thought of it not as snide, cynical observation but as a compliment.

No, came a response she had not expected, and for one brief moment, she was mortified her thought had arced to him. *I think I only read from your mind what might give you pleasure—and how can I deny aught to a lady of your station who is both friend and* shanora?

Though they were still tightly intertwined, they both burst out laughing—at the ease of the contact, at the way she had not bothered to guard a thought she had not expected him to be able to read, at the adroitness of his response, at the poor way their surroundings matched the nature of their endeavors.

"Some men who lack experience of women," she said aloud, separating herself from him the tiny distance necessary to speak, "keep themselves aloof from fear—"

"—or yield their bodies but not their souls when they *do* yield?" he suggested, completing her thought though he was not sure with which of them the sentiment had originated.

She nodded fractionally, bit her lip though the action did not quite hide the way a smile tugged at the corners of her mouth.

He smiled down at her. "I was having a similar conversation with Deneth in the aftermath of your dream."

She laughed in disbelief. "There's an interesting leap from sharing your spells with me on the battlefield of my mindscape. Did you find the sight of a woman wielding a sword on her own behalf so alluring you had to discuss it?" Some gentle teasing here.

His grin became wry. "Oddly, we were discussing Carotian mysticism and how the *tal-yosha* gives Thalacian women a miss, and how Falidian men and women form no bonds at all in the sense your people do."

She reached up to touch his face gently. "I think your Johanna will have little to fear from you when it comes to yielding yourself body *or* soul."

"Johanna," he said pointedly, "will not even be born for a millennium."

"Ah."

"Ah."

The distance between them was so marginal, she could not have told who closed it first, but it suddenly ceased to exist, and they took uncanny, unlooked-for pleasure in those few moments of spontaneous effort.

A moment before they would have, as spontaneously, fallen apart, breathless from their exertions, there came a rumble like the one that had heralded Mistra's arrival. They looked up in time to see Anthraticus materialize in mid-air. He was clearly disoriented, and he was making no attempt to fly. They heard the softest "plop" as he landed head first on the floor.

The others had not been alarmed by Mistra's disappearance, especially with Deneth there to reassure them that she was with Mosaia, and that both of them were certainly as safe as it is possible to be in the jail of one's enemy. They made an intelligent guess that the large slave bracelet depicted on the new piece of tapestry indicated Mistra's alter ego: they would need her medallion to complete it.

They had been divided on whether to explore the rest of the place before putting the torch in the appropriate space in the fire room. The practical Habie had pointed out that the Pantheon alone knew what could be waiting for them in the unexplored rooms and hadn't they better use the torch while they still could, as it was not as easy an item to conceal as the thread and pieces of tapestry. Realizing this would mean diminution of the party by yet another member but seeing the sense of Habie's argument, the others reluctantly agreed. Anthraticus volunteered out of respect for the memory of his friend and fellow spellcaster Mistra. He also pointed out his disappearance would represent less loss to the group, as he wore no medallion essential to the completion of the tapestry. He agreed with Mistra's previous suggestion that his magic resistance was probably the strongest in the group. Privately, he thought his magic might be better used freeing Mistra and Mosaia than running hither and yon seeking out the rest of the physical pieces of the puzzle, but he kept this to himself.

In the fire room, Anthraticus took the torch between his teeth and awkwardly piloted it out over the circle. Hovering, he let it go. The room rocked, smoke billowed up, lightning flashed, the tiled design—a stylized flame, this time—appeared with another piece of the tapestry sitting atop it, and Anthraticus vanished. This piece of the tapestry depicted a harp. It took no great leap of the imagination to figure this one represented Deneth's alter ego Tallin. Deneth plunked his medallion down on the bit of cloth. It fused immediately, and they had another completed piece of the tapestry.

"What about Anthraticus?" Alla pressed him as he held the piece of cloth up triumphantly for all to see. His self-satisfaction at this juncture annoyed her.

He quit gloating on command and concentrated. "Mistra and Mosaia are aware of him, so..." His voice trailed off as he fathomed what the dragon's appearance had interrupted. His expression turned so thoroughly indignant so suddenly that Torreb, who stood facing him, stepped back a pace.

"We'd best go on," said the priest when Deneth burst out as suddenly with a raucous chuckle. "Deneth's showing the strain." The reason for the bard's volatility obviously escaped him.

Not so, Habie. "The mice playing while the cat's someplace else?" she asked him in a voice not meant to carry.

He scowled, then looked philosophical. He should have anticipated a little friendly rivalry, paladin or no: a man would have to be deaf, dumb, blind, and stupid not to find Mistra attractive. He thought even his friends who preferred the company of other men would have reconsidered their orientation if Mistra had but glanced kindly in their direction. "Nothing that anyone could call anyone else out over—yet."

They pushed on up the one hall they had not yet explored. There they found a pair of rooms corresponding to the spinning and yarn rooms. These, however, seemed to be devoted to sewing and weaving. Careful inspection in the sewing room revealed a magical tapestry needle. The weaving room, however, was as full of un-magical looms as could be. They despaired of finding anything useful there till Habie, in her eagerness to look over, under, in, and around all of them, bumped into one and heard a rattle. There, in a drawer they had not previously noticed, lay a spool of silver thread. Torreb, who had pronounced the needle magical, said the same of the thread.

"But what do we do with them?" he fretted. "Do the looms mean anything? Is there a part of the tapestry we have yet to make?"

"If you mean do we have to weave it up on one of these looms, I hope not," said Habie, rubbing her shoulder where she had bumped into the loom. "I mean, *I* have no idea how."

This resulted in the four of them staring at Alla. "Yes, I can weave as well as spin," she said. "Out in the forest, there are precious few dry goods shops to be found."

"It seems like one of these looms should be magical if we were meant to do any weaving," opined T'Cru, "and our good priest assures us they are all completely mundane."

"Still..." Deneth mused as he fingered the silver thread. "Why are there two colors? If we're meant to sew the tapestry back together and nothing more, why are there two colors?"

Alla shrugged. "I will try a small piece, if you want. I can't think of any harm it would do."

They assented. Alla's nimble fingers quickly made a warp of a portion of the gold thread and threaded two shuttlecocks, one in silver and one in gold. She set about making a simple design—another small coronet.

"Strephel's socks, Alla," remarked Habie, impressed by the shapechanger's unerring facility with such fine work. "You could be a better thief than me if you wanted to put in the time."

In a few minutes, Alla removed from the loom a piece of cloth that was very pretty and looked absolutely nothing like the rest of the tapestry. Those, now that she attended to them, were woven in heavy, non-metallic fibers and only accented with the silver and gold. She saw now that parts of the designs were embroidered on the fabric rather than woven in. With a sigh, she unraveled the cloth she had woven.

Torreb placed a hand on her arm. "It was well thought of, my dear," he comforted her, and she smiled in weary gratitude. "Some good will come of your effort."

The last two doors—those that would have corresponded with the elemental rooms of the east-west corridor—they approached with caution. Would they represent some sort of in-between sort of plane despite what Alla had told them—mist, perhaps, or magma? Only T'Cru harrumphed at their misgivings. After one good snuffle at each door, he dismissed them as perfectly mundane.

And they were. One was a storage room: a utility room replete with tools, ladders of all sizes, nuts and bolts, and the like. "Now what does that remind me of?" Deneth said, half to himself. They left without taking anything.

Opposite lay a small kitchen stocked with practically nothing—at least, they found no table service. But some poking around in the drawers and cupboards revealed two curious objects. One Deneth identified as a heavily insulated thermos. The other was a pair of gloves which, to judge by their thickness, were at least as heavily insulated.

"What do you do with a ther-moss?" Habie wanted to know. She had never seen one.

"Oh, it's like a wineskin, sort of," said Deneth. "Only the insulation makes it so you can take hot stuff like coffee or mulled wine with you and it stays hot, or cold mead or cold water and it'll stay cold as you want—for a few hours, anyway." He examined the thermos more closely. "This one would—gods!—I think it'd keep lava hot." He paused, digesting and processing what he had just said. Suddenly he brightened. "Or—what was it Mistra said was in the Mist Room? Liquid air! By Thalas herself! It would keep liquid air *cold*!"

They cried out in delight. Habie capered about clapping her hands.

"And those," concluded T'Cru, "those gloves would keep your skin from freezing as you took the sample?"

"Yes!" He scooped up both thermos and gloves. "Come on, let's have at it. Mistra was right! We'll be back to the inn in time for afternoon tea!"

⚜

Mosaia finished attending to poor Anthraticus. The spragon had been dazed rather than seriously injured, but Mosaia had seen to the small cut he had gotten on his scalp when he fell and lulled him into a light sleep to help him get over the shock left in the wake of the spell.

"He's sleeping quietly," he reported to Mistra, who was trying to negotiate the lock. "His only wound was superficial; he endured no concussion from the fall."

"Good," she replied, flicking him a brief glance. "I hope he doesn't feel he's fallen in with a bad lot."

Mosaia smiled down at her and shook his head. "I think we're a rather nice lot. Mistra?"

"Yes?"

"I, um, hope you don't think I was trying to, er, compromise you. Er- a few minutes ago." He cleared his throat. "When I was so forward."

She raised an eyebrow and flicked him a smile in addition to a glance. "No, of course not." She worked very hard to hide the way the small consideration of his broaching the subject touched her heart—she did not want him to mistake the sentiment for pity.

"I wasn't—I mean I didn't—oh, bother." He sat next to her, drawing one knee up under his chin. "It's just you were so vulnerable, almost like a little child, and when you lay in my arms, the mental contact was still there, and it was so intimate a thing in and of itself, and then you woke and I looked into your eyes, and they were so beautiful and *you* were so beautiful and so close and—forgive me—you looked so inviting, and a wave of tenderness the like of which I have never known swept me, and..." He had averted his gaze and withdrawn into his rambling, so when he stopped at the light touch on his arm, it was like being waked out of a pleasant dream. "I know I was teasing you a little at first, flirting, and—"

She smiled indulgently. "It's all right, Mosaia. You read my thoughts clearly enough to see how ill I took your overture! It—went nowhere that dishonored either of us. Really, two *shanoras* would effectively be prevented from going any-where from which they could not withdraw, still friends under the sweet morn-ing light of Thalas." She kept her eyes glued to her work. A sudden diffidence took her, as if she had less experience of men than he had of women. "I, too, felt that wave of tenderness, and..." She trailed off, not wanting to embarrass either of them by painting too vivid a picture. He could avoid acknowledging an im-age she had not let escape her mind; if she spelled it out for him... She settled on the one thing she *could* safely spell out. "Well, since I can hardly veil my mind from you anymore, I admit you piqued my curiosity long before this—a reac-tion no man who was a warrior by vocation has ever evoked."

But he brightened. "I had?"

"Mmm. And I've felt guilty about it from the time you first mentioned your fiancée. Of course, I don't imagine this—well, this lack of experience extends to her as well, and I was hardly ready to invite the comparison!"

"Oh, no!" he protested. "I've never touched her." A beat and he buried his face in his hands as if in realization that the unspeakable had passed his lips. "No, that's not what I meant!" he went on, aghast.

Mistra would not have reacted, as her own culture possessed no frame of reference for what motivated the flash of horror she felt smite him. She cocked her head and explored a little, then bit her lip in perplexity. Something about his culture seemed to say there were women you touched (and did a lot more with and wrote off) and women you didn't (and married). Something in that suggested exploitation to her—something she liked the sound of not at all—that women would allow themselves to be exploited and men would take advantage and exploit to their heart's content. *But not the reverse*, she thought. *How very strange*. He must think his attentions suggested their relationship had suddenly taken on that shade of meaning!

He faced her squarely while she was still pondering this strange element of what till then had seemed to her a very moral culture. "I told you it was an arranged marriage. I don't expect to do so much as hold her hand till we make our vows. Father in Heaven forbid you think I would use you for convenience's sake, or from idle curiosity! I would use no woman that way."

She turned back to the lock, in part to hide the fact that she was suppressing a grin at the discomfiture in his voice. He was trying so hard not to offend her— and digging himself in more deeply with every word! Still, she found the very earnestness of his attempt sweet beyond measure. "You weren't using me, Mosaia."

"But I—"

She turned to him. "Yes?"

He found the burden of her marvelous eyes heavy indeed. He drew himself up quite straight and spoke more to the wall above her head than to her. "I must admit I—had impure thoughts about you." He might have been confessing to the murder of his own infant child and expecting a sentence of death by slow torture to be passed. "Since I can hide from you far less easily than you can hide from me with this bond that has arisen between us—you see, my inexperience extends to many things with which you have facility!—I own it freely, in plain language."

The indulgent smile again. How best to respond without impugning either his honor or his manhood? Briefly, she toyed with the idea of teasing him about how he had described his initial reaction to her when no one in the party realized the *tal-yosha* was just taking her in its merciless grip, about how he had only ever reacted that way once, when he was arresting a lady of the evening who was actively plying her trade. But a gut reaction, owned and easily put down, was not truly in the same league as the thoughts he was now trying so hard to come to grips with. It amounted to the difference between random urges and desires evoked by a specific object toward whom one already felt tenderly. While the former could be dismissed, the latter had the potential to develop into something almost ineffably holy—at least, in her culture.

"I, too, had 'impure thoughts,'" she said at last, somewhat amused at the phrasing but finally settling on self-disclosure as the best angle of attack. Aware of his discomfort meeting her unimpeded gaze, she half turned back to the lock. "And to judge from what I picked up from your mind and what I *know* was in mine, your thoughts were far less vivid—not nearly vivid enough to give offense, at least." She giggled. "Being compared to a dessert was a new one on me."

He laughed, understanding she was trying to ease the way for him. The tension in his shoulders eased, and he felt things were all right between them again. "Vividness itself comes as a mixed blessing, does it not? Some women find their charms so vast that to have a man daydream less than vividly about them is to have that man *give* them offense. And, for some, the opposite seems to be true. To –ahem– *daydream* so about a woman I esteem, about one who has known the love of the spirit as well as the body and valued both—I think that would do her a grave disservice."

She shot him a strange little frown, but the smile tugged at the corners of her mouth again. "Sometimes, my dear, you are insightful to the point of being frightening."

He relaxed his posture and came closer to looking at her. "I told you my knightly vows included one of chastity?"

"Yes. It is a commendable goal."

His heart lifted at the idea that she would place value on that particular choice of all his vows. It must be a function of their Ethic that they would have no actual law dictating chastity yet would still strive for what he had heard Mistra and Torreb call "sharing the Gift with wisdom." "I've told you of my vow of chastity, but I think I've never made it clear to any of you why I set foot on the path of so restrictive a life as that of a paladin. I realized early on that I possessed the sort of will that could bend others to my way of thinking, or to my service. I could have had power, or women, or wealth, all of it of my own choosing. So—I needed to learn how to choose, for the safety of my soul, and for the well-being of those around me."

She regarded him with a thoughtful frown. In another, it would have been a wild boast, but in this case she knew it for a simple statement of truth. She could, if she wished, see into the corners of his soul and bear witness to the towering edifice that was his will. Were he to direct it, it could have no less effect than the greater Disciplines—or the Art itself. She could only think well of him that he had sought at so early an age to harness and direct it into channels conducive to the common weal. "And did all your training beat these impure thoughts out of you?" she asked, phrasing it humorously but meaning to pose the query in all seriousness.

He considered. "Say rather that it has made it easy for me to keep apart from situations where they could be easily provoked. The women of my father's court—women of the street, for that matter!—have little appeal for me though they make the most outrageous of advances. If lust that is a mere thing of the body has meaning for me, I have not yet encountered the circumstances that elicit it. Even my Johanna, comely as she is, stirs little longing in my heart. I do not *know* her, you see, nor any of the women who have ever sought commerce with me—none has ever engaged my heart or my soul or my mind. And, so far, my body has shown little inclination to go where the rest have not led first." He saw an arch of one slender brow. She did not open her mouth, yet her thought was clear to him—not only was she surprised to hear such a sentiment come from a man of his station but to hear a sentiment that so exactly reflected her own. *And why not?* he wondered. *An intellect so vast and a soul so bright would surely be driven to the brink of insanity were they not fully engaged by the man upon whom she wished to bestow her favors.*

"You and the rest of our good companions," he went on, "certainly engage me on all of the levels that have marked the relationships I have valued most in this life. But none of those relationships has been with a beautiful woman, one with whom I share a common, high aim and the details and adventures of my day to day life—and now this bond, of course. It has put me out of my depth."

She grinned. "You never thought to have a comrade in arms provoke these impure thoughts?" Her smile was impish, but her voice was all kindly understanding. Despite their brief acquaintance, she found herself ranking Mosaia with the best men she knew; the thought of making sport of him never entered her mind. Half his attractiveness stemmed from his character rather than his dark good looks and sculpted physique—and that character was a well whose depths she strongly wanted to plumb in its entirety.

She thought, though, that character alone could not quite account for the little thrill that had coursed through her at the way he had described her as a beautiful woman. "Coming from you, Mosaia, impure thoughts don't frighten me." Her expression became reflective. "They just make me feel supremely, deeply complimented." She finally hazarded looking up at him so their eyes met.

"And have you some thoughts about what we do about these impure thoughts?" he asked, feeling safe reverting to teasing mode.

She leaned over as if she might kiss him but only touched her brow and nose to his. "You help me work this lock." Her eyes twinkled.

Mosaia looked confused, abashed, and crestfallen all at once, then burst out laughing. "Wise *and* beautiful *and* spiritually enlightened? That should not be legal! What do I do?"

"Here." She slapped a chisel into his hand. A rudimentary tool kit was something she toted around in her wristband, along with the arsenal. "I've broken what I could of the spell on the plate. It'll have to be forced the rest of the way." She scooted out of the way.

They worked in companionable silence for a few moments till his curiosity got the better of him. "Mistra?" he asked. It was more than a whisper, but not by much.

"Uh-huh?" She succeeded in prying one corner loose and started down the side of the plate toward the second.

"What's it like?" No sooner had he gotten the words out than he became appalled that he had inquired. It was something he had always wanted to ask the friskier of his men, but he had always felt that even the admission of curiosity would somehow tarnish his reputation.

"What's what like?" she asked absently.

He groaned. Now it came to it, he could not bring himself to elaborate.

She looked up, took in his posture and the abashed, almost mortified look on his face, and smiled sympathetically. She returned her attention to her work. "Oh, *that*. I see."

The plate suddenly seemed more fascinating to Mosaia than anything he had yet set eyes on during their travels. He fastened his gaze on it and pried with renewed vigor. "I apologize. 'Twas not a proper question." He felt her eyes on him again and looked up to meet them. She looked very fair in the flickering light, even with the wisps of hair in her face and the smudge on one cheek—fair and kind, he thought, but somehow sad. "I mean for a man to ask a woman."

A smile tugged at her mouth again, but she let her gaze drop back to the locking plate. "Maybe that's exactly who a man *should* ask." She paused, working and considering. "Did you really want to know?"

"I wasn't asking for biological specifics," he hastened to reassure her, "or for details that are too private for you to share with your loss so recent. Just—" With a sudden effort, he pulled the entire plate loose. "Ah, there we are." He turned it over in his hands before he offered it up for her inspection. "Here. No, just—what's it like?"

She took the plate and inspected it with a practiced eye for any wards or runes she might have missed. Finding none, she sat back on her heels. She appeared to Mosaia so deep in thought that he wondered if she were avoiding the question by puzzling over how further to disenchant the door. Finally, she came back from whatever private place in herself she had been and said, "It's so complex, Mosaia—but then again, it's very simple."

She bit her lip and turned her vision inward for a moment, trying to sort out how best to go on. "If you share the gift as Minissa intended, with the kindness of Arayne and the unbridled power of Thalas, the wisdom of Caros and the spiritual vision of Eliannes and the touch of Dorlas that lets your every part mold to that of your lover—well, you may laugh to hear what seems like so purely sensual an act described this way, but to us it *is* holy, when the gift is shared wisely between two people who care enough to commit a portion of their lives to each other."

She took a deep breath as tears stung her eyes. "It's like you've been this empty vessel all your life and suddenly you've been filled to overflowing with a drink so sweet and strong and full of life you know it can only be fit for the gods themselves. You feel you should die of it, it's so strong, but you don't—you only emerge feeling stronger and spiritually nourished and at peace." She sniffled a little. "And I've sometimes thought the tenderness and the sense of profound union and ecstasy and the peace that follow in its wake are a blessing of the Pantheon to show us a taste—a small one, one our mortal minds can grasp without self-imploding—of what the reunion of souls is like in the next life. You do briefly enter a different, holier reality."

She snapped back from whatever reality she had drifted off to to frame the ideas for him. "There, I guess that's the best I can do." She turned on him a small, apologetic smile, not realizing her gaze had wandered so she had not truly seen the cell for the past several minutes. Other scenes had been playing in her mind: her consorts, her partners, stages splashed with spotlights, woodland glades splashed with firelight and moonbeams and starshine, one specific woodland glade where... She tried to shrug off the vulnerability she suddenly felt.

He could do no more for a moment than sit there with his mouth hanging open. If it was Deneth who carried the official title of "bard," clearly he was not the only one in the company with the soul of a poet! It took him a moment to realize he must look like a beached flounder and that she might be reading his expression as shock rather than awe at the grandeur of the vista she had just painted for him. He tried to send some of that feeling through the bond, thought he succeeded. "I don't think I fully grasped how or why you could hurt so much being wrenched unwilling from your consort," he said, and then sighed. "Sometimes my own Mysteries ring hollow in my own ears, they seem so shallow in comparison to yours. I could never have framed the thought that there are many ways of touching—with raucousness, with reverence. Or that in actively resisting this wedding of the spirits a man might be acting not in accordance with the will of my God or your Pantheon. Or, really, why there are so many terms for the same basic physical act." He touched her cheek, sensed her feeling that she had searched too deeply and revealed too much. He took her hand and kissed it tenderly, then drew her into his arms for a warm embrace. "Thank you, Mistra," he said, his voice solemnity itself.

He felt her open her mouth to speak, sensed the way the words refused to come, but he understood anyway: despite his words, she felt she might have looked too long and to deep inside the wounds in her soul. He drew her back into his strong embrace with no thought of doing anything but comforting her. He felt an echo of the ache she had felt as she spoke, both the fullness and the emptiness. He pulled her even closer as he felt her start to shiver again. Through the bond, he sent wave after wave of thought telling her how she could trust him with the deepest secrets of her heart, how he would never betray any confidence with which she entrusted him. She murmured something, but it had nothing to do with thanks or trust or raw nerves being soothed. He thought she was saying someone else was here.

He looked around, wondering if one of the others had teleported in very quietly while he had been involved with Mistra. The presence he felt was not in the cell, though—it was outside the cell door. There came a mocking laughter, and the squeak of the door swinging inward on rusty hinges.

CHAPTER 8

The Wizard's Workshop...

*"Why worry about who's High King here and who's a craftsman or
a crofter? No matter who you are, you're somebody else's peon."*
—Avador bent Ebron, having a bad day ruling the Union

WHAT IS IT, DENETH?" asked Alla.
"Yes," Torreb prompted in a rare moment of drollness. "You
don't look at all well. Not afraid of a little liquid air, are you?" The
instant the words left his mouth, he regretted them for the cheek they were.
They had just paused outside the door to the mist-filled room in debate over
who should enter first when Deneth abruptly reached for the nearest wall. He
paled visibly as he leaned against it. His eyes glazed over. He began to shiver
much as Mistra shivered at that very moment, had he known it.

Habie slipped her small hand into his. It disturbed her that, when he turned
toward her, she saw in his eyes no sense of recognition. "Deneth?" she asked in
a tiny voice that mingled hope and fear. "Deneth, you OK? Deneth, it's me,
Habie." Holding hands was not the best contact for empathic healing, but she
possessed enough of the raw Talent that even from that vantage point she was
able to bleed off most of the disorientation.

Deneth shook off the vision that had assailed him. The mist before his eyes
cleared. Still, he had to pat himself down and touch a hand to each of the others
to reassure himself everyone was real and no one had been teleported anywhere.
What he had experienced had been disturbingly akin to that nightmare of
Mistra's in which he and Mosaia had become involved. This time, however, he
had nearly been sucked into the battle as participant rather than observer. It
could only mean—

"We'd better hurry," he urged. "Sigurd's a little faster on the uptake than we
were hoping he'd be. They're in trouble."

Alla cocked her head in the gesture they eventually came to read as her
peering into the cracks between the segments of time. "Yes," she agreed.
"Sigurd's beginning to take us seriously." Not bothering to fuss over marching
order, she reached for the doorknob, which refused to budge. "Habie?"

"Right." Out came the lockpicks. When she applied the first to the keyhole, however, she received a shock that sent her flying into the opposite wall.

"This is interesting," said Deneth as he stooped to help her up. He recalled now that not only had the door been untrapped before, it had been unlocked.

"Allow me," said T'Cru in his what-pieces-of-work-humanoids-are voice. He gathered himself into a deep crouch and catapulted into the door.

It groaned.

He tried again.

It fell open.

In they crowded, Torreb looking at Alla as if to say, "Why bother with tools or even magic when brute force suffices?" but remaining silent. Without discussion, Deneth donned the gloves and lowered the open thermos into one of the wells from which the liquid air bubbled forth. In short order, he had the vessel filled. He popped on the lid, threw it into his pack, and drew his sword.

Not a second too soon! The mist between them and the door had already begun to swirl and coalesce. Four small vortices formed and, between them, an amorphous figure—that is to say, its body was amorphous. The four tendrils that snaked toward them had a shape that could be guessed, and the claws in which they ended were quite well defined.

T'Cru, still geared up from the exertions of getting the door open, gave a roar that made his friends cower—and sprang. The mist creature sent its claws groping for him, trying to pluck him from mid-air, but they could not match his speed. They closed on nothingness as the great Tigroid passed cleanly through the creature's body. He landed between the creature and the door, which surprised him. If he been a two legged creature, the undissipated force of the leap—he had leapt planning to tackle, not to transect—would have landed him on his face. Regrouping, he turned, hoping that having its integrity disrupted had destroyed the creature. Not so! It must have been capable of phase-shifting its body while leaving its tentacles intact, for its body reformed even as he watched.

The creature still faced the back of the room. With his friends' lives in danger and his enemy making use of the weirding ways, T'Cru had no qualms whatever about attacking from the rear. Accordingly, he swatted, all claws bared, at the nearest of the four tentacles. He came close to purring with pleasure when his claws bit. He dragged the tentacle toward him, opening his mouth to receive it. His teeth, too, bit, treating him to a delicious crunching sensation as he sank them into the filmy substance. A flick of his head and the tentacle broke loose from the creature's body.

At this, his friends attacked, taking their cue from the Tigroid to go for the tentacles rather than the body. Alla shifted to one of her reserve forms: a great bird of prey like a golden eagle. T'Cru having left them no way to bar the door against pursuit when he battered it down, she dived for the kill. Beak and claws sank deeply into another tentacle just behind the claw. She had not quite the strength to dismember, as T'Cru had done, but she was able to render the claw useless.

But the tentacle itself remained prehensile. It whipped around her neck even as she lamed the claw. She beat her wings furiously, first trying to pull away, then to back so as to give the tentacle as much slack as she could. Torreb took the hint—and his chance. The stroke the priest dealt with his mace completely crushed the tentacle. Unfortunately, having the tentacle taken out of play so abruptly sent Alla spinning out of control. She hit the side wall and slid to the floor, stunned.

Habie was learning that the longer the tentacles remained solid, the more dexterous they became. She had raised her sword to slash and been taken by surprise when the creature parried, the way a swordsman might with a foil. Unlike a foil, however, when the claw scored a hit, it grabbed and rended flesh. After one strike of this sort, Habie lured it, twisted so it struck her off arm rather than the one holding the sword, caught the offending tentacle on that wrist, and slashed. *So much for* that *tentacle*, she thought, but the injury forced her to retire from the battle to work the claw loose from her arm.

Simultaneously with her attack, Deneth hacked off the last tentacle: his longer reach with both arm and sword had let him keep the creature safely occupied till an opening offered. As the creature dissipated, another piece of the tapestry dropped to the floor. His movements a blur, Deneth pocketed it, scooped Habie up, and plopped her onto T'Cru's back. Seeing that Torreb already had already gathered Alla into his arms, he hastened from the room. As they moved at top speed toward the air room, the chamber behind them began to quiver.

⁂

Mosaia and Mistra broke apart and clamored to their feet. The presence confronting them was so utterly evil that, in concert, with no true volition on their parts, they clasped hands and backed away from it. Conscious thought kicked in after two or three steps. They stopped. There came a tense moment during which neither did anything, including breathe. The ghost of a thought passed between the pair, a whispered tendril that spoke of not resisting the mage for now. That it slipped by the mage—the presence could only be he—without his acting to stifle it in any way, was the only suggestion that it had originated with Mistra.

Mosaia came to himself a beat before Mistra did. He saw that, as yet, the evil presence was no more than a shadow menacing them from the doorway; it had not threatened them overtly. He relaxed his stance, but Anthraticus's small whimper prompted him to act. Here, after all, lay a helpless charge in need of protection, no matter that he could stand all the rest of them in a fair fight with one claw tied behind his back had he been awake. He drew his sword and gave Mistra a gentle shove toward Anthraticus as she drew hers. Sounding for all the world like he was heaping imprecations of the wizard's head, he prayed aloud.

He had gotten no further than a general invocation to his own Father God when the shadow crossed the threshold. The caster followed in short order—a human male garbed in the long deep purple robes typical of Falidian wizards of the day. Runes every bit as friendly as the designs on the workshop walls and floor were stitched all over them in gold. His hair and beard were long but well kept. They may have been black once; now they were the steel grey that looks dignified in middle-aged schoolmasters and men of business. His eyes, somewhat hidden by bushy grey brows, were nevertheless so keen as to be piercing. His features were the neat patrician ones of the Falidian nobility. His general appearance leaned to the haggard, but he could not truly have been called aged before his time.

Mistra, had she had a chance to expound, could have told Mosaia that the lines around the wizard's mouth and eyes were the result of his tampering with forces just at the edge of his control—and, like the demon they had already met, not happy to be within his sphere of influence at all.

"Put your swords up, my fine adventurers," he said. His voice had a sibilant rasp that struck the questors as disconcerting. It made him sound like a snake luring its victim into striking range—certainly not an inappropriate image given the circumstances. "You will have no use for them. You don't believe me? Then allow me to put them in a place of safekeeping for you."

There was no question of either Mosaia or the Retributor resisting: even with the protections placed on it by the gods who had forged it, the sword could not counter a direct spell commanding it to locomote. Whining and cursing, the Retributor slipped from the grasp that had held it firmly seconds before. Mosaia remained impassive, though he kept his eyes fastened to Sigurd's face as if he were attempting to probe the wizard's mind. Not so, Mistra. She had loosened her grip on her sword when, at Sigurd's appearance, she had lifted Anthraticus and cradled him in her arms. She made only a little grunt of annoyance at being outmaneuvered so easily when her sword went to join the Retributor on the floor. But she positively fumed when, at a flick of Sigurd's finger, a tiny muzzle bound itself so tightly to Anthraticus's snout he could barely breathe, let alone incant.

"There, there," Sigurd cut off her incipient tirade. "Spragons can be such a nuisance. The idle word, you know, and there you are giggling and hallucinating. Can't have that, can we? Now, step forward into the light and let me have a proper look at you. And just hand over the little fellow, would you?"

They made no move to do either. Mistra, in fact, clutched Anthraticus to her breast as if her were her own small child, wounded and in need of comfort. They took in Sigurd's look of irritation and both decided they liked it better than the knowing smile that came next. Another flick of his fingers, and the entire floor of the cell upended into an inverted conical section. The two humans went sliding across the floor, and the dragon went sailing through the air. Sigurd attended to Anthraticus first, catching him neatly and then locking him securely away in a bird cage that sat on one of the lab benches. Then to the swords second, sheathing them in a special rack before he turned to Mistra and Mosaia, who merely got to their feet and looked defiant. In this way, the two adventurers saw what the mage missed— behind him, Anthraticus was beginning to stir. But they gave the information away by neither word nor gesture nor facial expression.

"Now, what to do about you two." The veneer of affable inanity had fallen by the wayside; now he looked and acted as dangerous as he, in fact, was. "I must admit finding *one* of you in my dungeons was a novelty, but three? Usually so dramatic a disappearance of one adventurer discourages the rest of his company from doing anything but leaving by the most expeditious route. I had already written you off as inconsequential—what a motley crew you are! Not a tiny percentage of the discipline of the others who have braved the dangers of my little playground, not consistently armed, not consistently uniformed, not even consistently human. When three of you gated into that cell, I began to believe I had *over*estimated you. That you pressed ahead when one of your number had disappeared showed some mettle; that you were still about it when *three* of you had fallen by the wayside suggested that you were stupid, careless, or the most pig-headed, bloody-minded party of reckless fools I had ever run across."

He was interrupted by Anthraticus, who had now come fully awake. He was beating his wings furiously against the bars of the cage and uttering what was undoubtedly the worst malediction he knew against Sigurd and all of his relatives. Due to the muzzle, of course, all that came out was "grr mph ng" and so on, so the wizard was in no danger. He cast the dragon an arrogant smile and continued.

"As I was saying, my first inclination was to think you represented the resident idiots of whatever villages and hamlets you hailed from, but a second thought occurred—that you might simply be suicidally brave, or so intent on your mission that the loss of individual lives meant little to you. I have little use for such heroics, so I was still prepared not to give you a second glance—

till my first glance showed me what an uncanny resemblance you bore to a bridal party I had recently snatched up. I neither achieved nor consolidated my current position by being cavalier about threats, even those that seemed at first to be inconsequential ones. I gazed into the crystal you see there, and what I scried prompted me to trot out my best spells of divination. One of those I aimed directly at your party, and so had my initial impression confirmed, that you were a collection of country bumpkins out to make a name for yourselves, clearly not cognizant of the fact that you were already in over your heads. In that assessment, I think now I was mistaken, and as I look at you, I can see why. A direct mental scan would be easy to foil for, say, a child of Thalybdenos, especially a descendant of one of the royal houses." He looked darkly at Mistra. Her at-your-service bow contrasted sharply with the look of challenge in her eyes. "You deliberately misled me on that first pass."

"You can hardly accuse me of a breach of ethics when you attempted a mind probe with neither the knowledge nor the consent of your victims," she said, lapsing into her logician mode, which could be so imperturbable as to be infuriating. Completely aware of the effect, she happily trotted it out when she needed to as a weapon of passive resistance. "I misled you but little—I only made you believe what you were inclined to believe from the outset: that we were, at best, an inconsequential threat."

"That is to say, you think your presence of here is of some moment," he scoffed. "Well, little princess, you may discover through meddling in my affairs that you are all of less consequence in the grand scheme of things than you would like to believe." His complete absence of rage made the retort all the more chilling. "A spragon, for instance, is easily dealt with, as is any garden variety spellcaster. Even a paladin..." A snap of his fingers, and heavy chains appeared at Mosaia's wrists and ankles. Although they were not visibly attached to any outside object, they held him securely rooted to the spot. Furthermore, while Sigurd omitted to place a physical gag upon his mouth, his speech muscles suddenly stubbornly refused to cooperate with his brain. His first response was to struggle, but he quieted at a touch of Mistra's hand on his arm. A look of trust came to his eyes: if she still believed the time had not come to resist this blackest of mages, he would not gainsay her judgment.

"As for the sort of enchantress produced by the children of Thalybdenos..." He produced a wand from a hidden pocket in his sleeve and discharged it at Mistra.

Mistra's judgment that they should not act came in part from an intuitive sense that what their comrades needed most was for them to play for time. Something in Sigurd's little diatribe had cued her that Waterford's lost adventurers were typically teleporting to his dungeon by some mechanism other than the one that had landed her and her friends here. Their conjectures about the nature of the temple working to balance out the evil Sigurd represented had merit!

So she held perfectly still while a tiny golden bubble emanated from the tip of the wand and floated toward her. Her focus blurred for an instant as she did some calculating. When it burst a foot or so in front of her, she did nothing to avoid its effect. As it burst, it produced what appeared at first as only a curtain of golden light. The curtain, however, quickly reached out and folded on itself to envelop her in a golden bubble. Large enough to permit easy movement, it allowed her to see and hear well enough, but she had seen true force fields with less tensile strength. It gave slightly when she prodded it with her finger but showed no signs of breaking. She did some quick recalculating, then merely looked thoughtful.

"Anti-magicked?" she asked as if it were a matter of no great interest.

"Yes," replied Sigurd. "Even mute and bound, your kind can work magic by mental energies alone, so mere physical restraints are useless. With this little device, I can send a spell in, but you can't send one out. I would try to avoid contact with the bubble. Its very touch might have ill effects on one with so appallingly kindly a nature."

"Oh. Thank you very much for the warning," she said in a voice so dry it would have caused brushwood to catch fire had it recently been exposed to a monsoon. "If you think my nature is *that* kindly, you definitely need to get out of your lair more." She gestured, and a large beanbag chair appeared beneath her. She watched for a reaction as she curled up on it. She didn't see much—just a flicker in his deep eyes, and that may have been no more than amusement at the display of power. So she tried another approach. "You haven't by any chance been crafting nightmares on my behalf, have you?" She might have been asking how many lumps of sugar he wanted in his tea.

"Well, as a matter of fact..." He displayed the modesty of one who knows he has scored a great triumph and need not brag. "I wasn't aiming for you specifically. It simply gives me pleasure to disturb the hours of slumber of the holy knights in Barony Clear Water. The battle I wage here is a war of sorts; my battlefield is the hearts and minds of men. You see, the paladins of the surrounding holdings generate a great deal of goodly force, while my abode and I generate a great deal of evil. In slumber, when the spirit is released from the body, the two seek each other and form an interface, one that worsens with proximity, and with strength. When your party arrived in Waterford, you inadvertently interposed yourselves between me and my usual victims: the force

I had shaped into the horrors of the dreamscape lighted on you rather than on them. You attracted the brunt of those energies, so much so that you probably gave all the paladins of House Clear Water the soundest night's sleep they've had in months, while other members of your party may not have even realized their dreams were troubled. But, while I made the effort to do some re-crafting when I realized my nightmares were affecting someone other than those for whom I had intended them, I hardly perceived you as a threat. Virtue and competence often have little to do with each other."

"Well, yeah, I can't argue with you there, having met your prospective bride. I *did* repulse the attack."

"You had, I think, help."

She narrowed her eyes at him. "So, I think, did you." That got the reaction she had been after!

"What?" The sense of danger he emanated escalated a few notches as his easy pacing and gesturing stilled.

Back to the logician mode, since it seemed to provoke him. "You re-crafted them in a direction so specific I barely noticed the signature of a second mind at their heart. Nightmares bearing the exact images that bothered me here have plagued me since before we set out from Caros. Here, they merely possessed more detail, as if the energy that produced them had been sent through a step-up transformer. Yet you yourself remained blissfully unaware of the existence of me and mine till last night."

He stepped closer to the bubble and lowered his voice. "We all have our masters, little princess. Even you serve another Power beyond your liege-lord."

A rare feral look came to her eyes, but she kept her manner casual. "Know someone named Syndycyr, do you?"

Sigurd paled: a change visible even through the wealth of facial hair. "Speak his name not!" he hissed, leaning in even closer so his face nearly brushed against the bubble.

Her mouth curved into a mischievous grin; captor-baiting could be such fun! She leaned forward, matching her posture and volume to his. "Oh? Why not?" She had an idea about the reason for his fear but wanted to hear him articulate it.

"It may open the way for him to come through."

Her ears pricked up at that. Did this mean their nemesis *did* have access to realspace? If so, this was more information than she had hoped to glean; it vindicated in pentacles her feeling that she and Mosaia should not initially resist the mage's efforts to neutralize them. "You speak of him as though he were a demon," she ventured, "one apt to listen and appear in the contingent world the minute his name is uttered by the unwary."

If he noticed the way eagerness lit her eyes, he gave no indication: her queries evoked other concerns! His eyes shifted left and right as if he were at a railroad crossing with poor visibility and a signal whose reliability was chancy. "A demon? Not yet. But evil, and in the service of them, and with powers that are god-like. I do him homage, but, yes, I fear to invoke him unsolicited and without good cause. It would be well for you to do likewise."

"And if I have a bone to pick with him?"

"Leave it unpicked. Do not even mention his name in passing, for here is a place where the barriers between this world and the one that holds him are thin."

"Then summoning him might keep you busy enough keeping him entertained that we have a chance to unmake your spell," she summarized. A smile played about her lips, but she focused her eyes narrowly on him. "Why don't you let my friends go?" she purred.

He straightened, the arrogant pride filtering back into his bearing. "I think not." And the sense of danger.

She leaned back and tucked her hands behind her head. She and her brother-in-law, the High King, had never gotten along well, but she did subscribe to what people all over the Independent Trading Worlds widely referred to as Avador's Axiom, viz., "If you can't win, go out in a blaze of glory." She actually preferred to think of that blaze of glory as style or, in her own case, panache, so she was willing to push her luck a bit here. "When you play poker, you often lose, don't you?" she asked with a congenial smile.

If he was reconsidering calling this particular bluff, he hid it well. "What makes you think he will come if *you* summon him?"

If there had been a camera or an audience handy, she would have mugged for it. "Oh, we're old mates, he and I. I'm carting around something he wants very, very badly."

He laughed, a particularly evil sound. "I *do* like a prisoner who makes me think, my dear." He accented "prisoner" just a little. "When I destroy you for your insolence—after I destroy your friends as you watch, of course, most horribly and painfully—it will be with a thought to reaching new heights of creativity."

She and Mosaia were to have many long talks during the course of the quest about what constituted Fair Play when dealing with the enemy, but just now, the paladin stood across the room bound and gagged and Anthraticus and the Retributor were equally out of commission: it fell to her to play for the time the company needed to complete the tapestry. She laughed, partly in play-acted triumph and partly in unfeigned amusement at the thought of a mundane

magician, however powerful, thinking he could destroy her: better creatures
than he had tried and dashed themselves to pieces! She gave a loud wolf whistle
and called "Syndycyr!"

"I will silence you!" he blazed. "It will not be pleasant."

"Be my guest." She called Syndycyr's name several more times, adding the
occasional "Ho!" "Yo!" or "I'm ready to bargain!" before Sigurd could contrive
any spell that might hinder her. Before he could pronounce the first syllable of
the dwimmer upon which he finally settled, the room darkened. A penetrating
chill descended. Mistra held her breath, surprised at the alacrity of the response
and wondering if she had overplayed her hand. Sigurd looked at once enraged
and petrified as he searched frantically for some sign of his master's arrival.

Syndycyr appeared with no further warning. One instant, no more than
cold, dark air separated Sigurd and Mistra; the next, Syndycyr appeared in the
gap. He glared at Sigurd, cocked an eyebrow at Anthraticus and Mosaia, and
nodded at Mistra. "Who summoned me?" he asked in a voice that would have
made a thunderhead look like bright sunshine.

"I did," Mistra said without fanfare.

⚜

"I begged her to leave you to matters more weighty, more worthy of your
attention than those here," said Sigurd, admirably composed for someone who
must have been conjecturing how many legs he was likely to end the day with
(and what sorts of predators he was likely to be scuttling away on), but sniveling
nonetheless.

"Of course you did," Syndycyr said laconically. "Afraid I'd turn you into a
worm and crush you underfoot, no doubt. On the contrary, if you have not
the wit to introduce me to the most valuable prisoner you have ever captured,
you are beneath my notice and have no business being in my employ at all." He
turned his attention to Mistra. "You had the temerity or the insolence or the
desperation or the utter lack of discretion—I won't say the bad sense, I know
you better than that—to summon me. Why?"

Mistra felt her heart perform the contradictory actions of freezing and
quickening at the same time. The vision she had had of Syndycyr in Tuhl's
caves left her unprepared for the full weight of his presence in the flesh; the
sense of power she had gleaned there fell kilometers short of his actual authority
and majesty. Tall, with the looks and physique that transcended the measure
of mortals, he reflected in his glance the wisdom of the ancients and the wit of
the gods-gifted. He was dressed simply in unadorned black robes. No tingle in
the air suggested active spellcasting on his part; what she found so impossibly

overwhelming was the sheer force of his personality. God he could not be, but she felt in his presence about as omnipotent as an ant might feel in the presence of a storm giant.

Remember what he is and remember who you are, rang in her mind as she fought back the awe that would have struck her dumb. Knowing she had begun by dealing a dangerous hand and now had no option (at least, not one that included survival) but to play it out, she said, "I wanted to see you turn Sigurd into a worm." She suspected the poised half-smile she managed came off as less than seductive but more than coquettish. The interest she saw in Syndycyr's eyes bolstered her courage, although not by much.

"I see." He also wore a half-smile, but he kept any nuance beyond interest carefully hidden. "And? What else?"

The intensity of his gaze almost made her recoil, but she had a sudden strange sense of a core of brilliant light at the center of her being. *Gods of hell!* she thought with sudden vehemence. *I can play in this league, and all I need to do it is* me! With a force that surprised her, she reached out and seized control of the conversation. "You've been bothering me since this quest began. Why?"

"Because you have something I want—not that your own sweet self would not fit that qualification. I hope, when the time comes, you will surrender both to me of your own accord. You see, while you are justifiably incredulous when this minion of mine threatens to destroy you, I have the power, the means, and the motive—and I will, if that is what I must do to achieve my aim. I should hate to do that. You and your companions in arms are valiant and clever: both traits that good and evil might admire in each other. Your company is bound up with the powers of the artifact I seek—if I must destroy you or in any way take it by force, who knows what damage I might do to it?

"And you, my dear..." He reached one hand *through* the bubble to stroke her cheek as though there were no barrier between them at all. "I would not destroy such a precious flower. It may be that I can even render you aid and assistance when all other hopes fail." He stepped forward so he stood completely within the bubble. His voice had been pitched for all to hear who would; now he modulated so it reached her ears alone. "How did you know?"

Her control of the conversation faltered at the display of force. She had no more chance of escaping the weight of his gaze than a mouse has of escaping that of a boa constrictor, yet her thoughts and speech were her own. Despite his easy defeat of Sigurd's sturdy spell, she found herself fascinated but not afraid. A beat to regain her composure, no more, and she reasserted enough control that they could at least confer as equals. "The character of the dreams changed when we came here, as if an intermediary, a craftsman, had taken a hand," she explained—a succinct summary, since he clearly knew the rest.

He looked thoughtful. "Well, let me waste no more of your strength or mine by tormenting your sleep. I need you strong and well when next we meet, and I know now that the aid you needed against the phantasms I sent is in your keeping. Here." He reached inside his robes and removed a charm carved of what looked like living black opal. Moving in so close that his robes brushed against her and the heat of his body radiated till it burned, he fastened the amulet around her neck, stroking her throat with his fingertips as he withdrew his hands.

Mistra had to force herself not to react—not to give him the satisfaction of a reaction—but she could not deny the fierce heat that pierced her at his touch. It was a lazy caress, no more, but as he withdrew his hands, he closed the small distance between them till the only thing lacking to make it an intimate embrace was the use of his arms. She raised her eyes to his and saw an image that surprised her: a penetrating view of his castle. She saw his laboratories, his quarters, his bedchamber, felt the touch of his body on hers within those precincts. For a moment, she felt his personality and designs for the future threaten to subsume her, knew her doom had been written and that fate had inexorably linked it to his, understood that she could save herself time and her friends suffering—could save *herself* suffering—by yielding him everything he wished this instant. The vision danced before her eyes with such vividness she could feel the end of the suffering that had barely begun to take hold. The physical release would be exquisite, almost enough to divert her mind from the way her soul had lost its very vitality...

In the end, the same vividness that nearly undid her brought her back to herself. The pain of the severed consort bond outweighed the pain of the *tal-yosha*; how dare he offer her an empty shell, a mere counterfeit, when her deepest yearning was still a thing of the spirit? The fire blazing in the hearth, the black velvet bed curtains overlaying a drape of gossamer, the rustle of satin at her back—it all vanished, leaving in its wake only Syndycyr's eyes and the amusement dancing in them. That elicited a second wave of fury—how dare he toy with such raw nerves? Yet in that wake came a second sensation—the heat that had threatened to burn now seemed like an island of penetrating warmth in a sea of ice.

As she stood still puzzling over both his temerity and the power of the mind that could probe and evoke with such clarity, he resumed his speech, bending slightly so his breath tickled her ear. "You eject me from your mind with great ease in waking life!" he laughed softly. "Though a part of you yearns for that very vision to find fulfillment in reality. You have seen my castle and some of its mysteries," he went on in the whisper that in Mosaia or Deneth would have sounded only tender. From Syndycyr, it sounded as alluring but lacking in all warmth: the difference between seduction of a willing party and rape. He took her hand in his and closed it around the amulet. "This will guard you, however you come there: by chance or design, or at my calling."

"Nothing is written in the stars," she said, her voice a dangerous whisper. "Not even a god would dare to suggest otherwise. You can't cow me by pretending to a destiny that doesn't exist."

"More than you realize is written in the stars," he replied without rancor, "and you would be surprised how even what is written can be tampered with by a power who dares use the forces at his disposal."

She puzzled a little over both his words and his tone of voice; she thought he sounded sad. She gave over debate in favor of examining the amulet. Like the Sword of Rhydderch, it emanated a power great but unaligned. "Its power is neutral," she commented. She found the fact curious, yet her voice sounded toneless in her own ears.

He focused his attention on her once more. "It is, but it is carved with my sigil, which my guardians will respect. And if they do not, it will give you the extra power you need to dispel them."

"Its use will put me in your debt." Again, without rancor or alarm—or any emotion at all.

"Its use will put you in my *power*," he corrected, "a little at a time. Ah, ah, ah!" He cut off her incipient protest. "Do not say you will never use it till you have seen every circumstance into which your quest will lead you. I *have* seen your road, and it grows worse with every turning. Only a fool would refuse help freely offered."

She narrowed her eyes at him. "*I* have seen our road," she shot back, "and only a fool would think a mage of your inclinations would offer anything without a price."

The very ruefulness of the smile he gave her made it charming; he nodded as if in salute, or as if to accord her the point. "You are all less than I, as is the prince whose release you seek, but I do not fool myself into believing the sword is mine for the taking. This contest over its ownership will be the greatest Game of all." He stepped outside the bubble and bowed low to her. "I am pleased to have met you at last in the flesh, princess. And some of your companions." His smile no longer either rueful or charming, he nodded toward Mosaia and Anthraticus. "We will meet again."

He turned to Sigurd. "Well, Sigurd, I think Princess Mistra meant for me to divert your attentions, and we can't have that. However, neither will I hinder her party in any way whatever. You are skilled and on native soil; they are resourceful and determined. I must truly say I wish victory to the craftier of you, though I may ask for custody of what prisoners there are left alive if they fail at the last." As abruptly as he had come, he winked out of existence. The room seemed to breathe again.

Mistra touched the charm. She wanted to think the reason she hadn't just thrust the accursed thing back into his hands constituted a refusal to show fear before an enemy. *What is wrong with my brain*, she raged at herself, *that I could feel my senses inflamed by such a one as that?* And another part of her mind replied, *It is the same quirk of nature that allows a moth to be attracted to the flame that will destroy it—and he shares it. At least, it's bought us a little more time. Do I dare play for more?*

"So, Sigurd," she said, settling herself on the beanbag. "You must be pretty good for Syndycyr to give you even odds against a party of eight." She cast the most subtle of glances at Mosaia. He remained immobile, but the look of concentration on his face suggested the altered state of communion with his God.

Recouping from the encounter with his master, Sigurd sat on a chair that appeared behind him: a dainty gilt thing, all swirls and filigree that looked even more out of place in the lab than the beanbag did. Still, it suited him, which made Mistra wonder if there were anal retentive aspects to his personality. His smile was mild.

"You must admit," he said, urbane again now that his master had departed, "I already hold many of the high cards." He gestured as if to remind her how many of her party were prisoners, then leaned on the wand, which lengthened into a staff. "Now, if I may be reasonable for a moment, *I* must admit you are well on your way to unraveling my spell. I will even admit it took me till the moment your little winged friend appeared on this side of the chasm to realize what was happening. When I cast the spell originally, I expected the tapestry to be destroyed completely, to feather off into the Ether and be no more." He sighed but did not sound particularly dejected. "I suppose incurring phenomena like its reappearance was the risk I took when I assumed control of a disused elemental temple as my base of operations.

"Now, I have looked in the crystal and seen the way the forces arrayed here fragmented the tapestry—its embroidery frayed, the medallions that identified those on whom I cast it separated from the actual fabric, its pieces made discrete again after I incinerated the whole thing. I know the others in your company retain possession of most of the bits and pieces and will undoubtedly collect the rest, given time. Of course, reuniting all of the proper medallions with the corresponding pieces of the tapestry will be difficult with you, the paladin, and the other young lady here. Oh, yes, there's no reason you should not know my Gwynddolyn lies in the other cell, heavily enchanted. It would have been easier for me if you hadn't happened along, but, like my master, I admit to a certain affection for the thrill of the chase, for a well-laid game against a skilled opponent."

"You set your game board well."

"Yes. I considered removing some of the challenge at one point—so many have got their deaths here. But I am finding dealing with you folk most entertaining. The solution to the problem of the basilisk, for instance—most creative."

One unequivocally positive thing she could say about an encounter with Syndycyr was that after facing him, even for a casual chat, she would not be intimidated by anything less than an arch-devil! "Uh-huh. What's to keep me from just dispelling this thing and engaging you this minute?"

"Well now. I wouldn't be much of a wizard if I hadn't learned how to manipulate my spells so their effects achieved durability and near-permanency." Rising, he pulled from his robes three small golden statues: they might have been likenesses of Mistra, Mosaia, and Anthraticus. These he placed on the lab bench beside him with a flourish, so she was sure not to miss the point. "As long as these remain intact, so will your bubble, the spragon's cage, and the paladin's restraints." At this point, he gave up all pretense of civility. "Gold, as you know, is malleable but notoriously difficult to shatter. Tantalizing, isn't it? Your freedom so near yet so far away?" He had a point: he had placed the statuettes so that, had she been free of the bubble, she could have reached them without getting off the beanbag.

"Ah, me," he went on with a yawn and a languid stretch. "And now, I must be looking in on your friends and making some revisions in the topography of the receiving cell. You three took practically no harm from the teleportation." He frowned thoughtfully, as a serious player might over a chess problem, and spoke as if to himself while he made certain his prisoners could hear him. "Yes, three humanoids and a feline. A revision of the floor, I think." He walked over to the cell. The lock remained broken past hope of easy repair, and the floor still tilted. "Bottomless? No, too pedestrian. Something sharp—tacks, perhaps. No, they would be no more than a nuisance. Ah-bamboo! Grows very quickly, especially under the influence of magic, and long and sharp enough to skewer a charging bull, yes..."

If his placement of the statuettes with their concomitant instructions had been meant as a show of power, this bordered on sadism. Mistra quantified it that way when she tried to reach out to Deneth to warn him and found the bubble to be proof against not only magic—at least, *her* magic—but mentalic contact. She saw Sigurd spare her only a brief glance to show he knew of her dilemma before he turned back to his work. His posture showed he had dismissed the three of them completely. Ordinarily that alone would have enraged her, but now it gave her the chance she needed to communicate with Mosaia. If Sigurd's machinations denied her mentalic contact, at least she could gesture. She looked imploringly at the paladin and mimed out the impossibility of her contacting the party.

Mosaia had been watching Mistra interact with their captors with varying degrees of interest—and alarm. He couldn't decide at times whether she was being brave or suicidal, but he had to admire her style. But it should have been *him* drawing the attention of Sigurd and his dark master, *him* preparing to defend them all. He trusted Mistra's judgment, but if he had known beforehand that judgment would lead him to this forced state of incapacitation, he might well have fought for control of the Retributor and waded in swinging.

I can pray, he forced himself to remember, *and I can have faith that doing something to attract divine assistance is as important as the verbal game of cat and mouse Mistra is playing with our captor or the collection of the pieces of the tapestry Deneth and the rest are undertaking.*

So, as Mistra had noticed, he had been in a deep contemplative state for some minutes, keeping only as aware of his surroundings as he needed to to determine if he were free or if she required his aid. And now, apparently, she did. Either that or she had developed a very interesting sort of seizure disorder that manifested as a series of discrete hand signals repeated over and over. He regarded her for fewer than three seconds, though, before he got the gist of her message—he needed no mental contact to understand her plea. He, in fact, had already been mulling over the problem of who might arrive next. Reason suggested it would not be Deneth: the others needed to keep him with the dwindling company till the last possible minute so they could communicate with those of the party who had been captured. Would the bard sense the way Sigurd's magic prevented Mistra from communicating with him? Mosaia could only hope Deneth's sensibilities were that finely honed. That set him wondering why Sigurd had taken such pains to contain Mistra but had left him only secured physically. If Sigurd had written him off as presenting no risk when it came to contacting the rest of the party, it could give them an advantage. On the other hand, though the link existed, Mosaia would be dignifying his abilities by even referring to himself as a novice. Perhaps Sigurd, in writing him off as a point of contact, had not erred.

He had also been mulling over what Sigurd would have to do with the cell now that he and Mistra had rendered the door effectively useless. He would have to change the cell dramatically, but with the thought of killing or incapacitating or merely containing, Mosaia had not known till this moment. Could Sigurd be misleading them and depending on Mistra to find a way around the magicks of the bubble that encased her? Mosaia considered the placement of the statuettes, the delight with which Sigurd had bit by bit revealed his thoughts about the reconfiguration of the cell, the look of triumph he had shot Mistra when he knew she had found her attempt at contact thwarted—and rejected that line of thought. Sigurd fully meant to kill or seriously injure the next of their party to teleport; he wanted the three of them to be fully aware of the trap and to wallow agonizingly in their own helplessness while they waited for their doomed comrade to gate in.

This dismal thought led paradoxically to a ray of hope. Sigurd must be assuming all five of the remaining company were immutably earthbound. But if Alla had an avine form, he himself had something to work with. He sighed. Assumptions made for sloppy strategy. Still, when he considered possible outcomes of this scenario, none could be worse than the case in which he did not at least try.

He looked back at Mistra and reached out in thought: perhaps range was the problem with the bubble's powers. Although he was new to this form of communication, would his proximity to Mistra allow a few thoughts to slip through? He saw her stiffen with the depth of her concentration as she grasped his intent, as if she could attract his thoughts to her in defiance of every power of her prison. But the spell was too strong. Her shoulders drooped, and she whacked her fist against the side of the bubble in frustration. It struck him peripherally that, even in that small show of dismay, she looked beautiful, even fetching. He shook his head to clear it of an image of her rather than Johanna walking down the aisle with him. Then he saw her straighten and nod encouragingly at him. She meant for him to try to contact Deneth alone!

He knew his eyes must have widened like saucers and remained that way because she kept nodding encouragement. Then he realized he must have started shaking his head because those encouraging nods began to be tinged with desperation. Anthraticus joined in at that point, again beating his wings against the cage and making little incoherent noises that Mosaia supposed meant, "Do it, you fool," or the like. He took a precious few seconds to think it through. For Mistra to counter the spell effect of the bubble with the sort of power necessary to defeat it would surely attract Sigurd's attention. Inadvisable. To do nothing was to condemn one of his friends to death. Unthinkable! He had to try.

Sweet Father in Heaven, he prayed, *guide my thoughts*. He had been going to say "guide my hand," as he did when fighting or performing a healing, but that entreaty didn't quite fit this contingency! With an admonition to himself to keep it simple, he shut his eyes and sent forth his consciousness.

⚜

Deneth rubbed his brow. They had come to a halt in the Air Room so Torreb could tend Alla and Habie. They had been debating who should be allowed the dubious honor of pouring the liquid air onto the enchanted area. T'Cru had volunteered, and the consensus of the group had gone with him.

As they finalized their plans, Deneth abruptly silenced them. He sat cross-legged on the floor, twisting his neck this way and that as though he were an antenna trying to home in on a weak signal. The tension in the room became palpable as Deneth strained to tune in—something. Whatever he was doing, he was clearly pushing the very limits of his ability. Finally, after several minutes during which they ceased all activity, he relaxed, but he panted as though from physical effort. He had, in fact, been holding his breath for a full minute: even that small disturbance of motion and sound would have drowned out the message he had been receiving, it was so faint.

When he came to himself, cursing his own inadequacy, he found Torreb and T'Cru kneeling beside him. Both looked anxious. "I'm OK," he assured them. "Phino's fiddle, it was so faint! I can only think it was Mosaia alone signaling."

"Is Mistra in danger?" asked Torreb.

"Not any more than the others, I think, but I can't get a good fix on her mind at all. Feels a bit like, well, X-rays trying to pass through lead."

"Such spells do exist—ones that would block use of the Art or the Disciplines. Perhaps they have all been captured but she alone has been placed within such a shell."

"The message, Deneth?" T'Cru pressed.

"Well, it was more of an image, really," said Deneth, as if he himself were still puzzling it out. "Which, I guess, would make sense if it were Mosaia alone, since he's a complete infant when it comes to this sort of thing. Where Mistra could probably shoot through a detailed account with an annotated bibliography, he would have to focus on simple images and maybe emotive content."

"Speak to the point, man!"

He hadn't realized he'd been rambling, and he started just a little at T'Cru's near roar. "Oh, right, sorry. It was an image of flight, but it had such an urgency about it that, well, it was as though it were vitally important that the next person to teleport stay airborne."

Torreb looked thoughtful. "But *they* were all OK, and perfectly earthbound except for Anthraticus."

"But Sigurd's intervened here, my good priest," T'Cru pointed out. "At least that is my assumption if Deneth sensed danger to our friends and now cannot communicate in thought with Mistra. Perhaps his chamber of confinement serves well enough for one prisoner, or perhaps, in the history of this place, the disappearance of one of a party of adventurers has deterred the rest from continuing so he has not had to concern himself with dealing with a number. But Mosaia, then Mistra, then Anthraticus—their very number and powers could be daunting, and, giving them credit for enterprise, they may have attempted to escape. Suddenly we may seem a more formidable party than any others he has dealt with."

"Do you really suppose he entrapped them, then let slip what his new arrangements would be?" He sounded dubious.

"Perhaps he felt safe enough 'letting it slip' once he had Mistra contained in this shell you postulate exists. Perhaps he was being deliberately cruel, taunting them with what the fate the next person to arrive would suffer."

Deneth looked over at Habie and Alla, whom they had been allowing to rest while they debated. "Even if Sigurd has identified what we are, he may think none of us can fly or hover very easily. I had forgotten Alla had any avine shapes till that last encounter."

"Deneth, are you *sure* you got the import of Mosaia's message?" asked Torreb.

"Yes, as far as it went," said Deneth. "Why?"

"Because it leaves us no option but to send Alla, and our encounter with that thing with the tentacles left her head and neck a shambles."

T'Cru laid a velveted paw on Torreb's knee. "I understand your fear for her, but if Mosaia saw the situation as so urgent he must contact Deneth unaided, must we not act on his information?"

Torreb shook his head. "No—you're right. I see no option. If Alla will go, I will give her such blessing as I can and leave her to it."

They roused the women, who easily saw the need for the change in plan. Alla even cocked her head in that disconcerting way she had of peering into the Ether and confirmed Deneth's interpretation.

"Can you change form from one animal shape to the next without having to become human in between?" Deneth asked her as he got the thermos ready. When she nodded, he went on, "Do what you need to do to handle this thing, but afterward you might think about becoming a hummingbird, even changing as you teleport, if you can. Hummingbirds are small and maneuverable and easy to miss, and they can hover and fly backwards."

Habie chortled. "I was thinking of that hawk thing. Something that could power-dive and scratch this guy's eyes out."

Alla could have told them not to tell her her job, but instead smiled graciously. "I shall keep both suggestions in mind." Before she did any shapeshifting at all, she bade them pull out and arrange all of the tapestry pieces. They saw clearly after they did so—it was like fitting together a large, flexible jigsaw puzzle—there remained a single piece missing. Of the five of them left, Habie alone carried a locket that had not yet been fit to the fabric, yet none of the incomplete pieces bore a logo that suggested her station. The most recent acquisition bore a crown and must signify either Gwynddolyn or Mosaia—most likely Mosaia, they thought, since his had not fit the original piece they found in the tree stump.

Alla had become so lost in thought over it all that Habie finally said, "Don't you have to meditate or something if you're going to go zipping from shape to shape?"

"I *should* compose myself, since I'm not at my strongest." She showed no immediate signs of doing so.

"What?" It came out as impatient to the point of being frantic, as if she had just looked over Alla's shoulder and seen the basilisk and her face showed some alarm while her brain could not figure out how to get her mouth to explain.

"Well, I think I know what to do with the gold thread and the needle."

"What, like sew it together?"

"Uh-huh."

"Tsk. Go compose yourself. You're not the only one around her who makes her own clothes." She pushed Alla gently but firmly toward an isolated corner and dug out the needle and gold thread. She stitched happily away while Alla first meditated, then received such blessings as the others could give her, including a little tune by Deneth "for the easement of the spirit" and a final pass by Torreb with such healing energies as he could still spare while keeping some in reserve for whatever battles lay ahead.

When Habie finished, she sat back on her heels to admire her work, idly twirling both the gold and silver threads between her fingers as she did so. "Bit shabby still," she murmured, "and not from my stitching. Hmpf. Must have been lovely when it was first woven, magic or no. See, the emblems have lost their sharpness, like dye running, only they're embroidered, not dyed. Just worn a bit, I suppose." She brushed a few loose threads into place on one of the emblems: places where the thread had worn but not enough to pull out the entire stitch. "There, that's better. Maybe a few stitches redone here and there..." She looked at the silver thread. She looked back at the tapestry.

Suddenly she was rummaging frantically through her pack in search of her spectacles. She put them on and gasped, though her guess as to what she would see had been accurate. There weren't many of them, but the spectacles showed up the tiny holes in the fabric where entire stitches had come undone. Hurriedly, she changed from the gold to the silver thread and set to work. It all made sense now. Without these few stitches of silver, there would remain a flaw in the tapestry, even with all the pieces sewn in with their proper lockets in place: a final obstacle, easily overlooked, to its completion. With the aid of the spectacles, she could even see the general pattern of the stitches she needed to make: cross stitches here, leaf or satin stitches there, the odd Carotian knot...

By the time she had finished, the whole tapestry was humming: a serene little sound like the one made by a well-conditioned motor running or a cat purring. The others, attracted by her flurry of activity and the empathic sense that something important was happening, gathered around her and applauded her work.

"See where your locket fits, Habie, and get the last piece in before you follow me," was Alla's advice. "We'll still have Mosaia's locket to fit in, and Mistra's, and I guess Gwynddolyn's if she's here somewhere, and probably precious little time to do it in. If only we had thought to take their lockets before they vanished."

"It's possible some other delicate balance would have been upset if we had," Torreb offered. "It's time you went, my dear. We'll join you shortly."

"Time," Habie said to herself. "What does that put me in mind of?" She ran her hand carelessly through her pack as Alla took off. It came to rest on the scroll. "Precious little time..." she repeated, but before she could work it out, she had other things to think about. A new piece of the tapestry appeared, this one emblazoned with a tinier version of the slave bracelet on the piece left them when Mistra had disappeared. Habie set her locket to the new piece, which readily accepted it. A few more turns with the needle and the tapestry lay before them complete.

CHAPTER 9

...And How We Got There

*"Nought better can betide a martial soul than lawful war; happy
the warrior to whom comes joy of battle—comes, as now, glorious
and fair, unsought; opening for him a gateway unto Heaven."*
—The Book of Wisdom

I F WE HAVE TO have a plan, then," Torreb said as he regarded the tapestry, "I'd
say Mistra's locket goes where the larger slave bracelet is, Mosaia's where the
crown is and Gwynddolyn's where the circlet is."

"Yeah, I'll buy that as a working hypothesis," said Deneth. No sooner were
the words out of his mouth than the chamber rocked. Across the room, a section
of the ceiling caved in. "Yikes! I sure hope Sigurd has an emergency exit from
this place. Let's move."

They moved. Initially, they each moved in a different direction, but they
moved. Deneth whistled loudly and gestured in a way that precluded argument.

"Where are you going?" asked Habie as they ran. "The chasm's—" She
pointed in a direction other than the one they were taking. Deneth never broke
his stride.

"Yes," agreed T'Cru. "I could leap it, were there not the possibility of magic
being involved, but—"

"Do you have any doubt there's magic involved?" snapped Deneth.

"Well, no, but—where *are* we going?"

"The storage room. Ladders."

"We need breadth, not height."

"Hah! What is a ladder but an upended bridge?"

"Trust a bard to think poetically," he snorted. There had to be a flaw in that
logic, but he could not pin it down. When they arrived at the storage room,
they found none of the ladders came anywhere near the length they needed to
span the chasm, but Deneth's spirits were not dampened in the least. He had
each of them take the longest ladder he could—the longest *wooden* ladder, that
is. The metal ones he rejected out of hand, though some of them were longer.
But he remained silent about his reasoning till they stood at the chasm's edge.

There, he bade them line the ladders up end to end so they overlapped just a little. Then he sat down, pulled out the lute, and started playing. All around them were signs of the lair's impending demise, but he seemed quite unperturbed.

"Deneth, your music is transcendent, full marks, ten out of ten for form as well as function, sublime and so on," said T'Cru, "but I ask you, *is this the time?*"

"Maybe he thinks he's going to charm Sigurd to come over to this side of the chasm and give himself up," said Habie.

Deneth smiled up at the two of them inscrutably. As he did so, T'Cru felt his fur doing something very unnatural for a Tigroid of his age: it began to thicken and curl. Habie's, too, stood on end and waved in time to the primal thrumming of the music. Torreb was patting the top of his head, trying to determine what the tingling in his scalp meant.

But the more pronounced effect was on the ladders themselves. Before their eyes, the once living fiber began to sprout. First came thick, vinelike shoots that grew and interlaced so swiftly that, in a few short minutes, the ladders had become one long, fused length of wood. Then came the buds—large, deep red ones that opened into blossoms a good foot across that were fully as sturdy as the wood itself. These settled themselves between the rungs so their footing would be less treacherous. The ladders, under the influence of Deneth's peculiar art, had turned into the bridge they needed to cross the chasm.

Now, without interrupting his ballad, the bard nodded to the others to feed the makeshift bridge across the gulf. Once they had done that, he made a slight alteration in his composition. Alla, had she still been with them, might have characterized the new music as earthier. As they watched, roots began to sprout from the terminal ends of the "bridge." These bored deeply into the living rock of the passage. Deneth had not been able to give them a handhold, and the crossing would still be tricky, but he had given them a stable surface on which to walk.

"Wo!" exclaimed Habie. "Lethal! Go Deneth!"

Torreb, in the midst of her effusive display, cast his own spell—one that would allow him to determine whether an effect of Sigurd's were somehow undoing Deneth's work in a way they could not perceive at first glance. But all was as it seemed. The bridge would hold them, and there were no inclines or other irregularities on the other side of the chasm that might send them sliding into it once they crossed. He expanded the spell outward so he got a cleric's eye view of the other side of the chasm and found nothing truly worse than he had feared. So, although he had to admit the stretch of ground between the chasm and the massive doorway was littered with traps for the unwary, he also delivered the good news that the chasm itself bore no spells or traps.

They crossed—T'Cru and Habie easily, Deneth with little more effort, Torreb wishing fervently for the gift of flight. Now all that confronted them were a myriad traps and the massive portal that would lead them to their friends—and to the end of the second leg of the quest.

Mistra had found that, when she touched the outside of the bubble, the evil images from her nightmares momentarily obscured her sight. When, however, she pushed the beanbag against it, it merely wobbled like gelatin and she saw nothing macabre. If she applied sufficient pressure to the beanbag, the bubble would roll slightly. Clumsy and slow though the process might be, it gave her a limited means of locomotion—an advantage her two companions lacked. With Sigurd busy gloating over his adaptation of their former prison and waiting for the appearance of his next victim, she had some minutes to learn to what use she could put her meanderings.

Mosaia, his message sent, realized that, while Sigurd had rooted him to the spot, the mage had left his upper body secured only at the wrists. The rack where Sigurd had stowed their two swords might be in reach if he could twist and stretch just the right way. Hoping he could trust the Retributor to be quiet till he explained things if he could get it even partially drawn, he began maneuvering. He could not wield it properly, but perhaps it possessed some as yet undiscovered power that might serve them.

Anthraticus, too, had made a discovery. When he buffeted the cage rather than beating his wings against it, it moved. Just a little on each try, but it moved. He could not break free—Sigurd had sealed his cage as he had sealed Mistra's bubble—but perhaps he could cause mischief by slamming it against something. Those statuettes, for instance, sat on the same lab bench as his cage...

Mistra made her way slowly and methodically around the perimeter of the laboratory to the other cell. Sigurd, who had now vanished in the direction of what looked like his private rooms, was either very involved with his work or confident that they could do him no harm. In either case, he had not returned to the workshop. A third possibility—that he was giving her enough rope to hang herself—she thrust from her mind the instant she thought it, as being counterproductive.

Once at the cell door, she flattened out the beanbag and stood on it so she could see through the bars. A disconsolate-looking shape huddled against one wall.

"Psst!" she whispered. "Gwynddolyn? Hey, Gwynddolyn!"

It was indeed she. She looked up. Her face was drawn. Her eyes, though dry, were rimmed with red as if she had been crying. The enchantment seemed to have worn off, at least. It took her a moment to realize who was addressing her. She was, after all, seeing Mistra through the bars of a very small window and the haze of the bubble, and Mistra's head blocked most of the ambient light. She frowned, then looked incredulous. Finally, she rose and came to the window.

"What is it?" she asked. "What's happening? Are you—?"

"It's Mistra, not Lucia—and keep your voice down. We're trying to rescue you and break the spell Sigurd cast on you and your friends."

"Oh. Oh, thank you." She took in the bubble, and, beyond it, Anthraticus in his cage and Mosaia in his shackles. "Are you, um, optimistic about your chances of success?" she asked as diplomatically as possible.

"Oh, sure. He's only got three of us so far, and we've almost got him licked. He's tried to put us out of commission. See those little gold statues over there on the lab bench? They're the key to this thing—" She indicated the bubble. "—and the cage Anthraticus is in and the shackles he has on Mosaia. We could probably find a way to break the spell if we put our minds to it."

"Oh. Well, maybe I can get him to let me out so I can help you. He didn't think enough of me to do more than teleport me here and lock me up, although I was enchanted into a stupor for a little while."

"Has he mistreated you?"

"Not really. He's just taunted me, but he's fed me and been a perfect gentleman otherwise. I'd have despaired by now, though, if I hadn't met your company in the forest. What has to be done to the statues to break the spell?"

"They have to be shattered or destroyed, but they're solid gold, so it may take some creative thought."

"Let me see what I can do. Go further off, and I'll see if Sigurd will come to my call."

"Right." She looked back across the room and took in Sigurd's continued absence, Mosaia's thus far fruitless efforts to unsheathe the Retributor, and Anthraticus' efforts to reposition his cage. She turned back to Gwynddolyn. "You know what? Tell him you want to see Mosaia's sword. Get Sigurd to unsheathe it somehow."

"You mean tell him I want it as a memento or something? Before he, er, does you in? Is that what you call it?"

"It is, but I hope he doesn't. His boss will be very upset if he does *me* in, at least."

"What's so special about the sword?"

"It's intelligent."

"What?"

"It talks—somewhat incessantly—and has some magical powers. I'm not sure we've discovered them all yet; it keeps surprising us. You'll see. Follow any lead it gives you."

A bemused frown marred her delicate features for a few seconds, but she voiced no argument. She gave Mistra time to jostle and bounce her way back to the general area from which she had started. Then she called sweetly to Sigurd.

⁕

The wizard took several minutes to respond, during which Mosaia had the sense to quit groping for his sword and Anthraticus tried to reposition the cage so as not to look like he was aiming for the statuettes. Luckily for the three of them, Sigurd was so deliriously happy at having been summoned by the woman for whom lusted that he failed to notice any looks of guilt or practiced innocence on the faces of his prisoners. As he passed them, though, they saw a disconcertingly self-satisfied expression on his face. Before he went to Gwynddolyn's cell, he stopped before the door to the cell that had held them, waved his arms, and incanted a few words. It clanged shut with an ominous ring.

"Well, well," he said conversationally through the bars of Gwynddolyn's cell door. "My little caged songbird is singing a new tune." He directed his comments to her alone, but he pitched his voice so the rest could hear him easily.

Gwynddolyn cast her eyes down demurely. "I see you have taken prisoners on my account. They resemble my friends so, I wondered if I might be introduced to them before you do, um, whatever it is you were planning to do to them." And she batted her eyes adorably. At least, Sigurd thought it was adorable; Habie would have asked for a shot of insulin or a space sickness bag had she seen the display.

Sigurd looked back and forth between his prisoners and the ingenuous, lovely face of his would-be bride. Briefly, he considered. It was the first interest she had shown in anything since he had teleported her here. She had eaten little and had spent her hours alternating between prayer and inconsolable crying. Even if she were to play him false, what harm could she do? His captives were secure enough from any magic or mischief she could work. And as mistress-to-be of this place, he supposed she had a right to see whom he captured and how he dealt with them.

"Very well, little nightingale." He waved his hand before the locking plate, and the door clicked open. Out stepped Gwynddolyn, every bit a princess despite her state of dishabille. "Now, I know little of their histories but much of their types. Here, for instance, is a treat for your pretty eyes." He indicated Anthraticus, who now sat quietly, trying to hide any trace of ill will.

"Oh, a tiny little dragon!" she gushed, clapping her hands in childlike delight.

"No, no. A small species of coatl, and quite up in years by his markings, which for any coatl means venerability, wisdom, and power. That's why he's muzzled, you see. His folk can work physical magic, so I must keep him quiet so he can't utter the phrases that would activate his spells."

"Oh, what a shame. What a darling pet he would make." At that, Anthraticus folded his arms across his chest and looked so indignant that, if he had not been muzzled, he still could have not spoken for the way all the retorts he thought of making jammed together in his throat in their rush to get out of his mouth. But Gwynddolyn reached into the cage and scratched him between the ears, at which he made a sound like purring. The gesture allowed her to note the position of the golden statuettes. It also allowed her to feel for a release for the muzzle, but she could find none: like the cage itself, Sigurd had sealed it magically.

"Well, perhaps a way may be found to neutralize him for your entertainment. I will put his destruction on hold if it will please you."

"Oh, yes, please."

"Not so these two, I fear, except that the most powerful of my order has indicated an interest in the woman. She resembles one of your handmaidens, does she not?"

"Yes. Your master must have an eye for hidden potential if he sees anything in her. Still, I suppose if she were bathed and dressed properly instead of decked out like a savage and had her hair pulled out of her face, she might be comely enough." She caught Mistra giving her a glare that said, "Don't lose yourself in the part," but, with Sigurd standing right there, dared do no more than twinkle back at her.

"If she weren't attractive, she could appear so, I have no doubt. Her wizardry is such that the bubble in which she is encased must block not only the force of her words but of her very thoughts. Still, I have spoken with her, since the bubble obviates the need for a gag, and that has provided some distraction." He turned, and Mistra mimed strangling him.

"And here," he went on, "is, I fear, the image of your beloved. Bound for his strength, and magically gagged because he, too, is capable of spellcraft. He is a holy warrior, a paladin, as are many of your kin. Strength, skill at arms, and the ability to invoke his gods for magical aid—it is a frightening combination."

Gwynddolyn ran a hand along the sword rack. "He must have a marvelous weapon if he is all you say. Could one of these be it?"

"The larger of the two."

"May I draw it?"

"Oh, very well. I suppose a dainty thing like you could not wield it even if you had a mind to."

Oddly, he proved to be right. In fact, she could barely draw it for its sheer weight. The three adventurers, who had seen the sword accommodate itself to arms far weaker than Mosaia's, could only suppose it sensed Gwynddolyn's ruse and was attempting to play along. It did not fuss when she finally released it from the scabbard, but the companions could feel a sense like awe emanate from it at being confronted with so kindly a disposition here in this place of darkness. Sigurd had avoided physical contact with either sword: he knew a sword belonging to a paladin (or even an ethically-aligned warrior sorceress) might release sheets of flame or electrical charges if someone of a diametrically opposed ethos tried to draw it.

For once, the Retributor sputtered as if it were fumbling for words. "My lady," it finally managed. "Lay me at your feet that I may do homage!"

Mistra and Mosaia exchanged a glance, then both rolled their eyes heavenward. Still, despite the spontaneous, mutual show of vexation at the sword's histrionics, Mistra had a feeling the knight would lecture her about this ploy if they ever got out of here.

Gwynddolyn looked to Mistra for instruction concerning the sword's odd request. "Do it," she advised. "Or he'll threaten to disintegrate or ask to be melted down or re-consecrated to the service of someone like Ahriman as a punishment. It will be easier on all of us if you just do as it says."

"Just what else does this miraculous talking sword do?" Sigurd's voice was heavy with suspicion.

"In Mosaia's hand, quite a lot. As you may have guessed, he'd be like dead weight if *you* tried to wield him."

The Retributor, actually much more savvy than it liked to let on, assessed the situation from where it lay at Gwynddolyn's feet. "Oh," it cooed, "but if it might ameliorate the mood of Your Wizardry, and his attitude toward my friends, I can be the purveyor of many fine sleight of hand feats."

Sigurd grunted. "Sleight of *what* hands?"

"Why, sir, the lady's, or your own. That is why I said I am a *purveyor* rather than a *worker*. You provide me with my materials, and I tell you what to do. Card tricks, three card monte, tricks with coins disappearing and such. I admit it's nothing useful, but perhaps it would entertain?"

The Retributor had managed to touch Sigurd's humor. His traps were all set; maybe acquiescing to this silliness would put Gwynddolyn in a yet better frame of mind. He had her place the sword on the lab bench—comfortably far removed from any of his prisoners—but not before asking if they knew this to be the limit of its talents.

"I know of no other qualities it possesses beyond those useful for tracking and detecting evil presences," Mistra said, quite truthfully. It had been a guess that the sword could do anything at all that might help them.

"I hope, for your sake, that you are telling the truth. I can think of punishments that would be quite unpleasant and yet not mar you for my master's use. But I believe that you speak no lie in this instance." He turned to the sword. "Well, with what will you entertain us? Bear in mind that this is my bride-to-be, who will soon be your mistress."

"How much time has Your Lordship?"

Sigurd cocked his head, somewhat the way Alla did. "A very few minutes, I think—then I shall have another prisoner to attend. Still, if all goes as I have planned, that prisoner will be in a position to be ignored indefinitely. What do you require?"

It gave the impression it was pondering his question. "Ah, I know! Conjure me, of your courtesy, three playing cards, one of them the queen of pentacles."

"Done. Now what?"

"Good. Now, let's have the princess move them as I direct her, and you will tell me where the queen finally comes to rest."

Mistra, Mosaia, and Anthraticus exchanged very puzzled looks. Mosaia, in fact, wondered if the teleportation had addled the Retributor's wits. But Sigurd and Gwynddolyn became engrossed in the game, so much so that when a sound as of wings beating on a turbulent wind arose in the cell nearby, they took no notice. A second later, a hummingbird like a small Crowned Woodnymph fluttered through the bars of the cell window and came to rest, hidden from the mage, beside Anthraticus's cage. It was Alla, of course: Mosaia's timely warning had saved her life. The others permitted themselves three quick looks of relief. Now, could they find a way to let her know about the statues? And was there anything to hand that she could use to smash them?

While Mosaia and Anthraticus looked like they were casting about for a solution, Mistra's brain went into overdrive. She saw no tool that would serve, at least not for a hummingbird, and no magic of hers, Mosaia's, or Anthraticus' would work until the statues were destroyed and the three of them released.

She swore.

She stewed.

She had an inspiration.

"Gods, Mistra," she said to herself, "you're in a laboratory, for the love of Cilio. Use your head." She started scanning the reagent bottles as she dipped into her store of chemistry trivia. Wasn't that a vial of *aqua regia* above Anthraticus's head? And didn't gold dissolve in *aqua regia*? In fact, wasn't that a standard test?

She motioned surreptitiously to Alla. In a game of charades, the contortions she had to go through to communicate her intent would have been humorous; here, with lives at stake, they were frustrating. But Alla finally got the hang of what she was trying to say. Switching to the larger Berylline, she carefully prised the *aqua regia* bottle away from the others on the shelf.

Content that Alla was doing all that could be done about *that* problem, Mistra cast about for anything in the lab that could help them once Alla released them from their bondage. What was the story they had heard about all the magic and many of the mages in the area simply vanishing? If Sigurd were constructing huge repositories of power like the tapestry—if he were the one who was in effect stealing the very mana from the earth—he would need a reservoir in which to harbor it. If Alla could free them, her own first move should be to look for an artifact or reliquary or receptacle of some sort for that tremendous power. Indeed, there would be an accomplishment that might just save all their necks if they were forced to face both Sigurd and any minions like the demon he could bring into play.

Of course, at this point, Sigurd had become so absorbed by his interaction with Gwynddolyn, he wouldn't notice if she burst free of the bubble and began to dance a jig. And, limited though it was, she had a means of locomotion. *Hmmm…*

She kept her focus partially on Sigurd as she slowly started to move her bubble-prison about the lab. She worked tentatively at first, rolling a meter or two, then stopping, rolling, then stopping, to make sure the mage paid her no mind. But his absorption with Gwynddolyn only deepened. Now she thought he would not notice if, in addition to the jig, she pulled a brass band from the Ether, in full uniform and playing battle marches at triple forte volume. She began to move with greater purpose. As she rolled her prison here and there, going so far as to aim it in the direction of Sigurd's quarters, she felt the glimmerings of that focus of supreme power…

Across the room, Sigurd was suffering a losing streak. Try as he might, he could not determine where the queen would come to rest after each shuffle of the cards. He couldn't do it if Gwynddolyn were moving the cards. He couldn't do it if *he* were moving the cards. Gwynddolyn won occasionally, but he supposed the sword favored her for her beauty, her sweetness, and her ethos.

After about fifteen minutes of this, he looked up, wondering what could be taking so long for his would-be victim to teleport through and be impaled. As he excused himself to have a look in the cell, Alla succeeded in unstopping the bottle of acid and tipping it so it poured all over the bench top. Seeing it go helter skelter, she fluttered about madly trying to get the statuettes moved so they would be best exposed to the caustic fluid. To her surprise—having no frame of reference for anything related to chemistry, she had really taken Mistra's word on faith in this instance—the statues began to dissolve. At the same time, she heard the sound of a lock being sprung at the far end of the room.

There came a horrible moment in which Sigurd took in the empty cell, the hummingbird, the dissolving statues, Mistra's presence at the entrance to his private quarters, and the attack force coming in through his front door. The images struck him in succession so rapid the observations were almost simultaneous. Rage blazed in his eyes. Even Gwynddolyn, whose abilities with the magicks of the time were limited, could feel the forces he was suddenly massing. If he were to let loose even the raw unshaped energy he was calling to him, he would likely stun and blind the entire party. If he were to shape it into a spell, he could destroy them utterly!

But before he could act, the Retributor shouted three nonsense syllables and, with a towering effort, lifted itself just enough that it came down on the cards with enough force to cleave them in two. A brilliant flash of light accompanied by a small plume of smoke issuing from the cleft edges of the cards heralded the release of the spell's energy. Sigurd's expression became abruptly blissful. He sat—hard, as if his legs had just failed him. It must have hurt, but he betrayed no reaction either to the physical pain or the indignity of his position. Oblivious to the commotion around him, he started humming Falidian nursery rhymes.

"Now, lady!" the sword cried to Gwynddolyn. "Wield me to your best advantage!"

"What did you do?" Gwynddolyn wailed.

"Befuddled him."

"You've befuddled *me*!"

"No—I ensorcelled him to *be* befuddled. It will give us a breathing space."

"Smash the statues!" Mistra ordered when Gwynddolyn looked uncertain which way to turn. She could see that the acid was working, but not fast enough. Still, exposure to it certainly should have weakened the figurines structurally to the point where a good thwack with a blunt object—say the flat edge of the Retributor—should smash them.

"But—" Gwynddolyn gestured helplessly to convey the idea that she had barely been able to lift the sword from its stand and there was no way she could get it up high enough to smash anything.

"Just do it!" said Mistra and the Retributor together while Anthraticus and Mosaia added in pleas made somewhat incoherent by their muzzle and gag.

The young princess looked very much like she wanted to say, "I told you so" when she failed to lift the sword, then staggered when it proved so light she could easily have pressed it a dozen times. Heaving with all her might—not much, but she was making a splendid effort for a beginner—she raised the sword and brought it down. Her attempt was graceless but effective. She smashed the statues, narrowly missing Alla in the process. The bubble, the cage, the muzzle, and Mosaia's assorted fetters dissolved into smoke. Freed, the companions armed themselves and warned Gwynddolyn back. Alla shifted to Habie's choice of a great peregrine falcon.

The four of them turned to greet their comrades, who stood in the great archway at the far end of the workshop. As they did so, a pitch black cloud burst with a roar from one of the thaumaturgic circles on the floor. It swirled, then began to coalesce.

"I have a real doomed feeling about this," said Mistra. It came out perfectly conversational, as if she were commenting upon the time of day; consequently, it evoked in her companions more dread than if she had screamed, run for cover, and locked herself in Gwynddolyn's cell.

⚜

A few minutes earlier, the four remaining questors sat by the massive door while Deneth and Habie contemplated the lock. Torreb had surprised them all (himself included) by foiling all of the traps between the chasm and the archway with a single spell.

"The effect of the place on magic must just be random," he remarked. "Now I know how Mistra must have felt when she got stuck in her miniature form, only in a good way!" Deneth and Habie had stopped in their task of examining the lock—and exchanged a significant look over what they had just discovered. "What is it? Is it another trap?"

Deneth shook his head. "No."

T'Cru made a chuffing noise at the back of his throat: in a human, it would have connoted deep suspicion. "I think they're thinking such a place *should* be trapped."

Torreb jerked his head toward the chasm. "You think *that* wasn't enough? *And* the bats? *And* the mist creature? *And* that crystal thing? Not to mention half of us disappearing the gods only know where."

"They're all OK," Deneth said quietly. "At least, the crisis I tuned into earlier has passed. I think," he added in a voice so low the others did not hear the qualification.

"It must be a part of the magic that works in Sigurd's despite," T'Cru pontificated. "If not for their sacrifices, the tapestry could not have been completed and the spell broken."

"It's still *not* completed," Habie pointed out, "and the spell's still *not* broken. "Not till we get those other three medallions placed. I sure hope Mistra's is back to normal size."

"*She* is," Deneth chuckled, "even if *it* isn't." He went back to work.

"How do you know?" She set about handing him his tools as if she were assisting him in surgery.

He grinned mischievously at her, recalling his glimpse of the sorceress entangled with Mosaia and his own resulting twinge of jealousy. *That* would have made an interesting picture with the knight full-sized and Mistra barely tall enough to tap him on the knee. "Trust me."

"Uh-huh. When have you ever led me wrong, right?"

"You got it." He stopped again. "You know, Torreb, I still think we should be ready for something—you know—out of the ordinary." He took a moment to make certain his sword sat loose in its sheath and that the lute was handy and tuned the way he wanted it. Habie looked to her own weapons. Then they turned their attentions back to the lock.

T'Cru idly sharpened his claws on the stone floor while Deneth and Habie worked, but Torreb sat lost in thought for a full minute. He had readied his mace and the Balance after Deneth's caution and, ironically, invoked Ereb's blessing as well as Strephel's on the work of the two thieves. Now, moving as if he had hit on the obvious solution to a problem that had stumped him for days, he reached into his pack and pulled out one of the candles Tuhl had given him, as well as the medallion. He regarded both for a moment, weighing matters. Taken together, they represented a total of perhaps five uses: not even one per adventure. Tuhl must have intended that each use be saved for some extremity, especially in the case of the medallion: although it was a more powerful token than the candles, it could be used but once. They might yet have to combat the demon; they would certainly have to face its master, a wizard grown so mighty in his unreserved malevolence that his nature pervaded the very fiber of this place. He nodded once to himself, then stowed in his pack the medallion and all but one of the candles. He spelled the remaining candle to light the minute the doors swung inward.

"Here we go," Deneth announced. "Ready?"

Gripping his mace in one hand and the candle and Balance in the other,

Torreb joined Habie and T'Cru as the bard motioned them all to one side a moment before he kicked in the doors. The instant the doors opened, his sense of unease grew exponentially.

Before them lay a short hall that served as an anteroom to what appeared from there to be a wizard's workshop. As Deneth led them forward, Torreb noticed a second flash of light welling forth from his hand: the candle's flame paled before the radiance that suddenly issued from the Balance. He had done nothing to invoke the effect, but it had manifested all the same.

But the lights of both candle and holy symbol paled to insignificance in the face of the shadow that rose and took shape in one of the thaumaturgic circles that lay etched on the floor before them.

Although he had prepared for this eventuality, Torreb could not keep an oath from escaping his lips. Thrusting the candle and the Balance before him, he took the lead, shepherding the others into the workshop—and into the veritable maw of the demon with which they had tangled earlier.

Even as Torreb led them forward, Sigurd cast off the confusion with which the Retributor had ensnared him. Springing to his feet with an agility Mistra's dancer friends might have envied, he leaped forward and hurled his staff at the circle in whose center the demon had materialized. Alla dived for it but was not in time to keep it from breaching the circle's integrity. The demon, summoned from the treasure room automatically if anything but the right key were used to open the workshop door, stepped from the circle. He roared in glee and expectation of battle.

Mistra, now free of the bubble, made a dive for Mosaia as he prepared to wade into the fray and tore the medallion from around his neck. She then vaulted over the lab bench that separated her from Gwynddolyn. "Can you handle a weapon?" she asked the other woman, who shook her head frantically. She had done her best to smash the statuettes with the Retributor, but the recoil forced her to drop the blade: her muscles were too soft and her hands too delicately made for her to endure such a shock and maintain her grip. Mistra, armed with a contingency plan and seeing this was no time for delicacy, ripped the medallions from her own neck and from Gwynddolyn's and thrust all three of them into the princess's trembling hands. She hung back from the battle, using the precious seconds to instruct Gwynddolyn. "Look, one of our friends over there has a tapestry. These fit into it magically. You've got to find the tapestry, put it together if you need to, and place these wherever they seem to fit. It's the only way to break the spell."

Gwynddolyn blanched. "But I can't! Oh, my gods! Look at that horrible thing! What will it do to me?"

"We'll hold it off. Think of Gunthar and your friends and what Sigurd will do to *them* if we can't defeat him. You're their only hope. Off you go." Not willing to argue the point, she gave Gwynddolyn a little shove toward the side of the workshop, summoned her blade to her hand, and went to join in the battle.

They might as well have been facing an army. Even as she watched, the demon sprouted four more arms, each bearing a weapon born of the stuff of nightmares. Of the original two arms, one bore a weapon, and the other gestured as if readying itself to cast spells. ZZZZZZZZTTTT! From his fingertips sprang a bolt like blue lightning that forced Torreb to dodge or be incinerated on the spot. WHOOSH! and a cloud engulfed Mosaia and Deneth: in seconds, they were retching and gasping for breath.

Across the room, Sigurd displayed his command of battle magic by pulling weapons one right after the other from the rack that had lately held the Retributor and Mistra's sword. In rapid successsion, he would grab a weapon, enchant it, and toss it into the melee to engage anyone not kept completely occupied by the demon. Mistra and Anthraticus, hanging back to deal with him specifically, bore the brunt of this attack, but the six companions engaging the demon were forced to guard their flanks and backs as well as their fronts as the occasional weapon gave the two spellcasters a miss and came at one of them from behind.

Sigurd laughed in gleeful malevolence at the chaos he had wrought around him. He could have gone on enchanting weapons, but his main interest, once he had all of his opponents fighting for their lives, became divining how much of the tapestry his opponents had found, what medallions they had fit into it, whether or not they had repaired the pieces and sewn them together, and who was carrying it—so much of its essential workings he had gleaned since his lair played him false and brought the tapestry back into fragmented being. With sight born of his art, he located it in Habie's pack. It dismayed him to see all anyone had to do to complete it was to place within the weave the medallions belonging to his three former captives. Habie as the bearer must be dealt with at all costs. He sent a silent command to the demon.

⁓⊱⊰⁓

The demon, having one foe engaging each arm and sensing he faced six warriors far more doughty than those he ever encountered in this place, plunged into the fight with reckless abandon. Quickly, even as he laid about himself with his weapons and readied his spells, he assessed his situation. To a one, his opponents were aggressive, imaginative fighters; the knight was elegance in motion, battling on his own account but whirling and diving to help the others when they faltered. The bard a bundle of energy unbridled but focused enough to keep him on his guard. The priest fought like a madman; the two beasts engaged with such ferocity, the feline from below and the falcon from above, that he feared to let their pounces and dives connect at all lest he lose a limb. Even the little demi-human, who seemed bent on incapacitating the hand he was using to cast spells, was giving him trouble—her accuracy with the daggers and other oddments she hurled was uncanny.

But he was no ordinary demon. He heard his master's mental command. He continued to fight competently, albeit more conservatively, as he acted on it. He felt a pang of remorse: he had rather liked the little thief. No matter. He could keep her with him for amusement's sake once he vanquished her, recreating her as an undead servant of some sort.

"Well, little one," he boomed, turning the full focus of his gaze on her—and anyone paying attention could, at that moment, see in his eyes every torment ever devised in each of the Seven Hells. "Well met! Come and know me better!" He raised the one weaponless hand.

"Eat drek, you overgrown—!" She never finished the sentence. A bolt of unlight issued from the demon's hand and struck her squarely in the chest. She stopped, stricken, and keeled over. Her body remained stiff, her eyes glazed.

But now the demon shrieked. His rhythm had faltered—barely—when he had cast the potent spell. As marginally, his attention had wavered. It was enough. He felt steel cleave his flesh: the knight had struck home, completely severing one arm. The blade he carried must be consecrated: no metal not blessed by a deity of good could sting like this when it bit. For that matter, no blade not forged by a god should have been able to cleave bone and sinew so cleanly. He came close to turning his wrath on Mosaia at the insult to his beloved etheric flesh, but he had seen earlier that the priest represented the greater threat. His body, being made of etheric substance, could be hacked and slashed quite a bit before he took damage enough to halt him in his tracks, and a severed limb would eventually regenerate; his spirit was another matter. *That,* the priest could banish or unmake with that candle in his possession. He redirected the weapon he had been using on Torreb and contented himself with attacking the knight simultaneously with two weapons even as he leveled his free hand at the priest. The priest, much too dangerous to be taken back to his own plane as a servant, would go down in ignominy while he kept the knight powerless to intervene. Then he would fall on the knight with both weapons and spells and destroy him utterly for his effrontery in severing his arm.

The true death that the demon had withheld from Habie now fell full force on Torreb: A second bolt of unlight—this one flecked with jagged bolts of livid green—shot from the demon's hand. This one took Torreb squarely in the chest. He fell, and the demon breathed a sigh of relief: incapacitating the priest cut off the recitation of holy verses that was, for him, an agony as wrenching as the spell cast by the candle. Then he roared in rage: Torreb had not collapsed but had sunk only to his knees. Impossible! Who *were* these people? The aura cast by both the symbol the priest held before him like a shield and the candle must have mitigated the effect of his spell: the force that should have killed had merely damaged. He prepared to fire a second volley, then stopped. He could see what those facing him could not. One of Sigurd's animate weapons, a brutal-looking morningstar, was coming up behind the priest. When it came crashing down, the stroke would be his death blow. The demon whooped in glee now. Both the knight and the bard had noticed the morningstar; the demon reoriented all of his weapons so they would have to make the choice between their own lives and that of the priest. If either turned to intercept, the demon would impale him; if neither had the will to sacrifice his life in that way, the priest would die. The demon gloated at the horror and indecision he saw in their eyes.

The stroke fell, but not on Torreb. Seeing the dilemma in which the demon had put her friends, Alla took a hand (or a claw). She separated herself from the main battle, power-diving and plucking the weapon from mid-air at the last possible instant. Gripping the morningstar in her talons, she lobbed it at Sigurd with such smooth efficiency it simply completed its arc of swing heedless of the fact that it had been driven from its opponent and was now attacking the master who animated it in the first place. It did not have the force of a fatal blow, but it did stun him long enough for Alla to carry out one more desperate measure.

All around her, her friends were embroiled in battle. Anthraticus and Mistra were both still pinned by half a dozen animated weapons. Across the room, Habie lay stunned or dead and Torreb knelt, stricken. Mosaia, Deneth, and T'Cru were making a brave stand against the demon, who now lacked for an arm and was oozing ichor from a dozen serious wounds. She knew her strength and stamina, never completely regained after the battle with the mist creature, were flagging; she also knew that, were man and beast to defeat the demon instantly, it would move them no closer to their goal of besting Sigurd and recovering Gwynddolyn's friends. If she could take but one last action, she must make it count in some other way than harming the demon or distracting the mage.

Gwynddolyn, she thought, *where* is *Gwynddolyn?* Casting about, she found the young princess—the only one of them to remain unoccupied. There she was, hiding behind a lab bench at the edge of the room. *Mosaia's description of the women of his day must apply equally well to women of the past*, she thought in what was for her an acrid humor. *They are decorative little twits groomed for form rather than performance. How do they even endure childbirth?* Gliding over to exhort the woman to action, she saw her first observation was not strictly true—Gwynddolyn was not cowering, only moving very slowly. Timidly, like a mouse, she was skirting the battle and aiming for—what? There was only one possibility, Alla thought as she caught sight of the medallions clutched in the girl's hand. Mistra must have coached the girl earlier about finding and completing the tapestry. Her attitude softened—perhaps the young woman was doing the best she could with the task Mistra had set her.

Well, she could no longer strike a blow that would make a difference to either battle, but she could take advantage of Sigurd's momentary indisposition to help Gwynddolyn along. Reorienting, she folded her wings and dived for Habie. She dug her talons not into Habie's flesh, but into her pack. Her strength was barely held to lift the girl so she could work the pack free, a bitter struggle that seemed to take hours. Even as she fought to free the pack, she sank her beak into one of the shoulder straps, severing it. Habie dropped unceremoniously to the ground, freeing the pack completely. Alla flew it over to Gwynddolyn, let it fall, then rounded on Sigurd, whom she had noticed stirring out of the corner of her eye. *If I'm going to drop in my airborne tracks*, she reasoned, *let me drop where it will do my friends some good.* She fought to gain altitude, then plummeted, using her final strength to set her claws before her. The speed of her dive would have let her tear the mage's face off had the stupor not begun to lift, but he had recovered. Flames leapt from his fingers. The impact of her collision with that wave of force was dreadful; it knocked her from mid-air as much from that impact as from the heat of the flames themselves. She dropped to the floor, completely spent, and knew no more.

When Habie fell, Gwynddolyn saw what no one engaged in the melee could take thought to notice: the way the girl's pack cushioned her fall. The pack bulged so she landed softly at an incline, then rolled to one side. The bulge could only be the tapestry. But how might she get to it? Her new friends were keeping the demon well occupied, but he had been forced to one side so Habie and her pack lay almost directly beneath him. If she made a grab for it, surely he would see her and deal with her as he had just dealt with the image of her maiden Nura. *I must approach at least*, she said to herself, willing her body to move, *so, if an opportunity arises I will have less distance to cross.* She tried to move, but her muscles responded sluggishly: her legs seemed suddenly to be supporting an unbearable weight.

But what was this? A bird like a great falcon was gliding toward her. Another of Sigurd's enchantments come to peck her eyes out for her betrayal? No, the bird had just attacked Sigurd; its previous opponent had been the demon. It must be a friend. As it approached, it looked at her with intelligent eyes. A moment before they would have come beak to nose, the bird veered off and flew back toward the battle. *Is this a lesson the gods have sent me,* she berated herself now, *that if a wild bird of prey does not fear to enter the battle, I should cast fear aside as well?* Putting thought aside, she shut her eyes and found herself able to force her limbs into action. Though she could not bring herself to do more than crawl on all fours, she moved forward. *I bet there are snails that can move faster than this,* she observed with something between anger and the beginnings of hysterical laughter.

Plop! Something landed on the floor before her, impeding her progress and forcing her to open her eyes. *Oh, bless the Quatrain Godhead!* she rejoiced in her heart. It was Habie's pack! Still keeping low, she gathered the pack into her arms and scuttled back to her cell to complete the tapestry as Mistra had instructed her.

If Mistra saw little else of the battle, she saw Sigurd's attack on the nearly spent Alla, and it enraged her. In her fury, she sliced with such force she cut in two the animated sabre she with which she fought—the last of the half dozen that had engaged her. It, too, dropped to the floor. "All right, magician," she muttered. "Let's see you fight one of your own kind." This last escalated in volume till Sigurd could not have missed the challenge she issued. She made an inviting little hand gesture, and turned an inviting little smile on him, too. Something about confronting him head-on made her more keenly aware of that core of strength—of blindingly white light—she had felt when Syndycyr had come close to daunting her. She had no idea how to conceptualize it: reality or cheat or fevered imagining brought on by battle rage. But she drew from it hope and renewed confidence. Sigurd turned toward her, but she gave him no time to reply. Up went her hand. From her palm issued a beam of light as radiant as the beam released by the demon had been dark. Sigurd, taken by surprise despite her warning, reeled.

"Gotcha," said Mistra. It hadn't been a definitive strike, but just the sense of the spell connecting felt very life-affirming.

The demon, aware of the attack in the instant it occurred, turned to defend his master, losing a second hand to a slash of Deneth's sword as he winked out. He reappeared hovering over Sigurd's body, his hand raised. Mistra, having anticipated such a turn of events, directed a second beam of radiance—this one blue with silver highlights—at the demon. It struck him so he roared in pain—but not before he got off his own spell. This time no unlight issued from his hand; what came forth took shape as a cloud. It welled outward gently and quietly but very quickly—and its coming stifled all light.

For a moment, the fighting ceased. Darkness enfolded the entire party at once, for the cloud did not travel by simple diffusion but reached out to engulf the enemies of its caster. From the darkness came sounds: the eerie clanking of chains, the drag of shackles through haunted crypts, the howl of werecreatures. Mosaia felt the half-guessed touch of a shroud on his neck and stopped dead, wondering which of the animate weapons would strike him next, and where, and when. Deneth smelled the stench of decay and wondered if it emanated from his own rotting flesh. The beasts felt the drag of nets and ropes. Torreb understood the darkness to be his own sepulcher; accepted numbly the fact that he had been entombed while still alive.

Mistra alone beat back the images. Rather, she perceived them but knew they had no more power to touch her than if her soul had been girded with armor made of several centimeters of quantum steel. But because of her house's history of direct interaction with demonkind, she knew what the others did not—that mere exposure to this cloud of clinging blackness would sap them of strength, of breath, of life itself, till those illusions of death manifested themselves in reality.

And such a death would be subject to no law or power of any god in the Pantheon.

Gwynddolyn experienced the feeling of entombment on a far more visceral—a far more *terrifying*—level than the rest. She had reached her cell with the tapestry and unfolded it. She had been about to set the first medallion in when the darkness caught her, and the metal fell from her nerveless fingers with a clang that reverberated in the sudden stillness. The adventurers had each known something of despair, of terror, of confronting a superior enemy. Gwynddolyn had known nothing but the life of comfort of those born to privilege. The others had seen despair turned to victory; Gwynddolyn could not conceive of the despair that did not feed on itself till it spat back utter calamity. Where the adventurers feared but tensed themselves to confront what lurked in the darkness, she merely cowered, wondering how she could go on amidst the terrors of the blackness.

But as the dark and quiet threatened to rob her of her last vestige of breath, something arose to cleave them. She heard the tiniest sound, saw the tiniest speck of light. The sound itself was so small she thought she might be hallucinating; the light could have been a trick of a mind addled past its ability to comprehend. But they persisted and grew. Five seconds of looking and listening convinced her of their existence in fact; ten, and she could put character to them. The sound, though still small, was glad and wise; the light was sanctity incarnate, and it seemed to center on Mistra, the only one of her new friends she could see through the door of her cell and the last thing she had seen before the darkness had enveloped her.

The sound was the voice of a sprite, she thought, or a naiad—earthy and full of the rhythms of nature. If there were words, she did not know them, but she caught their meaning: the richness of life renewing itself; the simple courage of men tilling their fields, of women giving birth; the downfall of tyrants. As the song grew, so did the light. It began as an argus—faint, but pure and holy—surrounding Mistra alone. Her friends took up the chant, hesitantly at first, only Deneth initially singing with any sense of conviction that his ears were not betraying him. But as they joined in, expanding on the melody with flourishes or harmonies, the light grew to encompass them, too. It grew till the darkness constituted no more than a thin band at its outer edge; it grew till it thrust the darkness back; it grew till it illumined every centimeter of Sigurd's lab and the demon quailed at the sight of it.

And ever after, no one could be certain just who had started the song. Though most thought it was Mistra, since the light seemed to well out from her own body, she always maintained she had caught the tune from Deneth, who maintained that a woman had already been singing when he joined in, but that that woman was not Mistra.

Whoever started it, it broke the spell. At least, although the darkness hovered like a noise on the edge of hearing, the spell had mitigated its effects for the moment. Gwynddolyn suddenly found she could act. Something in Habie's pack caught her eye in the growing light: a spell scroll. She grabbed it, tore it open, and read it through. It was a temporal stasis spell. She knew enough of magic to know the spell was written so its casting could affect only one person or creature. A terrible choice now confronted her. The demon controlled the darkness, but Sigurd controlled the demon. Encapsulating either in a bubble of temporal stasis would effectively disconnect him from any magicks he had currently in play. Mistra and the others were holding off that baneful darkness, driving it back and keeping it at bay, even tormenting the demon while they did so. But how much more could they endure? Brilliant and plentiful as the light had become, if the demon rallied and attacked them so he interrupted the chant, would the darkness not simply engulf them once more with redoubled force? If she chose the demon, the darkness would dissipate immediately, and the demon would be effectively removed from the battle. Sigurd, however, had many other weapons as potent—she noticed him rousing even now and knew he would quickly bring those weapons to bear. If she chose Sigurd, his hold on the demon would be broken: the demon would have no one to control him. That might mean freedom for them all, or instant death.

She chose Sigurd. She read the scroll aloud, then, not waiting to see the effect, she turned her attention to the tapestry. Still, as she worked, she *felt* the darkness retreat in earnest, *heard* the few remaining animate weapons dropped clattering to the floor, and she reveled in her newfound freedom to act. As she set the medallions in their proper positions, they fused instantly, and the tapestry lay before her, complete. She took up the bulky cloth and dragged it into the workshop, bearing it before her like a shield.

The demon, she saw as she emerged, had shrunk somewhat; two of his remaining four arms were dissolving like so much mist. He remained, she thought, a formidable opponent. What would he do? Had she just condemned them all to a life in bondage to this abomination?

Rather than scooping them all up and dragging them off to the Abyss, however, he let go a hearty laugh. "Well met, little maiden," he greeted her. "You have freed me as well as your friends by suspending this viper's power." He touched Sigurd's shoulder. The groggy magician disappeared in a shower of sulfurous sparks, attaining at the last moment just the level of consciousness he needed to emit a blood-curdling wail at his fate. The demon laughed again. "Now *he* will serve *me*. I will no longer trouble those of you who live or who fell by a hand not my own, but these others I claim as my spoils of war. The body of the little thief I shall reanimate; the body of the priest will serve as proof of my skills to Ahriman himself, with whom I shall seek service and so cleanse myself of memory of this period of base servitude." He reached toward Habie and toward Torreb—the stricken priest had clung to life till the moment the cloud of darkness struck and drained him of his last vestige of breath.

Loyalty meaning more in this instance than sanity, the five remaining companions closed ranks around their stricken comrades before the demon could act. No one of them cued or led the others or initiated the action at all. It was as if both the thought and the impulse to act occurred to all of them at the same instant. Gwynddolyn, still clutching the tapestry, found the courage to join them a heartbeat later. Several of the companions grinned at her sudden display of temerity, at the sudden defiance in her posture. Then they turned a collective look of challenge on the demon. No one raised a weapon; they let posture and stance convey their message, which the demon might have taken to mean "This far and no farther" or simply "Not a chance, fella." Whether he chose the more or the less formal interpretation, he backed. Slightly.

"You think to thwart me, little mortals?" the demon boomed, sneering.

"We are not all mortals," retorted the Retributor, "and you do not know your peril! Make my day! *Make my millennium!! MAKE MY LIFE CYCLE!!!*"

Deneth muttered, "Just make him mad, you stupid sword. Good strategy" at the same time that T'Cru, at his most regal, pronounced, "You will not have them while we live." He turned so the demon could see the Stag on his haunch. For the first time, he bore it, *displayed* it, with unadulterated pride.

Taking their cue, the other three so marked bared their left shoulders, although Mosaia and Mistra trotted out the Circle and the Tree as a gentle reminder that there were more consecrated champions of good here than just Torreb. Light welled from the marks as well as from the holy symbols—a power that might shake the foundations of this planet kept in abeyance till the battle resumed. That light and that power were bad enough, but the demon saw this in their posturing: during the initial battle, he had had both the partnership and the power of his late master to back him, and the pair had possessed the element of surprise. If he chose to fight them now, he would do so on his own. They had had the chance to rally, they were battle-ready, and there is no more dangerous opponent to tackle than one who has a well-loved, stricken comrade to defend.

No one spoke for a tense minute, nor did anyone move. The demon himself looked cowed, though he tried to hide it. Even so, he reached twice more for his victims, and twice more he jerked his hand back as if he had been stung or repulsed.

"What are *you* going to do with them?" he asked as a final ploy. "At least where I take them, they can have a semblance of life. I will give my word in the name of my lord Ahriman that I will even reanimate the priest, if you like. I owe that much to a worthy opponent."

And now he read in their collective stare only a single message: Forget it.

He hovered, regarding them in stillness for a long moment; then he sighed, bowed as if acquiescing, and dematerialized.

Something in the demon's penultimate position affected them so they turned as soon as he had vanished to look behind them: it appeared that he had been focusing on something behind and above them in those last few seconds, had not, in fact, bowed to them at all. They saw nothing, but there came to the air around them something indefinable, like the scent of far-away lilacs caught on a warm breeze and wafted toward them on the first day of summer.

⁂

Only now that the danger had truly passed did they realize the plight of their friends. Alla, although not badly wounded, had spent every ounce of energy she had to give and had fallen unconscious, but Torreb lay at death's door—really, he had partially crossed its threshold—and Habie lay in that horrible twilight that was almost, but not quite, beyond. None of them knew whether Torreb would follow her into that land of shades and spectres if they could not rouse him quickly. Mosaia saw immediately that, with Torreb down, he was Habie's best, and maybe her only, hope. He took charge, saw that the rest looked to him to *take* charge; a trace of grimness in his eyes alone betrayed how intimidating he found the tasks before them. He nodded to Mistra to help Torreb, and to the beasts and Deneth to see to Alla. No one argued. Indeed, they seemed happy to have someone in whom they had confidence directing them!

"God be with me," he prayed as he knelt beside Habie. Clutching the Circle and bowing his head, he sought fruitlessly for some sign of life. Tears came to his eyes at the thought of such a bright, merry spirit suffering so cruel a fate. He had healed a myriad battlefield injuries, had brought men back from the brink of death. True resurrection in his faith took one man praying for hours before he could even attempt the restoration while at least one more kept vigil over the body and laid on hands to keep the soul from going too far beyond the Veil to be recalled. He had never before encountered this state of un-life, and he was not sure he was prepared to face its ultimate consequences. If his ministrations resulted only in his restoring Habie to undeath rather than to true life, his only choice would be to kill her outright in the moment he realized his error. Still, he must try. It must be as Deneth had once suggested: he could play nearly any stringed instrument anyone handed him because he knew the basic principles behind playing any stringed instruments. And it must be as Torreb had said when confronted with the dragon Postumous on Astra: he could at least manage the healing mindtouch on a sentient beast because he knew how to employ it on his own kind, and humans and humanoids were really only another sort of sentient beast. So, still praying fervently, he laid his hands, one over her heart, one over her brow, and began his work. But he begged he be spared that terrible choice even as he prayed into his hands the power to restore her.

So deep did his concentration become that it took the gasps of his friends to rouse him to the point he noticed that what he knelt on was not dressed stone but grass. He looked up. The last traces of the workshop were just dissolving around them. The lab benches, the cells, the runes and thaumaturgic circles, the reagent bottles, the very floors and ceilings, all of them were fading like morning mist in strong sunlight. In minutes, the only evidence that remained of Sigurd's presence or his machinations—indeed, the only tell-tale signs that he had ever existed—were the tapestry and the huge gazing crystal. By the light of the torch he had lit in his cell—the torch now hovered in the air above them, as if held by an unseen hand—he could see they were back in the woodland glade where their adventure had begun.

"What's going on?" Gwynddolyn ventured timorously. She clutched the tapestry more tightly.

"Someone is, I think, helping us," said T'Cru.

⁕

Mistra cocked her head in a way she knew told the others she was peering into the Ether much as Alla might have done, as well as taking in the physical scene around her. Around her, Alla had resumed her human form; she breathed easily and her color had improved—she saw Deneth and the beasts had been able to achieve that much, at least. Habie was another story: she still lay inert despite Mosaia's best efforts. She herself was not doing much better with Torreb. She had gotten his wounds to seal and his internal bleeding to stop, but that simply meant he was getting no worse. It would take a Torreb, she thought with grim humor, to heal a Torreb. A moment ago, she had been praying to Minissa (or Thalybdenos, Tuhl, Avador, and anyone else who might be listening) for assistance, even if that help were only a hint about what to do next. Now she thought her prayers and Mosaia's had been answered: an idea had come to her whose origins could not but have come from beyond.

"Mosaia," she said quietly. "Bring Habie over here."

He complied without hesitation, lifting Habie as if she weighed no more than the dolls Mistra had played with when she was a child. "What are you thinking?" he asked as he did so.

"The tapestry. If it had the power to undo the spell, mightn't it have the power to undo the harms incurred along the way to defusing it?"

His face told her all she needed to know about the way his heart lightened at the thought. *He has seen magic that fits his paradigm of its misuse on this adventure,* she thought, *yet he allows for the possibility that it can also heal.* She helped him to arrange the bodies of their friends side by side, then signed to

Gwynddolyn to bring the tapestry. The three of them draped the cloth lovingly so it covered Torreb and Habie up to their chins. When they had finished and Mosaia was kneeling across the tapestry from Mistra, she saw inspiration had struck him as well. He reached a hand out to her. She did not even have to ask what he wanted. She placed her hand in his so their clasped hands met over the bodies. Together, they bowed their heads in prayer. She was content to let him direct the contact, to do no more than lend such strength as she had—after all, he was healer by trade and she only now and again by necessity and the grace of the Pantheon.

The two times he had healed her, she had experienced a sensation like cool rain on parched grass; the sensation of healing him had not been that different. Now, as party to the contact that would heal another, she marveled at the depth of his devotion, at his facility with guiding the healing energies at his disposal, at the way his hands could deal death so efficiently in one heartbeat and life in the next. To be invited into a healing circle with such a one was a heady feeling indeed!

She felt a gentle touch on her shoulder, and suddenly Deneth entered the contact as well, followed shortly by Anthraticus, T'Cru, and Gwynddolyn. And music the like of which she had never heard, as if the spirit that animated the lute were somehow communing directly with her soul. Even the Retributor somehow joined that mystical circle. *Our minds must be so foreign to his,* she thought, *and yet he trusts. I wonder if there are any more like him at home...*

They broke off in the absolute stillness that heralded the imminent approach of dawn. Nothing seemed to have happened. Gwynddolyn spoke what the rest of them did not dare for fear of affronting the gods whose help they had sought: "It's not working. The tapestry is all fixed, and my friends haven't come back, and your friends don't look any better, and it's not working."

For no logical reason, however, Mistra could not find it in herself to give in to despair. Nor, she thought, could the rest of her companions. A stillness came over them, as though they felt without voicing the opinion that their own solemnity would allow any spell that had taken shape to work itself to its necessary conclusion.

The sky in the east was just beginning to grow lighter when Anthraticus sprang without preamble into the air. He fluttered so erratically as to be capering, his buoyancy like optimism made flesh. "How lovely will be the sunrise," he said in a voice as animated as his movements. "How symbolic is it always of reversal. How lovely the turn of any tide, be it time or water or battle or life itself." He indulged in a somersault. The others, he noted, were not amused, although

Mistra and Mosaia looked very much like they wanted to believe his assertions. But on the whole, they looked like they thought his behavior out of place. They weren't getting the picture at all.

"In many places, you see," he went on, determined to make them understand he had not taken leave of his senses but rather had a vital point to make, "the people feel the dawn and dusk are invested with mystical potency, with magic, or the favor of the gods. The veils between the worlds of flesh and spirit thin. Take your wounds, Princess Mistra. Wouldn't you say they felt miraculously better than they did, say, ten minutes ago? My eyesight isn't what it was a hundred years ago, but, yes, I'd even say they seem to be healing."

He watched as the princess responded to his suggestion. He had observed that while she never balked at getting her hands dirty, as the humans might say, right now she was looking at herself with barely-concealed distaste. Her clothes were in complete disarray, torn and dirty, her braid was a shambles, she saw grime over nearly every inch of her body. But after giving herself a once-over, she looked up at him and nodded: under the tears, the throbbing of the wounds she had forgotten about in her concern for Habie and Torreb had stopped. A particularly nasty gash she had gotten on her thigh had stopped bleeding; the skin had knit almost completely.

He looked at the others. In the growing light, he saw that, although the rents in their clothing went unmended, his friends' wounds were healing before their eyes. Alla's breathing slowed and deepened and she actually began to stir; both Torreb and Habie were making some respiratory effort now. A gentle breeze broke the stillness—the same one they had sensed in the workshop before it dissolved around them, or one very like it. He thought it smelled like the leaves after rain, but quizzing the others, he found each perceived it differently. Mistra thought it smelled like musk, but Deneth thought of honeysuckle and the Falidians of spiced wine.

⁂

Alla and Torreb opened their eyes at precisely the same moment and inhaled deeply. Alla likened the scent to flowers in spring, but Torreb said, "By every deity in the Pantheon! There be seraphim here!"

That was the missing puzzle piece for the Carotians. To Mosaia and Gwynddolyn's puzzled expressions, Torreb responded, "They are like the archangels of your own cosmology: mighty dwellers of the Celestial Concourse, servants of the Pantheon who are sent to intervene in the physical world from time to time."

"At least one seraph must have manifested in the lab," said Mistra. "That must be what the demon actually acquiesced to; it knew it could fight till the

Seven Hells froze over and never defeat a party backed by such a power."

"Perhaps that was the source of your inspiration to use the tapestry to accomplish the healing we could not," offered Mosaia.

"We must be favored of the Pantheon, of Ereb himself!" Torreb said, as if the discovery of the Stag on his own body had not convinced him of the Pantheon's blessing.

"We've been *favored* of the Pantheon since we were chosen for this mission," Deneth said sourly. "If that's what you want to call it. You were unconscious and had something like nine toes in the grave when your celestial buddy first showed up. It helped us to keep the demon from toting you and Habie off to his larder. I'd call that a reasonable extremity, and I think it was reasonable—*real* reasonable—that we got some help." He thought Torreb looked like he expected a roll of thunder, and possibly a lightning strike on the ground at his own feet. "Well, I don't care *who* hears," he announced in response. "I've always said Minissa chose the wrong man for the job here, that I'm not holy or even reverent or anything else like it, but the way this stupid mark keeps sitting on my shoulder shows me she's too bloody-minded to admit she made a mistake. But I've tried to do my best, cuz I like you guys, so, faced with a demon, an almost undead creature who used to be my live friend, a half-regularly-dead priest, and none of us without battle scars after all our hard work, I can't say I'm *impressed* she noticed we needed a little help and sent it. In fact, my usual veneer of cynicism might have been bolstered or tilted over the edge into complete disbelief—in *anything*—if she hadn't, although you'll notice no one showed up till the battle was over. So thank you, whoever you are, but I think it's only fair you graced us with your presence."

The others were caught between cringing and laughing out loud at the tirade but were saved the agony of the choice when a warm golden light welled up before Deneth. It phased into what could only have been a seraph, one in the service of Ereb by his colors. They variously bowed or knelt to show their respect, even Deneth, who had colored slightly and whose face became a study in wonder. In fact, he did not kneel volitionally so much as have his knees give way. The seraph touched a hand to his brow. He was never sure if the seraph spoke the words aloud, but he heard them all the same and never forgot them: "Most recalcitrant and most beloved son of Phino." A remarkable statement in that he had never been consecrated to any deity whatsoever: some customs kept by the Carotians and Erebites were taking a while to make a comeback on Thalas.

The seraph then turned and blessed the others, even the Retributor, and this time Deneth and all the others were sure they heard the words "Hand of Minissa and Ereb" whisper in their minds. The sun was just coming above the horizon when he took Habie's head between his hands and breathed gently into her face. Her eyes fluttered open seconds later. As Torreb helped her to climb out from beneath the tapestry, the seraph touched a hand to it as well. It began to fade slowly. As it did so, they heard voices around them. From the very air of the glade materialized Gwynddolyn's friends, the questors' doubles; a very beautiful effect, and a very symmetrical one. As the tapestry became more translucent, Gwynddolyn's friends became more opaque and solid, so they had completely solidified just as the tapestry disappeared completely. It took them some minutes to orient themselves, but when they did, they rushed up first to Gwynddolyn then to the questors and bombarded them with questions about what had happened. And by that time, the seraph had vanished. With him had gone the tapestry—and the crystal.

⚜

The seraph left but one thing in the wake of his passing, and only Mistra seized upon it—but, after all, she had been the one who had been seeking it in the first place. On the grass where the spirit-creature had knelt lay a small golden statue fashioned in the likeness of Sigurd. Such power emanated from it that it surprised her when none of the others noticed. Like the Sword of Rhydderch Hael and the amulet Syndycyr had given her, the power emanating from the statuette had no orientation, and that gave her pause; she had expected anything the mage had tampered with to have become corrupted. The power, while clearly the raw stuff of which a mage crafted spells, was redolent less of Ether than of earth. It was as if someone had drained the Orb of Caros of its energies and deposited them in a vessel charged to receive such force.

She stashed the statuette in her pack for later consideration, then, on a guess, removed the Portal Stone from her the pouch at her waist. It glowed brightly. A very little maneuvering told her the Portal must lie on the other side of the glade.

"It was here all the time," she said to herself. "Sigurd must have tampered with the very fabric of time and space here when he set up his stronghold and cast his spells." She stood lost in thought for a moment before allowing her double to draw her into the reunion.

⚜

Now that Sigurd had been dealt with, Gwynddolyn and Gunthar were able to return safely to the Clear Waters' ancestral home, and they would not hear of it but that the questors would come to stay with them and celebrate their union properly. What Gwynddolyn's family would say at the sight of an entire duplicate set of her friends, no one knew, but they all agreed it would lend credence to an otherwise outlandish tale.

Fortunately, the horses had remained where the questors had left them. After a little rearranging and doubling up, they mounted up and headed toward the Clear Water lands. It represented the better part of a morning's ride to cover the distance to the castle, but no one was particularly keen on sleep after the adrenaline rush of the past few hours.

Gwynddolyn's parents received them warmly—indeed, they thought, too casually until they realized she had really only been gone overnight and her family had no inkling a wedding had taken place. That their entire adventure had taken less than twenty-four hours finally hit home; it seemed like they had done enough reasoning and fighting to fill a week's hard adventuring. At the moment, a long rest attended by every luxury Barony Clear Water could provide seemed beyond praise as a reward for their travails.

"What I'd like to know," said Habie, still weak from her bout with undeath, "is, does it get worse?"

"The gods test us according to our abilities," Torreb reminded her. "And I *suppose* we're supposed to be getting better."

"It is in the very nature of such challenges," agreed Mosaia, "that if you survive them, you come out stronger, and so better able to meet the next trial sent by your Pantheon or my God."

"What doesn't kill you—or *un*kill you, like what happened to me—makes you bigger and meaner, huh?" the little thief asked glumly.

"I suspect," said Deneth, "that by the end of our adventures, we will be looking back on this time and deciding that thus far the universe had not even taken its gloves off, let alone started slapping us silly."

"Can we quit getting better?" Habie groaned.

"Yeah, and get zapped for sitting on our hands," said Deneth.

"No matter," said Mosaia. "Here I think we may find refuge for a few days, at least. Unless anyone feels a pressing need to move on, I think we all need time to rest and recover from our wounds, the better to meet the next adventure God sends us."

Mistra admitted then that, with Sigurd cast down, the Portal Stone was functioning once again; although she had not been able to pin down the Portal's exact location, she knew it lay in the glade somewhere. "Still," she went on, "I think one of us would have had a sign or a feeling or something if it were important that we push on immediately."

She got no argument.

Gwynddolyn's folk, once the story had been explained to their satisfaction (which took most of the afternoon), blessed her and Gunthar. They then proceeded to fête their exotic guests in style and to provide them with welcome comforts. There were hot baths for all who wanted them: one large sunken tub (it fit ten without crowding) was fed by natural hot springs that dotted the property and outfitted by means of rudimentary engineering with whirlpool jets. Five minutes in the tub left a strong man's muscles feeling like limp spaghetti; ten sent his mind into a stupor of delight. Those who preferred the human touch (or a combination of the mechanical and the biological) learned the household included several full time healers who specialized in massage— apparently Baron Clear Water went to great lengths to ensure the well-being of his knights and to get them back on their feet expeditiously when they were injured. Of all those who made use of the masseurs and masseuses, Mistra was the most pleased—she had expected to be obliged to offer her services in this area, not to be a recipient of them.

Everyone had been attended to by evening so well that they all felt themselves deep in the Clear Waters' debt. Baron Clear Water did not see it that way. The questors had saved his child and, through her, his entire family. They were his honored guests, and he felt there was little he could offer them even should he put his entire holdings in their name, that could expunge the debt.

"You are complete strangers to us," he intoned, "yet you have been the salvation of my house and have taken great pains on our account." At his phrasing, Mistra's head snapped up. For the second time, she looked within and found a response struggling to free itself from her very soul. But again the sensation passed: the baron had spoken a word too many or a word too few or deleted or added a word to the phrase that would release that response. She frowned and shook her head to clear it of the glamor: it was fruitless to speculate about any knowledge that had been implanted subject to specific release conditions during her long period of training in the use of the Sword of Rhydderch.

The baron had a feast prepared for them that night; even with so little notice, the meal he commanded was sumptuous. Fine wine and food, accommodations that far excelled those they had left behind at the inn, and entertainments that met even Deneth's exacting standards—he provided for it all. Two days and a night of sleepless activity followed by a surfeit of amenities left no one wanting for a good night's sleep. Even Mistra slept peacefully, but she saw when she awoke that some time during the night she had taken Syndycyr's charm in her hand and not let it go.

CHAPTER 10

Baron Clear Water's Story

"Though he should conquer a thousand men on the battlefield
a thousand times, yet he, indeed, who would conquer himself
is the noblest victor. Great as is war in a just cause, the most
excellent battle is the one for the conquest of self."
—The Book of Wisdom

ND HOW IS IT," Titus, the current Baron Clear Water, asked at table the next morning, "do you suppose, that you came to be cast in the images of my dear Gwynddolyn's friends? Surely there is some will of the gods at work here." He had tactfully avoided raising the subject last night. The mere story of the abduction and rescue provided plenty for him to digest at that point. Now, after rest and refreshment, such questions and the threat of the answers they might bring came more easily to his mind.

A hale man of sixty, he had clear grey eyes that were as piercing as Sigurd's, but that contained the kindliness and wisdom the wizard had let fall by the wayside long ago in his quest for power. They were, in fact, Mosaia's eyes, a curiosity that had escaped neither man's notice. His brows were just greying, as were his moustaches and the hair at his temples.

For their role in rescuing his daughter and friends he wished to hear their story told in full. Falidia at this point had not even harnessed electricity, so fireside storytelling was an important means of entertainment, especially on cold winter nights. Baron Clear Water was always on the lookout for a new tale that he could catalogue (and possibly embellish) for later use. A final reason, a far more personal one, one more likely than the others to be important in the mystical order of things, he kept to himself till he heard the full tale.

"Take you, young Mosaia," he went on, for Mosaia had given his first name only, deleting his titles and lineage and making himself out no more than a holy warrior sworn to the service of the Falidian gods. It had been a wrench for him to refer to his deity in this way, but to have expressed his vows properly would have required the explanations they had all been at great pains to avoid last night. Mosaia was no pragmatist, but knightly courtesy bade him think first of the comfort of his host in this instance; he had phrased his responses the previous night as truthfully as he could without breaching his own sense of decorum. "You named yourself as no more than a goodly knight-errant, yet there is about your carriage nobility, and I noticed the charge upon your sword harness incorporates the tokens of my own house. Are you some long lost relative—a distant cousin perhaps?—trying to make his way in the world without benefit of the name of your house to gain you acceptance?"

An uncomfortable silence ensued during which some of the travelers looked at one another, and some suddenly found things of immense interest on the ceiling, out the window, or on the floor. "Come, come," he continued. "There is no name any of you can give that will earn my enmity or distrust after all you have done on behalf of my dear Gwynddolyn and her husband. Fear not if your houses are out of favor or brought low by circumstance or become dens of iniquity. Even if you were all highway robbers and murderers, still I would welcome you."

Mosaia, being a relative and native of the planet, supposed the others were waiting to take their cue from him. "Very well," he said at last. "But our story will sound strange to you. Do you believe, lord, that Go–er–*the* gods have all power?"

"Yes." He said it with conviction. Like all ruling barons of House Clear Water before and since, he was a pious man.

"And that there are different pantheons in other lands, pantheons that, like the ones you worship, are all good but cast in a different mold?"

"I am not unfamiliar with the premise."

He looked accepting enough, so Mosaia went on. "I am Lord *Mosaia* Clear Water. I am not a distant cousin, but a direct lineal descendant of your lordship. My friends, except for Anthraticus, come from a place called the Carotian Union, and we have, as you have guessed, I think, been sent on a quest, by their goddess Minissa. To complete this quest, we must pass seven magicked portals. These portals may transport us, as we are learning, anywhere in space and time. It is by the decree of the gods that we have come here. Do you not believe me?" The change that came over Baron Titus's demeanor prompted to ask this last. In fact, the older man's eyes had widened and his jaw had simply dropped. It took Mosaia a moment to understand that what he was seeing was not skepticism but awe. In fact, Baron Titus's entire posture spoke eloquently of both expectancy and recognition, as if he had been alerted that a predetermined battle signal, one for which he had been waiting all his life, had just been sounded.

"Fantastical," he replied, "but perhaps not as fantastical as you deem I make it out. Pray continue."

Mosaia looked to Mistra, who best knew the tale in which they had become embroiled. She told the baron the story of Eliander, the Lost Prince of Thalas, of the circumstances of his disappearance, of the way in which he represented the hope of her people. Guessing they had arrived in an era where there was no concept of life on other worlds, she followed Mosaia's lead and blended that concept into the story one thread at a time till it was clear Baron Titus had accepted it. She tried to keep the tale brief, but the baron stopped her frequently to clarify some aspect of her story. She understood the importance of some, but others that interested him especially seemed to her quite trivial. Still, in the end, he nodded as if satisfied.

"And of what type are you each?" he pressed on. "I mean, what were your titles or trades before you began this noble enterprise?"

While she had told the tale of the quest with great eloquence, Mistra turned suddenly shy, as if she and her accomplishments were of no account. "I am the third child of the Royal House of Caros—a princess with no pretense to a throne, or to any responsibilities at all! I was chosen for this quest because I'm the third child of two third children. I have some skill with maths and most of the sciences, but in real life I'm just a ballerina—that's a dancer who practices a type of formal theatrical dance."

"There's no *just* about it," Deneth corrected her. "She was the leading ballerina in a galaxy class troupe when she'd barely come of age—quite respectable and very celebrated."

She beamed at him—dance and the theatrical arts had a wicked name some places she had been, and she had hoped to circumvent a direct confrontation over whether her cherished art represented some sort of harlotry here. Deneth had just saved her the trouble of delving into it. "All Carotians are born magicians with innate powers of the mind. We learn the battle arts as a matter of course, and I can't say I haven't fought to defend my life or my friends'. And all royal children become honorary clerics of the deity to whom they're consecrated. I serve Minissa, who sent us on the quest. You have no equivalent here. All things that grow or move upon the land are her province."

"I'm a bard," said Deneth. "I think you call us minstrels here. I do a few other things well: fighting and thieving were a necessary measure if you wanted to stay alive and healthy where I grew up. My father is a minor nobleman on the world I come from, but on that world the nobility have spawned so much treachery and heartbreak we really should think up another term for the ruling class."

Mistra squeezed his hand and shot him a fond smile. "He works more poetic magic with his music than I do with all my skills combined."

Lord Clear Water smiled at that, then nodded encouragement to Habie. "I'm an orphan," she said as if daring him to make something of it. "I've had to live by my wits all my life. I guess what I'm best at is stealing, though I've done it only to help us along in our adventures since these guys adopted me. My people, the Lemurians, are born empaths who can draw strength from another mind or sort of absorb injuries from other people to heal them." She looked uncomfortable. "About the thieving bit—you can search me and my things, if you like, now or before we take off."

The baron chuckled. "Unnecessary, little thief. I trust in the judgments of the good gods."

She smiled, undone by his simple acceptance.

Torreb said, "My story is simple. I'm a priest in the service of Ereb—that's our god of justice, or of war in a just cause, as some make it out. I fight, too, if I must, though I don't like to."

"Battle lust is not all it's made out to be in epic poetry. There is wisdom in your feelings, and they do you credit."

"He's too modest to say he was on his way to being the youngest high priest of Ereb his world had ever seen when Minissa called him," said Alla. She got from Torreb the same sort of grateful smile Mistra had given Deneth. "I am of the oldest race on the face of Ereb, Torreb's home world. We are shape-changers, that is, *aranyaka* in the language of my mothers. I can alter my appearance to look older or younger, or I can completely change form to that of a beast. *I* don't think I work magic, but these others seem to think I have a knack for being in harmony with the natural world and sensing its imbalance. I can tell things that way—not true divination, but that same basic result."

T'Cru propped himself up on the table on his forepaws. "I am T'Cru, the crown prince of my people—at least, I was till I was marked by Minissa. Like Habie's folk and Alla's, we Tigroids are an indigenous race on our homeworld. Ours is a highly stratified society; one's caste is denoted by the shadings of one's coat. Our society is changing at the behest of Minissa and under the guidance of enlightened rulers like my father, but with the purity of my coat marred—you see how the mark of the goddess, the Stag of Minissa, stands out white against the black of my fur, where it appears as a shade of brown or tan on the skin or fur of all my companions—I may be prohibited from ascending my own throne." A small feline frown came to his face. "Funny—that used to matter a great deal more. I haven't thought of it in days."

"And what of you, little spragon?" Baron Clear Water asked Anthraticus, who had been perching atop his great chair at the head of the table. "I see no sign of this Stag of Minissa on you, yet you travel and quest and fight with these others."

Anthraticus's face went indigo—his way of blushing. "I, er, oh, dear, this is embarrassing. A coatl of my years should have known better, but there you are." He hopped onto the table so the baron did not have to crane his neck to see him. "We met when I—it was in jest, you understand, and I think they've forgiven me—played a small practical joke on Mistra and Deneth, who were merely bringing a gift to my queen." He forbore to mention what they had been doing at the exact moment of the encounter. "Upon a time, for the pleasure of my queen, I developed a cantrip that induces euphoria, much as I'm told your ethanol does. In fact, it seems to turn a part of the blood into whatever fermented substance would induce that state in that species. Inherent in the spell was my own race's immunity to its effect, else the worst pranksters among us could have wreaked havoc upon our small colony. And we have little use for the other intoxicants you humans use, partially because we always assumed we would be immune to *them* as well. Later, after Deneth finished his errand, he introduced me to the potions you call wine and brandy. He was called away, and I must admit I stayed and overindulged. In a drunken stupor, I curled up inside his rucksack for a nap. Next thing I knew, we were on Falidia. Serves me right, though they've been all the company a coatl—a *spragon*—could wish for, and adventure has shaken off the complacency that sets in at my age in a creature of my station."

The others variously grinned or laughed at his account, but Baron Titus still wore his look of expectancy. He did so till Mosaia said, "Oh, I'd almost forgotten. There's one more of us, in a manner of speaking. My sword. It's intelligent—well, *sentient*, anyway. As a matter of fact, it may be quite put out that I left it in its scabbard. I brought it to table with us, but I left it sitting against the wall just there at the behest of your steward. I did not wish to suggest a weapon was needed here, and it was a difficult thing to explain without telling our story in full."

"Well done," said the baron. "Pray bring it and draw it that we may become acquainted."

He said nothing but let go a resigned sigh.

"You wish not to unsheath it? I will not look at it as a token of disrespect or of offense, I assure you."

"No, of course not. It's just that, um..."

Mistra bailed him out. "You see, my lord, the sword is a Holy Retributor, forged by our god Ereb. It has proven a true and worthy companion, quite deadly to our enemies in Mosaia's hand. But it is said that Phino, our god of performing arts, took a hand in its forging as well, and maybe even Strephel. That would be our god of humor. It has, well, a histrionic streak?"

"Streak?" muttered Deneth. "It covers the entire canvas."

"The seraph *did* refer to it as 'Hand of Minissa and Ereb,'" Torreb reminded them all. "I suspect that means it has *some* redeeming characteristics."

"Then I would see it, by all means," the baron laughed, "and hold converse with it."

"All right," said Mosaia, but there was an unspoken "You asked for it" in his voice. He brought the sword to the table and drew it before Baron Titus' seat. It began instantly to tirade against them all for having left it in its sheath for so long while they enjoyed themselves. It took some minutes for Mosaia to quiet it and introduce it to their host, his ancestor and the fair Gwynddolyn's father.

Its manner changed immediately. "Forgive me, lord, for my unseemly outburst. Due to my master's oversight—" It made a noise that in a human would have meant he was kicking his master in the shins, "—I did not realize that I lay before my host and benefactor. I sense the high quality of your character. Allow me to pay my humble respects. Nay, let me atone for my behavior. Leave me unsheathed in the company of lesser weapons, I beg. Or better still, douse me in cold water and allow me to rust, just a little—"

"Enough!" commanded the baron, clearly amused rather than affronted. "Your silence will be fitting punishment for the moment, I deem." He rose and paced the length of the room twice before he spoke again. He stroked his beard and looked like a man who, seeing the miracle he has wished for all his life, is still inclined to doubt his senses. "By the gods," he muttered, "all the signs are made manifest. Can it be? Can *I* have lived to see it?" He went to the mantel above the fireplace and pressed a stone in the tilework design set above it. A panel on the upper surface of the mantel sprang open. He reached inside and pulled out a small velvet pouch. He considered it a moment longer, then turned to them.

"For some generations, it has been the custom of the master of the house to hand down to his eldest child—to the one who will become baron or baroness after him—the contents of this bag and the means to keep it secret. No reason has ever been given for their existence or purpose, but they were given to one of my forebears whilst he knelt at private prayer in our chapel. He had a visitation, or a visit from a celestial messenger, or a vision—whatever you are wont to call such things." He stopped, aware of the reverence that crept into his voice. He had discussed this but once with his eldest son, and that briefly: now here he was telling the story in full to a company of complete strangers! He looked from face to face, as eager now as they were a few minutes ago to believe his listeners would not mock what was to him sacred beyond measure for all it seemed bizarre. Seeing rapt attention rather than the most minute trace of skepticism (but then, would not holy questors know when a story, however outlandish, concerned them and their mission?), he went on.

"Well, the story goes that the messenger blessed him and praised the piety of

our family and said because of that holiness we had been chosen as the repository
of a special trust. The contents of this bag were left with the understanding that,
some day, a party of travelers would come to whom the bag should be given,
their mission being somehow tied up with it. A verse was left, by which the
party was to be known, but I confess that, until this morning, it made little
sense to me. Listen!

"They will come at time unlooked for.
Many shall they be, to the number of House Clear Water.
Pressed by need desperate,
Yet will they aid you in your direst need.
Portals they must pass, not of this world.
Two will lay behind them and five ahead.
How will you know them?
Of royal blood is she that was first chosen, third of third and third
with body and soul touched by each of the twelve Graces,
She danced for the stars before time began.
Of imperial blood the second, bound to lead his people,
Touched by the shame that is no shame to bear.
Of the blood of two kings a third, your own progeny,
warring only for the right, radiance is his adorning,
he is destined to have kingdoms fall at his feet.
Of noble lineage a fourth: cloud and mountain,
river and all sentient-kind
Are moved by the melodies of his soul.
Touched by the hand of one Grace the fifth,
A child of his kind,
His healing hands were taken from the service of many
To serve the few.
Touched by the hand of a second Grace the sixth,
A wise-woman among children
Her flesh takes many forms
From her a new race of men will spring.
Touched by all and none the seventh
Healing is in her hands
As are things belonging to others.
Spirit but not flesh is the eighth, the last of the first
His home is in abode dark and deep
A weapon in the hand of the holy
A thorn in the side of the sober.

A ninth devised his own place in the pack
Wiser than wise, older than old
Merrier than merry
Power for mischief and good are his."

He got out no more than the first line before Deneth had fished a pen and paper from somewhere and begun scribbling furiously to get down the entire poem.

"A curious verse, is it not?" Titus continued. "You perhaps understand better than I each of the references to your own selves, esoteric though they be, but I find in this verse and in your tales enough similarity that I am convinced you are the party for which my family has waited all these generations. One thing only you may not know, or Mosaia may know it if they still teach the Irfan system of numerology on Falidia in his day. The reference to the number of House Clear Water—applying Irfan numerological codes gives the name of my house a value of nine."

"*Our* number!" exclaimed Habie. "Or it is if we include Homer."

"Homer?" her friends chorused.

"The Retributor," she said as if that should explain the odd appellation. When they still looked puzzled, she went on as if explaining how to add two and two to a cadre of scientists who should have been way past calculus, "You said this seraph guy called him 'Hand of Minissa and Ereb.' HOMEr. What's that thing where you take all the first letters and make a word out of them?"

"An acronym?" Mistra asked weakly.

"Yeah, that. Hand of Minissa and Ereb. Homer."

"The acronym of 'Hand of Minissa and Ereb' would be HOMAE," Deneth pointed out.

"Well, that would be a stupid name. Look, maybe 'Homer' isn't exact, but it's pretty close. And it's better than calling him 'Hey, you stupid sword' or even just 'sword' or 'hey, you' all the time."

To that logic, they had to bow, especially when the Retributor itself said they could call it that if they liked, and that it had always rather fancied itself as a masculine rather than a feminine or gender-neutral entity.

"It would seem your paths were laid out for you long before you set out on them," Titus took up his tale once they settled that, "even yours, Anthraticus, though your coming seemed to you an accident. It may even be that the fulfillment of this quest is the purpose to which you were all born."

"It is as you once said to me," Mosaia said, directing this to Torreb.

"What did I say?" asked the priest.

"That you were surprised there were only seven of us appointed to the party when the number of best mystical significance to your culture is nine."

"And now you are," said Titus. He sat again, this time closer to the center of the table so that they could more easily see what he was about to show them. The pause he read in their faces, induced by his last remark, did not escape him. He opened the pouch with a studied reverence. Inside lay a large platinum copy of the medallion that Gunthar and Gwynddolyn had worn, the one depicting the cross within the circle and all four elemental symbols. Alongside the medallion sat a set of crystals of assorted shapes and colors.

"They are common enough items," he said, "though the platinum is quite valuable in this time period and the stones are all magical." He handled the articles one by one, as if his decision to surrender them had infused each with new meaning. He felt as if he were really seeing each of them for the first time. He knew it would also be the last; the moment for which generations of his family had been prepared had arrived. Yet, in looking at the items with which his family had been entrusted and comparing their simple appearance with the obvious worth and valor of those assembled before him, he wondered if he had been led astray and if this weren't all some great cosmic joke the gods were having at the expense of a House Clear Water grown too cocky in its own piety. "Perhaps," he suggested, "they are enchanted to appear other than they truly are?"

"Who cares?" enthused Habie, making a dive for one of the crystals. "They're pretty, and they're magical, and they're—" She burst out giggling as she grasped one of the crystals, a pale blue parallelepiped. "It tickles!" The sensation forced her to drop it, but, instead of plummeting to earth, it hovered before her. "What's it doing?"

"It's, hmm. I think that particular one makes people take to you instantly."

"We do that already," Deneth said graciously. He gave her a companionable wink.

"It'll follow you around now that you've handled it. Go on, give it a try."

Wearing a completely bemused expression, she hopped up on the table and walked a few steps. The crystal bounced along behind her like a happy puppy. She walked faster and finally hopped off the table, breaking into a jog, circling the table twice, then pulling to an abrupt halt. When she turned to look, the stone remained bobbing in the air behind her.

"The stone, at least, is made your friend," chirped Anthraticus. He fluttered over and hovered, eyeballing it from every direction his lengthy neck would allow. "Baron Titus, are these not the magical trinkets my folk call Stones of Enhancement?"

"Here we call them the Stones of Esmee, for the enchantress who first created them. I daresay in the hands of one so skilled as yourself, they would appear as trinkets. Their magic is not strong, but useful for all that. Each marginally improves some quality of the user: strength at arms, insight, memory. Consider what you think of your larcenous friend now," he added with a chuckle.

It was true! To the other questors, Habie's recklessness now seemed as bravery, her sarcasm as wit, and her quick eyes and ears the senses of the hunter rather than the assassin. To Mistra and T'Cru particularly, her markings seemed fair, far more beautiful than the most true of any of the delineated Lemurian clan markings they recognized.

The stones were seven, which suggested to them that one had been intended for each of the original (flesh and blood) questors. To Mosaia, they accorded the medallion as an emblem of his people, but, "Share and share alike," he said. He gave his own stone, one that enhanced strength, to Anthraticus (he traded it to Mistra, who had one that improved reasoning), although in his heart of hearts, he suspected that the true ownership of the medallion lay with all of them. Perhaps it had a use related to the quest that none of them had yet fathomed.

They enjoyed the hospitality of the Clear Water family for some days. Baron Titus took them riding (and running and flying) over his vast lands of rolling green hills and verdant forests. Mosaia initially resisted saying anything about what was to be found where in his own time, but Baron Titus's enthusiastic curiosity about the future of his lands won him over.

"It's not all that different," Mosaia said, wondering himself why that should be. "There are settlements and villages, and the place is more heavily farmed, but the parklands have changed little." He pointed out a spot nearby where a belt of grassland clove an expanse of forest cloven in two: the effect from the air must have been that of two butterfly wings. "There, for instance. In my day, a hamlet is there, yet it fits itself comfortably under and between the eaves of that forest, never having disturbed so much as a sapling. I like to think of my people and their land living at peace with one another, the better for them both to prosper." He caught a strange, appraising, and completely appreciative look from Mistra at this bit of news. "What?"

"I'm seeing more and more reasons why Minissa chose an outworlder for this quest," she replied with a warm smile.

She cantered off, leaving him feeling like a barbarian who had just found favor in the eyes of a young elven queen.

Baron Titus provided for the diversions each of his guests liked best. Deneth found places to attend to his music and Mistra to her dance, often together. Mosaia and Torreb kept vigils in the chapel on behalf of the quest and studied long in the library. Habie picked locks to her heart's content, with Baron Titus's complete approval. The Baron reasoned that if her gods had chosen the girl for such talents, the least he could do was to help her to hone her skills! Alla, shifted into various of her animal forms, and T'Cru spent much time in the woodlands, revivifying themselves by contact with their native surroundings. The five of them who fought with weapons not of their own flesh joined the knights of the barony at combat practice at whiles; Mistra joined Torreb and Mosaia at prayer and at their diverse studies periodically, as did Habie—a fact that surprised no one more than herself! Anthraticus peeked in on them all at one time or another, but he danced attendance on Gwynddolyn on those rare occasions when she made herself publicly available (she was evidently a very happy bride).

⁓⁓⁓

"I wonder what it all means," Deneth mused an evening later. He had transcribed Baron Titus's verse about them for later consideration from his first hasty scribblings and was now poring over it as he, Mistra, and Mosaia waited for the others. She had called them together to discuss something she would only call "a matter of great moment."

"According to this," he went on, addressing Mistra as she perched on the arm of his chair, "you existed before the One called the universe into being."

She chortled, amused both at the idea and at Deneth's attributing anything to the One. "Yeah, Deneth. I'm a goddess come among you in human form."

"It is a stirring picture," Mosaia said with a reflective smile. "I have only seen you at practice, and I can still imagine you dancing among the stars before heaven and earth were joined, giving light to the cosmos and bringing joy to the heart of what you call the One."

She dropped her eyes but could not hide the small flush of pleasure his assessment gave her. "It's poetic exaggeration, I'm sure," she said, brushing the thought aside despite the appeal of the image he painted.

"And you needn't be a goddess come among us. In the Falidian theology of my day, the Great Ones—the prophets or revelators—are said to have had an existence apart from the Creation before time began, much like your *kanami*. God in His infinite wisdom is even said to have schooled them in Heaven to prepare them for the day they would walk among us. Some feel He even determined the time of their arising. What puzzled me in the poem was the reference to Graces."

"Oh, that bit's easy," said Deneth. "Twelve Graces—twelve gods in the Pantheon."

"Our gods, too," Mistra said, chiefly for Mosaia's benefit, "were said to have been schooled by the One before the Creation came into being. And while prophets, as you know, the use of the term on Falidia ceased giving us instruction an age of the world ago, reading between the lines of the *Book of Life* and the *Book of Wisdom* makes me wonder if your prophets and our *kanami* are the same sort of being."

"Must have been some schoolhouse," Deneth chuckled. "Gods, prophets, the *kanami*... I wonder what they all did for recess, let alone class."

She swatted at him playfully. "I've often wondered if my sister were of that kin—she and my brother-in-law, anyway. You don't get heroes of their caliber who go on to rule an entire star system branching from every dynastic tree, not even in our neck of the galactic woods." She flashed Mosaia a wry smile. "Anyway, if *I* danced for the stars before time began, *you're* destined to have kingdoms fall at your feet."

Deneth chuckled. "I though you were at heart a man of peace, Mosaia, one who waged war only for the sake of the defense of your homeland. Are you planning to go home and become a warlord after we've found Eliander?"

Mosaia surprised them both with a show of extreme diffidence, as if the subject pained him and he were reluctant to discuss it. He looked at the ground and mumbled a reply—the first time either of them had heard him swallow his words at all.

Deneth and Mistra exchanged a helpless glance. How had they trespassed, and on what? "Or perhaps," Mistra said gently, feeling her way by observing the knight's response, "you will return more of a hero than ever and kingdoms will simply beg you to rule over them for your sense of justice and piety."

The knight flashed her a grateful smile—his expression said that, if she had still not found quite the right words, he appreciated her effort (and, by extrapolation, Deneth's). He looked like he would have explained further, but at that moment, Habie waltzed in. She took in the scene, ripped the paper from Deneth's hand, flounced over to an easy chair, and threw herself into it.

"Deciphering the non-rhyming rhyme, huh?" she asked, giving the poem a perfunctory scan. "Making any headway?"

"Yes," Mosaia said drily. "Mistra's been promoted to godhood and I'm going to unite my world under my own good government whether the people will or nil."

"Oh, good. That leaves me becoming a priest and Alla mothering a new race of super-beings. How Baron Titus decided this was us at all is beyond me. So, Mistra," she said, abruptly changing course, "whatcha want? Don't you know there are locks to pick and walls to scale here?"

With an indulgent grin, Mistra reached into the small satchel she had brought with her. "I suppose there's no harm in the three of you contemplating it till the others get here." She pulled out the figurine of Sigurd, noting with interest that the features that identified the mage had blurred somewhat over the hours since she had discovered it.

Their reactions were diverse but marked. Mosaia braced himself as if for an onslaught; Deneth sat forward and gave a low whistle. "Holy draffing drek!" gasped Habie.

"What is it?" exclaimed Alla as she, Torreb, and the beasts entered the room. They all but stumbled into the room together in their haste; now they entered by hugging the walls, as if the statuette had sent out giant hands of power to crowd them away from itself.

"You said that magic had disappeared virtually overnight," Mistra said, directing the remark to Mosaia. "I think this is where it went. At least, Sigurd's other two constructs, the tapestry and what I'm fairly sure was the gazing crystal, vanished into the Ether with the seraph. And this was left in his wake. I had postulated the existence of just such a repository based on comments I heard from you and from others at the inn." She smiled wanly. "I was trying to home in on it and had just started to feel I was making headway at the time the demon dropped in to say hello."

"You mean Sigurd like *absorbed* all the magical power from the earth around here or something?" asked an incredulous Habie. "And he stuck it in *there* so no one could use it?"

"*He* could use it. It strikes me now that he was enchanting those weapons very quickly during the battle, and it must have been he who gave the demon his extra arms—quite a number of feats to pull off simultaneously! But possible if one has a repository of power like this at his disposal."

"Lethal! We can take it with us! Use it to whup Syndycyr if we run into him again!"

"*Can* we?" she asked archly. "Tuhl hinted that the Orbs of Caros and Ereb— and so on—powered the unique talents of *all* of our people—my access to the Art, your empathy, Alla's ability to shape-shift. Can any of *you* draw on the power that lies hidden in this thing?"

While the others either tried or sought for a way to make the determination, Mosaia said, "I think it matters not if we *can* draw its powers. They were stolen from the substance of my home world, and I think here they must remain."

"Well, no problem then, right?" Habie said with forced cheerfulness. "Mistra can just put it back where she found it and..." She looked around and saw little beyond a sea of morose stares. "No?"

"In *this* day," Mosaia said slowly, "there *are* sorcerers of Falidian stock who can draw the power, or so I suppose. But as Sigurd fell to the lure of its power, so would others. A repository of magical force like this will be a danger to my entire world as long as it remains within its precincts."

A brooding silence ensued.

T'Cru first moved to break it. "The options, then," he reasoned, "would be to learn the means of releasing the power back to the earth from which it came, or to turn it over to some authority who could keep it eternally safe from misuse—or to find the authority who would have a chance of learning that means of release, I suppose."

Another silence.

"What would your counsel be?" Mistra asked Mosaia as if she heard in his silence a counterproposal forming.

"I think T'Cru has the right idea when he suggests an authority who could release the energy or find a way to keep it safe forever. My counsel would be to turn it over to the church."

"They don't exactly *have* a church," said Deneth. "It's not like in your day when they have a monotheistic creed but just can't agree on the dogma or who the most recent prophet is. They have four separate deities. Whose priests could you turn it over to without insulting the clergy of the other three?"

"I think," Torreb said, brightening, "that that is not an insoluble problem. Haven't any of the rest of you heard anyone swear by something called the Quatrain Godhead? I think at heart, earth, air, fire, and water are just aspects of one supreme deity, much as the members of our Pantheon are aspects of the One." He grinned. "Perhaps if their high clergy do not yet meet as a body, it's time they began. We can give them the problem of the disposition of this very figurine to begin their deliberations, just to get the ball rolling. I've made the acquaintance of the house priest here, a bright-eyed little fellow who serves Aquea. Perhaps he can introduce us to the local religious brass."

"Us?"

"All right, me. If there are formalities I overlook or taboos I violate, he will react more favorably to me as one priest to another."

"It's your trinket, Mistra. What do you say?"

She flashed Torreb an approving smile. "I say my 'trinket' is in good hands." She looked to the rest for any sign of objection. Getting none, she took the figurine and handed it to the priest.

Seven days after their adventures with Sigurd, one reason for Baron Titus's indulgence of them became clear. He gave his daughter and son-in-law a proper wedding feast complete with ball and tournament. No one from that time seemed to regard this as an unusual length of time—it took half that time for him to get word to his neighbors and the rest of the family about the events that had transpired. The mail service being what it was in those days, he kept the messages brief and reserved a full telling of the tale for the feast.

It was a grand day. The travelers were mistaken for their counterparts as often as not; for advantage or fun, they often went along. Deneth supposed he damaged—or, at least, added spice to—the reputation of Tallin the harper by sweeping as many ladies as he could get away with off their feet. The women took turns with their own counterparts attending Gwynddolyn so friend and handmaidens could reap some of the advantages of the treatment the fêted guests were receiving. Food plain and exotic abounded, activity was non-stop, and at night there were pavilions under the stars for those inclined to prolong the day's revelries.

Mosaia called Mistra aside shortly before the tournament began. "You're the first one who hasn't had to ask if I'm Mistra or Lucia," she laughed. "Deneth even tried to assert his rank as a nobleman and compromise my virtue as a woman of subservient status."

Mosaia chuckled. "He undoubtedly knew it was you all along." And sobered. "Before, I would have thought that in character, but now that he is here—" He tapped his brow. "—I see he is too fundamentally decent a man to toy with a woman so." He grinned again. "And you are far too intelligent and insightful a woman to fall for such a transparent masquerade." And tapped his brow again. "Lucia is not here," he explained. "And—oh, bother!—I see the resemblance, but my kinsmen are fools who cannot see how much brighter is your spirit, or how much more beautiful you are." He tried to avoid her gaze as he said it, but her response forced him to look up.

She smiled fondly and regarded him for a long moment, then, reaching up to brush a lock of hair back from his face, said, "I would have said the same of you and Gunthar, radiant though he is with new-married bliss. But you did not bid me come away that we could compliment each other till the skies fall."

"No," he said with a smile like summer. "'Twas but an unlooked-for and delightful bonus." He was suddenly all business. "You said once that, as you and Deneth have a language in common, so do you and I. Therefore I ask you this as the only person here I *can* ask who will understand. I wish to try my skill in the tournament, but I wished to do so anonymously. Gunthar is more than willing that I should use his armor, as we are much of a size and he has no use for it—he has no wish to risk injury to himself, to his body *or* his pride, by competing during his honeymoon!"

"I see. Then Gunthar and the others would see Gunthar's armor and standard and suppose that it is you carrying them, and you wish to give them a surprise."

He smiled with a shyness she found endearing. "And for other reasons. I wish to be tried truly, and maybe the other knights will pull their strokes for an honored guest, one who might be identified by his own arms and armor, or for Lord Gunthar, if they are not in on the ruse and so think I am he."

"A matter of honor," she laughed. "Of course I'll help you. What can I do?"

He beckoned her to the private stable used solely by House Clear Water. In one of the stalls stood a chestnut destrier, even-tempered but vigorous. A set of full plate armor stood there: both the breastplate and the shield had the distinctive blazons of a rising sun. Mistra handled several of the pieces, appraising with the eye of an expert. "These were made by a master smith," she commented.

"I hoped you would know somewhat of arms and armor."

"My father is a king, after all. We may favor our personal shields in real life, but we learn about such things in our courses on heraldry and the older forms of combat. I think the reason we're actually made to fight a time or two in armor like this in school is so we appreciate the lack of encumbrance the force shields give us! Now, did you need an esquire to help you gear up, or do you need me to do something about the blazons and things?"

"The blazons, certainly, and, well, if you were to help me dress and arm, my secret would be the better guarded." His eyes twinkled.

With a conspiratorial wink, she turned to the armor and shield. She considered a moment, then flicked a finger against both the breastplate and shield. The design on the breastplate winked out of existence; the shield went completely black. Both were still clearly of the finest workmanship; they merely lacked identifying features. At a wave of one hand, the destrier became a Pinto rather than a chestnut. Mosaia cleared his throat, and she turned. "Did I do it wrong?"

"I thought the vergescu might be better than the black for the shield," he suggested.

"But you are no unblooded knight out on his first adventure," she protested.

"In a sense I am. I have never jousted, never been in a tournament at all, really."

"But you..." She trailed off. But he what? Maybe she was making assumptions about present day Falidia that were unwarranted.

A trace of melancholy came to his eyes, though he smiled understanding. "Nor have I ridden much on errantry. My homeland has been at war for most of my life, so I am blooded in truth, but—well, tournaments and errantry are pursuits for a time of peace that has only just come upon us."

"So you have yet a third reason for entering," she mused. She held him with her eyes a moment, evaluating. He did not so much go up in her estimation as flesh out.

He nodded. "'Tis a way to test whether, in the pursuit of victory, I have lost my ability to wield my weapons elegantly and to keep foremost in my mind the courtesies of the field that should be the adornment of any sworn to chivalry. In war, one hacks and slashes and does what one must to protect one's men while securing a humane victory."

His noble sentiments evoked in her a fleeting wish that he would ask her to run away with him, a desire in herself to throw herself at his feet and beg to be the mother of his children. In body as well as in temperament, he seemed destined to become a hero out of legend. No wonder women fell all over themselves trying to attract his notice!

Waving off the flight of fancy, she flicked another finger against the shield so it went from black to unadorned white, then helped him into the cumbersome armor. They worked in companionable silence for the most part, both getting the strange feeling they were marking the steps of a dance they had learned in isolation but practiced in the full knowledge that one day a partner would arise, or that they had gone through this series of movements together many times before. Only occasionally did she stop, knowing from even her minimal experience how an improperly sized bit of armor could slow one down or limit one's range of motion or tire one needlessly with fighting against its burden. She adjusted a strap here, a joint there, occasionally invoking a little cantrip to do it. By the time she finished tailoring, the armor might have been made to his own measure rather than Gunthar's. He flashed her a grateful smile as he took a few practice swings with Gunthar's sword.

What she hadn't a clue about was the actual squire's role in the tournament—what weapons got handed when, and how. Against type, she posed as Lucia and pulled out the frilliest of her flirtatious mannerisms to secure Mosaia a proper squire who would help and not hinder, one who bought her story of Mosaia being a long lost friend from the temple of Erda, god of earth, whom she had known from her days in the temple of Ignea. She let Mosaia kneel and kiss her hand, then took her place in the stands.

He watched her go, knowing she had pressed something into his hand but not looking to see what till he turned to go to the lists. He threw his head back and laughed when he knew it for the last article he needed to complete his disguise: a strip of cloth he might use for a token. But he sobered as he showed it to his *pro tem* squire and noted its delicacy and design. Made of scarlet gossamer, it bore, blazoned on it in gold thread, a rampant ki-rin, the central element in her personal sigil.

"A king's daughter, indeed," he murmured as his squire fixed the token to his helm.

CHAPTER 11

Who Passes the Portal?

"When I sojourned on Earth, I happened on the writings of a
wonderful female mystic who, for my money, out-mystic-ed
anyone Caros has ever produced. She said things like 'When
you are showing off your spiritual goods in the worldly market,
they should be things which your fellow men cannot display'
and 'How long will you keep pounding on an open door
begging for someone to open it?' If we had been able to find
her, I would have given up trying to make the universe safe for
constitutional monarchy and settled down to be her disciple."
— Mistra bas Carthanas

FROM MISTRA'S JOURNAL
It was nearly midnight when I found Mosaia in the deserted clearing
in the wood where a bardic circle had been held earlier. His soul was like
a beacon guiding me, that's the only way I can describe it. If he had been lost
in the pathless wood or had somehow conveyed himself to the other side of the
planet, still I would have been drawn directly to him.

He had been completely, utterly, almost ridiculously victorious in the
tournament this afternoon, yet he was in a strangely pensive mood when I
found him. Not sure if he was aware of me, I leaned against a tree across the
clearing from him and attempted to look so casual he would know it was an act.

"I don't pretend to understand you," I finally said, just to announce my
presence, "but I'm enjoying immensely the mental gymnastics I'm going
through, trying."

A rueful smile, but he refused to meet my eyes. "And what would you like
to understand?"

"The way you courteously struck your opponents from their horses,
courteously dismounted, courteously waited while they re-armed, courteously
proceeded to trounce each of them in hand to hand combat, each with his own
choice of weapons, and let's not forget the way, after all that, you evoked such
adoration they offered you their undying loyalty to a man. And then you let
Gunthar take all the credit."

"Oh, my reasons were many and varied," he said. "Gunthar is a worshipful man. Perhaps I wished to give him a wedding present that increased his honor in the eyes of his bride and kin and left him a little re-enfranchised after he suffered so cruelly at Sigurd's hands. It was not easy for *me* to be Sigurd's captive, and I was not the man who bore the brunt of his rage for trying to make off with the woman for whom he lusted. And really, it was the only instance in which I could ethically get some amusement out of having traded places with my double." He was clearly referring—amiably—to the way Deneth was out adding to Tallin's reputation with the ladies of the barony (not sure if that means giving him more status or more notoriety, but both men seemed to be enjoying the ruse the last time I ran into them).

"Anything else?" he asked. I crossed the clearing to stand over him and brushed a stray lock of hair from his face before I replied. His eyes in the starlight were a marvel, a sea I could lose myself in for an age of the world.

"The way you've been left unembittered by years of war." I think I hit that note that had more typically been coupled with the words "I love you" when I'd spoken them to Isildin and Pezeshka. "The way you think of your Father God as loving parent rather than capricious warmonger, and think the best of everyone you meet."

He took my hand and drew me down next to him, and then he was brushing aside stray strands of *my* hair. He didn't ask aloud and he didn't send the words into my mind, but I knew he was asking *Can I trust you? Do I* dare? And I swear I'd experienced moments of intimacy with my consorts that were less private and fraught with tension.

He must have found what he needed in my eyes, for the next moment, he was speaking. "Where to start," he mused. "I did not claim the victory publicly because it was enough that *I* knew."

"Knew what?" I asked.

He sighed and looked solemn (and oh! does solemn look good on him). "I told you I wanted to be tried truly. I wanted to know that I could still fight with some grace and elegance and that, when my life was not in danger, I could resist the expediencies brought on by the fog of war. I guess I learned I was capable of a little more than hacking and slashing."

Well, duh. He'd managed to stand as many as ten opponents at once this afternoon, and he wasn't actually defeated—they just sort of gave it up as a lost cause when he was still on his feet after ten minutes.

It took me a moment to frame what I was trying to ask next. I came up with the remark that I felt that, after all that effort, he was acting almost frightened by his victory. He asked if that was the bond talking. Actually, he asked, "Is that...?" and trailed off and touched his temple.

"That, and observation," I replied. "It certainly isn't logic." We laughed together at that: I know it still puzzles him mightily that Carotians can combine logic and passion and a profound sense of the mystical all in the same package.

"On this quest," he said, "we go to look for the one who will provide the best hope of uniting your people. At home, many of us look for the same thing, but we look for two figures: a Prophet Whose teachings will at last unite the whole of Falidia and a king who will be the greatest exponent of those teachings. It is said that their coming will be heralded by a time of turmoil unprecedented, by war and pestilence and bloody revolution. You ask why I am not made bitter by my years on the battlefield. It is because I see war in that light, that it is not just hardship but a sign that those times are upon us. I believe I may have lived to see that time spoken of by the prophets of old, by the very Lord I serve. In fact, I believe that at least the holy soul who is the Supreme Prophet of my world may be alive and living somewhere on Falidia even as we speak."

I can barely find the words to describe the effect his assertion had on me, or to sort out the thrill of the intellectual interest from the sense of wonder. Chills swept me as if not Minissa but the One Herself were about to manifest—and in a sense, She was. I recalled the words of an ancient text regarding the Great Ones who appear in the noble form of the human temple and suffer and sacrifice to free sentients of their bondage: "We, indeed, set foot within the School of inner meaning and explanation when all created things were unaware. We saw the words sent down by Him Who is the All-Merciful, and we accepted the verses of God, the Help in Peril, the Self-subsisting, which He presented unto Us, and hearkened unto that which He had solemnly affirmed in His tablet... And We assented to His wish through Our behest." Here was an irrefutable demonstration of the way the One cared for Creation, for every individual soul in it, of the way She laid down a Divine Plan for the entire cosmos before Creation itself came into being. To feel through the aegis of the bond the hope, the profound awe and sense of reverent joy that this one thought brought to Mosaia's heart: it was as if that joy were my own. And that brought tears to my eyes.

"I pray daily that I am right and that I may do Him service in my own way when I return," he concluded. "Do you see the source of my fear now?"

I frowned and shook my head. The future is always born in pain on a world as young as Falidia, and I told him I thought his Prophet could only benefit by having a battle lord as pious as Mosaia flock to his banner. I certainly would have said that, of all of us, he was the closest to being the stuff of which heroes are made, less apt even than Torreb to stray from the most direct path to the Home of Homes.

"The easy victories I have won here and at home," he said, "coupled with my not inconsiderable social position, could easily lead to arrogance, to outright hubris. In my Lord's time," he said, "there were certainly those who rejected Him out of hand because accepting Him would have meant they lost their positions in the church or government of the day. Others missed the call not for fear of loss of temporal power but because they had decided ahead of time how prophecy would be fulfilled; they could not accept that my Lord fulfilled the prophecies in a way other than the one they had pre-determined, perhaps in a metaphorical or symbolic way rather than a literal one. The greater my skills become, the more I fear I will fall into one of those traps."

"It takes no sage like Tuhl to tell you that the language of faith has always been metaphor," I responded, "or that truth and fact do not always coincide. As for the rest, a truer soul I have not met." The coin suddenly dropped. "That's why you were so mortified when Deneth joked about your becoming a great warlord and having kingdoms fall at your feet. You feel you might vie with this king rather than bending the knee before him, or might demand proofs of his or your Prophet's station just to stall embracing your own convictions."

He nodded. "That would not only be blasphemy—our own Scriptures say man does not put the Lord God to the proof!—and my worst nightmare, it would mean I was working to delay the unification of my entire world. And there are days, Mistra, when I think only unity under one government like Caros has will save my world from destruction. Most of the cultures on Falidia seem to speak of this time and of the two figures: some call them the Great Uniters and some simply The Twins, but I believe they all describe the same holy pair. Yet our disparate cultures see the differences that would divide them rather than the commonalities that would unite them. Either way, Deneth's words painted an ugly picture, one that played to my worst fears."

There seemed little way I could respond to that beyond taking him in my arms to comfort him. "I promise you this: When the quest is over for good or ill, and if you wish it," I said, "I will come with you and seek this Holy Pair with you, and I will convince as many of the others to come as will join us."

That seemed to pull him out of his funk a little. "You would come here?" he asked. "In my time? To a benighted backwater wallowing in its own spiritual gloom?"

"Mosaia, how bad can it be?" I asked. "It produced you. And even if it *was* that bad, of course I'd come."

He flashed me a very private sort of smile. "You're offering to divine or pray or research to help me in what really relies on my making a leap of faith."

I punched him lightly on the shoulder. "No, what we'll really be there for is to pound you till you come to your senses if you feel you've found one, or both, and then deliberately turned away."

His laughter came like a rubber band snapping, the outrushing of a deep well of mirth that swept me along in its current. As it felt good to discuss matters so close to his heart, it felt good to laugh together. To have someone to whom you can open your heart and with whom you can then laugh like children is a rare and precious gift.

I wondered what he could read in my face just then. Probably a combination of "You're too good to be true" or "Where have you been all my life?" or simply "Please may I be the mother of your children—and the longer and harder we have to work at begetting them, the happier I'll be." And my look must have engendered a response, for he looked at me oddly and suddenly said, "What?" As in, "You are looking at me in a way I can't quite fathom—and I hate it."

Even working out what my expression might have been suggesting, I had to think to frame it in a way that would come out coherently. I had admired Mosaia for many things during our short acquaintance, but this show of reverence and piety in discussing his world's twin Redeemers had gone straight to my heart as no mere show of raw intellect could. I had never really thought of piety or reverence for the divine as a quality that could pique my interest. Yet in Mosaia it seemed to blend with all of his other fine qualities—indeed to crown them—like a rich icing on an already mouth-watering cake. Neither of my consorts had lacked for faith, but neither conceptualized it as the center of his life in quite this way. *Odd,* I thought, *to be shown the nature of my own heart by an outworlder who worships a Father God!*

"I'm grieving what is nearly the worst loss my people can endure," I finally got out, "and yet you've shown me exactly where my heart is likely to lead me should I choose to give it again." I laughed at the absurdity of it. "I'd never thought of piety as a stimulant of desire." It seemed to take him a moment to register what I'd said and during which I feared I had offended him, and then we were laughing like raucous children again. I know he didn't take it as a come-on, nor had I meant it to be. Between us, we could have given a dozen reasons beyond my loss and his engagement why even considering acting on the warmth that had arisen between us was a stupid idea. We're just too different. Our *worlds* are too different. Falidia abjured as evil the very Art and Disciplines we hold sacred, for the love of the Pantheon! And I think that, while our moralities seemed very similar on paper, his world's left a certain amount of latitude for hypocrisy.

"I have known men who have availed themselves of the favors of a willing woman," he told me, "and then abjured her, saying they had lost all respect for the woman, when I think who they hated in truth was themselves, for sating an appetite it was not meet to sate, and for debasing another human being to do it."

Well, I couldn't argue with that! Still, it seemed to point up a basic difference in the way our cultures approach relations between the sexes. I'm not sure the chaste women in their culture are supposed to enjoy themselves even with their legal partners, where we are taught to give and receive pleasure as part of our adulthood training at home. To do less, to withhold oneself or not to find joy in union, is to violate the sanctity of Minissa's Gift to us. And no one would make an overture with the thought that it was the other's job to call a halt to the proceedings!

Yet I think we both realized that, as Deneth and I had needed to get our bearings after that insanity in Tuhl's wood, Mosaia and I needed to get our bearings after our little interlude in the dungeon. Through the bond, I caught an echo of his thoughts about me: *a companion whose own best interests are mine, a friend who could no more seduce or compromise or even vamp a man than she could slice open a vein for the sake of frivolity. A truer heart I will not find, though it professes faith in my own God and is sworn by those self-same vows I took upon myself long ago.* That was a heady enough assessment, but I heard him add this: *Yet she is a woman all the same, and in the company of no other have I ever been so sharply aware of my own masculinity.* That took his assessment from mere heady to completely dizzying. Well, I really had tried to look nice today: my hair was loose, Lucia had waved it for me and set tiny flowers in it, and I had found this lovely, flowing azure gown that bloused in all the right places. Maybe that helped. Still, a dancer is not used to getting unqualified remarks about how womanly she looks on a daily basis.

"I actually sought you out so we could talk about what to do about Anthraticus," is what I said.

And "I know," is what he said.

And we did, but not till the moon had come and gone and the stars were beginning to fade in the pre-dawn light.

The next morning found Mosaia kneeling, keeping prayerful vigil for Torreb as the priest prepared to divine an answer for them about Anthraticus. That had been the upshot of his discussion with Mistra—when they had finally gotten around to discussing the problem. They both felt the poem presented to them by Baron Titus gave them a fairly clear message that fate—or the Universe, or the gods, or the One—had decreed the spragon continue on with them. Indeed, it seemed to suggest that his participation in their quest had been fated, perhaps from the moment his soul came forth from the Void. Unfortunately, their discussion left them with one insurmountable and somewhat frightening question: what if they had misinterpreted? What if the poem simply meant that Anthraticus was meant to make it to the Falidia of the past but to go no further? They had still seen nothing that looked like the Stag of Minissa anywhere on his scaly body.

"We need to gather as much information as we can," concluded Mistra, "and then present it to him and let him make the choice."

"And if that information is metaphysical rather than physical?" Mosaia used.

"Metaphysical may be all we have to go on."

Deneth being busy enhancing Tallin's reputation and the rest having called it a night, they waited till morning and went their separate ways, he to find Torreb and she to find Alla. The two men would use their priestly callings to divine what they could; the two women would use their woodland skills and the Portal Stone to try to pin down the location of the Portal. They hoped not only to find it but to see if the Portal itself would offer further guidance.

When Mosaia tracked him down, Torreb had been finishing up his morning prayers in one of the small prayer rooms that dotted the palace. The young priest had been thinking along exactly the same lines. He had, in fact, been about to direct his footsteps to the Clear Waters' private chapel. Mosaia saw this as a confirmation of his and Mistra's decision: he himself had been about to suggest that very chapel as a place from which to work. To him, it seemed the place had the same feel of goodly spiritual residue as that of a chapel consecrated to a saint who had in life possessed great powers of healing.

The pair set out for the chapel together. Since Torreb had enough experience with divination that he had even acquired a personal spirit guide or two, they decided that he would cast the spell while Mosaia prayed and lent his own strength to the contact.

Now he watched while Torreb first bowed his head, then opened his arms in supplication, the better to receive the blessings of his gods. He had heard the priest invoke the name of Eliannes, their goddess of meditation. He wondered at that till he recalled that the place where Mistra had given them that first awful vision of Syndycyr—the earthly vessel from which Tuhl had drawn their quest gifts—was called the Well of Eliannes. She must be their bringers of visions as well. He himself had had Sendings—visitations or inspirations—but never a true vision. He wondered if he might be about to see his first, through Torreb's eyes. He held his breath expectantly, hoping.

And whether it was his hopes or Torreb's prayers, or the whim of the Pantheon to be dramatic at that moment, or just the way the gods of the Union did things, an image began to form above the altar in short order. Of blue light it was at first, yet as it took shape, Mosaia saw glints of all the other colors of the spectrum. At first, these were distributed randomly; they had the matte quality of the best oil pigments. Soon, however, sparkles appeared here and there amidst the splashes of color. This effect, too, was random at first, but, as sparkle after sparkle appeared, each staying in place longer than the last, they organized themselves into a pattern that resembled nothing so much as the glint of sunlight on running water. This whirl of coruscating light and color presently resolved itself further into the shape of a fountain. Living lights became living waters spurting high into the air, then arcing gracefully to fall into a little pool from which issued a small cascade.

While Mosaia was still marveling at all of this, another wonder met his eyes: a face formed in the center of the column of water. It was fair and unblemished, neither male nor female. It took in Mosaia as its gaze swept the room, but its eyes came to rest on Torreb. It regarded the priest solemnly for a moment, then nodded—an indication of its readiness to begin the formal audience. Torreb spoke no word, nor did the oracle, but Mosaia found he could follow the flow of their conversation as each nodded or gestured. Mosaia felt in those moments the delicacy with which Torreb had balanced the powers he used in the casting of his spell; he hardly dared breathe lest he disturb them and disrupt the fragile web Torreb had woven. The oracle was the only thing he had ever seen that was at once so beautiful it pierced his heart and so pure and holy it stirred him to the depths of his soul, though now it occurred to him that he had found that exact blend of qualities to a lesser degree in his new bond-sister. Loath was he for this audience to end!

He watched, rapt, till the vision nodded a farewell and vanished in much the same way it had come: face to fountain, fountain to ripples on a lake, ripples to swirling lights. He thought the audience had taken mere minutes, but when he looked around, he saw that the shadows had shortened and the sunlight had brightened considerably. It must be nearing noon.

Torreb rose, then dropped onto the front pew so heavily he appeared to have had his legs cut from under him. He heaved a long sigh. His face was beaded with perspiration.

Mosaia rushed forward, knelt beside the priest, and chafed his hand. "Torreb, are you quite all right?" he asked, frowning in concern. "Are you well?"

"Yes," Torreb assured him. "I just feel like I've been bench-pressing my own weight at twenty times normal gravity for an hour, is all. Whew!" He flashed Mosaia a weary smile. "Sorry I took so long. I haven't augured all that much, but that's the guide I've gotten most of the time. Nice enough being, but very talkative. We got into, um..." He looked evasive for a moment. "Destiny and free will, and the way they interact, and the philosophical repercussions of one's actions, and I got lectured a bit on keeping my priorities straight and ordering the course of my life. I think he—or she, I've never been sure—likes me to feel I get my money's worth, so to speak, when he-or she—appears."

Mosaia laughed, although he didn't look at all certain they weren't about to be struck by a bolt of lightning for irreverence. "You and your folk speak with such candor about your holy things! What of Anthraticus?"

"Yes, well, the best I could get is that, as far as fate and the Pantheon go, it's his decision. Yes, your forebear's poem means the Pantheon chose him to pursue the Quest of the Lost Prince, but that also means he's been given the same choice as the rest of us, to go on, to stay, or to turn aside at any point along the way. He will face the same risks we do, and his departure would compromise us the way the departure of any of the rest of us would. The oracle did tip me to one thing: we were in our own present time when we were on Astra, but that's the last time we'll be in present time and real space and anywhere near our own corner of the galaxy altogether till we get home. So if Anthraticus wants to *get* home, like any of us, he'll have to ride out the quest till we find Eliander and make it back to Caros." His lips and brow puckered in thought.

Mosaia also frowned. "I like it not that he faces the choice of facing danger with us or never seeing home." He cracked a smile. "Of course, knowing Anthraticus, he'll probably volunteer to be at the forefront of any battle we fight!"

"I, um, asked it one thing more—which was where the lecture came in," he said with a rueful grin.

"Yes?" the paladin encouraged.

He raked a hand through his hair. "I—well, you may have noticed I've begun to develop rather warm feelings toward Alla. Or maybe you haven't. I know of all of us, I'm one of those least likely to go gushing all over everyone with my feelings."

"Except where obtaining new knowledge is concerned," Mosaia pointed out. His voice and smile were kind. "It is one of those things I admire most about you."

Torreb smiled diffidently and cast his eyes down. "Yes, I guess if I have a true passion, it's learning all there is to know about everything in the entire universe. And I've never been in love before—and I don't know that I am now, and Arayne knows that a woman of an entirely different species is probably not the best choice for a simple man like me to cast his eye on for his first affair of the heart. But we can't always choose. Can we?" When he lifted his eyes to Mosaia, it was with a far cannier look than the paladin would have expected from the way Torreb had been going on about his own concerns.

Mosaia thought that from another, the remark might have caused him to take umbrage. But this was Torreb, who was about as capable of guile and malice as T'Cru was of frivolity, so he said simply, "No, I suppose we can't."

"Would you like to know what my oracle said?"

"Yes, if you would care to share. I have no wish to trespass on something too private," he amended hastily.

"Well," he began, hiding a little initially behind bravado and theatrics, "when I forced from the depths of my soul the temerity to inquire about myself and Alla, the oracle's reply was cryptic—very hard to render into speech, now that I try, so I will understand if you ascribe it to no more than the ravings of a not-quite-lovestruck lunatic."

He smiled indulgently. "I think you are no more a not-quite-lovestruck lunatic than I."

He nodded and turned to face Mosaia, his eyes brightly intense with his fervor to convey the sense of the message. "All right, here it is, though it does fall a bit flat now I try to put it into words. It *did* sound frightfully profound and meaningful as the oracle delivered it, you must understand. It was something along the lines of 'order your priorities and see what you're prepared to give up for each other.' And, of course, the greatest priority those of us from the Union could have right now is the quest to find Eliander and put him on his throne. And, really, what can a poor country cleric actually have to sacrifice? I suppose I was hoping for something out of what your folk might call a fairy story. You know, 'Here, Torreb, go look under the third rock from the left by the old oak tree near the well, and you'll find a magic wand that will turn Alla into a human or you into an *aranyaka*, your choice, and you'll both live happily ever after in wedded bliss.' Still, it could have been more discouraging. I mean, I was almost expecting a clear-cut 'Torreb, you've really gone around the bend on this one!'"

"'And Mosaia has, too'?"

"No," he chortled. "If you want my opinion, if I'm half-way around the bend, you haven't begun to see the curve in the road yet. He did say one other thing of interest."

"Go on."

"It was about Mistra. Not that I asked in so many words, you understand—I don't have *that* much temerity. But the oracle said her future husband is someone she knows but knows not, although I couldn't make out if it was a pun on the archaic sense of the word 'know' or just a common usage like it's someone she knows of but hasn't formally met."

Mosaia regarded him thoughtfully for about ten seconds. "You're an insightful fellow, Torreb," he finally said. "For what it's worth, I'm not about to run off and find a way to terminate my engagement." He grunted. "I guess it would take a better logician than Mistra to figure out how to do that while we're traveling in both time and space!"

"Your Johanna," Torreb said sympathetically. "She is very beautiful."

"Yes, she is. She may be many things more, but I won't know what they are till we marry. Knowing Habie and Alla and Mistra *now* and seeing what a woman—a female of any species, I suppose—can make of herself and her life given the opportunity... It makes me wonder if it's not only Johanna who might have benefitted by living a less sheltered life! All three of them seem so skilled at what they do, I feel quite humbled in their presence. And to think of women as true comrades is totally outside my ken. Yet there they are, striving shoulder to shoulder with us."

Torreb nodded. "My true belief—with all my *vast* personal experience—" He made an outrageous face, "—is that striving shoulder to shoulder is the best way for men and women to become informed of one another's character. You see, I do have more than a little experience observing couples who are courting and counseling those who wish to wed. I think those best prepared are those who have worked together to serve the common weal rather than those who have engaged in the more superficial of courting activities like dating or walking out. In fact, on Caros, I'm not sure they date in the conventional sense at all." He chuckled. "No wonder the Thalacians don't see eye to eye with them when it comes to social norms!"

"Nor would we, I guess," said Mosaia. "Yet here are Mistra and Deneth and I, sealed in one of your people's most sacred bonds. Baron Titus told me of a saying from this time that would fit."

"What's that."

"If you want the gods to laugh, tell them your plans."

Anthraticus was, at that moment, perched on the back of Habie's chair. She, Deneth, and T'Cru were sitting in one of the castle's many salons playing poker. Gwynddolyn was there, holding T'Cru's cards for him and following his instructions rather than playing her own hand. Anthraticus cocked his head and frowned. He was quite certain a knave he saw in Habie's hand had not been there a moment ago: in fact, he was sure it had been an eight. He craned his neck down on the assumption that old age might be making him myopic rather than that Habie might in any way be cheating. He got swatted for his efforts.

"But—" he began, but a small, furry hand clamped his snout shut.

Deneth looked up sharply. "You had something to say, Anthraticus?"

"No, I guess not," he sulked once Habie had released her grip—not without a glare of warning that left him with the impression he would be in dire peril if he said another word.

"I'm in for five," Habie cut him off. She tossed in five of the local coins they had been using as chips.

"Call, if you would be so kind," T'Cru instructed Gwynddolyn. He nodded encouragement as she touched the pile of coins uncertainly.

Deneth regarded the two of them levelly, thinking as he did so that non-humans were notoriously difficult for him to read. What passed as a poker face in some cultures might appear to him as gales of riotous laughter. With a shrug, he threw in eight coins. "I'll see that and raise you three."

Unruffled, Habie called, but T'Cru instructed Gwynddolyn to fold. Habie and Deneth regarded each other impassively for a moment before he said, "OK, munchkin, whatcha got?"

Habie smiled smugly and set her cards down. "Full house, knaves up." She reached for the pot, but Deneth clapped a hand over hers.

"Uh-uh. I, too, have a full house—or a house full—of pentacles." He smirked, perfectly well aware his smirk was as charming and attractive as any of his high voltage smiles.

"You have a *flush*?" Habie exploded. "But I dealt—" She clammed up before she implicated herself.

"Yes?" he teased, his eyes bright with mischief.

In response, she folded her arms across her chest and threw herself furiously back in her chair. The pillows that had served as a lift so she could see over the top of the table went flying.

T'Cru curled up on the rug and yawned in what could have been disinterest but probably constituted disdain. "You see, my dear," he explained for Gwynddolyn's benefit, "Deneth and Habie cheat with equal facility. The outcome of each hand is a matter of who's cheating more creatively at any given moment. It's a wonder I even allowed you to play with such cutthroats." He purred as the princess scratched him affectionately behind the ears.

Anthraticus, though he had not been playing, did not take the matter with such aplomb. "You cheat at cards?" he fumed in what for a spragon must count as a roar as he circled Deneth and Habie. "*You cheat at cards?*" He fluttered back and forth between them now, and this must have passed for pacing in the spragon world. "How ignoble! How unseemly! I had been under the impression that, though you are not all nobility, you were at least honorable people." Tiny wisps of steam curled from his nostrils.

"Oh, come, Anthraticus," T'Cru said lazily. "They're only humanoids. You can't expect them to hold themselves to the same rigid standards we beasts set for ourselves."

Habie opened her mouth to respond but clamped it shut at the realization that his remarks had made her too exasperated to talk.

"Ah, come on," Deneth admonished. "We both know we cheat, and that we do it as outrageously as we can get away with without being caught. It's part of the game. Look!" He took his winnings and divided the pile into three roughly equal stacks. He eyeballed them, kept the largest, and slid the others toward T'Cru and Habie. "See? It's not the money. It's the challenge. I wouldn't cheat in a true gentleman's game, and I'm sure neither would Habie. Right?" He looked to her for support.

"I've never been *in* a gentleman's game," she sulked. "I wouldn't be caught *dead* in one."

"I was making a point."

The arrival of Torreb and Mosaia cut the argument short; Mistra and Alla came in almost on their heels. Torreb took in the scene and burst out laughing: Anthraticus had flown in a huff to the nearest window, where he perched aggressively, his back to them, and alternated between ignoring them and regarding them with complete contempt. "What's happening here?" asked the priest.

"We were cheating at cards." Deneth was the picture of insouciance.

"We were *caught* cheating at cards," Habie corrected sourly. "*I* lost, and Anthraticus is more put out than I am."

"It's the principle," the dragon announced haughtily, without turning around.

"Come, friends," Mosaia said in his best tones of reconciliation, "we have weightier matters to discuss than who cheated whom at cards."

"Sure," Deneth agreed, then added, "I bet even Mistra cheats at cards."

"I do not," she said with affected indignation. "My skills are so highly refined I don't *need* to cheat." She cast the bard a covert grin and an even more covert wink.

"Let us put our differences aside," Mosaia reiterated. He kicked his volume up a notch, and his diction, always crisp, was now so sharp that one could have cut an aged cheese with it. They all gave him their attention, some having started visibly at his tone of voice. "While some of you were wiling away your time engaged in frivolous pursuits, others of us have been taking thought for the fate of our friend Anthraticus."

"I can take thought for myself, thank you," the dragon snorted.

"Can you?" Alla asked gently. "Can you take thought for your actions without knowing whether one course or another may get you your death?"

That sobered him! He took to the air again, landing gracefully on the table in front of Alla. "Your pardon, lady. I, too, had wondered if, should you ask me to come with you, I should push on—well, push my luck with the Portals, really—or if I should impose upon the hospitality of these good people for what might amount to the rest of my life—that would be *all* of their lives, and their children's, and their children's children's, and then some."

"We took the liberty of trying to learn what the Pantheon purposed for you," said Torreb. "We knew from the outset death *would* come to any who accompanied us unbidden." If he saw the shadow pass over Mistra's face at that remark, he gave no indication. "We initially thought their mercy protected you this time, since your presence in Deneth's pack was accidental."

"More or less," Deneth said under his breath.

"But, of course, to listen to Baron Titus' recitation," said Mosaia, "you are our ninth, and your presence seems to have been fated."

"Yet each of us was given a choice when Minissa called us," said Torreb, "and you should be extended the same consideration."

Anthraticus gave a curt nod to show he was thinking, but was still put out with them.

"That excels anything we learned about *Anthraticus...*" Alla began, interpreting the nod as tacit approval to continue with her part of the story.

"...but we *did* get the Portal to materialize," Mistra offered brightly. "That's the good news. The bad news is there's a barrier like a force field across it."

"And the good news," Alla continued, "is that we think we discovered the means of defeating it."

"And the bad news," she went on as Alla fished her Stone of Esmee out of her pack and tossed it into the air, "is that all but two of us lose these little gizmos in the accomplishment of the task. When the Portal appeared, we saw that the lintel had been carved with five geometric shapes that looked remarkably like the Stones of Esmee the Baron gave us. I took mine and inserted it into the shape it fit—shed a few tears over the depth of my sacrifice, please! It clicked in as though the slot had been made for it."

"And it started to metamorphose! The lintel looked to be made of rowan wood; the instant Mistra put her stone into the slot, it began to change, to lose its luster and its color. Five minutes later, it was only a geometrically shaped protrusion made of rowan wood. The barrier is still there, but the volume of the hum that defined it began to drop off the minute the transition was complete."

Anthraticus, drawn in now despite his earlier ire, relaxed his posture in a way that said he was grateful for the actions they had undertaken on his behalf. "When do you propose to move on?" he asked, his small brow furrowing.

"*I* had hoped tomorrow morning," said Mosaia, "but we haven't had a chance to discuss it."

Gwynddolyn's mouth turned into a comely pout. "I had hoped you would enjoy the hospitality of my family's house for some days yet," she said diffidently. "But if you have an errand that will not wait, I cannot put my family's wishes ahead of that."

"We would like nothing better than to reside here in peace for some days yet," said Mistra, "but our worlds are waiting for us to save them."

In the end, they stayed several more days, and Anthraticus, with many apologies to Gwynddolyn and her family, made it known that he would push on with the questors.

"My reasons are mostly selfish," he confessed to them. "I sense wonderful adventures ahead of you—unique places, unique people. And if it is the will of the Great Spirit Dragon..." He shrugged, then turned on Deneth and stabbed a claw in his direction. "And don't you expect me to run off and play, varlet! I have more powers than any of you guess, and I would use every last one to protect any of you from harm."

CHAPTER 12

The Sword of Rhydderch Hael

"In my part of Falidia, we are told 'A good man brings forth good things out of the good treasure of his heart.' And sometimes, those good things come back to him."
—Mosaia, Lord Clear Water, on some events that transpired on old Falidia

THE EVENING BEFORE THEY knew they must set off, the house priest approached them. His manner constituted an odd blend of the sober and the diffident. He held something in his hands, but he was concealing it in the folds of his robe till the moment he knew he and the companions had found a place of privacy and security. When he had drawn them close so they formed a tight circle with himself at its center, he set the object on the table before him.

It was the statuette of Sigurd.

To a creature, everyone in the party either started or gasped.

"You're giving it back to us?" Mistra asked in amazement that was part awe and part frank horror. She reached out to touch it, then recoiled, mystified. The day they had surrendered the figurine, the facial features and other details that had made the statue distinctively a portrayal of Sigurd had begun to blur. Now the features were barely recognizable. The most that could be said was that the statue evinced human characteristics—a faceless, hairless head; arms; legs; a garment that might once have been carved in the likeness of a robe but now clung to the figures limbs as if it had been recently drenched in a downpour.

"After a fashion," replied the priest. He flashed a shy smile at Torreb. "I did as you recommended and humbly suggested a conclave among the high clergy in the district. They accepted this suggestion, and Baron Clear Water has been kind enough to host them in his great meeting hall these past few days. Ignea, Erda, Aguea, and Etherea—all were represented. I am told they had a vision." He turned to Mosaia. "Is it true, the tale I have heard, that most of you come from a different place in the cosmos, but that you, my lord, come from a time far in Falidia's future?"

Mosaia, seeing no point in denying it, nodded.

"And that, in Falidia's future, the people worship not many gods but one?"
Brightening a little, he nodded.

The priest, too, nodded, as if Mosaia's response but confirmed a belief he had held for some time. "I am told that, in this conclave, a vision unfolded in which the symbols of earth, air, fire and water appeared as separate entities, hovered above the assemblage for a moment, and then blended into one another, resolving at last into the form of the symbol your lordship bears. Many in the highest echelons of the clergy took umbrage at that, for the suggestion hung in the air like the scent of thick incense: if the Four become One so the distinctiveness of earth, air, fire, and water is lost, much of the power that accrues to them as priests and priestesses of the individual deities will be lost. Yet there were those in that august assemblage who saw it as a portent, who believed that it was a sign of what many had long believed, that Ignea, Erda, Aguea, and Etherea were ever only aspects of a supreme deity who rules above all, and that the time was coming when this doctrine of the essential unity of the godhead would be proclaimed. And did you not hear the commotion last night? At the setting of the sun, a new star arose to take its place in the heavens. I beheld it, as did a goodly number of the household and the conclave, yet there are those who believed it to be an ephemeral phenomenon—a comet, maybe, or a shooting star with a longer life expectancy and a stranger trajectory than most.

"But before the assemblage fell to arguing about the nature of the Four—or the One—we all serve, they agreed on this point that is of moment to you. We stand—so they said—upon a cusp between one age and the next. If man's folly has grown to the point where *one* man can create an artifact that will suck the magical life out of the very earth, perhaps it is time that the use of magic be denied to man. The ability we can do little about, but the *means...*" He looked from one to the other of the company. "Is it not also true, this rumor that you travel, on your quest, from place to place through the aegis of portals that transcend time and space?" He waited till he got a few nods before he went on. "The conclave's decision was that the church as it stands is not capable of managing this engine of sorcery that was once turned to evil use and might be so turned again. Nor can they find a means of releasing the power back into the earth. A great and powerful mage, maybe, could do it, but to follow the course of allowing such a one to manage the artifact would require first that the conclave seek him out and then that they pray with all their strength that he would not simply take the artifact and make use of it for his own dark purposes. The thought of unlimited power has done that to many a kindly one before this—Sigurd himself was not an evil man in his youth.

"It is possible that, if the time has come for the church to be renewed and a new doctrine to be preached, that the One Who arises to do so will give us the means of dealing with this thing—that is *my* belief, and that of many who think that a new day may be at hand. But even those who believe know the time of that One's arising may be years in the future, and not all could agree that the time has come for such a One to arise. Some doubt that another *will* arise and feel that revelation is complete with the prophets who spoke of the Quatrain Godhead. So not all could agree on a way of handling this artifact that involved leaving it in this world. Therefore, they turn to you good people—favored of your own gods, *marked* by your own gods—and beg you to take this engine of evil with you into the interstices of time and space, that the burden may go and remain forever beyond the grasp of my folk. Will you assume this task on behalf of our world?" He looked at the sea of diverse faces, mildly but with sincere hope.

A silence ensued, during which nearly every one of the companions at some point thought all the rest looked to him or her to speak on behalf of the party. But there seemed little room for debate: implicit in their decision to turn over to representatives of the dominant church this repository of such extraordinary power had been the commitment to abide by the clerical body's decision.

"We shall see to its safe disposition," Mosaia said at last, though it was Mistra who reached for the statuette and placed it with her own belongings to guard it till they came to the interspace.

❧❦❧

FROM THE JOURNAL OF MOSAIA, LORD CLEAR WATER:

That evening I went out for myself to see this star, this new body of light that had arisen to take its place in the heavens. And there it was, visible for all to see who would. Neither comet nor meteor, but a star so bright it cast pale shadows. *Could it be?* I wondered. Much has been made of the impossibility of establishing the facts surrounding the One who first brought us the doctrine of the one good God. Those of the Orthodox Church go so far as to say that He did not bring the doctrine but merely refined it, that the Law existed in His day and that He only tried to boil it down to an ethic like the one espoused by Mistra's people. No matter. All agree that He was born under a star like this, in this time whose events have been blurred by the passage of time and by the willing misdirection of the fathers of the early church. Now I understand why they would have moved to obscure the facts such as they were—such as I and my good companions have discovered them to be. But for our intervention, Falidia would have become a different world, a world forged in the image of Sigurd the Magician—and what shape would that message of essential goodness and light have taken then? How long would it have taken to take root? What person not directly involved with our adventure would have believed that it was no pious Falidian of his day—not knight, not priest, not goodwife—who spared my world such a fate but a troupe of outworlders and time travelers, none of whom owned this concept of a Quatrain Godhead, all of whom journeyed here upon another errand entirely.

"It is curious," Mistra said to me as she joined me in my observation of the star. "On Thalybdenos, attainment to facility with the Art was looked on as having been a sign of the maturity of my race—well, of the best folk my race produced. On your world, it seems to have been a sign of man's innocence." She cast her eyes to the heavens. "Was not the One it is your privilege to serve, born under just such a star as this?"

I nodded. "Would that we had not purposed to move on tomorrow," I said, for a great desire had arisen in my heart to make the journey to the village where He is said to have been born, and to do Him homage.

"You would travel to the place of His birth, I think, on foot, in the utmost poverty, and across vast distances. I think you would crawl on your belly stripped to the skin were the way made entirely of ground glass." Her voice, as always when we discussed matters of the spirit in which our cultures differ, was sympathetic.

"Would that I had realized that the time of our arrival coincided so closely with that most blessed Event. I would have struck out the moment we saw Sigurd and his lair destroyed to find the place. If you and the others were not depending upon me, keeping me from casting my life away frivolously, I would say I would dare all dangers for the sake of a single glimpse of Him, for one look or one touch of His tiny hand, though He be newly born rather than come to the flower of His manhood and the effort cost me my life. Yet we all know that the time has come when we must move on if we are to come to Eliander before Thalas writes its own doom."

"You truly believe He has been born and that you know in what place you would find him?" she asked with surprising earnestness.

I nodded.

She nodded in sudden decision, as if after a long debate with herself, or as if at the direction of another will—that is the only way I can describe it. Then she gave me what I can only describe as a cryptic smile. "Such faith should not go unrewarded, not when it is coupled with such an overwhelming sense of responsibility." And she reached for my hand.

I do not know if what happened next was real or not, for when I came to myself completely, the sun was rising and I found myself in my own bed in

Palace Clear Water. Yet when Mistra took my hand, the balcony upon which I stood seemed to dissolve around me. Without a word passing between us, I knew that Mistra was somehow supplying the magical force to bring me face to face with my heart's desire and that I had but to tell her where lay the object of my search. She was the engine that powered the vessel and I was its rudder; she was the raw, driving force to which I gave direction. And I steered truly, led forward first by the star and then by the sense of the Ineffable as we neared the rustic surroundings into which a King was being born. Were we borne aloft? I know not. Did we merely step through a gate in the Ether? I know not that either. I recall the wind rushing past my face and the sense that we trod the spaces between the stars, yet the journey seemed to take no time. But as we traveled, I had the distinct impression that others of the company had joined us.

We lighted in a dusty street without sign or lamp to light our way, yet I have never been so sure of my steps. We might have been shades one and all for the notice we garnered from those in the street, yet when we came to that sacred, snow-white spot, all were aware of us—mother, father, child; shepherds, beasts, and the few nobles and priests who had understood the Sign and its significance and made the journey here before me. My friends hung back: this was the savior of *my* world, they seemed to be saying. This was my moment to bask in His naked glory, and it seemed fitting to them that I tread the last few steps of our path alone. Yet I know behind me they knelt in homage—those dear creatures, servants of another aspect of the Divine who venerated this manifestation of His glory from afar.

And I, the least of His servants—indeed, the least of men who walk upon the green earth of Falidia—dared approach. One step, two steps, a dozen, and then I was falling to my knees before Him and weeping as if my heart would break, pouring out for all to see the sorrow and longing in my soul (yet I felt from friend and stranger alike not scorn but only infinite understanding of the profound effect this meeting had on me). And amid that turbulent upwelling of dross from my soul, from my very heart of hearts, I felt a touch on my head. His small hand had signed my brow in blessing, and when I dared raise my eyes, I saw that He looked upon me and smiled...

"How is it," I asked Mistra later, "that you bent the knee before this strange prophet of a strange world, before this representative of a godly construct you do not yourselves own?" And she replied with the same cryptic smile that had set me on the path of this adventure (yet now I saw the beatific reflected in the pools of her eyes), "The One before Whom I poured out my heart, the man of

Earth who set me on my road home so I could take up the burden of the quest—
his soul and the soul of the One you serve are made of the same cosmic stuff.
And of such stuff were the souls of the Revelators we had on Thalybdenos for
long eons before we knew anything of magic or the gods who walked with men,
who covenanted monarchs. Of such stuff are the *kanami* of our worlds made.
It is fitting that we do honor to all such that we meet in the cosmos." Flawlessly
logical and flawlessly mystical, as was her way, yet that show of homage remains
with me as one of the dearest, most tender, most humbly endearing gestures I
have ever beheld. Their regard for *my* Mysteries seemed at that moment to color
vibrantly their regard for *me* so I felt doubly blessed. Who, I wondered (not for
the last time on this quest that would span a dozen eons and as many parsecs)
were these people who seemed to comprehend to a far greater degree than I with
all my schooling, the essential verities of my own faith?

The next morning, they set off. Their doubles, Gwynddolyn, and Baron
and Baroness Clear Water saw them to the Portal, where they all took a few
minutes to puzzle over the geometric impressions. In the hope that pointing
out the focus of her own contribution would ease the grumbling of the others
over being forced to give up the magical trinkets they had so recently acquired,
Mistra showed them the spot where she had fit her own stone into the frame.
Her gesture failed miserably. Nevertheless, in a very few minutes, everyone
but Habie, Alla, and Deneth had surrendered his Stone of Enhancement. As
each stone became one with the lintel, the entire Portal glowed transiently.
With the addition of each successive stone, the glow lasted longer; the hum
that seemed to indicate the presence of the force field diminished. By the time
Deneth grudgingly fit his stone into the doorframe—his was the last that would
actually fit—the Portal's glow had neared permanence and the hum had sunk to
a whisper on the edge of perception.

They stood before the Portal and considered what this might mean. A full
minute of silence ensued. Finally, Habie, without consulting the others, bent
over, picked up a small rock and lobbed at the Portal. Her aim was true, or
else Fate directed it, for it entered the space defined by the Portal in its exact
center. At first, the rock looked like it would sail through that space unimpeded,
but at the last instant—just before it winked out of existence and entered the
interspace—it volleyed back. The overall effect resembled that of a ball bearing
striking an extremely elastic, extremely resilient swath of rubber sheeting.

"OK," she grumbled. "*I'm* out of ideas now."

"*Look*!" exclaimed Gwynddolyn.

At the failed demonstration, the questors as a group had taken to slouching and casting their eyes toward the sky, toward the ground, toward the wood around them—in short, they had completely stopped regarding the Portal. At the urgency in Gwynddolyn's voice, however, eight heads snapped up, down, across, and in whatever other direction they needed to go to orient once again on the source of their woes. They saw immediately the young bride was not imagining things! Amidmost, where the stone had struck, a patch of pale radiance was materializing. It tricked the eye so it was difficult to determine if it was a large patch being viewed at a distance or a smaller one appearing right before one's nose or even a form slipping into this world from a place in the Ether where dimension has no meaning. Whatever its size and shape, it definitely had not been there a moment ago. It shimmered in the early light like a spider web hung with morning dew.

Habie wrinkled her nose. "It's another slot—I think," she pronounced. She rummaged in her pack for her special glasses and slipped them on. She wrinkled her nose further. "But it's not shaped like my stone or Alla's, or like much of anything. Here." She pulled off the glasses and offered them to anyone who wanted a look.

Mistra, her curiosity seriously aroused by now, donned them and peered at the shimmering slot. She could see its margins peering back at her as if daring her to identify the item she had come by on this adventure that would fit the space they described. No very exotic shape this—it looked to her like an upended bullet, or like the elongated niche one could find in a myriad temples scattered across the cosmos in which stood the figure of a saint or deity. "I wonder..." she murmured. She passed the glasses along to Deneth, then dropped her pack and sought for the figurine that at one time had borne so striking a resemblance to Sigurd. Sure enough, when she removed it from the bundle of clothing in which she had wrapped it, its shape had changed again. Now, rather than looking like the wax cast from which a human figure might be detailed, it looked like the elongated lump of wax from which that same human figure would first have to be chiseled. "What do you think?" she asked, holding it up for inspection while the rest variously observed the niche through Habie's glasses and inspected what had now become little more than a nondescript lump of gold.

"It's like the punchline to a bad cosmic joke," commented Deneth.

"It is further confirmation of the reason we thought we came here," said Mosaia.

"And of the trust the high clergy placed in us," said Torreb.

Alla smiled enigmatically. "We took something from the earth on our first adventure. It seems fitting that we give something back on this one, the gold no less than the enchanted stones. It's balanced, like the principle that drove the temple."

With the aid of Habie's glasses, Mistra extended the figurine and manipulated it into place. As the lintel had done with the Stones of Esmee, the force field seemed almost to reach out to embrace the item that completed it. The shimmer that had been little more than a distortion like a heat curl coruscated as it took the gold to its heart, waxing in grandeur till it became a light too brilliant to bear unaided. Just as it reached the edge of tolerance, it flashed out and all who were there assembled really *were* forced to look away for a moment lest they be blinded. When they dared look again, they saw that both light and shimmer had gone; the hum that had characterized the persistent presence of the force field had vanished as well. The Portal itself now shone without flicker or wink.

By that time, even the Falidians had noticed a change in the feeling of the very air around them. It tingled and thrummed; had they visited the hill and the tree around which had circled those marvelous horses at the very beginning of the companions' adventure here, they would have likened the two sensations to one another. With one significant difference: where that impression of the throb of life had been permanent and connected with the existence and growth of the tree, this one would clearly be self-limiting. They knew their friends must leave them on the instant, now that the Portal had been fully activated.

The questors said rapid but heartfelt good-byes as they stepped through one by one. The last few to go took in the reaction of the Falidians as the first few disappeared. Awe came to the faces of the observers; a few registered frank shock, as if they had till that moment looked upon the entire tale of the questors and their true homes elsewhere in time and space as a fiction, a tall tale meant to take advantage of the gullible and the ignorant. Now, nearly all the Falidians made some show of reverence, kneeling or genuflecting. One or two actually prostrated themselves at the feet of the remaining questors.

And so the companions departed, singly and in pairs. Last came Mosaia, who had spent his last few moments on the Falidian side of the Portal in quiet, urgent conversation with Gwynddolyn and her father. By the time he came to the Portal, its light was beginning to flicker again. He stepped through into the tranquil wood of the interspace before the light died, but on the breeze that followed him came the sound of applause and many cheers.

"Pity we couldn't tell them we'd write," Torreb remarked to Mosaia as the knight joined them. "They are a fine people, your forebears."

Mosaia smiled in bemusement. "Gwynddolyn found a way. That's why she held me back for a moment. She had her father explain to me how to open that compartment where the medallion and the stones had been kept. She said they'd all write us letters and place them there while they live. Since the secret of opening that compartment won't be passed down now, the letters should still be waiting there when I get home."

"Not bad for a bunch of antediluvian mundanes," laughed Deneth.

"How mundane were they really at this point in their history?" mused Anthraticus. "The more I looked about me, the more I was convinced that every last one of them had *some* facility with the Art, though it was minuscule."

"That is truer than you know," said Mosaia. "Baron Titus explained *that* to me as well in our final moments. 'How is it,' he wondered, 'that you retain the gift in your time when we are being cut off from the very means of making magic in this age?'"

"So our deliberations over the disposition of the statue went less unobserved than we had hoped!" chuckled Torreb.

"I think there was no eavesdropping, really. A house priest is, after all, responsible in some ways to those he serves, and Baron Titus was a man of great perspicacity. When I was silent a moment, he said, 'Let them turn to the Quatrain Godhead if they want magic—that's what some of the high clergy are saying of this decision to rid the world of the power. Have you somehow regenerated the powers we are losing by turning to your gods in the future?' I could but nod. I had not realized the healing powers of priest and consecrated knight in this time period were but an orientation in discipline, much as the skill of the Erebites is, that the discipline itself was no different in substance than Sigurd's having summoned his demon or enchanted weapons to throw against us in the fray. It gave me pause! But I think it gave the Baron hope, that such useful magicks as the healing arts were not gone from his world forever."

"After that business with Sigurd," observed Torreb, "I should think it would be a relief to learn those powers would again only be wielded at the behest of church and deity."

"Do you think they understood about the star?" Mistra asked dreamily.

Mosaia nodded. "I was hard put to decide whether or not I was tampering with the future if I told them all I knew. House Clear Water is said to number disciples of my Lord among its forebears, but whether that means (as much of this adventure has meant) that such events came about through my direct intervention or not, I was unsure. So I commended their attention to it and urged them to contemplate their own Scriptures and the sentiments of that landmark conclave of clergy we instigated and left it at that."

"You left them with one thing more, I think," said Alla.

"What's that?"

She smiled serenely. "The light that came to your face in the night. It has never really left you."

They found themselves in the same green, growing place they had come to when they had left Astra. At least, if it was not exactly the same place, it was of the same sort. "A world between worlds," Mistra tried to explain it when she got back to Caros. "Growth was there, and life, and healing, but other than that it seemed like nothing ever really happened. But that doesn't describe the effect of being there, not by a long shot."

This time, not having Anthraticus' or Alla's well-being to worry about, they took advantage of the place and stayed for several nights—if, indeed, "nights" was not a misnomer. The sky lightened and darkened much as it did on their worlds of origin, but never did the companions have a clear sense of time actually passing. In this environment of timelessness, the interspace demonstrated its finest magic. Their physical wounds had mended since Sigurd's downfall, but many of the party had suffered subtle wounds of the spirit that could find no healing in the mortal world. In the interspace, those wounds not of the body fled and troubled them no more.

On what they knew would be their last "night" there, Mistra worked a wondrous magic for them. Of the eight of them, she alone had been vouchsafed a clear and lengthy look at the Prince they went to rescue, and that in a single vision long ago. The rest had been afforded a brief glimpse of the Prince lying on his woodland bier while they sojourned in the wood of Tuhl the Loremaster, but Anthraticus had never had the benefit of a single glance. Now, as they sat lazing around their campfire after dinner, she took the Tree, the holy symbol she carried secured to her wristband, between her fingers, rubbed it as if some of its substance could be worked free, then gestured as though she were casting something into the fire. And, indeed, those who were paying attention thought they saw a fine silver dust leave her hand. Deneth was playing an old Thalacian folk tune on the lute—something in an exotic and mournful mode that might have been Phrygian. Somehow, it seemed to the rest that it became part of her magic, or fueled it, or she may have only been waiting till he could set the mood properly.

"Look!" she said softly. The flames billowed up and out, paling till they gave way to an image. At its heart lay a wood much like the interspace, within which sat a structure much too beautiful to be a crypt, yet this was how she described it. It had been constructed of a gleaming white stone that reminded them of the stuff from which the Portal Stone had been cut. Carved upon it were fine scrollwork traceries, abstract designs that enfolded a myriad bas-reliefs that told of the Exodus and the founding of the three realms that had become Caros, Ereb, and Thalas. Inside on a bier of the same workmanship lay Eliander. His buckskins matched his tawny coloring, so that, with his build being much like Mosaia's, his aspect was somewhat leonine. His face was very fair, yet, even in repose, it spoke of an appealing combination of wit, kindliness, and solemnity. The spellcasters could sense an innate power emanating from him, the sort that could cast worlds from their orbits—or ignite hearts grown cold from the ravages of a planet too long at war with itself. He wore a wristband like Mistra's from which hung a medallion set with the token of the House of Thalacia—a two-headed serpent, its necks crossed so its heads faced outward. Inside the circle formed by the snake's body lay what must have been his personal sigil, a high-headed harp.

"Lethal!" breathed Habie with more reverence in her voice than the remark suggested. "Lethal," she repeated for effect, but her voice had sunk to a whisper.

"Do you find aught in him that would move you to swear fealty?" Mosaia asked Deneth. His own eyes suggested that, had it been necessary, he himself would have sworn allegiance to this alien king and followed him into the Maw of Hell itself.

Deneth, clearly bemused, kept playing but nodded once. A silence fell while the eight of them contemplated the image. It lasted perhaps a minute, then fizzled like a wet firecracker.

"Sorry," said Mistra, embarrassed by the spell's inelegant finish.

"Nothing to forgive," Deneth said with a reassuring smile. "Much to thank you for, in fact." He winked at her, and she grinned amiably.

"Might we see the sword again?" asked Mosaia. "Or is it best kept hidden?"

"It is the right of any of you to ask at any time," Mistra said formally. She pulled the scabbard from her pack—another magical encasement which, like the one that held Deneth's lute, compacted whatever its owner put into it. In that sheath, the dimensions of the Sword of Rhydderch Hael—really a great two-handed broadsword every bit the size of "Homer"—shrank to the proportions of a longish knife. "And I was hoping someone would ask, for I had a point to make apart from dazzling you with my spellcraft and the comeliness of Eliander's visage. All of our speculation evoked by the thought of my dancing for the stars before time began and by our brush with the heavenly body that signified the birth of one of the Great Ones, all of our talk of history and prophecy and a plan laid by the One before Creation itself was begun—all of it prompted me to show you this. Did you notice the device on Eliander's wristband?"

"The Serpents," said Torreb with a sagacious nod. "The two-headed snake shaped just so," he said for the benefit of the rest, crossing his wrists before him so his arms took on the aspect of the serpentine body and his hands that of the serpentine heads.

"The traditional device of the House of Thalacia," added Deneth, "the first Thalacian monarch."

Mistra nodded. "Now, bear in mind that this blade was forged on another world in a time that would seem a while ago even to Alla or Anthraticus." She drew the sword and showed it to them. They emitted a collective gasp. The body of a two-headed serpent circumscribed the great leaf-shaped blade; its necks crossed below the quillions so its two heads faced outward. The questors had all seen the blade as Tuhl had delivered it to Mistra—that evening seemed an age of the world ago now; that chamber where the quest gifts had been bestowed, a room on the other side of the cosmos! But in the press of excitement that had taken them as Mistra had held it aloft and chanted the cry that would set them on their road, much of the detail of the scene had blurred, and the significance of what she now showed them had been completely lost. "Its name is Dyrnwyn. It means 'white hilt.'"

"How did *you* come by it?" asked Alla.

Mistra passed the blade along so they could examine it while she told them what she knew of its origins. "Ariane came across it while she and Avador were off making the galaxy safe for constitutional monarchy. It was part of an archaeological exhibit of some things unearthed on Thralham IV, one of the first planets in the sector colonized by humanoids from outside—or so many archaeologists speculate. See the runes traced on it? They comprised a ward so powerful that, when she tried to decipher a mere copy of them, they blew up in her face. Later, she had a vision in which the sword's eternal guardian appeared to her and bestowed its custodianship on my family. The ancient Terrans of a magical land called Britain or Merlyn's Enclosure called him Herne the Hunter, though he has had many other names besides in the cosmos: I gather he is a distant cousin of Minissa's. When he gave my family the custodianship of the sword, he told Ariane that its powers, with their magnitude and lack of absolute orientation, could be so easily abused that the blade deserved both an eternal guardian—him—and a temporal custodian—us—that could keep the sword safe from falling into the hands of the unrighteous while it awaited the next time its powers would be called upon—to free Eliander, in our case. Undoubtedly once we've done with it, Herne will pluck it from our grasp and trot it off to some other part of the cosmos where godlike powers are needed to right some wrong, and the custodianship will pass to others." She grinned. "Apparently the whole scheme involved some creative pilfering, for the exhibit is still making the rounds, intact with one exception—what they're exhibiting is not Dyrnwyn but an excellent but magically inactive copy."

Deneth chuckled. "I knew there was something about your family I liked."

"Yeah," Habie agreed, "all the truly great have *some* redeeming characteristics."

"They *stole* it?" was all Mosaia could say.

"It is not stealing, my friend, if a deity means for something to be yours," said Torreb. "Their majesties remain, in my eyes, the most wise and just of rulers and the most honorable of folk."

Mosaia sighed. "I have heard the names of both God and the Fiend invoked as an excuse for committing thievery and other crimes, and it has never been more than delusion. But—ah, well, that is Falidia and not the Union."

"Actually," Mistra went on, "if it assuages your conscience, an outside party pilfered the entire exhibit before my family got involved. All they did was –oh– *guide* the archaeologists in their choice of which sword to keep. I don't blame Herne—I think he was absolutely right about this being a very dangerous artifact to have on the loose. He left its true purpose unstated. For all my family knew, it would become an heirloom of our house and not be called into service so soon after they brought it home."

He smiled at her, trying to make up a little for calling the High King and Queen, her kin, thieves. "Herne left it in good hands, whatever the circumstances." From his seat on a log near the fire, he sketched her a little bow.

"I do know a little more. Rhydderch Hael—that is, Rhydderch, the Generous—was a king on ancient Earth. The sword comes into the old lists of the Hallows—the royal, sacred regalia, in this instance of Merlyn's Enclosure, after an enchanter in Rhydderch's service. Its property was to shoot jets of flame out of the serpents' mouths when it was drawn. I imagine it was careless handling of those wards that led to tales of that property, though Tuhl made out that it *would* spew forth flame in the hands of the valiant."

"There are other runes than just wards here," Anthraticus said, perching on her shoulder and snaking his neck down. "Many of them, in fact."

"Yes. Once Herne showed Ariane how to defuse the warding runes properly, these appeared. There are many more here than even *you* can see at first glance, like a stereogram image that seems to gain more depth the longer you look. They tell how one draws on the power of the sword. There's so much to them that I had to be ensorcelled so I could pick the information up directly from the sword—not a far cry from the spell you gave Deneth, except I have imprinted in my mind now every syllable of every word in every spell it will take to invoke those powers. Evidently all of the Treasures of Britain were of this sort—repositories of great power."

"How came such things into the world?" asked T'Cru.

"They seem to have come from what the legends call Faerie, or the Underworld—something like what your folk, Mosaia, think of as dwelling in the Hollow Hills. Some were sought after, some were brought to the mundanes by folk who were immortal or gifted in the Art."

"Rather like one of you Carotians popping up on Falidia one day and handing Homer to Mosaia."

They all laughed at that thought. "I can't say I haven't heard it postulated that the blood that runs in the veins of the children of Thalybdenos is the same blood that ran in the veins of fairy folk like the Sidhe and the Tuatha de Danaan of Merlyn and Rhydderch Hael's world." Mistra's eyes shone with an inner fire as she spoke again. "There is another point that might interest you. Merlyn, who was supposed to have taken the Treasures out of the world to guard them till they should be needed once more, was said to be keeping them against the time that the king should come again."

"What, like he was off on holiday?" asked Habie.

"No, like he suffered a fatal wound at his last battle and was carried out of the world to be healed, so that he might come again when his people most needed him." She grinned. "Not unlike Eliander."

"That is Arthur of whom you speak, isn't it?" asked Deneth. "Not this Rhydderch fellow at all. Arthur, or Artos, Ursus, Beur the Magnificent, N!xaou!, LLyrrell or any of the scores of kings and queens who were and will be. It seems like nearly every world has one."

"The king who was and will be is a powerful figure in galactic mythology," agreed Mistra, sheathing the sword.

Mosaia sighed wistfully. "It has been a great lesson to me to understand why and how magic departed from my world, and I should count myself fortunate that I came to be numbered among this company that lives to serve Eliander: a king that was and will be, a king out of legend. Still, I wish the earth of the Falidia I know could be the stuff from which such a legendary hero would spring."

Deneth and Mistra exchanged a glance. It said that if this was what he thought, he had never taken an extensive look around the corners of his own being. But it was Torreb who spoke.

"But your own scriptures speak of such a one, I think," said the priest.

Mosaia grunted a little non-committally, and he and Mistra exchanged a surreptitious glance. She shook her head fractionally to say she had never even thought of betraying the story with which he entrusted her, and he shook his head fractionally to say he never doubted her, and then they both looked helplessly at each other as if to say, "Well, it's Torreb; who else would walk blindly into the most private recesses of another's soul and mean no harm?"

As for Torreb, who blundered blithely ahead, if any had asked him why he missed the nuances of body language that told him to drop the subject, he would have responded with wonder that any could hang back when the mysteries of the universe lay before one like an open book waiting to be read. "Your faith regards your prophets as monarchs in the spiritual sense, does it not?" he said. "From that point of view, when one revelation fulfills the one before it, the king that was has come again. Have I misinterpreted?"

The paladin's eyes widened even as the tension seeped from his shoulders: he now saw Torreb's scholarly enthusiasm as that rather than an attempt to trespass on ground too private to reveal to the whole party. "Always you folk amaze me!" he chuckled, and the sound reflected both the ebb of the adrenaline rush and the returning flow of comradely feelings. "No, you do not misinterpret. That is merely a very sophisticated and lucid interpretation of our sacred texts—of our whole civilization, really. Hearing you say it so plainly is rather like my not expecting you to know your numbers and suddenly hearing you spout off theorems that require the use of calculus. I guess the Falidia I know *can* give birth to these heroes out of legend." They all shared a good-natured laugh at the observation.

"I think the reason the Arthur stories and others like them exist on so many worlds in so many variations," said Deneth, "is that they're more than just stories told for the sake of entertainment."

"Well, they're at least that or you'd be out of a job, pal," laughed Habie.

He held his hands up in a show of conciliation. "Normally I'd say I just redact 'em, I don't explain 'em. But there's more to them, isn't there. They touch the heart as well as the mind."

"They're teaching stories, Deneth," Alla said quietly. "You're meant to get something out of them, often something quite new, no matter where you're standing on the wheel when you hear them."

"Wheel?" asked Habie. "What wheel?"

"Alla's folk might call it the great wheel that is life, or the great spiral dance," Torreb said, obviously feeling like he was putting himself forward in the presence of an *aranyaka*. "And her folk tell some of the best stories of that type I've ever heard. They often tell stories not about kings and knights, or about humans at all, but about woodland creatures, or creatures of the field and plain. Isn't that right?" He directed this last to Alla.

She nodded, obviously pleased at the thought that someone in the party knew this.

"Can you tell us one?" Habie asked Alla eagerly.

Alla looked around the circle. The cumulative weight of their gaze forced her to drop her eyes. "I'm not a very good storyteller," she stammered out.

"Oh, come on. You're among friends."

"Here, *I* know one very short one," Torreb offered in an effort to get Alla off the hook. At her nod and at gestures of encouragement from the others, he said, "OK. An elder *aranyaka* was trying to teach an *aranyakan* child something of the way of the *aranyakan* people. 'There are two wolves that live in the heart of every *aranyaka*,' he said, 'and they are constantly fighting. One is the wolf of kindness, purity, charity, and love; the other is the wolf of indulgence, selfishness, attachment, and hate.'

"'Which one wins?' asked the child.

"The elder smiled and said, 'The one you feed.'"

There was a beat of silence, then an outburst of appreciative laughter. Alla's eyes actually shone at hearing even a short tale of her people told by a human.

The next morning, they pushed on—and immediately wished they had not. The vast burning waste that confronted them had to be a mistake, or some deity's idea of a joke, or some sort of horrible mass hallucination.

"Can we please go back and try again?" asked Habie.

Epilogue
And More Interludes...

*"If the Great Mother put it there, it is in the right place. The
soul would have no rainbow if the eyes had no tears."*
—Aranyakan tradition

So THAT'S WHAT HERNE gave you," Avador said to Ariane as Mistra finished her story. "I always was a little unclear on the sword's significance."

"So was I," Ariane admitted with a silvery laugh. She patted the gazing crystal as if to commend it on a job well done. "Mistra just related about ten times the amount I ever learned by *studying* the runes graven on it. As a sister enchantress, I envy her the experience of having *invoked* the powers that let her learn all she did."

"It must have been like the difference between studying a book's table of contents and reading it."

"But a book that not anyone could have opened! Even though I defused the wards that made Dyrnwyn's serpents spit flame at all and sundry, the same power would have been activated had any but she tried to access that information. Apparently that history is tied up with the spells that bring the full powers of the sword to life."

He threw an arm around her shoulders as they left the chamber of the Nonacle and the care of the crystal to the good offices of their Thalacian counterparts. "Two things about that disturb me."

"Only two," she mused, mostly teasing.

"Yes—well, two that I feel like bothering to enumerate just now. The other questors will certainly guard Mistra as if their lives depended on hers—which is, to a certain extent, true."

"How so?"

"Well, we know releasing Eliander is dependent on the use of the Sword of Rhydderch. We don't know whether the questors' ever reaching home again is dependent on releasing Eliander, or on some other use of the sword. If something *does* happen to Mistra, and the others survive, is there a way the quest can be achieved and the remaining questors brought home?"

She pursed her lips. "I truly don't know, love. Of course, since only Mistra ever had access to the, well, to the *owner's manual* for Dyrnwyn, who's to say that those instructions didn't provide for an emergency bail-out procedure. Perhaps there's a back door permitting access to one of the others, like a private password to a computer program." Looking speculative (and slightly edible), she turned to him, placing her hands on his chest and fixing him with the violet eyes that poets had suffered and died trying to describe. (Others have commented on the designer colors with which the Pantheon seemed to have endowed the Union's royal families, as if simple brown hair or blue eyes abruptly go out of style in any year that produces a royal heir. Dorlas usually gets the blame, although the most outrageous—hair the color of flame or eyes the black of the eye of a dead ant—are attributed, like the temperament of the Retributor, to Strephel.)

"With all she learned in her trances," Ariane went on, "Mistra might not even *know* what she knows. There are spells that allow knowledge to be imparted in such a way the recipient himself doesn't realize it's there till the need for it arises."

"Gods of my father!" he laughed. "You're reminding me of one of our most basic axioms, one that at least as titular clerics we should both know and remember."

"And that is?"

"Faith manages. If a way needs to be found, trust that the Pantheon will provide for it, and Mistra will discover it."

"You have confidence in her abilities?" It was more statement than question, and she asked it coyly, as if trying to coax a dark secret from him.

"Oh... Yes," he admitted. His tone said he would have preferred to have all his teeth pulled with no anesthetic.

"We have got to get you two talking when she gets back. You could be great friends if you'd get past these walls you keep putting up. What was 'two?'" she asked before he had a chance to rebut her suggestion.

"What? Ah, 'two,' yes, well—with Mistra in that induced state all that time—"

"The one you started calling her 'trance-endental state'?"

"Mmm. If she had to be made that suggestible in order to absorb all that information directly from the sword, or whatever source it was serving as the conduit for—" He paused, not liking what he was about to say. A light touch on his arm and a wealth of understanding in those amethyst pools encouraged him to speak his thought, however distasteful he might find it. "All right, Ari—for your ears alone, hmm? With her in that state, and the way you've explained the possibility of back doors and subliminal messages responding only to certain triggers and so on, why couldn't someone who had a vested interest in the mission failing have implanted some detrimental suggestion?"

The amethyst pools widened and shifted toward the sapphire. "Avador, she was guarded by at least one of the Council every second she was entranced, and there were priests and priestesses praying and bards playing soothing music to facilitate the trances and—blessed Arayne, Avador! Who among them don't you trust?" The suggestion of a raised eyebrow quieted her, as did a thoughtful flicker of gold in the depths of his sea-green eyes.

"All right, all right," she continued quietly. "I grant you it's possible— theoretically. But—who? Why?"

"Who, I don't know, but the mercy of Arayne runs true in you, my love. You trust the good motives of everyone. One of us has to question. *Why* is easier: if Mistra's mind could be, well, booby-trapped, for lack of a better word, then what other tampering with the quest would be necessary? A saboteur could lay out red herring after red herring, each just good enough that the questors would learn of it and stop it in the nick of time and think themselves very clever, and very much only a single jump ahead of the pursuit."

"And the real pursuit would have already made it to the finish line and been patiently awaiting their arrival," she mused. "It is a grim thought." She brightened. "But, really, what we've seen of their obstacles has suggested no one guiding hand, no commonality. The pirates were privateers, that whole scenario on Falidia wasn't even in this time frame, no one in the party has tried to harm anyone else in the party." She looked to him in mute appeal.

He nodded. "There is a commonality—our friend Syndycyr—but, unless he has a true minion among us, there's no way he could have been present during Mistra's indoctrination. He was very close with her those few minutes in Sigurd's workshop. I can't get over the feeling he was giving her something, or instructing her in some way."

"And if he had a minion there and then, why not here and now?" She frowned, trying to scrutinize the idea, and ended by only yawning broadly. "It's late, Avador. I think, for now, I am content they've finished two adventures with no more harm taken than the generation of a few hopeless passions."

"Passions, did you say?" He flicked his eyes suggestively.

The silvery laugh again as she beckoned him toward their inner sanctum. He saved her the trouble of responding in a way that, had the chamber not been magically soundproofed, would have called out every guard in the palace.

⁂

"What have you done, my pet?" Lilith asked, almost gushing in her eagerness to know. "Tell me."

"You will see," Syndycyr replied enigmatically. For once, he mused, he was the one being guarded in his responses. He found the effect on his companion most gratifying!

She stopped following him around the workshop long enough to reason it out. "Ah! You said you would soon have a way to ensure they had a way to contact you and seek your help. Is that it? Is that why you answered the princess's call?"

He continued to fuss with a dust he was compounding of newt's toenails and other such paraphernalia. "I answered her call to discommode that wretch Sigurd." His lips twisted into a malevolent grin. "It was too good a cue for a dramatic entrance for me to pass up."

"It was an opportunity to enter the physical world," she taunted, "and you have all too few of those."

His dark eyes flashed. "Keep on like that, my dear, and you will never learn what I did."

She frowned petulantly. "Was it a token of some sort? Will it corrupt its bearer or bring ill fortune?"

"It is a token, but its actions are far more subtle. I guess you and your kind would not understand, but our adventurers are reaching the point where they would dare much for one another."

"Death?" she enthused.

"Death and what is, for their kind, worse." His tone was grim, but his eyes reflected sadness.

She barely noticed. "Damnation?" she enthused. "How delightful! How infernal! My father will be delighted with such a catch!"

He regarded her. "Think of what you are saying. Your father is obliged to offer delights of the flesh (and so on) when he tempts. How would he respond to someone who entered his lair willingly, with no temptation offered, for the sake of friendship alone with no purpose save the salvation of the life of another innocent?" It pleased him that she paled at the thought. "The very proximity of such a one as that would be like the stench of death to a mortal. I should think he would try to banish such a one to the higher planes with every spell and artifact at his disposal. No, damnation was never my purpose."

"Yes, I see that now," she whispered, and shivered as if the room had gone chill.

"I would quit trying to learn the workings of my charm, if I were you, and quit gloating over the capture of souls which are as yet neither yours nor mine to command—souls for which, for your daring to present them to your father— for your even allowing them to enter his realm—he would condemn you to eternal torment. No, my dear. The souls will come, but they will be mine."

Arayne entered the pavilion she shared with Ereb. He was just dismissing his seraph and being somewhat more effusive in his praise than was usual for him-a concession to the angelic creature's uncertainty (also uncharacteristic) about the propriety of his own performance. Noticing his wife, the god held out a hand to her. "Come, my good lady, join me and assure our friend that he did well."

The goddess of mercy's smile outshone the brightest stars in magnitude when she wished it to, and she wished it to now, so it would gently belie her words. To needle one of their immortal minions was not in her nature as it might have been in Strephel's, but she could, if she chose, force them to hang for a brief moment on her every word. "My sister Caros would say it was un-wisdom to intervene in a matter our questors could manage alone," she said as she joined Ereb on the wide divan, "as my lord Ereb would say such was un-justice."

The seraph had gone down on one knee at her approach, and there he remained. All three pairs of wings drooped a little at her assessment. "Such were my thoughts, my lady," he said. "Yet they seemed in such desperate straits with that foul creature of the Pit to torment them, and what powers they had, they seemed either unaware of or incapable of harnessing in that extremity." He cast his eyes down sadly.

Humor flickered in the eyes of the god of justice. Unseen by the seraph, he winked at his wife. "And how says my lady herself?"

Arayne placed a delicate hand under the seraph's jaw and lifted his face so their eyes met. "I would say it was no mercy to them to force them to their limits so early on, or ever to force them to those limits so they achieved their aims yet were broken by the experience. Nor would that be wisdom or justice, but it might be a wound even the great Thalybdenos with his arts could not heal, and a misery all the kindly laughter in the great heart of Strephel could not kindle to happiness."

The seraph's brightest smile would not have outshone the stars, but the one he flashed them now might have kindled a few. He kissed Arayne's hand, bowed to Ereb, and vanished.

Ereb chuckled. "I *was* going to ask if he felt himself answered, but he has let his deeds speak for him! Thank you, my dear."

She nodded graciously, then looked out across the gardens as if descrying something even her sibling deities might miss if they turned a less discerning eye on the scene. "I have seen things in the pool of Eliannes that convinced me that what your servant did was right in an absolute sense, even as it was right in the sense that it was motivated by pure intentions."

"Then Eliannes knows of his mission in my service?"

"I believe they all know, my husband."

"Ah. Well, I did not command him to be discreet, just effective. And how think they?"

She laughed—a silvery little sound like Ariane's. "They will not ask you to recall him, though none of them would have thought to set one of his own minions to this task."

"Indeed. And why is that?"

She sobered. "I have heard Avador ask my dear daughter Ariane in jest why we didn't just zip off and collect Eliander ourselves, why we left all in the hands of mere mortals if we were powerful enough to ensure that the quest did not fail—and she jested back that she knew not, but that he should ask a priest!" She allowed herself a small smile at the thought that her headstrong namesake—one to whom knowledge and truth were as meat and drink—would palm *any* question of theology off on a poor, unsuspecting member of the clergy. "But truly, my dear, do not the two questions—why we do not act and why the seraph, if he does act, must do so guardedly—do not the two have the same answer? The One has decreed that only the sentient mortals can know pain and have free will to endure it, that some greater good beyond their own happiness be achieved. Likewise, the One has made it so that such sacrifices hold a power that, once released, might set the entire Creation ablaze. There is no act, no thought, no intention of which we immortals, powerful though we be, are capable that can possibly hold such power. That is why it never occurred to the brethren of the mighty Ereb to seek a capacity in which their minions might serve the quest beyond keeping prayerful vigil."

He nodded. "It is for the very reason you describe that evil will never gain a lasting foothold in the Creation. Evil knows no other measure than its own gain; it will never give up the chance to please itself in favor of acting for the common good. It admits the existence of no such phenomenon." He took Arayne's hand as he had on the day the One had joined them. "My seraph—he will not prevent those sacrifices being made when the time comes."

She nodded acquiescence. "Our questors—now is the time for them to find harmony and balance, to forge the bonds that will unite them. He has allowed them a chance or two they might otherwise have missed."

"It is so. The time for sacrifices, from the smallest to the ones that will shake the Union to its foundations, will come soon enough."

ὄιReCὭORu oF ChΑRACὭeRS

THE ORIGINAL QUESTORS

MISTRA, PRINCESS OF THE royal house of Caros. She has already distinguished herself in the galaxy at large in both the arts and the sciences. Need someone to tweak the Ether with the Art or determine truth from falsehood with one of the Disciplines? She's your woman: her gifts in both are prodigious even for a member of the royal family. She also swings a pretty mean sword. Her presence is critical to the success of the quest, for only she has the skills and knowledge needed to work the magical artifact whose power will free Eliander. Can't believe all this comes in one slender package? Hmm. Maybe there's a reason . . .

At the beginning of the quest, she learned she had been smitten about two years early with the tal-yosha, the hunger to find a bondmate Carotian women endure every eight years under normal conditions. Definitely not the best time to be traversing space in the company of three brave, wise, and devastatingly handsome and spiritual men..

DENETH, A MINOR NOBLEMAN from Thalas, and the most gifted bard in the Union: his music can make flowers blossom and stones rise up and dance. He is a terror in a fistfight, a capable opponent in a sword fight, and almost as good a thief as Habie: one learns much of the arts of self protection in the streets of postwar Thalas City, where he received his bardic training. He is not reluctant to go on the quest as much as he is disbelieving that the gods would have chosen him over someone who openly acknowledges their existence.

ALLA, OF THE RACE of aranyaka (Forest Dwellers) that are the planet Ereb's indigenous race. This dwindling race inhabits the woodlands and live so closely with nature that they have many skills of detection and tissue manipulation that defy explanation (they maintain that they do not use magic). Alla's folk worship only the Great Mystery, but she becomes one of very few who have spoken with Minissa and heard the voice of the great Stag who is her minion.

MOSAIA, LORD CLEAR WATER, a nobleman and holy knight from the world of Falidia, which is about as far from the Carotian Union geographically as it is ideologically. His clarity of sight keeps him from profaning or dismissing out of hand Mysteries not his own; while most of his countrymen would shy from adventuring with a party that worships a pantheon of deities (and one that includes goddesses as well as gods), he sees only that the Pantheon has a reputation for benevolence and takes ship for the Union with a high and eager heart. He is, obviously, the stuff of which heroes are made.

TORREB, A PRIEST FROM Ereb in the service of Ereb, the god of justice and war in a righteous cause. He was about to become the youngest chief priest the order had ever ordained and take over his first parish when Minissa marked him. Disappointed as he is at being chosen for such a great work at this point in his life, mystified as he is over why Minissa would choose him in the first place over an older, more experienced priest, Torreb knows his duty and obeys the call without a glance backward.

HABIE, AN ORPHAN WHO makes a passable living on the streets of Caros' capital city by stealing. She is of the people of Lemur, a race of demi humans who are one of Caros' indigenous peoples; they are powerful receptive empaths who can use this ability to heal. For Habie more than the others, the quest represents an amelioration of her fortune

T'CRU, CROWN PRINCE OF the Tigroids, Caros' other indigenous race. The Tigroids are great hunting cats who live within a caste system so strict that the color of one's coat is a determinant of rank, with unbroken black denoting the highest nobility and mottling the labor class. The Stag of Minissa appears as a white mark on his heretofore pure black coat. His question as he starts his journey is, has Minissa blessed him or cursed him?

A FEW WE PICK UP ALONG THE WAY

MOSAIA'S SWORD IS A blade fit for a holy knight. Forged in the deeps of time by Ereb, the Pantheon's god of justice and war in a righteous cause, it is a fearsome weapon. Unfortunately, as the companions find out, the sword is sentient and highly opinionated about its role in the battle against Evil. They also learn that it was blessed at its forging not only by Ereb but by two others: Phino, the god of performing arts, and Strephel, the god of humor. Imagine the personality you get with this combination . . .

NTHRATICUS, CHANCELLOR TO THE queen of a colony of spritely
A dragons (or "spragons," as Habie dubs them) the companions encounter
late in their adventure. Although they consider themselves cousins to the larger
dragons whom the adventurers set out to heal, they are actually a species of
coatl and are covered with tiny feathers rather than scales. Because of his age,
Anthraticus is the wisest member of the party and may be a more powerful
worker of magic than even Mistra, but his naivete about the workings of the
universe at large get him into trouble. In fact, he never realized how unworldly
he was about some things till he first met Deneth! Ah, well, life in the colony
was getting a bit dull . . .

SUPPORTING CAST

UHL (INITIALLY REFERRED TO as The Sage) serves as the Guardian for the
T Orb of Caros. He is a Lemurian who bears no resemblance to Habie or
any other Lemurian on the planet. He is a mage who can out cast the strongest
Carotian, a technician who can out tinker even Mistra, a sage whose wisdom
and knowledge rival those of Caros and Cilio themselves. He sets the questors
on their way and watches over them from afar. Unlike the rest of his people,
he remained true to the promise of his race when the humans arrived from
doomed Thalybdenos. Where nearly all of his people used their empathic skills
to draw strength from the humans when their own energies flagged, he kept
to himself, struggling to master test after test and building up his own reserves
of power. He was the last Lemurian known to have undergone the Lemurian
Sleep of Transformation, which changed him into the one Being capable of
protecting the Orb.

ERI (INITIALLY REFERRED TO as The Chronicler) is Tuhl's apprentice,
P although she is clearly not another Lemurian. Her great task (think of
it as a doctoral dissertation before Tuhl turns her loose) is writing the story of
The Quest for the Lost Prince through interaction with the questors after their
return and the aegis of a lot of mystical gadgets that Tuhl possesses that let her
see the events as they actually happened. She is, as Tuhl suggests, a distance
runner rather than a sprinter. Her only complaint is that she doesn't get why
all the indigenous races of the Union were represented except one. One of her
weaknesses in translating the various dialects of the colorful characters who
people the quest is really one of her greatest strengths: she has a keen sense of
how to render into Galactispeak the nuances of almost any language. This is
why you will see a character like Mistra compliment Deneth with a phrase like

"Nice shootin', Tex!"

Her studies with Tuhl even allowed her to find Scriptural parallels for the worlds on which Adventurers is being published. In the case of Tapestry of Enchantment, the citations made from the Books of Life and Wisdom translated most easily from the Terran Holy Books belonging to Christianity, Islam, the Bahá'í Faith, several Native American Traditions, Buddhism, and Hinduism. Mistra felt strongly that she wanted the Terran mystic who so impressed her identified, since female Sufis of repute were so rare. The Sufi saint in question was Rabia al-Adawiyya. If you look, you may also find oblique, sly little references to other historical figures like Shakespeare.

A RIANE, High Queen of the entire Carotian Union. She is Mistra's older sister and the eldest child of the King and Queen of Caros. A great heroine in her own right, she traded in her role as crown princess when the Union was formed to become the newly-formed confederation's joint head of state.

A VADOR, High King of the entire Carotian Union. Another great hero in his own right, he is the eldest child of the King and Queen of Ereb. His and Ariane's parents were divided when he and Ariane fell in love, as both were well-suited to rule their home worlds and one would have had to abdicate had they married. The formation of the Union and the sudden need for a High Monarchy allowed the pair both to follow their hearts and fulfill their political obligations.

S YNDYCYR, a sinister figure who has taken an interest in the quest to free Eliander. Like the Lost Prince, he seems to be incarcerated on a plane that exists outside normal space-time. Mage, priest, warrior—if the questors could come face to face with him, he would be a formidable opponent. He has minions who are free to enter normal space-time and already displays a knack for thinning the veils between the worlds. Who is he, and why is he so interested?

L ILITH, Syndycyr's mistress and the daughter of Ahriman, the ruler of the Seven Hells. Syndycyr's goals are her goals unless, of course, they conflict with the wishes of Dear Old Dad.

OUR GUEST STARS

GWYNDDOLYNN OF HOUSE CLEAR WATER. Under normal circumstances, she might be Mosaia's cousin and betrothed, but the whole party has moved 1000 years into the past. The waif-like princess was about to be married, but to Mosaia's ancestor and double, LORD GUNTHAR CLEAR WATER. In fact, all of the questors have doubles known to GWYNDDOLYN. She knows Deneth as Gunthar's harper TALLIN, Torreb as their priest ERIC, Alla as her best friend ELLA, T'Cru as TALLIN'S friend PROWL, and Mistra and Habie as her two handmaidens LUCIA and NURA. Even Anthraticus does not upset her world view, as she tells the questors that Lucia has a familiarity with the woodlands that frequently causes her to bring home odd little pets of his sort.

SIGURD, A FALIDIAN MAGE of great power and dark intent. His story ties into the mysteries of Falidia's deep past. To overcome him, Mosaia must unlearn everything he ever learned about the evil name that magic has on the Falidia of his day and whether lore of a Falidia on which magic existed is legend, untruth, or intentional misdirection. That Sigurd wields such great magic suggests he has great knowledge, and all knowledge must have a source...

THE CAROTIAN PANTHEON

The six gods and six goddesses of the Pantheon represent some of the great dualities of life. The planets in the Union, including doomed Thalybdenos, have been named for the deity to whom their first ruling monarchs were consecrated.

ARAYNE, GODDESS OF MERCY. She sanctifies marriage and childbearing. Her colors are sky blue and silver; her symbol is a heart within a heart. She most often appears as a tall, beautiful woman dressed in long robes of sky blue trimmed with silver. She has very long dark brown hair and violet eyes.

EREB, GOD OF JUSTICE. He sanctifies war in a righteous cause and so is sometimes misinterpreted as being just "the war god." His colors are moss green and rust. His symbol is a pan balance. He most often appears as a warrior in the full vigor of youth. When he goes to war on behalf of the Pantheon, he wears golden armor but more often appears in a long tunic and hose that match, respectively, the green of his eyes and sandy brown of his hair.

Together, Arayne and Ereb represent the duality of mercy and justice. They stand at the head of the Pantheon but are more firsts among equals than true authority figures.

MINISSA, GODDESS OF NATURE. She sanctifies the physical union of man and woman. Her colors are white streaked with rainbow pastels. Her symbol is the Stag. Like Arayne, she appears most often as a beautiful woman robed in white belted with colors and crowned with foliage appropriate to the season (most typically spring flowers or autumn leaves). Her hair is long and dark auburn; her eyes are the green of fine emeralds.

BRONYS, JUDGE OF THE dead. He sanctifies acts associated with death like ritual suicide, dying curses, and acts likely to result in sacrificial death for a good cause. His colors are black and silver. His symbol is the scythe. Like Ereb, he appears as a hearty warrior and is more likely to be seen in his black armor or in a black tunic and hose with silver trim than in his judicial robes. His hair is silver; his eyes are midnight blue. He is good, though he comes of as taciturn, dour, and somewhat aloof because he has to judge impartially the souls who come to him.

Minissa and Ereb represent the duality of life and death.

ELIANNES (SOMETIMES CALLED THE Dreamer), goddess of meditation. She sanctifies prayer, visions, and other endeavors in which the powers of the spirit are focused inward. Her colors are lilac and gold. Her symbol is a mirror. She most often appears as a woman smaller and younger but every bit as beautiful as Arayne and Minissa. She has long golden hair and azure eyes and dresses most often in robes of lilac shot with gold.

THALYBDENOS (SOMETIMES CALLED SIMPLY The Healer), god of healing. He sanctifies all the healing arts including herbcraft (so his name is also invoked by practitioners of the culinary arts). His colors are burgundy and platinum. His symbol is the Healing Hand. He appears most often as a youth in a burgundy cassock trimmed with platinum alchemical symbols. His hair is platinum blond; his eyes are cerulean.

The duality these two represent is that of mental or spiritual forces turned inward vs. the same forces turned outward.

CAROS, GODDESS OF WISDOM. She sanctifies child-rearing and education. Her colors are teal and copper. Her symbol is a two-headed serpent (it may also be represented as a caduceus). Although she can appear as a young woman like her sister-goddesses, the form she most often takes is that of an apple-cheeked matron. In either aspect, her dress will bear the tell-tale colors of teal and copper. Her hair is raven even when she appears as a matron, her eyes the blue of cornflowers.

CILIO: GOD OF SCHOLARSHIP. He sanctifies the mental disciplines as Eliannes sanctifies the spiritual. His colors are tan and slate blue. His symbol is a lamp. Like his consort, he can appear in the full vigor of youth, but his favored aspect is as an irascible older man. In his elderly aspect, he wears robes of rough homespun in his colors (although they may be so spotted with ink and dust that the colors are hard to recognize). His wire-framed glasses may often be found perched atop his head. What hair he has is grey, as are his eyes.

Their duality is wisdom or judgment vs. pure intellect, intellectual pursuit, or book learning.

DORLAS (SOMETIMES CALLED "THE Maker"), goddess of handicrafts. She sanctifies all craft work, visual arts, and any work done in the spirit of service to sentientkind. Her colors are umber and a more muted gold than the shimmering gold of Eliannes, a Florentine finish to The Dreamer's shining brilliance. Her sign is a loom overlaid with a spindle or paintbrush. Her usual aspect is that of a mature woman with a long braid so that her beauty is more earthy than dazzling like Eliannes or Minissa, and closer to the human heart. As her colors suggest, she has a vaguely leonine appearance, especially when the Greek-style robes she wears in her colors are blended with her ash blonde hair and brown eyes.

PHINO, BARD OF THE gods and the god of performing arts. He sanctifies not only the performing arts but any idealistic pursuit. His colors are hunter and grass green. His symbol is a high-headed harp. He appears as a fully mature man dressed in bardic robes of his colors, although they shimmer with hunter and grass green and all the shades in between when he moves. His hair is medium brown, his eyes golden flecked with the same brown, a hawk to Dorlas' lioness.

Their duality is the physical or visual arts vs. the performing arts.

THALAS (ALSO CALLED LADY of the Elements), is Minissa's counterpart. Where Minissa concerns herself with all that grows and lives, Thalas' domain is the physical side of nature: rock, water, and weather. She sanctifies the tilling of the earth. Farmers know that, while they find their livelihood in that which grows, without the nourishment of the soil and the coming of rain and sun in good measure, their crops will fail and their livestock perish. Her single color is a multi-shaded silver. Her sign is a cloud cleft by a lightning bolt running from upper right to lower left. She, too, appears as a beautiful woman with waist-length hair. Her beauty, though, is other than the warm beauty of Minissa or Arayne or the spiritual beauty of youthful Eliannes: it is a beauty bordering on the terrible, as if she were a power barely in control of itself (and, indeed, she has a stormy temperament). Her hair has been best described as "the grey of a stormy sea," and her eyes are silver flecked with black. Combined with the her flowing, shimmering, many-colored silver robes, she gives the impression of being a storm cloud, although her clerics say that when she smiles, her smile comes as a sunbeam piercing those same clouds.

STREPHEL, (ALSO KNOWN AS The Trickster), the Pantheon's fool and its god of humor, he fills the role of many pantheons taken by the trickster god. He sanctifies humorous pursuits but also suicidal risks, but he looks favorably on suicidal risks taken in the name of a good cause. His colors are brick red and bronze. His symbol is a stave with bells. His appearance is ageless, although as he dresses in motley or in a parti-colored cotehardie (both in his associated colors) and wears a matching fool's cap with bells, his age would be difficult to determine. He tends to caper when he appears to his supplicants. His hair is auburn and his eyes a tan that feathers out to true bronze.

If these two represent any duality, it is sobriety and light-heartedness. The legends say that when the One created the Pantheon to govern the worlds of the Carotian system, He (or She) saw that only Strephel had the humor and lightness to balance Thalas' stormy temperament and only Tha

Made in the USA
Lexington, KY
12 December 2010